THE SPIRIT OF THUNDER

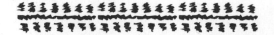

THE SPIRIT OF THUNDER

Kurt R. A. Giambastiani

A ROC BOOK

ROC
Published by New American Library, a division of
Penguin Putnam Inc., 375 Hudson Street,
New York, New York 10014, U.S.A.
Penguin Books Ltd, 80 Strand,
London WC2R 0RL, England
Penguin Books Australia Ltd, Ringwood,
Victoria, Australia
Penguin Books Canada Ltd, 10 Alcorn Avenue,
Toronto, Ontario, Canada M4V 3B2
Penguin Books (N.Z.) Ltd, 182–190 Wairau Road,
Auckland 10, New Zealand

Penguin Books Ltd, Registered Offices:
Harmondsworth, Middlesex, England

First published by Roc, an imprint of New American Library,
a division of Penguin Putnam Inc.

Cover art by David Cook
Cover design by Ray Lundgren

 REGISTERED TRADEMARK—MARCA REGISTRADA

Printed in the United States of America

PUBLISHER'S NOTE
This is a work of fiction. Names, characters, places, and incidents either
are the product of the author's imagination or are used fictitiously,
and any resemblance to actual persons, living or dead, business
establishments, events, or locales is entirely coincidental.

ISBN: 0-7394-2457-2

For Ilene—
welcome to the next level

ACKNOWLEDGMENTS

First and foremost, I wish to acknowledge once again the Cheyenne people, whose law, legend, and history have been such a continued enlightment and inspiration. Without them, this book simply would not exist.

This past year has been one of discovery for me. That may be a bit of an understatement, but still, I owe a debt of gratitude to those who eased my journey through it.

Many thanks to my agent, Eleanor Wood, and my editor, Laura Anne Gilman, for enduring my numerous neophytic anxieties during the past year. I hope to do better next time.

For Mike Baker, friend and rock-solid supporter, I can only say that your enthusiasm made all the difference.

I would like to extend my sincere appreciation to Ulali, R. Carlos Nakai, and Hans Zimmer, for helping create the proper atmosphere. Thanks also to my *barristas*, Pete and Larry at Island Espresso, for keeping me properly caffeinated in the mornings. Trust me, guys, it helped.

Last and most important, for my wife, I must reserve the deepest thanks and say that if not for you, Dear, I would only be able to dream instead of do.

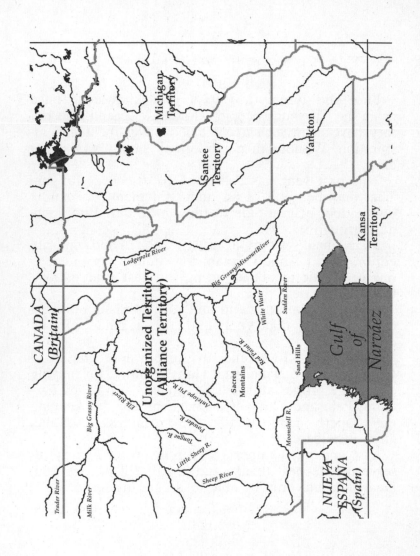

CHAPTER 1

Summary, A.D. 1886
Red Paint River
Cheyenne Alliance Territory

The sweat on the back of George's neck went cold as he stared at the lump of raw metal in his bandaged hand.

Gold!

Even encrusted with dirt as it was, there was no mistaking that yellow luster, deep and dark—almost as dark as the marigolds in his mother's garden.

It was gold, pure gold, and a sizable nugget, too, the size of a hen's egg. He felt the weight of it in his hand, his dexterity still off as he compensated for his missing finger. At seven or eight ounces, it represented the better part of a year's wages for a laborer or a clerk or . . .

Or a soldier, he thought with dim regret. Like I once was.

A voice, followed by the sound of gentle laughter, brought him back to his surroundings. George looked up from the nugget and into smiling faces.

The chiefs of the Great Council, the ruling body of what the Americans called the Cheyenne Alliance, sat around him, watching him. They were Indians—"savages," George would have called them just a few short weeks before. Now, as he himself looked around, he knew them instead as comrades-in-arms, as friends, and in a few cases almost as family.

They all sat cross-legged on the ground. The buffalo hides that covered the lodge's conical frame had been pulled up to let in the breeze of early summer. It was a double-size lodge—nearly twenty feet tall at its peak—and was reserved solely for the Council's use.

Beyond the perimeter of the lodgepoles the people of the camp had gathered to hear the proceedings. They sat and stood in the bright sunshine outside, waiting to hear what would be said next.

Within the lodgepoles and under the shade of the lodgeskin, the sixty chiefs sat. They sat with their backs to the place where the doorflap would have been, facing the place of honor at the back of the lodge, the place where the principal chief sat. Three Trees Together was ancient; his face was lined and deeply creased, turning his features into an unreadable mask. His long braided hair was altogether white. George had been told that he was more than a hundred years old, but the man's hooded eyes were lucid beneath wrinkled lids and when he spoke his voice was clear and deliberate.

With the old man sat two of the secondary chiefs, both elderly and respected men in their own rights.

George, as a guest invited to speak with the Council, sat near the front, among the elder, more respected members. With him was Storm Arriving, a warrior of repute and George's friend.

One of the chiefs near George said something else and the men laughed again.

"Stone Bear speaks," Storm Arriving said, translating into French for George's benefit. "He says that the yellow chief-metal does not make *vé'hó'e* crazy like we thought. It makes them stupid."

Vé'hó'e. There was that word again. It was the Cheyenne word for white men, but it was also somehow inextricably tied to their word for spider, web-weaver, and to the name of some ancient Trickster-god. George did not fully understand the implications of the word, but he had always known that he didn't like it.

"One Who Flies," Storm Arriving said, using the name the Cheyenne had given George, "Stone Bear is teasing. It was not an insult."

George calmed himself, aware that Stone Bear's teasing was meant in good humor.

Besides, George thought, I *am* a white man. A *vé'ho'e*. One of *them*.

"Stone Bear is right," George said in French. Storm Arriving began to translate. "But it only makes us stupid for a short while. Crazy comes later, and it is crazy you need to worry about."

He looked around the lodge.

Nearby was One Bear, a chief of the Tree People band and father of the woman who had found the exposed vein of gold in a granite outcropping a few miles distant. He looked at George with calm attention. His face concealed all except for the interest in his eyes.

From the *vá'ôhtáma,* the place of honor at the back of the lodge, Three Trees Together sat forward with his forearms on his knees. The old man's hands toyed with the medicine bag that hung from his neck and he chewed on his bottom lip and stared at George through squinted eyes.

They were all listening, polite and attentive, listening to what he, an outsider—a *vé'ho'e*—had to say. And George knew they would give his words just as much weight as those of any tribesman.

"Mâsêhavé'ho'e," he said. " 'Crazy white man.' I hear you say this all the time. *Vé'hó'e* are crazy. *Vé'hó'e* don't know how to act. We don't know where the sun is in the sky. We're deaf to the spirits of the earth. We bury our dead in the ground and pile stones up into the sky. We do everything backward. We're crazy." He held up the nugget. It shone in the shaft of light that stole in through the smokehole above.

"No matter how crazy we seem to you, this metal

will make us ten times worse. This gold can be a great tool for you, and with it a great many problems might be solved. But it also brings with it a whole new set of risks. Its presence here must be kept secret—if at all possible—for if the *vé'hó'e* out across the Big Greasy ever learn of it, you will never keep them from your lands."

He put the lump of gold down at the edge of the cold hearthpit.

"That is all I have to say." He waited for Storm Arriving to finish translating his words.

The chiefs were silent awhile as was their custom between speakers. Finally, Three Trees Together straightened up and put his hands on his knees.

"This seems like good advice to me," George heard through Storm Arriving's translation. "We should keep this knowledge with the People, and keep the *vé'hó'e* of the Horse Nations from learning it." There was general assent to this statement, and George saw the agreement pass beyond the perimeter of the lodge and into the crowd that surrounded it.

"I would be interested," the old chief continued, "in hearing more of how we might use this yellow chief-metal. Later, perhaps, One Who Flies can tell us more of his ideas. But at the moment, there is work to be done. We have spent nearly a moon here, waiting for our war party to return from the City of White Stone. The coup they counted on the chiefs of the Horse Nations was great, but now we must lay to rest those who fell along that path, and after that, we must move the People. The buffalo are far ahead of us, and there is hunting to do."

George looked down, flexing his wounded hand, remembering the past month. His lightning invasion and attack on Washington had not been without its cost. Physically, his only lasting scar would be the loss of the little finger of his left hand, blown off by an explosion in the Capitol rotunda. In his soul, however, the injuries cut much deeper.

He had lost a great friend, Laughs like a Woman, who had died saving George's own life from American rifles. He had lost any hope of reconciliation with his father, President George Armstrong Custer, Sr., for leading the Cheyenne to the Capitol building to force a parley with Congress. But the knife-edge across his heart had come when he overheard the treachery of his own country's congressmen—men who, while discussing peace with the Indian chiefs on the floor of the House, whispered how they might betray their own promises to achieve the greatest political gain.

Though he had hinted at it, George had not told the chiefs of the congressional subterfuge. The hope that some senators would keep their promise, the hope that by the time the cherries ripened in June some representatives would come to meet with the leaders of the People who lived on the great plains of the American interior—that hope still flickered in George's heart, wounded though it was.

Three Trees Together stood, signaling the end of the meeting, and the other chiefs did likewise. Though the sides of the lodge had been raised, the men all left by what would have been the doorway. As with all lodges, the doorway was on the eastern side. The east was the home of the rising sun, the place where all things began. For the Cheyenne, George had learned, and for the Great Council in particular, there was symbolism in everything. No chief would leave but by the proper direction.

The lodge was a circle with a doorway that faced the east. As George and Storm Arriving left the Council Lodge, they were in the center of yet another circle.

The Council Lodge was in a circular clearing in the center of the Cheyenne encampment. The clearing was about a quarter mile across, to George's estimation, and in it, along with the Council Lodge, were dance rings, racing tracks, and the two great lodges that housed the tribe's sacred objects, the nature of which George still had no notion.

As he looked around the clearing, George saw the camps that surrounded it, the camps of the ten bands that made up the whole of the Cheyenne people. They covered the undulating, green-carpeted landscape for a mile or more in every direction, bounded on three sides by the creeks and rivers that supplied such a large assembly with adequate water.

The ten bands were camped in their traditional sites around the circle. To the south, the Scabby band, the Hair Rope band, and the Ridge Men. To the west were the Poor People and the band that Storm Arriving called his own: the Tree People. To the north were the lodges of the Flexed Leg band, the Broken Jaw band, and the reclusive Suhtai. And to the east were camped the Northern Eaters and the Closed Windpipe band. These last two were camped on either side of an opening in the immense circle, the sun road, a gap left open to admit the rising sun as through the door of a lodge.

The camp was a circle; a lodge was a circle. The more George learned of these people, the more their symbols could be seen in everything they did.

The two men turned west, toward Storm Arriving's home among the Tree People band.

"How many people are here in camp?" George asked.

"All of them," Storm Arriving replied without hesitation.

George smiled at the misunderstanding. "No, not how many of 'the People.' I meant how many people, how many men and women."

Storm Arriving looked around as they walked. "Ten thousands? Two times ten thousands? More? We have never counted. Besides, what does it matter? By the time a man finished counting, the number would have changed." He gave George a sidelong glance. "That sounds like a *vé'ho'e* question."

George chuckled at the jibe and looked at the ground. "Not exactly," he said. "It's more of a soldier's question."

"A bluecoat question, you mean," Storm Arriving said, meaning a soldier in the U.S. Army. "But you threw your blue coat away. You do not need to think like them anymore."

George shrugged. "Perhaps, but not so for you, I fear. In order for you to succeed against the *vé'hó'e*—in order for you to *survive*—I think the People will have to start asking bluecoat questions."

Storm Arriving stopped. "You are talking about war, no?"

George looked at his friend, so different from himself. Storm Arriving was a tall man with skin like tightly stretched leather. The hair on the right side of his head—his temple and back over his right ear—had been shorn close, while the hair on the top and left side of his head was long and pulled back into a braid that fell to the middle of his back. Sunlight glinted from several silver earrings that dangled from his right ear, and the white feather at the nape of his neck lifted in the prairie breeze.

His chest was bare, the scars of his recent skin sacrifice were still harsh and angry on his breast. He wore a breechclout for modesty, and his leggings, fringed and painted with geometric designs, dragged on the ground as he walked. His moccasins were decorated with colored quills. Over his shoulder hung a leather quiver and a horn and sinew bow, both festooned with fox tails and feathers, silver circlets and strips of red cloth. On one side of his belt hung a knife in its sheath and on the other the tail of a white-tailed deer.

He was, in every aspect, the picture of a savage that George and every other American had learned as a child: uncivilized and murderous, a creature and not a man. But as George had learned, that image was wrong. This was a man who knew the subtle play of politics, who knew the sting of injustice, and who knew the heartache of a frustrated love affair. He also knew the meaning of war.

Storm Arriving had not looked at George as he asked his question, and even now he kept his gaze fixed on the west, toward his clan's camp, toward the flocks of whistlers, toward the sacred mountains that rose up from the horizon.

"Yes," George answered. "I am talking about war. War like the People have never seen."

"Worse than our war against Long Hair, your father?"

George's father had fought the Indians back in the seventies. In a terrible and bloody series of battles, Custer, Sr., had taken the Missouri, Kansa, Yankton, and Santee territories away from the people who had called them home for untolled years. George had seen for himself, from both sides, the grief that the losses of that war had left behind.

"Worse than that," he said, "especially if there is gold to be had."

Storm Arriving pursed his lips as he considered this news. His gaze still fixed on some distant point, he said, "There are perhaps eight thousand soldiers in the camp of the People. And twice as many again are the women, children, and the men too old for the path of war." He turned and looked at George. "But we have our allies: the Sage People and the Cloud People of the south with perhaps three thousand soldiers of their own, and the Inviters and the Little Star People to the north, who are nearly as great in number as the People."

George scowled. "Twenty thousand soldiers. What about the other allied tribes?"

"Like the Ree and the other Earth Lodge Builders?" Storm Arriving dismissed the idea with a gesture. "They are few and have no soldiers to speak of. They are farmers and do not walk the war path."

"And your other neighbors?"

"No. The Cradle People and the Crow People are bitter enemies of the Alliance. Any other peoples are either too small or too far away to be of any help."

"So," George said, "twenty thousand it is, then. It will have to be enough."

"It seems to me to be a great number of soldiers. There has never been a war fought with so many, not even against Long Hair."

George sighed. "My friend, when my people fought their Civil War, they sometimes lost twenty thousand men in a single battle."

Storm Arriving gaped incredulously. "You are joking."

"No," George said. "It is true."

Storm Arriving laughed. "Then we will have no trouble beating the bluecoats. What kind of war chief loses twenty thousand men in one battle?"

"The kind who starts with a hundred thousand."

Storm Arriving took a breath before he spoke. "One thing I have learned: It is not always numbers. Having greater numbers makes a war chief confident, but having fewer numbers makes him smart. Do not count us lost before we have even begun."

George smiled, appreciative of his friend's wisdom. "You will make a good chief someday."

They began walking once more and soon were among the lodges of the Tree People band. Women were out tending the meat on drying racks or tanning hides. Younger men were working on arrows or shields. Old men sat in story circles and smoked, and children ran to and fro between the lodges. Many people greeted the two men by name as they passed, and Storm Arriving greeted them all by name in return.

Each family had five or six lodges, some even had more, and they set them all close to one another in a circle around a main family lodge. Between family circles there was more room—fifty yards or so—and thus the camp was spread over a large area. Storm Arriving and his family had set their lodges at the western edge of camp, so the two men had over a mile to walk before they reached home.

"Why don't you camp closer to the center?" George asked. "We will meet often with the Council in the weeks to come, and it would be a shorter walk."

"My mother is old, One Who Flies, and now has only one daughter to help her when I am gone. At the edge of camp, she is closer to the river and it is not so far a walk to get the day's water. Besides"—he tapped George in the chest—"we are here already. You have survived the journey."

George spied the familiar decorations on the lodge ahead. The buffalo skins that covered the frame were painted on one side with black handprints over the white spots and jagged lines that represented hail and lightning. The other side had on it blue stars around a white moon.

Storm Arriving had a small family—smaller now since the tragedy of his sister's death—and so, apart from the main lodge, there was only one other, the women's lodge where his mother and sister lived during their monthly cycles.

Nearby, however, alone and by itself, was a single lodge. The newly stripped sapling trunks that made the conical frame were still orange where they extended above the skins. The skins, too, were new, and nearly white in the strong sunlight of the late afternoon. The lodge was empty—or at least, George corrected himself, it had no living inhabitants.

"Who will take care of him?" he asked.

Storm Arriving looked at the lonely lodge. "Laughs like a Woman had no family. They were all killed years ago, during the war against Long Hair. The father of Laughs like a Woman died in the battles. His mother and two sisters died in the fires along the Big Salty."

Fires my father started, George thought. "And yet . . ." Realizing the fullness of the man's story, George's emotions threatened to overcome his control. "Somehow Laughs like a Woman ended up dying to save my life."

"He thought well of you."

"Not at first."

Storm Arriving laughed. "No, not at first. There

were two times on the day the cloud fell when I thought he would surely kill you."

"Well," George said, "he *was* a Contrary."

"That is probably what saved you. Anyone else would have done it. I nearly killed you myself, but my reasons for keeping you alive were different."

George did not like discussing those reasons. They had to do with visions and prophecies and a woman who could see into the future: Speaks While Leaving, daughter of One Bear, and the woman whom Storm Arriving intended to marry.

"So who will take care of Laughs like a Woman?" George asked, getting back to his original question.

"I will," Storm Arriving said. "He was a brother to me, my special friend from years past." He turned and looked at George. "You would be welcome, too, if you wished."

George put his hand on the knife that hung from a strap across his shoulder, a gift from their fallen friend.

"What do I need to do?"

It was the second time Storm Arriving had made this trip in as many moons. The first time, he had come with his family to lay his sister to rest. Blue Shell Woman had died during a surprise attack by the bluecoats, an attack that had killed more women and children than warriors.

On that occasion, his heart had been sore and raw. In her funeral bed, his sister had been young and beautiful, still untried by life. She had died on the brink of her own future, and Storm Arriving had wept for her loss as well as his own.

This time, though, his heart was well. He did not rejoice at the death of Laughs like a Woman, but neither did it pain him. Laughs like a Woman had died well, fighting a strong enemy, and saving the life of a friend. He had died very well. Often, that is all a man can hope for, Storm Arriving thought.

He rode with One Who Flies and Big Nose, another lifelong friend of the deceased, south toward the traditional burial grounds. In the distance they saw other travelers on similar errands. Of the four hundred warriors who had traveled to the *vé'hó'e* City of White Stone, less than three hundred had returned, and the landscape was dotted with grieving burial parties all bent on the same destination; all traveling alone, but all traveling together in similar purpose.

Storm Arriving and his friends all rode whistlers, even One Who Flies, who owned none. His belonged to Laughs like a Woman. Each man had a spare mount, and it was on these that they had loaded the body of their fallen friend and all the other necessities of the task before them.

The whistlers ran across the landscape with effortless strides. They were large, lizardlike creatures with long, powerful hind legs. Their forelegs were small and used only for digging up roots or pawing through mud or snow to find forage.

Storm Arriving's whistler fluted a call to the others, and the sound reverberated through the long bone crest that curved up and back from its head.

Storm Arriving interpreted his whistler's call. "Squirrel-dog village," he warned. He used the Trader's Tongue as One Who Flies did not yet speak the language of the People. "Let us slow a bit."

The whistlers dropped back to a long trot and Storm Arriving heard the first short yaps of the small squirrels-that-bark-like-dogs. Ahead, little squirrel heads poked up out of their holes and then ducked back down into their burrows.

At a full run the whistlers could easily have harmed themselves if they stepped in one of the burrow openings. At this speed, though, they could see and avoid the dangers.

They ran across the squirrel-dog village without difficulty and Storm Arriving pressed the pace again.

"When will we get there?" One Who Flies asked.

Storm Arriving looked at the sun, now just past the top of the sky. "Before the sun sets," he said. "We have made good time. Two days out, maybe three back."

"Why longer on the way home?"

"Because," Big Nose said, "the People have already moved on to the north to follow the herd. We have to catch up with them."

"Ah, yes," One Who Flies said hesitantly. "I see. And you know where they have gone?"

Storm Arriving laughed. "Don't be such a *vé'ho'e*," he said. "We will find them. It will not be hard."

One Who Flies smiled and rode on. Storm Arriving noticed that he rode almost like one of the People now. He looked comfortable on whistler-back, straddling his mount's narrow spine, his feet in the loops, his legs tucked up, almost kneeling as he sped along. He rode as one should ride a whistler, as part of it, not sitting on one's rear like the *vé'hó'e* rode their horses.

Crazy *vé'hó'e*.

They rode on without further conversation, and Storm Arriving watched as the land around them began to change.

They were coming to the edge of the long blanket of buffalo grass that had covered the flat plains behind them. The constant whisper of his mount's feet through the short blue-green blades began to give way to soft thumps and scratches as they ran over hardier bluestem grass and spots of bare earth.

The Sand Hills were ahead, rising out of the featureless prairie like the humps of buffalo bulls above the rest of the herd. The folds and creases in the landscape made it easy for a man to lose his way. Here, the sun and the westerly wind were important allies that helped direct any who traveled across the dunes.

They headed into the hills and for hours coursed up and down their flanks, passing stands of prickly pear, butterfly sage, and tall sedgegrass. As evening came and the air began to cool, they caught the taste of the wind off the Big Salty. The whistlers caught it, too, and sang a long rising song to greet the tang in the air. The riders crested the top of a tall hill and saw, in the distance, their goal.

The westering sun made the shadows long and turned the hills before them into bright ridgelines separated by dark, shaded slopes. Beyond the hills, however, they could see the glittering waters of the Big Salty. Each wavelet shone like a star in the pale road of water that led off to the misty horizon.

"Why do you lay your dead to rest here?" One Who Flies asked.

"It makes the journey shorter for the spirits." Storm Arriving could see that One Who Flies did not understand. "Wait until tonight. Then you will see."

They started off again, riding into the slow rhythm of chilly climbs up shadowed inclines and warm descents down each hill's sunlit flank.

The sun was preparing to set when they reached the bluffs at the rim of the sea. All around this northern limit of the Big Salty—in front of the riders and as far as they could see along the coast to either side—the higher lands of the prairie ended in cliffs so high that a man at the bottom could not shoot an arrow to clear the top.

All along the base of the cliffs was a wide belt of forests and swamps in which lived creatures similar to the lizard-like denizens of the plains.

The frond-leafed forests were home to huge hardbacks with spiked tails and horn-faced beasts larger than a buffalo. Man-sized shadow-hunters stalked their prey in packs, springing in ambush from behind the huge boles of fern trees. In the salt swamps lived whistlers with ducklike bills and no crests, twice as large as any beast found on the prairie. There were also waterwalkers, lizards that walked on two legs, stepping across the water plants at high tide as they hunted for the mud-skimmers that hid in the cool shadows.

But beyond the forests and the swamps, beyond the rocky islands and the bars of white sand that protected the shore, was the Big Salty. The air above it was hazy with spray and filled with fishing lizards and flyers. In flight the man-size creatures were graceful and agile, turning easily with a flip of their paddlelike tails or the slightest change of their leathery wings. On the cliffs where they nested, however, they were clumsy, hobbling and twisting like crippled old men, their wingtips folded up behind them like unused walking sticks. It was these creatures that Storm Arriving and his people depended on to help speed the journey of their loved ones' spirits. If the three men worked quickly, Laughs like a Woman would be on his way to Séáno before the moon set.

Storm Arriving searched the coast to the east. "Where is it?" he asked of Big Nose. His friend scanned the nearby shoreline, squinting against the sunlight that came in low from the west. He pointed to a bluff some little distance away where the dark green sedge was thinned by the pale clumps of white sage.

"Hip-ip," Storm Arriving said, urging his whistler into a run. They were there within moments and the mixture of the heavy salt air and the redolence of sage crushed under his whistler's feet filled the coolness with a sacred scent.

He stretched his hand out toward the west. The sun was three fingers off the horizon, the growing crescent of the waxing moon more than a hand behind.

"Plenty of time," he said.

They unloaded the whistlers of their burdens. Storm Arriving carried the poles and rawhide strips that would form the catafalque upon which their friend would spend his last earthly night. Big Nose took down from his spare mount the bundle of buffalo robes in which they would wrap the body. When they were done they went to help One Who Flies, and together the three of them took down the body of

Laughs like a Woman and the articles that would accompany him on his journey.

Laughs like a Woman had been dead for ten days. To prepare his body for the journey back to his own lands, they had wrapped it tightly in long lengths of white cloth. Even so, the body had begun to ripen and the carrion smell was strong, even through the layered windings.

They laid him down on a bed of white sage and set to building the catafalque. Poles were set deep in the soft, sandy earth, and other poles were lashed between them as beams. With rawhide strips they created the lattice that would support the body. One Who Flies worked hard to help despite the recent loss of the small finger from his left hand. As the sun met the horizon, they pounded stakes in beside the poles to stabilize them.

Overhead, the sky darkened through a host of blues. The red light from the setting sun touched the thin, feathered clouds and made them glow with a shell-born pink, and the wings of the flying lizards soaring beneath them burned with ruddy fire.

Storm Arriving instructed One Who Flies with gestures alone. Words seemed somehow profane in this sacred place, and the three men continued their preparations in silence.

On the lattice they laid out a fine buffalo robe. Of thick fur and soft, supple hide, it was sewn with thousands of colored porcupine quills. It had been the finest thing Laughs like a Woman had owned.

Together, they lifted the shrouded body up and laid it on the fur-lined bed. Beside him they laid his bow, his quiver and arrows, and a bundle that held his finest shirt and leggings. Storm Arriving regretted that they could not dress Laughs like a Woman in his best clothes—the necessities of war had prevented it. More important, he felt, that they had brought him to his homeland and to this place. The spirit of his body, once released, would find the spirit of these fine clothes and all would be well.

Storm Arriving tucked a parfleche filled with dried meat beside the body, folded the ends of the buffalo robe over him, and stepped away from the scaffold.

The fire had gone out of the sky and was replaced by fires on the nearby bluffs as other mourners completed their rituals. Above, the moon brightened, stars gathered their courage, and the flyers became dark-winged shadows against a darkening sky.

Storm Arriving kindled a small fire and fed it with gathered sage and juniper. Big Nose took out his drum, a piece of shaved buffalo hide stretched taut over a rim of bent willow-wood. He began to sound a rhythm.

The drum's voice was low and basic—a heartbeat in the air—and the sweet smoke from the fire was like the breath of the world. One Who Flies squatted near the fire, respectfully silent, as Big Nose began to sing. The craggy-faced warrior sang of brave deeds and a hero's death. He sang of the impermanence of life and of the eternal earth. He sang, and One Who Flies fed the fire.

Storm Arriving stood up and went to the whistlers. He picked up the halter rope of the spare mount that One Who Flies had led here. Laughs like a Woman had not had many whistlers—the life of a Contrary was one of deprivation and solitude. Of his few, however, this one, the one that had borne his body to this place, had been his favorite. It was a huge drake and had been Laughs like a Woman's war mount for seven years. If Laughs like a Woman had given him a name, he had kept it to himself, for he had never told Storm Arriving what it was.

Storm Arriving led the drake over to the scaffold. It snuffed and crooned at the smoke from the sage-brush fire and the dark green color of its muzzle flared red and white in agitation. Storm Arriving calmed the beast with soothing words and gentle scratches in the place-that-whistlers-love, the spot on the withers that neither beak nor claw could reach. The big drake relaxed and the angry hues drained from his skin.

"Hámêstoo'êstse," Storm Arriving said, and the whistler lowered himself to the ground. He continued to soothe the beast, lulling him into a state of near-sleep.

The pulse of Big Nose's drumbeat and the cry of his song touched Storm Arriving's heart. The scent of the smoke from the fire enfolded him as he stood beside the whistler. The smoke cleansed him, purified him. On the catafalque behind him, Laughs like a Woman lay dead, his spirit awaiting release. Laughs like a Woman had all that he needed for his journey— food to eat, finery to wear, a bow and arrows for the eternal hunt. He only needed one more thing. A mount.

Storm Arriving drew his knife from its sheath and in one quick move he cut deep across the whistler's throat. The blade was sharp and gave little pain. The drake's eyes widened in surprise, then glazed as his blood drained out. He laid his head down on the bed of sage, breathed once, twice, and died. The drake's spirit would soon be free to join Laughs like a Woman on the road to Séáno.

Storm Arriving looked up. The flying lizards were closer now. Drawn by the songs, they were moon-silver phantoms that flew past in the night. Their chatter was chilling, oddly human, like old men complaining about the lateness of dinner. One flyer, more brazen than the others, landed on the scaffold. It was the size of a boy, but its wings extended over the edge, reaching nearly to the ground. It folded up its wings, tucking the tips up under each arm, and looked at the trio of men that stood nearby.

Its beak was long and black and lined with the tiny teeth that gave it its name in the language of the Sage People. It glared at the men, the iris of its eye bright yellow, glinting in the firelight. Storm Arriving heard a flap and a rustle and another flyer landed, this one on the ground near the drake at the foot of the cata-falque. The first flyer raised its head and cried up to the stars and the moon with a high, keening call that raised the hairs on Storm Arriving's arms.

The whistlers began to pull at their tethers. With silent looks, the three men agreed it was time to go. They climbed atop their mounts and bid them rise. In moments they were on their way, but after three strides, Storm Arriving pulled up and looked back.

Another flyer had come to ground near the slain whistler, but along with the other two, it only crouched and stared at the retreating men, as if waiting for some privacy before beginning the feast that would release the flesh-bound spirits and send them on their way.

Storm Arriving looked beyond the flyers, toward the sea and the star-filled sky.

"There," he said, and pointed so One Who Flies could see.

The moonlight bedecked the dark salt waters with glittering shards of silver. In the distance, the glints of light merged into a shimmer that flowed the length of the Big Salty, flowed all the way to the horizon and blended there with the milky glow of the star-road that climbed up the night sky to Séáno.

"There. Can you see now? Can you see the road?"

One Who Flies studied the vista. "This is where the road to heaven begins," he said. "That's why you bring them here."

"It makes their journey much easier."

"A spirit can get lost in the world," Big Nose said. "Spirits get lost every day." He turned and looked at One Who Flies with a dead-eyed gaze. "A lost spirit can really ruin your day."

One Who Flies looked at Big Nose with puzzlement, but a quick smile told him that he was being teased. He shook his head.

"I still can't tell when you people are joking."

Big Nose laughed and leaned forward. "A man may not tell you when he is joking, but he will always tell you when he is serious. If you are not sure, guess a

man to be joking. You'll be right most of the time."
He straightened up and looked off into the dim night.
"Shall we go?"

"Yes," Storm Arriving said. *"Nóheto!"*

The other two started off but Storm Arriving held
back. More flyers had gathered, here and at the other
burial sites he could see. He was well pleased with
this. Tonight the dead would rest.

A few days later they were riding past the sentries.
The People had moved north, leaving the Red Paint
River for the arms of the Antelope Pit River. Aside
from the new location, everything else was just as the
three men had left it. All the bands were encamped
in their customary places, the Council Lodge and the
lodges of the sacred artifacts stood tall and impressive
in the center of camp, and the flocks of whistlers
cropped the blue-green grass out to the west.

The men rode down the sun road into the center of
camp. Big Nose clasped his friends' hands and turned
toward his home with the Hair Rope band. Storm Arriving and One Who Flies continued onward to the
camp of the Tree People band.

Storm Arriving's mother and sister were waiting
outside the lodge when they rode up. Picking Bones
Woman greeted them with a nod.

"Was it done well?" she asked.

"Yes, Mother." He dismounted and embraced her.
"It was done very well."

"It will be a long time before we see another man
like him."

"Yes," Storm Arriving said. "A very long time."

"Your sister did as you asked," she told him.

Storm Arriving looked at Mouse Road. She smiled
timidly and glanced off to the side. He followed her
gaze.

A lone lodge stood close by. It was Laughs like a
Woman's lodge, still new and bright. Mouse Road had
taken it down when the People moved and had set it

up in this place. It was not so close to his own family
lodge as to be a part of Storm Arriving's family group,
but also not far enough away to be all by itself. She
had put it in a place of transition, a place of possibilities.

In front of it, tethered to a stake, stood a whistler—
a hen that, along with the drake One Who Flies rode
and the drake they had sacrificed at the burial, comprised the whole of the flock that had belonged to
Laughs like a Woman.

"Thank you, Mouse Road. That, too, was done
well."

Mouse Road blushed at his praise but said nothing.

His sister was a young woman of fifteen summers.
Already, she had most of the beauty of her deceased
sister, and showed signs of a quick mind like her mother's. But while just a few moons past she was a loqua-
cious child who would offer an opinion on anything,
now—since her sister's murder—she was quiet and
taciturn. Storm Arriving knew that her spirit had been
bruised. He prayed it had not been broken.

What she needs, he thought to himself, is to be
drawn out. He resolved to discover a way to do so.

He turned to One Who Flies and gestured toward
the lodge his sister had raised. "This lodge belongs to
Laughs like a Woman," he said in the Trader's
Tongue. "But he is gone and no longer needs it. Now
it belongs to you, and his two whistlers, as well."

One Who Flies was surprised by this. He stammered
his words as he spoke. "But . . . but there . . . Certainly, someone else . . . a family member . . . a close
friend. Surely there is a widow who could use it
more."

Storm Arriving smiled at his friend's discomfort. "It
is good that you should speak so," he said, "for it
shows that you appreciate the gift. Laughs like a
Woman would be pleased. But no, there is no family,
and there is no widow or lonely grandfather in the
whole camp who has less than you, One Who Flies.

What do you have? Nothing. Only the clothes you wear and a single mount you never ride."

"That walker makes me nervous. She's so big—"

"So now you have two whistlers, and a place to stay dry when it rains." He touched his friend's shoulder. "Laughs like a Woman thought well of you, One Who Flies. He liked you. He gave you his best knife. If he had been able, he would have given you these gifts himself."

One Who Flies sighed and Storm Arriving saw acceptance clear the trouble from his brow.

"I will remember him until the end of my days."

"Good," Storm Arriving said. "Then everything has been done well."

"Why Jacob," Libbie said. "How nice."

President George Armstrong Custer, Sr., watched over his newspaper as his wife got up from the breakfast table and walked across the room to meet the Secretary of War.

The room in which he and Libbie took breakfast was a long, narrow room on the south side of the third floor, not far from the family's residences. The drapes had been pulled back to let in the early morning sunshine. Even in June, the White House was a chill, damp place. Custer was sure that if he went down into the basements he would find the Potomac lapping at the bottom stair. Still, after a lifetime in tents on battlefields, in barracks on the frontiers, and even a few years in low-rate hotels as a representative in Congress, he had to admit that the White House, with all its faults, constituted the best accommodations he and his family had ever known.

As Libbie walked toward her unexpected guest, the pale yellow cloth of her dress caught the slanting shafts of morning light, rebounding them through the room like a gossamer breeze. She met Jacob with outstretched hands.

"It seems like a year since I saw you last. Will you join us for something to eat?"

Custer turned the page of his newspaper and took a sip of his coffee, feigning disinterest.

The coved ceiling carried Jacob's whispered query across the room. "Is it an 'Autie' day, or a 'Mr. President' day?"

"I heard that," Custer said without looking up.

Jacob cleared his throat. "Ah, a 'Mr. President' day, I see. Perhaps just some coffee then."

Libbie led Jacob back to the table with inquiries after family and friends long absent. In truth, it had not been all that long since she had seen their old friend—a month, perhaps, six weeks at the outside—but on that last occasion as at many others before it, business had intervened and Libbie had had to forgo even the smallest portion from the feast of friendly gossip that Jacob could always provide.

Today, though, Custer was determined to let Libbie have her fill, and his earlier churlishness guaranteed at least some of it. Jacob, thinking Custer to be "in a mood," would not speak to him unless spoken to. In the meantime he could natter away without feeling guilty about keeping his Commander-in-Chief waiting.

Custer peeked surreptitiously around his paper to catch a glimpse of his wife. Elizabeth Custer leaned forward as she chatted amiably with their old family friend. Custer was glad to see the glint in her eyes and the hint of a smile on her lips. The last two months had been so hard on her—their son, first a captive, then a turncoat; the attack on the Capitol building, led by their son; the disgrace, the worry. For all this, rightly or not, she had blamed her husband, and Custer knew that arguing about their son's own role in events would do nothing to help melt the wall of ice that currently separated them. Any thaw, if it came, could not be pressed. Libbie, when she cared to be, was a force of nature. Custer resigned himself to simply wait for a warmer season.

Jacob Greene, on the other hand, was anything but a force of nature. Jacob was solid, as dependable as they came, and loyal beyond call. Physically he was everything Custer was not, dark where Custer was fair-haired, stout where Custer was thin. Only in his capacity as a leader had he shown the same qualities Custer prized, and as a friend, he had proven to be a most trustworthy adviser.

As a result, Custer had kept Jacob close by through their years in the military. When Custer had moved on into public service, Jacob had accepted the invitation to come along.

Jacob caught Custer looking at him and his side of the conversation began to flag.

"Well," Libbie said, "I suppose there is some business that has brought you here. Something already delayed too long by idle chitchat?"

"Yes," Jacob said. "I mean no. I mean it wasn't idle chitchat." His eyes shifted nervously from Libbie's smile to Custer's imperiously lifted eyebrow. "But there is some business. Now that you mention it."

Custer released his friend with a chuckle. "Jacob, relax. Libbie, don't we have a free evening some time next week?"

Libbie thought for a moment, then nodded. "Thursday next."

"Why don't we have Jacob and Nettie over for dinner that night? Just a quiet evening with old friends."

His wife's eyes lit up with genuine excitement. "Oh, what a wonderful idea," she said, but quickly tempered her enthusiasm. "That is, if you two have no other commitments for that evening."

Jacob beamed. "There is no place we'd rather be."

Libbie's smile was contagious and Custer found her gazing at him with a tenderness that he'd not seen since he'd first told her the news about their son.

He smiled himself, and thought: We win the war with little battles.

"But now," she said, "I think I have kept you two from your business long enough. If you will excuse me?"

The men rose as she got up from the table.

"Thank you, dear," she said to Custer and, still smiling, left the room.

Custer folded up his newspaper and laid it on the table. He drained his coffee cup and waved off the servant who came to refill it.

"Well, Jacob," he said at last, "what brings you?"

Jacob's face became serious.

"You are going to hear something today. About a new bill in the Senate."

"Oh?"

"Yes. It came to my attention because it will affect our policy regarding the Unorganized Territory."

"Really?" Custer sat forward. The Unorganized Territory—those lands currently controlled by the Cheyenne Alliance—had cost him plenty, both politically and in the budget, and he had nothing at all to show for it. "In what way will our policy be affected?"

Jacob drew invisible lines on the tablecloth with his finger. "It calls for a major' railroad extension that crosses the entire state of Yankton and bridges the Missouri River; all for the purpose of opening up the Frontier and encouraging active settlement of the region."

Custer sat back. This all sounded familiar. He searched his memory, trying to recall the conversation. "This . . . by chance, is this bill from Bob Matherly?"

Jacob gaped. "You know about it?"

Custer laughed. "Know about it? Hellfire, I told him what to write."

"What? You—" Jacob sputtered, unable to complete his thought. Custer stepped into the gap.

"Now what did you want me to do about the bill?"

"Do? I want you to oppose it. To veto it if you have to."

"Veto?" Custer said, perturbed. "Why would I do that?"

Jacob calmed himself. "Mr. President, we have had more than enough trouble with that region this year.

You in particular have been pilloried for your actions—"

"I read the papers."

"Um, yes, Mr. President. What I mean to say is that, well, we just thought—"

"*We?*"

"Yes, Mr. President. Samuel and I. A few others in the cabinet. We're concerned."

"How so?"

"Sir, the Democrats are making a lot of hay on this whole issue. Between that and the railroad strikes out west in Chicago . . . Well, sir, we just thought that this whole bill was nothing but a political powder keg."

"You're worried about a second term."

"If you just let this die away—"

"But, Jacob, don't you see? This is the perfect tool. I don't want to run away from this with my tail between my legs. What kind of political future will *that* provide me? This bill, it takes our two greatest problems, the Frontier and the railroad workers, and puts them in the spotlight."

"But, sir—"

Custer held up a hand. "It puts *them* in the spotlight, and takes it off of me. I say we support this bill, support it to the hilt. It will take public attention off our failure and allow us to focus it on the future."

Jacob shook his head. "It's risky, sir. What if the project fails?"

"Then it fails. But remember that if it does, it will do so more than a year from now, and if it does"— he winked—"it won't be *our* fault."

Custer could see Jacob's anxiety melt away. An impish smile touched his friend's otherwise cherubic lips. "And by then," he said, "the election will already be won."

Custer held up a finger of warning. "Assuming I even decide to run for another term. Believe me, I've not decided on that. But if I do, a success or two under my belt will help. If this succeeds, it's our win. If it doesn't, it's their loss."

Jacob shook his head again, this time in mild disbelief. "All right, Mr. President. We'll do it your way."

"Was there ever any doubt?"

The sun was only a breath of pink along the prairie horizon, and the cloudless sky above was still brilliant with stars when Storm Arriving heard someone stir inside the lodge. He shivered in the chill air. He draped his Trader-wool blanket over his head and pulled it close about his shoulders, and then stepped back, away from the lodge so as not to overhear any conversation from within or frighten anyone who came out.

In the distance, he saw another suitor waiting outside another lodge. The other suitor was much younger than he—Storm Arriving could tell by the young man's thin legs and by his anxious pacing. The doorflap of the other lodge opened and a man came out—the girl's older brother, most likely.

"Go home," the brother said and shooed at the suitor as to drive off a dog. "Go home."

The young man did not move until the brother picked up a stone and threw it. It hit him with a thump and the frustrated suitor ran off.

Storm Arriving chuckled silently. The young suitor had a long and difficult courtship ahead of him. Such a brother would make sure only a worthy man wed his sister.

More voices awoke within the nearby lodge. Storm Arriving pulled his blanket tighter to hide his face. From other family lodges the womenfolk began to emerge. Empty waterskins in hand, they walked down toward the river with whispers and silent glances sent in his direction.

"Good morning, Storm Arriving," one of them said, though he did not know her and she could not see his face. Her companions laughed and Storm Arriving smiled. His own courtship had lost its secrecy years ago.

By the time the lodge's doorflap opened, the dawn sky was orange and the sun was ready to lift its head above the rim of the world. A woman stepped out into the morning air and stretched. Storm Arriving sighed. It was not the one for whom he waited, but her mother.

"Ah," Magpie Woman said, seeing him standing there, "it is a fine morning, Storm Arriving." She patted him on the shoulder as she headed off to the river. "She will be out in a moment."

The first rays of the sun ran down the sun road and touched the front of the lodge. The doorflap opened and she stepped outside.

Her moccasins were beaded with blue and white, and her leggings were stitched with red bits of Trader's cloth. But between the moccasins and the leggings there was a patch of skin that made his heart leap. The curve of her bare ankle was the finest thing he had seen for a very long time.

After the ankle and before her knee came the hem of her dress, and as the whole of her emerged from the lodge, he could only smile. She wore a wide, quilled belt about her waist that emphasized her form without endangering modesty. The fringes of her sleeves fell to her waist, and her left sleeve was untied along the top in the old tradition, leaving her bow arm almost bare.

Thick braids hanging down past her belt, she stood in the orange light of the newborn sun. She took a deep breath, closed her eyes, and let the sun warm her skin for a few moments. Then she opened her eyes—they were large and dark and round—and she turned. She saw him, anonymous beneath his blanket, and smiled a happy smile, though she said nothing.

She slung her empty waterskins over her shoulder and headed toward the river. She ignored him studiously, but her smile remained.

He reached out and plucked at her sleeve as she passed by.

"Speaks While Leaving," he whispered.

She stopped but did not turn, playing the courtship game to its utmost. "Who is it?"

"I am Storm Arriving," he said. "The man who will be your husband, if you will take me."

Now she did turn, and her smile was even broader. "Husband? To me? What makes you speak of marriage now, when you have said nothing of it so far? How many years have you courted me, Storm Arriving?"

"Seven," he said.

"Seven years. And in all that time, not one word of marriage."

"We were arguing for four of those years," he pointed out.

"True," she agreed. "But that hardly matters. There are still three years without a proposal. Why now? What made you decide to talk marriage today?"

"It was something that One Who Flies said to me."

Her teasing tone turned to curiosity. "Really? What was it he said?"

"One Who Flies said: 'Why haven't you asked that girl to marry you?' "

She laughed. "Now you are teasing me," she said and turned to walk away.

"No," he said, following her. "It is true. He said it last night."

"And what was your answer?"

"I did not have one."

She stopped. "You didn't."

"No," he said. "I didn't. So I came straight here and waited all the night like a moonstruck youth for the first sight of you. I wanted the very next words I said to be the words I should have spoken years ago: Will you take me as a husband?"

She took a step closer, then another. She reached out and touched the edge of the blanket, and he opened his arms to her. She took a third step. Her hands slid around him and she laid her head on his chest. He let the blanket slip to his shoulders and wrapped it around them both.

"Yes," she whispered, her voice barely audible.

"I am sorry I took so long."

"Who will you send," she asked, "to speak to my father?"

He sighed. "I do not know. I would have sent Laughs like a Woman, but now . . . I do not have an elder or a truly close friend to act as intermediary."

She gave him a playful tap but did not release her hold of him. "Don't be silly. Of course you do."

"Who?" he asked. "One Who Flies? I couldn't ask him."

"Why not?"

"He's never done it before."

"And Laughs like a Woman had?"

"He doesn't know what to do."

"So teach him. It is not a difficult thing. He comes over. He asks. He leaves."

"But . . ." Storm Arriving was stymied, caught between his head and his heart, and not caring for what his heart was saying. He felt Speaks While Leaving grow still in his arms, as she guessed his reasons.

"It is because he is a *vé'ho'e*," she said.

Storm Arriving grit his teeth, ashamed of his unreasonable feelings.

"Then what about Big Nose?" she asked, attempting to find a solution. "Or one of the chiefs of your soldier society?"

"No," he said. "You were right the first time. It should be One Who Flies." He took a deep breath and let it out again, trying to calm his mind as well as his spirit. "In the fall, before the People depart for winter camps. He will come to visit your father in the fall."

She hugged him tightly. "You are a good man," she said. "Now let me go so I can help my mother get the day's water."

He opened his arms. "I am not keeping you."

"Yes, you are," she said, her cheek against his shoulder, her arms still around his chest. "Yes. You are." Then she stood on tiptoe and kissed him swiftly and was gone, running down the river path.

CHAPTER 2

Autumn, A.D. 1886
Elk River, Western Reaches
Cheyenne Alliance Territory

George crouched down next to his walker and waited for the signal that would begin the hunt. The lizardlike beast lay as flat as she could in the long, dew-damp grass, though her flanks were plump with fat from the frequent summer hunting. George leaned up against her to steal some of her warmth, for though she was the cause of a great deal of his anxiety on these hunts, he was not so afraid of her as to forgo what comfort she could provide. He nestled up against her and waited under the metal-lidded sky of the northern prairie.

The People had moved, picking up camp several times throughout the summer, following the herd as it wandered north toward the greening regions of the higher latitudes. It had been a peaceful time of hunting and trading with allied neighbors like the Inviters and the Cloud People, free of conflict with the more antagonistic tribes like the Crow and the Cradle People. As the weeks passed, George became accustomed to the slower, more deliberate rhythm of the Indians.

His life now progressed in time with the land around him. He rose earlier, feeling refreshed. Each morning he bathed in river waters and watched grown men, even old grandfathers, act like boys, though it be just for a hand of time. The days were filled with chores and duties—though fewer for him than for others—and the evenings were busy with feasts and dances and always, always the drumbeat of ceremony.

He knew the day by the arc of the sun and not the hands of a pocket watch. In learning this, he learned how the earth moved and where the moon and the sun and even the stars were. At times, he could almost sense where he himself was in the world, could almost feel the presence of lands and places far removed from a single man on the lonely prairie.

Only in hunting did he still feel completely out of place. Hunting was a man's one great duty of the summer months, and the tribesmen worked hard to feed their families and put aside meat for the winter months. Though George had no family to feed, he did have the burden of a walker, and he had no intention of dealing with her when she was hungry. Unfortunately, he had no rifle, and could not use a bow with any accuracy. More than once he had been forced to rely on the generosity of his walker-riding comrades to help fatten his own beast for the long, dark winter months ahead.

Walkers moved much like whistlers, standing on long hind legs, but they were larger than their herbivorous cousins. George's walker was twenty feet long from the tip of her narrow, tooth-filled mouth to the end of her striped tail, and she was more muscular than any whistler. Walkers were predators—perhaps the largest on earth—and several weeks before, George, in the thrall of what had seemed to be a good idea at the time, had acquired one.

He laughed silently at the notion of a man acquiring a walker. No, it had not been his doing. It had been hers. He had found out too late that an unaffiliated walker often bonded with a new rider and would let no other ride her.

He sighed. It *had* seemed a good idea at the time. Now, though, the novelty of caring for a fifteen-foot-tall, meat-eating monster was wearing very, very thin. Every week during the heavy hunting season, walkers had to eat, and eat they did—with enthusiasm. The fat his mount put on now was needed to see her through the winter when she entered into a state of semihibernation.

George waited for the hunt to begin with growing impatience. He began to hum a wordless tune.

A hiss issued from the grass nearby. He poked his head up above the grass to find Blue Arrow scowling at him. George shrugged and gestured. *Yes. Quiet. Stay low.* Blue Arrow, still scowling, ducked back down into the tall grass next to his own walker.

When will the signal come? he silently asked the clouds.

But then he heard it—a whistler call, three long notes. It came again. They were coming!

"Ame'haooestse."

It was Blue Arrow again. He was standing up in the waist-high grass, calling George by his Cheyenne name.

"He'kotoo'êstse," George said in a harsh whisper. Be quiet!

"Ame'haooestse," Blue Arrow said, and pointed. George heard the whistler call again. He stood up and looked.

A man on whistler-back was riding their way. It was Storm Arriving. George waved.

"One Who Flies," Storm Arriving said, speaking in French. "Three Trees Together would like to speak with you."

"Now? I'm rather in the middle of something."

Storm Arriving frowned, puzzled, and George wondered if he had used the wrong French idiom.

"I am trying to hunt," he added to clarify.

"Ah. Yes, I see. Your walker will have to stay hungry today. Three Trees Together was very insistent."

George sighed. There was nothing else to do but go along. Storm Arriving would not have ridden a whistler out into the middle of a walker hunt without need. George clambered up onto his walker's back. The "saddle" was no more than a rope tied around the walker's keellike breast with a small wicker wedge tied to it to keep him from sliding down the beast's knobby spine. He slipped his feet into the two rope loops that served as stirrups and bid his beast rise to her feet.

"Good," Storm Arriving said as the walker stood. "Come, please, One Who Flies."

They rode off. George's walker grumbled, and Storm Arriving maintained a cautious distance between his whistler and the unhappy carnivore. George looked back toward the hunting ground. Already the waiting walkers were invisible, hidden by the tall grass.

"I was hoping," he said to Storm Arriving, "to at least make a kill today. She's been getting impatient with my lack of skill at hunting."

"Yes," Storm Arriving said without embellishment.

George grew concerned. Storm Arriving was taciturn only in times of danger. "What is wrong?" he asked. "Why does Three Trees Together want to see me now? Why couldn't it wait?"

Storm Arriving did not say anything and George could see the muscles in his neck and shoulders were tense.

"What is it?" George asked again, sure now that something was very wrong.

"It is not for me to say." Nor did he say anything else as they covered the miles back to the camp.

Storm Arriving led him not to the Council Lodge in the central clearing but around to the south of camp. They rode up into the group of low hills from which came several of the freshets that ran through and around the encampment. The hills were thick with tall birch and aspen. As they rode into the wood, the gray light of the cloudy morning took on a different hue, transformed from silver to gold by the fading leaves of coming autumn. Storm Arriving's whistler shifted color from pale prairie dun to mottled greens and golds. George's walker, unable to change the color of her skin, merely concerned herself with navigating her bulk along the whistler-sized path.

Storm Arriving slowed down as they wended their way past paper-pale trunks. Birdsong filled the air and George heard, too, the *hup-hrrr* of a red squirrel warning his kind of trespassers entering their domain.

They came to a place where the trees stood slightly back and a small rill tumbled over mossy rocks to create a canopied pond. The surface of the water was dotted with golden, heart-shaped leaves and the darting dimples of water-striders. There was the smell of clean air, damp earth, and the fragrance of nature's renewal.

An ancient birch leaned out over the water. Near it was a tiny fire in a circle of stones, and next to the fire was spread a buffalo robe, hide side down. On the robe sat Three Trees Together, cross-legged, staring intently at the pond's quiet waters. He made no notice of their arrival.

"Hámêstoo'e," Storm Arriving said, and their mounts settled into a crouch for the men to dismount.

They walked over to the old chief. George did not say anything, but left it to Storm Arriving to announce their presence. Storm Arriving said nothing, however, merely stood there near the edge of the buffalo robe, waiting.

Three Trees Together watched the water's slow progress from the moss-clad rocks down to the hidden outlet some yards away. He seemed a statue, with only the strong pulse in his neck and the nearly imperceptible turn of his head as he scanned the scene giving evidence that he was flesh and blood.

Finally, he spoke, though still without looking at them. His voice was quiet and measured, and it was as if he spoke not to them, but to the forest before him. Storm Arriving translated his words.

"Two nights ago," he said, "I had a dream. It was not a good dream, but it had a lot of power, and so

I paid attention to it. In the dream, I saw a river—I do not know which one—and out of the river came a man, a bluecoat, and this bluecoat, he carried a sack in one hand, and a sword in the other.

"This man seemed very sad to me. I could see in his eyes that he was sad. He looked at me and he held out the sack. I took the sack and opened it. The sack was full of cherries, nice and fresh, but as I watched, they broke and turned rotten and their juice seeped out of the sack and made a pool on the ground like blood.

"I looked at the bluecoat again and now his eyes were angry and there was blood on his sword. He held out his sword to me, but I did not want to take it, so he turned away and walked back into the river."

The old man stopped speaking as a newt climbed up out of the water and onto a nearby rock. Its brown, pebbly skin glistened with moisture and it cleaned its onyx eye with a carnelian hand.

"Do you remember," the old man continued, "what the *vé'hó'e* chiefs said when you left the City of White Stone?"

"Yes, sir," George replied. "They said they would talk again with the People when the cherries were ripe."

"Yes. That was it." The chief's breath seemed labored, ponderous. "It has been more than a moon since the cherries were ripe. I have sent soldiers to the bluecoats to ask for a chief so that we could talk more. There is so much still to talk about." Again, the heavy breaths and still Three Trees Together had not looked in their direction. George noticed for the first time that the old chief's hands were not fingering his medicine bag as was his habit. Instead, they were clenched into fists and tucked into his lap, as if he were trying to hide them.

"It is not a good thing for a grandfather of the People to grow angry. That is for the war chiefs, and even then, anger must be tempered by good judgment. But I find it hard today not to be angry."

He turned to face George and Storm Arriving, and within his deep-set eyes lived a silent rage.

"The first soldiers we sent to the *vé'hó'e* came back with no answer, and that made me sad, just like the bluecoat in my dream. But today, when the soldiers returned from their journey, one of them was dead—killed by a bluecoat while approaching a fort across the Big Greasy—and this has made me angry, just as the bluecoat in my dream became angry."

George's heart fell. The idiots! Trust the Army, he thought, to make a bad situation worse. The sentry had probably warned the Indian soldiers away in English, which they did not understand. "Sir," he said to Three Trees Together. "It is probably just a terrible misunderstanding. I am sure if they knew . . ." His words trailed off, too weak to have any effect.

"I do not understand you *vé'hó'e*—"

George winced inwardly at once more being lumped together with all others of his race.

"—but I think I must," the chief continued. "I think it is the most important thing I will ever do."

The old man took a deep breath, but this one was not in anger. It was an attempt to control and dispel his ire.

"Sit," Three Trees Together said, patting the buffalo pelt. "Let us smoke a bit. Then I want you to tell me about this yellow chief-metal and what we can do with it."

Storm Arriving translated the words of One Who Flies and Three Trees Together for several hands of time, stopping occasionally to drink from the clear water of the nearby brook or to enjoy a bowl of smoke from the grandfather's pipe. As was the way with Three Trees Together, the conversation often wandered from the topic, sometimes covering vast stretches before finally, but always, coming home to what the old chief really wanted to know.

They talked of gold and of guns. They talked of what One Who Flies called "artillery," which Storm Arriving could only translate to Three Trees Together as "bigger guns." They talked of the Horse Nations, of Long Hair, and of the way in which bluecoats made war.

Oddly, it seemed to Storm Arriving that these were not the chief's main concern. One Who Flies, buffered by the translation of his words, was unaware of the subtleties of the grandfather's questions, but Storm Arriving could hear it.

In a discussion of his life as a soldier with the Red Shield men and of the tactics he used when he walked the war path, Three Trees Together said, "You used to be a bluecoat. How is it that you threw your blue coat away?"

Storm Arriving knew that the old chief had already heard the story—everyone had—of how the bluecoats had killed Blue Shell Woman who had loved One Who Flies with all the fervor of a young woman's first infatuation; and of how One Who Flies, in disgust and anger at the acts of his people, had thrown away his own blue wool soldier's coat and vowed never to wear it again.

Three Trees Together knew this story, though One Who Flies had never personally told it to him. Now he asked to hear it. As Storm Arriving translated the tale, he could tell that the chief was not listening to the words. Even though he did not understand the Trader's Tongue, he listened as One Who Flies spoke. He watched his hands as he gestured and wrung them. He watched the expressions that crossed the face of the former bluecoat as he told the sad but familiar story. The chief was trying, Storm Arriving could tell, to see into the heart of this man. Storm Arriving found himself trying to see into it, too.

Who are you? What do you feel? How much like me are you? How different?

Storm Arriving once thought he knew the answers to these questions, but as he listened to One Who

Flies tell his tale, as he heard the varied emotions in his voice, in his words, he saw that there was more to this man than he knew. Perhaps more than he would ever know.

Later, when the conversation came around to home life, Three Trees Together said, "I have heard you have a lodge of your own. How is it?" And again he watched more than he listened as One Who Flies answered.

"It is a fine lodge and I am very grateful for the gift. Storm Arriving's sister has taught me the proper way to raise it and take it down. It still flaps a little in the wind, but I am learning."

Three Trees Together leaned forward, elbows on his knees, and began to toy with his medicine bag. "Tell me, One Who Flies," he said and his steady gaze was fixed on the former bluecoat. "How long do you think you will stay with the People?"

The question surprised Storm Arriving and he hesitated before he translated it. What was the old grandfather really asking? Was One Who Flies not welcome to stay? Or was he hoping he would stay? The questions raced through his mind and he could see as he translated the chief's words that One Who Flies was asking them, also.

"I . . . I do not know." His hands fell to his lap as he searched for an answer. His words were halting as if unsure of themselves, as if they were new and had never been spoken before. "I am a . . . traitor . . . to my own country. I will never be welcome there. Never." His hands began to move again, palms up, and then they fell still once more. "But even if I *was* welcome there, I do not think I would return. Things are too different."

Now his hands moved without words to guide them. They grasped at the air as if searching. Three Trees Together said nothing, giving One Who Flies time to find what he wanted to say. When One Who Flies spoke, it was in a soft voice, heavy with emotions barely held in check.

"I would like to help the People. I think I *can* help. But I know that you may not want my help. I am a *vé'ho'e*. I am the son of Long Hair. I am the *enemy*. I would understand if you no longer wished me to be here."

"Do you miss your family, One Who Flies?"

It was a dangerous question, and the answer was slow in coming.

"Yes. I miss my family. My mother and my two younger sisters. I wish I could tell them I was safe and well." He looked at his left hand, the one that was missing its little finger, lost in the battle at the City of White Stone. "They may still worry about me and I would like to put their minds at ease."

Three Trees Together sat back and began to fill his pipe. "It is a hard thing, to be banished," he said. "When a man of the People kills another, he is banished from our society. He will often go to live with the Inviters or he and his family may live alone. Many years will pass, but eventually the smell of death will leave him and he can come back to the People."

"I do not think my people will ever forgive my crime," One Who Flies said.

"Hmm," the old chief said. "That is unfortunate. I think you will make a good man someday." He reached over and took a small twig out of the smoldering fire. The tip of the twig glowed orange and left a rising trail of smoke in the still air.

"You are welcome to stay with the People until you want to go back among the *vé'hó'e*. But now, I think you should leave me. In a few days the bands will be leaving for winter camps, and you have some business to take care of, don't you?" This last was said to Storm Arriving.

"Yes, Grandfather," Storm Arriving said. "I do."

"Then go." He waved the glowing twig. "You have wasted too much time already."

Storm Arriving nodded to One Who Flies and they rose.

"Thank you," One Who Flies said.

"Go," the old chief said with a wink and a gap-toothed grin. "Get this man married."

Speaks While Leaving poked at the fire. She and her mother sat before the hearthpit on the packed earth floor of the family's lodge, knees together and feet tucked in close to their left.

Speaks While Leaving's father sat at the *vá'ôhtáma,* farthest from the door, and talked quietly with his mother. Healing Rock Woman worked on a sewing project while she spoke with One Bear. She kept most of her work hidden in a large sack, and pulled out only the section she was quilling. That way, no one could see the whole of the design until she was done and it was ready to give away.

It was a quiet evening. The air in the lodge was still strong with the lingering scents from the evening's meal of braised antelope meat and a porridge of cracked maize and rose hips. From a nearby lodge came the chatter and laughter of the seed game being played. Speaks While Leaving would have liked to attend the gaming, but tonight was not a night to be out with her friends.

She put another piece of wood on the fire and embers rose from it like flying stars trying to reach the sky.

"Leave it be," Magpie Woman said. "It is burning well already."

"Yes, Mother." She put her hands in her lap and sat, outwardly quiet.

"My granddaughter-who-can-see-the-future," Healing Rock Woman said from her place near the back of the lodge. "Can you not tell what will happen tonight?"

Speaks While Leaving smiled. "No, Ke'éehe. My father has not made his mind known to me. I can only guess."

"Ha!" the old woman scoffed. "Guess, indeed. Even a one-eyed hardback could see that—"

There was a disturbance outside—the sound of many feet and the fluting of whistlers. There was much whispering, and then the sound of feet running away.

"Speaks While Leaving?"

The voice came from outside the door to the lodge and by the accent, she knew who it was. She took breath to speak but her father spoke first.

"*Qui parle?*" her father asked.

"*Je suis 'Un Qui Vole,'* " was the reply.

"*Entrez vous.*"

The doorflap opened and One Who Flies peered inside. Speaks While Leaving gasped as the former bluecoat stepped into the lodge.

He was not wearing his *vé'ho'e* clothes. Instead, he wore moccasins and full-length leggings with long green fringes down the side. He wore a breechclout painted with symbols of grasshoppers and storm clouds, and a deerskin tunic with a wide belt of braided hide. Over his left shoulder was the strap of his sheathed hunting knife, and on his right shoulder and on his left hip had been pinned the white, flaglike tail of a timber-deer-waving, the ancient symbol of love. His hair had been pulled back—as best as possible—with a piece of leather, and his face had been shaved clean of the stubble of beard that was so unusual among a people who did not grow beards at all.

It was a startling transformation, and she saw by her parents' exchanged glances that she was not the only one who thought so.

One Who Flies took a step farther in, away from the door. He walked to his right, to the guest portion of the lodge and, after a gesture from her father, sat down next to him facing the fire.

"How are you?" he asked her father in the Trader's Tongue. "I hope you are well."

Unfortunately, her father had expended his entire knowledge of the Trader's Tongue with the conversation at the door, so now he turned to Speaks While Leaving with an expectant look.

"He asks after your health, and hopes you are well," she said to him in the language of the People.

"I am well," One Bear said, "as are we all." He pointed to his guest's garments. "You have changed your clothes."

Speaks While Leaving translated and saw One Who Flies smile at the words. He plucked at the fine garments he wore.

"I must admit, these are borrowed clothes. I did not have any clothing appropriate to my visit here tonight."

"And how," One Bear asked, "do you find wearing a breechclout instead of the all-over-leggings you usually wear?"

One Who Flies considered his answer. The breechclout was an important symbol of a man's virility and maturity, and Speaks While Leaving worried that her *vé'ho'e* friend might say something inappropriate.

"It is," he said, "colder than expected."

Speaks While Leaving blushed at the words but translated them anyway. Her father was wide-eyed, shocked by the candor of the reply, but Healing Rock Woman began to laugh, and by the smile that spread over the face of One Who Flies, they all realized that he had made a joke.

"You surprised me," her father said. "You are not known for making jokes."

"It is something I am trying to change," One Who Flies said. "But in truth, I have come here to ask you a question. It is a question about which there is no joking."

One Bear sat straighter and assumed his position as the head of the family, a chief of the Closed Windpipe band, and a man of long and solid reputation. "What is it you wish to ask?"

One Who Flies swallowed hard as the purpose for his visit arrived. "I come on behalf of Storm Arriving," he said, "son of Yellow Hawk, respected soldier of the Kit Fox, and a man whom you know to be brave and honorable. He requests the privilege of being taken as husband to your daughter, Speaks While Leaving, and in honor of her he gives you several gifts which wait outside. Among these gifts are eight whistlers—two drakes and six hens—three buffalo robes taken during the Hard Face Moon when the fur is thick, two Trader-wool blankets, and a metal cooking pot."

As Speaks While Leaving translated her own bridal negotiation, tears filled her eyes. The list comprised everything of value that her betrothed had to offer and more. It was an honorable bride-price for any man to give, much less Storm Arriving, who was not rich.

"I hope that you receive these gifts," One Who Flies went on to say. "But Storm Arriving will accept whatever answer you make."

As soon as Speaks While Leaving had finished translating his words, One Who Flies stood. To wait for an answer would have been the height of rudeness and so, without another word, he left the lodge.

No one spoke for a time. Even her grandmother stopped in her quilling while the women waited for One Bear to speak. His decision, whatever it was, would be final. If the gifts were still outside the lodge in the morning, the offer was refused.

One Bear sat at the back of the lodge, immobile. Finally, he sighed and glanced at his wife. "It is more than I gave for you," he said.

Magpie Woman smiled at her husband. "I know," she said.

"It does not mean that I love you less," he said.

"This, too, I know. Shall we bring the gifts in?"

Storm Arriving did not sleep. When the sun peeked over the horizon in the morning, it found him just where the moon had left him, sitting outside his lodge, wrapped in a buffalo robe.

With first light, One Who Flies came, fresh from his

morning bath and, without a word, sat down beside him. So, too, came Big Nose, and when the sun was two fingers above the horizon, Two Roads and several of his Kit Fox brethren came as well, men to whom he owed so much. They all sat down and faced the morning sun. Its light warmed them and pulled the moisture from their hair and clothing. No one said a word. They simply waited.

Standing Elk came running in from the east. "They come!" he shouted, and all the men stood and let out a great whoop of jubilation. All except Storm Arriving.

He remained cross-legged on the ground. His friends, jumping and shouting for joy, pulled him to his feet. Big Nose retrieved a piece of charred wood and went around laughing and smudging the men's cheeks and brows with thumbprints of sooty black, the color of victory, but Storm Arriving could only stare.

From around a distant lodge, the procession came into view. Ten whistlers walked, heads nodding and voices fluting with high spirits. Their ropes and bridles were festooned with furs and feathers and jangling bells of brass and silver. Each mount bore a gift—a bundled robe, a folded blanket, a stack of hides. From one hung a rifle and a shield. On another were a bed-roll and a willow-wood backrest. But the one in the middle carried the greatest gift of all.

Speaks While Leaving sat on an immense drake. She wore a dress of whitened buckskin upon which had been sewn hundreds of elk teeth and long strings of red-dyed leather that swayed with the drake's every step. Her waist was cinched by a wide belt decorated with quillwork of concentric circles in black and red, representing the sun and the moon, days and nights. On her wrists were gauntlets of stiff hide, also quilled with the auspicious symbols. Her leggings, like her dress, were of whitened buckskin, and her moccasins were new and had never touched the ground. Her hair was plaited in two braids bound by white leather windings and eagle's down, and along the part of her hair had been drawn a line of red paint—red for home and warmth—to match the small red circles painted on her cheeks, her chin, and her brow.

She sat atop the whistler, serene and beatific, her unwavering gaze locked on the face of her beloved, her smile peaceful.

All the neighbors gathered as the bride-party approached. The old women began to sing.

> *Breathe life into life.*
> *Bring happiness home.*
> *See your future, see your past.*
> *All is one. . . .*

The party stopped in front of the elated crowd. One Bear stood next to the drake that carried his daughter, and Storm Arriving saw his new father-in-law's happiness. Magpie Woman was there, too, but Storm Arriving dared not look at her. She was now his mother-in-law, and custom forbade them to speak for years to come. In time, after the proper exchange of gifts, the taboo could be lifted, but for now their friendship was at an end.

"Storm Arriving," One Bear said, his voice deep and strong. "You have courted my daughter for a long time, and in some strange ways." There was much laughter at this, and Storm Arriving's friends poked at his ribs until he smiled.

"But you have won her heart, and offered generous gifts for her hand. My heart is happy to see in your faces the great love you share. And so, I bring her to you. I bring also these gifts in thanks for the many years of happiness I know you will bring her. Tonight, stay with your family to celebrate your marriage. Tomorrow, you will join your new family with the Closed Windpipe band."

Big Nose and Two Roads and the others whooped and surged forward. They took a blanket and held it by the edges, beckoning to Storm Arriving. Moving as in a dream, he stepped up to the tall drake. He reached up to his beloved and she slid off the mount and into his arms.

She smelled of sage and rosemary. The elk's teeth on her dress—a gift in themselves worth ten whistlers—rattled and chattered. Her scent, her warmth, her touch; the gifts arrayed before him; the friends and family—old and new—surrounding him; it all swarmed his brain and made him giddy. He looked at his new bride, the woman he had loved since boyhood days. She beamed at him and nuzzled his cheek.

"Put me down," she said. "Plenty of time to hold each other ahead."

He grinned and set her upon the blanket his comrades held taut. As a new bride, her feet would not touch the earth for several days. The men cheered again, and carried her into the family lodge.

Picking Bones Woman and Mouse Road stood by the doorway with his mother's friends. They held blankets and new clothes—their gifts to the bride. His mother and sister were happy for him—he knew this without thinking on it—but there was a sadness, too, in their eyes, and perhaps, as well, a bit of worry. The marriage of a son or brother always meant a loss as the groom went to live among his bride's family. With winter coming, the bands would go their separate ways. Picking Bones Woman and Mouse Road would soon be alone.

The men, including One Who Flies, emerged from the lodge, having deposited their charge within. The women then entered, to dress the bride in their gifts and to begin preparations for the evening's feast. Mouse Road hesitated at the door, gazing back at her brother. Then she, too, entered.

The problem of Mouse Road still dogged at him, but when he saw One Who Flies standing quietly, smiling but not comprehending the jabbering celebrants around him, Storm Arriving saw a solution, or at least part of one. He went over to One Who Flies.

"The Tree People have taken you in the place of Laughs like a Woman," he said. "Your name and his are tied together."

"I am honored by it," One Who Flies said.

"Since I will not be with them this winter, I would like you to spend the winter with the Tree People."

"What do you mean, you won't be with them?"

Storm Arriving wondered at how much One Who Flies really understood of what had transpired. He seemed to have missed so much, it only strengthened Storm Arriving's resolve.

"When a man marries," he explained, "he goes to live with his wife's people. Forever. Tomorrow, I will no longer be of the Tree People."

"Ah," One Who Flies said. The worry in his friend's voice was obvious.

"Would you watch over my mother and sister?" Storm Arriving asked. "It is a thing I would have asked of Laughs like a Woman."

One Who Flies nodded—his way of signing an agreement.

"There is another reason for this . . ."

One Who Flies looked up from beneath a troubled brow, expectant.

"My friend, you need to learn to speak the language of the People. Not enough of us speak the Trader's Tongue, and none of us speak the language of your people. You must be able to speak to any of us. You have learned some, but not enough. Not nearly enough."

The door to the lodge opened. Mouse Road came out and started off on an errand.

"Mouse Road," Storm Arriving called. "Come here, my sister." She did so without a word.

"I need you to do something," he said to her. "It is very important and will take much of your time this winter."

With a move of her hand she signaled her agreement.

"I want you to teach One Who Flies how to speak our language."

His sister paled and looked at One Who Flies as if he were a rogue walker. Then she pointed her thumb to her chest.

Me?

Yes, he signed.

I don't want to, she said.

I am your brother, he told her. *Do this,* and with his hand palm up added, *please.*

She sighed.

"Good," he said. "And teach him the proper way to make signs, as well. He looks like a raven in a tree whenever he nods his head. By the time the bands gather together next summer, I want him to speak as well as you."

She acquiesced, sullenly, and after a final glance at One Who Flies, headed off.

Of this One Who Flies had understood enough. "She will be a reluctant teacher," he said in the Trader's Tongue.

"Perhaps," Storm Arriving said. "But she will teach you." He slapped his friend on the back. "Come. I want to swim in clean water before the feast. There will be games and dancing and more food than even you can eat. Maybe a pretty face in the crowd will please your heart."

One Who Flies smiled and they headed off toward the river.

A storm broke over the camp the day the bands began to head out, and George reflected on how much the weather echoed his mood.

Cold and gray, the clouds were so thick as to make the sky unknowable. It might have been noon, or daybreak, or twilight from the looks of things. Only his inner sense of time told him that it was the forenoon of the day. The wind, edged and honed sharp by the season, cut through clothing with an icy knife.

The rain, when the thunder finally loosed it, fell in thick sheets that drenched a man clear through in moments.

George began to take down his lodge and pack it for travel. He felt cold inside, and angry without good reason. When the lodgepoles all slipped their ties at once and clattered down upon his head in a loud and bruising pile, his temper at his own ineptitude in handling anything Indian built and burst forth.

"Hellfire," he cursed. "Damnation and hellfire!" He sat down in the mud and the driving rain and wished fervently for a horse, a tent, a pan of biscuit, and a pot of hot, steaming coffee. He wished for something, anything, as long as it was old and familiar.

Someone laughed and he glared from beneath a shock of rain-soaked hair. Speaks While Leaving was standing there, a stiff hide held above her head for protection from the storm. His glower cut short her laughter and she came toward him instead with a look of mirthful pity that, though less derisive, made him feel even worse.

"Oh, One Who Flies," she said, holding the rawhide up to cover them both. "You are so miserable." She could not keep the laughter out of her voice and his temper began to abate.

"I suppose I am rather ridiculous."

She reached forward and set his hair back out of his eyes. "This is not what you expected, is it?"

"No," he admitted quickly.

"Do you regret?"

"No," he said, just as quickly. "I regret nothing."

"Good." She reached for a small pouch that she had tucked under her wide belt. She crouched and handed it to George. "A gift," she said, having to speak up a little to be heard over the drumming of the rain. "For your friendship. For your advice." She smiled, and George felt his heart lighten at the sight. "And for falling from the clouds."

She stood.

"We will meet soon," she said. "During the Hatchling Moon. Keep well, my friend."

And she was gone, swallowed up by the hammering rain.

He looked at what she had given him. It was a small bag of stiffened deerhide, fringed at the bottom and painted with blue and red stripes. George worked at the leather tie at the top, his fingers fumbling in the cold and wet. When it finally gave way to his efforts, he opened it and dumped the contents into his hand.

Despite the gloom, the nugget shone. Speaks While Leaving had scrubbed it clean of all dirt and detritus, and it gleamed and glistened in the rain that fell upon it but could never change it.

He looked up. Mouse Road was standing over by her family's flock. She stared at him for a moment with an expression he could not fathom, and then turned away without comment.

George chuckled. He hefted the nugget and put it back into its bag.

"Crazy *vé'ho'e*," he said, and with a buoyant heart, he turned back to his packing.

CHAPTER 3

Winter, A.D. 1886
Washington
District of Columbia

Winter in D.C. had always depressed Custer. Never enough snow for a boy from the Michigan Territory, but more than enough rain for any man alive.

This winter, however, as the Christmas holiday approached, it seemed to Custer that the Almighty had taken pity on the people of the region.

Custer looked up from his report, squinting as the afternoon sun broke through the clouds and sparkled from the still-wet panes of his office window. The reprieve was brief, however, and the light was doused as clouds returned. He sighed and turned away from the window.

His office was on the second floor of the executive mansion. A large square room, it still showed the touch of several of its previous occupants.

On a nearby occasional table rested a silver tray upon which stood a cut-crystal decanter and four crystal tumblers, a gift left behind by the Grants. On the wall was a map of the Frontier as it looked during Sherman's stormy tenure. And the chair in which Custer now sat—with its leather upholstered seat, straight back, and heavy oak arms—had been Lincoln's for many years and the one in which he reputedly sat as he freed the slaves with a stroke of his pen. It was not an impressive office. Custer, like Sherman, preferred working at a large table rather than at a desk. It was, however, serviceable.

That's fine, Custer said to himself. It's a room for business, not politics. Plenty of other rooms with which to impress the enemy. He turned his attention back to the report.

There was a tap at the open door. It was Douglas, the old Negro butler who saw after the family's needs and kept the household staff in line. His skin was night-black and his fringe of curly white hair provided a high contrast to his bald pate. His eyes were dark and expressive and, as Custer had come to know, held no artifice. He had come with the house, having seen to the needs of eight presidents, and Custer had grown quite fond of him over the past two years.

"Yes?" Custer said.

"Excuse me, sir, but your afternoon guests will be here soon. Will you want any . . . refreshment?" He glanced at the crystal decanter which, by Custer's standing order, was kept empty.

"Oh, yes. Good idea. Find out what the general drinks and fill it up. Check with Samuel. He'll know. I wouldn't know a rye from a whiskey."

Douglas picked up the tray with its decanter and glasses. "A rye is a whiskey, sir."

"Exactly my point. Is Mr. Greene here yet?"

"Yes, sir. He's speaking with Mrs. Custer out in the conservatory. Shall I bring him up?"

"Just send him up, Douglas. No sense your climbing that staircase again. He knows the way."

"Very well, Mr. President."

Custer went back to reading the report that had already taken up too much of his morning. After two years in office, he was still staggered by the amount of seemingly useless information that required presidential review. He thumbed to the back of the report.

One hundred fifty-seven pages. One hundred fifty-seven pages of gray, washed-out type, rambling on and

on about the completion of the Canadian-Pacific railroad and its expected effect on American trade
relations.

He took off his reading glasses and massaged the
bridge of his nose to ward off the headache that
threatened to scuttle his day.

"Mr. President?"

Custer looked up to find his Secretary of War at
the open door. "Ah, Jacob," he said. "Thank you so
much."

"You're welcome, sir. For what, sir?"

Custer held up the report. "For rescuing me from
this." He tossed it onto the far end of his long table.
"Come. Sit down. Matherly and the general will be
here shortly. You met with him this morning?"

Jacob eased himself onto one of the straight-backed
chairs that were always around Custer's table. "General Herron? Yes. He and I met for breakfast at his
hotel."

"What was your impression of him?"

Jacob ticked off points on his fingers. "Gruff. Un-
pleasant. Crass. But thoroughly committed to the
idea."

"You think so?"

Jacob poked the tabletop with a finger. "This man,"
he said, "will follow orders. Without question or remorse. Herron will not give us a repetition of that miserable performance Stant gave us this last summer."

"You're damned right I won't," said a voice from
the open doorway.

Herron's frame filled the available space. He was
tall and broad of shoulder but ominously lean in a
way that Custer had only seen in Indian warriors: a
slenderness forged by a life of athleticism and warfare,
built of quick reflexes and a quicker mind. His pale
green eyes looked at Custer and Jacob with a keen
gaze. He wore his uniform as if he could wear nothing
else. The dark blue wool of his double-breasted frock
coat was dry, but his black slouch hat was beaded

with droplets of rain. He was younger than Custer had expected, or at least he appeared so.

Behind him was an aide, also in blue army wool, and Robert Matherly, dressed in a riding coat and high-collared shirt. Behind them all was Douglas with coats of Kersey blue and congressional black draped over his arm.

"Beg your pardon, Mr. President. General Herron and Senator Matherly to see you."

"Thank you, Douglas. Come in, gentlemen."

The general removed his hat as he entered the room. Now Custer could see the man's age, as his thinning hair was shot through with silver, especially at the temples. His square jaw was clean-shaven beneath a still-dark mustache. He moved to one of the straight-backed chairs across the table but did not sit. Custer saw the deep lines at the corners of his eyes and the tautness of the skin across his angular cheekbones.

"You've spent a long time on the Frontier," Custer said, extending his hand.

"It's a land that leaves its mark," Herron said. His handshake was firm and stable.

"Mr. President," Matherly said as he came forward. The portly senator presented his hand as well. "So nice to see you again."

"You're to be congratulated, Robert. The passage of your first bill. It went about as smoothly as you could have hoped."

"Smoother than I could have dreamed, thanks to you, Mr. President." Matherly pumped Custer's hand in both of his own. "I can't thank you enough for your help in getting it passed before the election. Now, with the Democrats in control of the House, I could never have gotten it to the floor."

"Yes," Custer said. "That may be. But I can't take all the credit. It was well presented by you."

"Could we dispense with the niceties," Herron growled, "and get down to business? Sir?"

Custer glanced at Jacob, who made a "See? I told you" shrug.

"By all means, General. All of you, please, have a seat."

They all settled into their chairs except for the general's aide, who remained at silent ease behind his commander. Douglas reappeared, carrying the silver tray and crystal decanter. The butler silently mouthed a word and Custer turned to Herron.

"Scotch, General?"

Herron raised a dark eyebrow and nodded.

Douglas poured two fingers of the pale brown liquor into a tumbler and handed it to the general with a white-gloved hand. Herron sniffed, then sipped.

"Very nice," he said showing white, even teeth. "Single malt?"

Douglas answered quickly, acting as if the question had been put to him. "Yes, sir, General Herron. Lagavulin. Sixteen years old."

The general bristled—at being addressed by a servant or by a Negro or both, Custer did not know—but the tall man made no further complaint. "Very nice," he said again, though his smile was strained.

"So, now," Custer said, drawing the meeting together. "I asked for an overview of your plans for the execution of this bill."

"Yes, sir." Herron motioned to his aide, a young second lieutenant, who opened the end of a leather map case and shook out a roll of parchments. Herron took one and rolled it out on the table, setting his tumbler at one end to keep it flat.

It was a map of the state of Yankton, from the Mississippi to the Missouri, and beyond.

"Crossing the state with a new railway is the easiest part of the venture," Herron said. "And the quickest. We've already laid out our path, a straight east-west corridor from the existing bridge at Davenport-Rock Island." He pointed to the site on the state's eastern border and drew a line with his finger. "We extend the line straight through to Washita and onward to this spot on the Missouri shore."

"The state legislature has already set aside the land we need," Matherly put in. "We've had to displace some of the local residents, and there's been some unpleasantness in the—"

"Yes, yes," the general interrupted. "Can't make an omelet, as they say." He tapped the spot on the state's western border.

"This," he said, "is our challenge. The Missouri starts to meander here. It is wide and deep along most of its accessible length, but my engineer says that those facts, in and of themselves, are not the problem. The problem with the Missouri is seasonal flooding, much like the problems they had bridging the lower Mississippi. Whatever we build, it will have to be strong enough to withstand a serious flood. That means wider and stronger than the minimum required."

Matherly leaned forward in his chair, a smile of appeasement on his lips and a wheedling tone in his voice. "I am sure that General Herron's concerns are well intentioned, but to accomplish his goals will increase the time and money required well beyond that already allotted. And since my state is responsible for a large portion of that cost, I would like to entertain some alternatives."

"Alternatives?" Herron made a rude sound. "You can build a ferry in a fortnight for a double sawbuck," he said, "but it won't do what you want." He turned back to Custer. "The plan calls for a bridge that will carry over a million souls; transport the goods to supply them, the livestock to feed and transport them, the army and weapons to protect them, and the machines to haul it all; and do all that for ten or twenty years. Frankly, I'd build a pontoon bridge and call it done if I thought it would suffice."

"Do it once, do it right?" Custer suggested.

"Precisely, Mr. President. Senator Matherly's worries about cost aside, you have to take longevity into account. My engineer tells me that if this bridge is to survive even a mild storm season, it must be longer and stronger than originally estimated."

"Who is your engineer?" Jacob asked.

"Lieutenant Colonel Craig M. Shafer. Top-notch. Bit of a perfectionist, but the man knows his business. Did work all over the world before he joined the service."

"Why did he join up?"

"Wants to build bridges, and the army builds more bridges than anyone, these days."

"So," Custer said. "How much will Colonel Shafer's recommendation affect the project?"

Matherly jumped in again, saying, "It will double the construction time to a year or more, and it will quadruple the cost!"

Custer held up a hand of gentle placation. "Nevertheless, it is often foolish to ignore the advice of experts."

Jacob sighed. "Already over budget. Now this *is* a military operation."

"But Mr. President," Matherly whined. "How can you expect Yankton to shoulder such an increase in costs? We're only two hundred thousand in population, almost all of it in farmland. How can we possibly—"

"The same way everyone else does," Custer said. "Borrow it." He got up from his chair and walked around the table to where Sherman's map of the Frontier hung on the wall.

"Look," he said, pointing to a long squiggly line that traveled north and west from Yankton's border. "That's the Missouri River. And this . . ." He spread his hand over the blank area west of the meandering river and north of the Gulf of Narváez. "That, Senator, is a plain of fertile farmland six *times* the size of Yankton. We are going to flood this plain with settlers and you, Mr. Matherly, you *and* the state of Yankton are going to be the beneficiaries of that flood. This plan—this bridge—is going to make you rich."

"And famous," Jacob said.

"And famous," Custer echoed. "Do you have ambitions, Senator? A committee chair? A cabinet post? Even . . ." He motioned to the room and the building around them.

Matherly was wide-eyed. He swallowed hard, but laughed nervously and gave a small nod.

"That kind of ambition takes vision, Robert. Strong vision."

"And guts," said Herron, not helpfully.

"And guts," Custer said, "but mostly vision. You've got to be able to see beyond the dollars you'll be spending, to the fortunes that you'll reap."

Matherly chewed his lower lip but Custer could see that he was taking the bait. "It will be a hard sell to the state legislators," he said.

"Small fry," Herron growled.

"Little minds," Jacob condemned.

"Precisely," Custer said with a smile. "Not like you, Robert. This whole plan was your idea from the start. You've taken it all around the track, and admirably, too."

"Admirably," Jacob and Herron said in banal unison.

"Don't fail now in the home stretch."

The senator shook his head. "That kind of debt. It would be crushing."

"You know," Custer said, turning to Jacob and tapping the bridge site on the map. "Senator Matherly has been so instrumental in this . . ."

"I've an idea," Jacob said, picking up the hint. "I propose that this bridge spanning the Missouri River be named in honor of the man who made it possible: The Senator Robert J. Matherly Bridge."

"Oh, well done," Herron said without enthusiasm.

Matherly gaped and then beamed. "Such an honor, Mr. Secretary. I could hardly—"

"Nonsense," Custer said. "It's well deserved. I'll brook no further argument. General, would you please include a groundbreaking and dedication ceremony into your plans?"

"Done, sir."

"Thank you. Good." Custer clapped his hands and rubbed them together. "What's next?"

Herron leaned back into his chair. "That pretty much covers it from the civilian side of things. There are the military aspects that I could present, but we needn't waste the senator's time with that."

"Yes," Custer said. "I should like to hear of your strategies. What do you say, Robert? Is there anything else you'd like to discuss?"

"Unh, no," Matherly said, still dazed. "If you gentlemen will excuse me?"

They all nodded and the portly senator rose. He was somewhat paler than when he had arrived, and Custer was sure that he was a little weak in the knees. He managed a slight bow of farewell, and walked to the door, which Douglas opened for him. He hesitated, and Custer thought he saw him shake his head, once, as if to clear it. Then he strode out and down the hallway. Douglas closed the door.

"That was a bit thick," Herron said.

"It got the job done," Jacob offered.

"Please," Herron retorted. "The man's an idiot."

"Perhaps," Custer said. "But he's *our* idiot. And a useful one, too, so far."

Herron's sidelong glance was disbelieving and insolent.

"General Herron," Custer said tersely. "What you saw here today was politics, and not that watered-down jockeying for position and power that military men call politics. I'm talking about real politics, with all the lies, flattery, double-dealing, and brazen flat-out pandering there for you to see. It isn't pretty, and it is rarely honorable. It *is* however, as I learned during my years in Congress and my time here as president, necessary. It got you the money for your long bridge, and the time to build it. Be grateful."

Herron looked at Custer for a long moment. Finally,

he came to some sort of decision. He nodded. "As you say, Mr. President," he said.

"Now," Custer continued. "How do you intend to hold this territory when others have failed for so long?"

"Begging your pardon, sir, and with all due respect, but the men before me failed because the men before you failed." He pointed to Sherman's Frontier on the wall behind him. "An army can't protect a half million square miles of open country. An army can't fight an enemy that disappears like water through a cupped hand."

He motioned to his aide and the young lieutenant produced a second map. Herron laid it out on the table.

"This is the new map of the Frontier. Here is the Missouri, here's the bridge that will cross it. This line here is our new railroad, and all along it, every hundred miles or so, is a fort. And I mean a *fort,* sir." He stood and began to pace. "None of these tent cities with a few clapboard houses that I saw during our civil conflict. No, I mean forts. Forts with walls, with lookout towers. Places of strength to attack from—"

"Or retreat to?" Custer asked.

"Yes, by God, if needs dictate it. A fort that is a haven for civilian and soldier alike. A place where we can stand at the walls and pick them off one by one. Let them try their open ground cavalry tactics against a squad of riflemen behind crenellated walls."

Jacob chuckled. "You make it sound almost . . . medieval."

"Perhaps I do, but it will work where other strategies have failed. Never attack the enemy on his own ground. Draw the enemy to you, and attack him on *your* terms."

Custer pointed at the blank area on the map. "All right. I think I see where you are going with this. So boil it down for me, General. What will be your end result?"

Herron smiled and to Custer it looked a grim, relentless thing.

"By the end of the first year, a single railroad line extends deep into the Frontier. Along it, walled forts with ample fresh water have been raised at strategic points. Around each fort there is a community; little towns at first, small enough so that the population is able to retreat within the fort walls if trouble rides in.

"Then, by the second year, spurs from the main line branch out from the existing forts and towns, all leading to new forts and towns. The perimeter expands, and the old towns along the mainline grow larger and the old forts are shut down. It is, as Mr. Secretary pointed out, almost medieval, but it has everything that previous administrations have failed to provide. Active goals, defensible targets, and a plan by which we can measure our success."

Custer could not help but smile. "General, you have me convinced. When does it all start?"

"In the spring, sir. We'll break ground for the bridge and begin staging supplies. Progress on the western bank will be slow until the bridge is operational, which should be by spring of the following year."

"1888."

"Correct, sir."

Custer glanced over at Jacob.

"Election year," the secretary said.

"Sir," Herron said. "There is still one outstanding problem."

"And what is that, General?"

"The Indians, sir?"

"What do you mean? It sounds like you'll have the whole Alliance under your thumb in a couple of months."

"On an engagement basis, yes, sir, I will. But I'm talking about the long term. What do we do about the Indians in the long run?"

"Hmm. I see," Custer said. "Yes, the methods used

so far in Santee and Kansa have not achieved truly satisfactory results."

"There's the plan that Senator Dawes has introduced," Jacob said. "To give each Indian a plot of land?"

"And turn those savages into farmers?" Custer dismissed the thought with a wave of his hand. "Let him try. It won't work."

"I have a suggestion," Herron said. "A military one."

"Oh?" Custer said. "What?"

Herron reached for his tumbler. The maps rolled up into his waiting hand as he lifted the glass to his lips. He tossed off the last finger of Scotch and looked Custer dead in the eye.

"Kill them," he said. "Kill every last one of them."

Early-morning snow fell through the stands of silent spruce. The whole of the world was hushed. George stopped to rest at the top of the trail that led back toward camp, sweating despite the cold, the wet load of lichen-robed deadwood heavy on his back. Snowflakes, fat and lazy like eiderdown, fell reluctantly from a steel-gray sky. Tree branches laden with white winter coats hung low over the trail, waiting, it seemed, for the slightest touch so that they might dump their icy burden on unsuspecting passersby.

George sniffed at the scents of winter: the sweetness of evergreen boughs burning in lodge fires, the musk of damp buckskin from his Indian-style clothing, the earthy aroma of deadwood on his shoulder, and the crisp, empty smell of winter's chill, a smell that had no true odor of its own but which sharpened and heightened all others. As he waited for his breathing to slow, he craned his neck to peer past tree trunks and snowy branches.

The winter encampment of the Tree People band was much different from its summer arrangement. Instead of the summer circles of tribe and band and family, winter lodge sites were scattered in and among the trees without pattern. A family might raise three lodges side by side, and put a fourth a quarter mile upstream, near the high pond. George spied the lodge of Picking Bones Woman—it was no longer the home of Storm Arriving—a mile away across the ravine formed by the still-trickling streamlet. He recognized the dark handprints and the whimsical over-the-smokes, the fox-tail and feathered streamers tied to the tips of the lodgepoles. He could not see his own lodge, but he knew where it stood, a discreet distance farther uphill from hers. He had picked the spot carefully, wary of the interpretation his neighbors would give to even the smallest choice made by the man who fell from the clouds. He had chosen a spot uphill from the family he was to watch over, but screened by two large spruce trees. Beneath these trees he had directed his walker to make her winter nest. There, she would represent a second guardian, a second pair of watchful eyes, for although she would be in a somnolent state through most of the winter months, her eyes would remain open, lidded only by milky nictitating membranes. She, with her immense strength and ferocity, carried a strong spiritual force that helped establish George in the role of protector.

Not that I'm doing any protecting, he thought contritely, reshouldering his burden. More like the other way round, if anything.

He headed on down the trail.

The short winter days brought his neighbors out of their lodges later than usual. On his way downhill he met a line of women walking uphill, heading out on errands similar to his own.

"*Pévevóona'o*," he said to them—good morning— and stepped aside to let them pass on the narrow trail. A few of them stared at him warily as they passed. One, a young woman named Fern Tree Woman, was wide-eyed. She pointed to his face, then touched her own chin. She said something to her friend, of which

George only understood "He looks like . . ." George smiled shyly and scratched at the growth of new beard that covered his face. He had stopped shaving during the last moon, for although he preferred to be clean-shaven, staying so without a razor and strop was an agonizing process. His new beard still seemed a novelty to his neighbors, especially the women, and George assumed it was because their Indian men simply could not grow them. He was the first *vé'ho'e* most of them had known and, even with his Indian clothing, was a continuous curiosity.

Fern Tree Woman's mother urged her on, not wanting her daughter to become the object of gossip for dawdling around a man. The procession of women passed, and George continued once more down toward the creek.

He heard children sledding down the valley. Two weeks before, the ice had finally covered over the lower pond's placid water, and a few days ago the community elders had pronounced it safe to play upon. George caught a glimpse of a circle of girls playing football, and a group of boys spinning tops and betting on the outcome. He walked on, and the pond was hidden by a twist of the vale and the heavy growth of evergreens.

The band's lodges stood on either side of the quiet streambed like flotsam strewn on a rocky shore. He followed the path past several lodges. Some of the men were up, too—some bare-chested in spite of the cold—preparing their whistlers for a hunting trip, or heading off on an errand or visit. George smiled at the men he met, greeting a few by name. None smiled in return and none stopped to speak to him. While his neighbors were never given to loquacity, primarily due to his still-limited command of their language, today it seemed that they were actually avoiding him.

As he clambered over the rocky creekbed and started up the far side of the ravine, he saw Long Jaw come out of his lodge. The Indian saw George and ducked back inside his lodge.

George stopped in his tracks, dumbfounded. He spun around. Wherever he looked, eyes were suddenly averted and backs were hastily turned.

He stood there, his jaw clenched and his breath coming out in frosty clouds. "For months I've tried," he said through gritted teeth, "and still you shun me." Months of frustration at his isolation and loneliness came to a boil within him.

He lifted his burden up over his head and with a roar he threw it down the steep path. Firewood clattered down the slope but still no one looked at him. He shouted again, a wordless howl of rage, and then turned and stomped straight uphill toward his lodge.

He growled and stormed his way through the branches, angry at everyone and everything. He cursed every time a tree dumped snow down his neck, his bursts of profanity growing longer and more heated with every step until, when he came to the last trees before his lodge, he was spouting a continuous flow of malediction in every language he could muster. "God damn it!" he snarled. *"Tu me casses les couilles. Quelle tas de merde!"* Then, as he kicked his way through the undergrowth, he stepped on the trailing edge of his own leggings, tripped, and fell headlong through the trees, landing facedown in the snow.

He lay there a moment, the powdery crystals melting against his skin, and listened to the utter silence that rushed in on the heels of his tirade. There were no sounds of nearby neighbors, no jeers from blue-crested jays; even the children down by the pond were silent.

He groaned, sure that his tantrum had only worsened his situation.

"Ame'haooestse?"

George scrambled up to his knees, blinking through the snow that stuck to his beard, brows, and eyelashes.

It was Mouse Road. She stood before his lodge, a parcel in her hands and fear in her eyes.

George sighed and sat down, regretting it immediately as Cheyenne leggings did not cover one's rear end and his bare rump was now in the cold snow. Calmly, deliberately, he began to brush the snow from his face.

"*Pévevóona'o,* Hohkeekemeona'e," he said. Good morning, Mouse Road.

"*Pévevóona'o,*" she said meekly.

"*Éoseetonéto,*" he said as he stood and continued brushing snow from his clothing. It is very cold.

"*Héehe'e,*" she said slowly, still wary of him. "*Eho'eéto.*" Yes. It is snowing.

George stood up, trying to make small talk, but Mouse Road's obvious uneasiness drove nearly everything from his mind. That he should have so affrighted such a fine young woman was unchivalrous at best; that he had done so to one supposedly under his protection rankled him even further. He clamped down on another surge of frustrated temper, refusing to make the same mistake twice in so short a span of time.

The Cheyenne words—so long and layered in their construction—eluded his ability. Finally, he settled on a simple statement of fact. "*Tsêhe'êstoo'onahe, énâhestovóhe,*" Long Jaw, he stays away from me.

Mouse Road's features relaxed, softened, and he thought that maybe she understood his anguish. She pointed to him and then touched her own cheeks and chin.

"*Ée'tótahe.*" He is afraid.

She continued, speaking slowly so that he could keep pace, explaining that his beard was like a fur covering his face, and many of his neighbors feared that he was turning into a wild animal.

Wonderful, George said to himself. And I'm sure my running around screaming didn't help.

He scratched at his beard. "I will . . ." he began in

Cheyenne. He made motions as if shaving. ". . . cut it," he completed.

"That is good," she said. Then she showed him the parcel she brought: a small parfleche of folded hide. She lifted one flap and steam escaped into the chill air.

"Vétšêškévâhonoo'o," she said.

George was not familiar with the word. He shrugged and made the sign for "no," a flip of the right hand from palm down to palm up.

She reached in and took out a small golden circle of fried dough. *"Vétšêškévâhonoo'o,"* she said again, and George's stomach gurgled with anticipation. Frybread. "From my mother. Are you hungry?"

Now he signed *yes,* and said, *"Héehe'e. Náháéána. Néá'eše."* Yes. I am hungry. Thank you.

She took a step, offering him the food. He met her halfway and smelled the warm, grainy aroma of the fried bread in the crisp air. Reaching under the top flap, he pulled out a piece. Steam rose from it as he broke it open, revealing the tender inner pocket lined with moist bread. He took a bite, careful of its heat on his tongue.

"Very good," he said. "You want?"

She reached in and took one for herself and they stood there for a while in silence, enjoying the food her mother had provided.

Mouse Road had been a patient teacher, even though somewhat hesitant about correcting his mistakes. Usually they met at her lodge or sometimes at the lower pond, where elder eyes could oversee and ensure propriety was met. Even though she was only fifteen or so to George's twenty-five years, she was of courtable, if not marriageable age. This was the first time she had come alone to visit him at his lodge, and he wondered why Picking Bones Woman had not come as a chaperone.

"Your mother," he said. "She is good?"

Mouse Road signed *no.* "Moon-time," she said around a mouthful of hot bread. "You cannot go there." She pointed to her lodge, downhill through the trees.

"I understand," he said. "Picking Bones Woman moon-time. Her medicine big. Stronger than my medicine."

Mouse Road signed her agreement; another hurdle passed. George regarded his teacher as he took another bite of the hot bread.

Mouse Road was pretty, as her sister had been, with a broad brow and a narrow chin, strong cheekbones and a smile filled with wide, even teeth. Her nose, too, had the family stamp: long, high-bridged, and straight. Her eyes, though nearly black in color like her sister's, were quite different in shape. Where her sister's eyes had been round and doelike, Mouse Road's eyes were long and almond-shaped. To George, she seemed to be always looking into a bright light. In repose, her eyes gave her the aspect of being wary and aloof, but when she smiled, they turned up into cherubic crescents that danced with the light. George tried to make her smile as often as he could, and lately she had been obliging him more and more.

She pointed to the snow-covered pile of branches and leaf litter beneath which George's walker slept. "She will wake soon?" Mouse Road asked.

"Yes," George said. He took a bite of fry-bread. "She too will be hungry."

Mouse Road smiled and it gladdened his heart to see it.

"Only," he continued, "I am not a good hunter. When I hunt, I do not catch." He pointed to the mound that hid his somnolent walker. "She catches. Not me. But I *want* to catch so others do not need to help me. How can I learn to hunt like the People?"

She thought and ate the last bit of her fry-bread. "You must speak to Little Creek. He is old and knows how to hunt all things. Bring him wood for his fire and he will teach you to hunt. Come." She bundled up the remaining fry-bread and put it inside the door of George's lodge. "I will bring you to him and help you with the new words."

She smiled for a second time and headed off down the trail, beckoning him to follow.

More wood to carry, George sighed to himself. But at least there's some company to be had for it.

So, trying not to feel like a puppy tagging along behind, he headed off after the young woman.

CHAPTER 4

Spring, A.D. 1887
Bank of the Missouri River
Yankton

General Charles Brandeis Herron stood under the canvas awning and listened to the drumming rain. He did not pass the time by participating in the conversations of the men around him: congressmen, mayors, aldermen. Their debates about the prime planting time for corn or the relative qualities of competing breeds of hogs did not interest him. Not even the representatives from the railroad company intrigued him with their complaints about the accommodations and cuisine.

Whining milksops, he thought to himself. What in Hell did they expect? This is the Frontier, not Fifth Avenue.

And so he simply stood by and listened to the rain and waited, waited, for the weather to clear, for his engineer to show up, or for the president to arrive, whichever came first.

Beyond the canvas-roofed pavilion and the tiny telegraph shack, the riverbank was a disaster. Immense stacks of timbers, girders, crates, and barrels filled the wide slice of land that lay between the quay and the roadway. The ground was a bog of slick goo and ankle-deep muck crisscrossed by a webwork of board-plank walkways. The rain—now in its third day—had saturated the entire region. The Missouri, so warm and stately in summer, now resembled more its Indian name: the Big Greasy.

It shuffled past, swollen and viscous beneath the heavy clouds. Choppy wavelets covered it shore to shore, and at the water's edge flecks of foam collected among the inundated clumps of cattail and sedge.

"It's a miserable place with miserable weather," Herron muttered to himself, "but at least we're under way."

His aide, Quincy, standing nearby, took a step closer. "Sir?" the lieutenant asked solicitously. "Did you say something?"

"Yes," Herron growled, irritated at having been overheard. "I said where in Hell is Shafer?"

"I'm sorry, sir," his aide said. "He assured me he'd be . . . Oh, here he comes, sir." Quincy pointed toward a stack of timbers.

Lieutenant Colonel Shafer spotted Quincy and waved, grinning as if spying an old friend. He walked straight across the mire, ignoring the wooden boardwalks and dirtying his trousers to the calves. He looked up into the rain as he approached, squinting through the fogged lenses of his spectacles like a man enjoying a sunny Sunday in the park.

"G'd afternoon, General," he said as he sauntered up to the pavilion, his Manitoba accent flat and hard. "Hey-o, Quince." He took off his glasses and smeared at them with a wet handkerchief. "Helluva bit of weather, eh?"

"You are late, Colonel," said Herron. He pointed to the unbuttoned collar of Shafer's Army frock coat. "And out of uniform."

Shafer's grin widened as he settled the temple pieces of his glasses behind his ears. "I suppose you're right to be a stickler on such points, General, especially on an important day like today." He winked at Quincy as he buttoned the collar of his uniform. "At least I got here before the big man arrived, eh?"

"I've never known a politician to be on time to

anything," Herron said. "The president may have been a soldier once, but he's a politician now. Ah, this must be they."

A covered carriage pulled by two huge drays slogged its way over a rise in the supply road that would eventually be covered with rails. The carriage teetered and swayed down the puddled, muddy track and Herron did not envy those inside for a moment. As the carriage came up and pulled to a stop, the door to the telegraph shack opened and out came the men of the press like hornets out of an opened nest. They ran toward the carriage just as the doors opened.

Custer stepped down onto the carriage step, took off his tall hat, and waved to the gathering. His features, well past youth, were beginning to look haggard and his mustache and long, pale hair were starting to whiten with age.

"Mr. President," shouted one of the newspapermen. "How was your trip?"

Herron rolled his eyes. "Jesus," he said so that only Quincy and Shafer could hear. "He just spent five hours locked up in a carriage that swayed like a drunken sailor with no other person for company than—"

"Senator Matherly," shouted another of the reporters as that man appeared from within the carriage, "is it true that your father-in-law is a major shareholder in the iron foundry chosen as the supplier for this project?"

Matherly stepped down from the carriage, waving. "It's a pleasure to be here," he said, ignoring the question completely.

The president and the senator, with a handful of aides and a bevy of Army privates holding umbrellas, came toward the pavilion. The officers saluted their commander-in-chief. Custer shook the rain from his lapels and returned the greeting.

"Mr. President, Senator Matherly," Herron said, "may I present Lieutenant Colonel Craig M. Shafer, chief architect and engineer for this project."

Custer gave Shafer a frank, up-and-down appraisal. "Get caught in the weather, Colonel?"

Shafer grinned and snapped off a superfluous salute. "Yes, sir! Actually, sir, I did, sir!"

Herron glared at the engineer. "Don't get cheeky, Shafer."

"Sorry, sir!"

Custer raised an eyebrow. "This is the man you want, General?"

"Yes, sir. He's the man I want for the job."

"And if he can't do it?"

"Then I kick his ass into the river and get someone who can, sir."

Custer smiled. "I'm glad to see you don't think too highly of this man here."

Herron's mouth twitched in a wry smile. "Sir, excepting you and me, of course, I don't think too highly of *anyone* here."

Custer chuckled.

The weather chose that moment to send a blast of wind in from the west. The pavilion shuddered, the men all held on to their hats, and the newspapermen protected their notes from the rain. Herron shivered at the sudden cold from off the river. The wind blew for a long minute and then the air fell quiet. It took a moment for everyone to compose themselves, and as they did Herron realized that the weather had changed.

"It's stopped raining," he said.

"So it has," Custer agreed. "How providential. Colonel Shafer, what say you give us a quick tour of the site before the clouds open up again?"

Shafer prudently looked to his general for instructions.

Herron nodded. "Stick to the walkways, Colonel."

"Yes, sir," Shafer said. "Mr. President. Senator Matherly. If you would follow me, please."

Shafer led the way. Custer, Matherly, and Herron followed. Behind them, the press followed along in a clump, notepads up, pencils scratching. The other guests came along at the rear, straggling along the narrow walkways.

Shafer took them first out toward the piles of supplies.

"Naturally," he began, "most of this so far has come to us via the river." He pointed to the stacks of logs, timbers, lumber, and iron girders and plates. "Eventually, of course, we will be receiving our matériel by rail. That will be some time from now, however. Besides, we'll need the barges for the construction process as well as toting supplies up from the Gulf."

He looked at the president when he spoke, but his voice was pitched so the reporters and guests could hear as well.

"The logs and timbers will be used for pilings and in the construction of the two main footings for the bridge. The wrought iron I-beams and plates will be used in the superstructure for the main span."

"Main span?" Matherly asked. "I thought there was to be only one span?"

Shafer nodded as he led them along the narrow boardwalks toward the quay. "One main span, yes, Senator. But look." He pointed to the broad river before them. "That water is five hundred yards wide. It would take a decade to build a single span to bridge it, and you don't want to pay for *that,* eh?"

Matherly's nervous laugh was echoed by the assembled state dignitaries. "No," he said, "we don't."

"Didn't think so. I've planned then for two smaller spans, one from either shore, built of simple, efficient trestlework." He set his hands apart to depict the breadth of the river and then drew them slowly toward one another. "These shore-based spans will reach out across the water to where it hits a depth of about thirty feet. There we'll build two large bulwarks that will serve as the footings for the main span." With his hands he described a bridging curve. "The main span will be a long, graceful arc that will rise high enough above the water to accommodate the largest steamers on the river." He pointed to the middle of the river. "The deck will be sixty feet above the water and a clear eight hundred feet from end to end. It will be a bridge unlike any other in America."

"How so?" asked a reporter.

Shafer smiled, and Herron saw a gleam in his eye. "When I was in China," he started.

"You were in China, Colonel?"

"Yes. I served for the British during the Opium Wars."

"General," said one of the reporters, "have you enlisted a foreign national to lead this project?"

"The colonel is an American," Herron said.

"Born in Santee Territory," Shafer said. "But raised in Canada. And as I was saying, when I was in China, I studied the bridge-building techniques of Canton, Nanking, and Kowloon. Later, in Europe, I worked with Eiffel on his bridge that spanned the Douro at Oporto. This bridge will incorporate the newest ideas of Eiffel and Roebling, with the ancient methods of the T'ang Dynasty. The best of the old *and* the new. A bridge to last a thousand years. Large girder structures will travel upward and *inward* to form an arch that resembles the handle of a basket. From this arch, the deck will be suspended from cables. This bridge will incorporate the functionality of beams, arches, and suspension—"

The president raised a hand, halting Shafer midstream. "Colonel," he said, "your enthusiasm is infectious—I feel I can see it there already—but you lose me with such technicalities."

Shafer expelled the breath he was holding. "My apologies, sir. I do get wrapped up in the details sometimes."

Shafer's tour had brought them back up from the quays to the pavilion that stood at what would be the foot of the new bridge. Herron stepped forward and took charge of the proceedings.

"Thank you, Colonel," he said. "Mr. President, Senator Matherly, if you would follow me, I'd like to put you both to work."

He led them under the canvas awning where Quincy was waiting with two polished steel shovels. The first lieutenant handed one to Custer and one to Matherly and directed them over to a place at the top of the riverbank where the uneasy Missouri and the wide, empty land beyond it could act as a backdrop.

The local dignitaries looked on as the president and senator sank their spades and turned over a shovelful of mud. A photographer quickly exposed a plate.

Herron stood back after the formalities were complete and watched as the locals and the reporters buzzed around their president. Custer worked the crowd, spoke to everyone, and deftly deflected questions when they grew too pointed, but his glance began to stray, pulled with greater frequency by something out across the water. In time, Custer excused himself and made his way over to where Herron was standing.

"Rain's starting up again," Custer said, looking for the fifth time out across the Missouri. "We got lucky."

"I try not to depend on luck, sir."

Custer looked up at the canvas roof over their heads. "I see that." Another long look across the water.

"Mr. President, is there something bothering you?"

"Are you married, General?"

"No, sir," Herron said, not flinching at the change in subject. "Widowed, sir."

"Ah, I see. Any children?"

Herron scowled, unused to such personal probing. "No, sir," he said. "Marguerite and I . . . we didn't have long together."

"Well, now, that's a shame," Custer said. He looked across the Missouri again and this time his gaze did not waver. "I have children."

"Yes, sir."

"Two daughters. And a son."

"Yes, sir," Herron said. "So I've heard."

"The girls. They're at home with their mother."

"That's a good place for them, sir."

"My son, however, you may also have heard . . ."
Custer pointed toward the dark shore on the far side.
"He's over there . . . somewhere."

Herron heard the weakness in his commander's
voice. Custer looked not so much like a president than
a man struggling with the tragedies of his life. "Mr.
President," he said, "if I may speak freely . . ."

Custer nodded, but did not look away from the long
dark line of the prairie.

"Mr. President. The Frontier does not give men
back. It either kills them, or it keeps them." He took
a breath to decide whether to say more, then continued. "I know about loss, personal loss, sir, firsthand,
and if I may be allowed to give you a piece of advice—
one that has helped me—I would tell you this: Your
son is gone. You will never see him again. Consider
him dead. Grieve, to be sure, but do not pine, for that
way lies madness. Your son is not 'out there,' sir. He
is gone, and the sooner you get right with that, the
better you'll be."

Custer stared at the steel-gray waters and the land
they bordered for a few moments longer, then turned
to look Herron right in the eye.

"Thank you, General Herron. I will keep that in
mind." Then he walked back to the gathering.

Now that, Herron thought with satisfaction, is the
look of a leader.

Carefully, George tied the thin snare line into a
noose and draped it across the narrow track that ran
among the bushes near Two Fingers Creek. He dusted
the ground with dried pine needles and mulch and
camouflaged the rest of the noose with bracken. After
a final check of the stake that held the line to the
ground, he picked up the grouse the snare had trapped

and backed away slowly, gently repositioning branches and fronds in his retreat.

He retraced his steps back through the thickening brush of springtime, to where his walker lay, silent and still. George added the grouse to the three rabbits, one fox, and brace of pheasant that hung from the wicker backrest. They were the fruits of the snares, traps, and deadfalls he had set throughout the mountains that surrounded the band's winter camp. He scratched at the stubble on his chin and grimaced.

"Have to shave again," he said to his walker in the language of the People. She only huffed a misty breath and rolled one eye around to look at him.

"A lot you care," he said to her. "You don't have to scrape your face clean with a"—he tried to construct the word—"a knife-that-cannot-cut-butter." He smiled with self-satisfaction. "Come on," he said as he mounted. *"Nóheto."* Let's go!

The walker stood. George lay down flat along her spine but still the lower tree branches brushed his back. It was not a comfortable position. His walker had not eaten during the winter months, living off her stored summer fat instead, and her spine was now quite pronounced.

"A little lower," he told her and she complied, giving him more room. Then, with a gentle nudge of his toe, she started off; a cautious walk at first as they threaded their way through the low-limbed evergreens, but soon she moved up to a slow trot as they came to the established trails used by deer, elk, and bear.

With another nudge of his left toe, George steered his mount downslope. Despite her size, she made no more noise than an elk trotting down the trail.

They came out of the trees and into a meadow and George was glad for the opportunity to sit up on his knees. His walker chuffed—a harsh, throaty sound—and then roared. George looked out ahead and saw a herd of elk pounding away from them, clods of moist turf flying as they ran.

"Nóheto!" he shouted and held on as the walker burst into a full run.

She had one chance: She had to catch one of the fleeing elk before they reached the meadow's lower edge or she would lose them in the trees. From his vantage point, George saw that a wide creekbed lay across the herd's path. It would force them to the left before they could cross it. He nudged his walker with his left heel and she obeyed, veering off her course slightly. She ran in a huge, lunging lope, her legs pushing with all the urging a season's hunger could provide. George kept her at an angle to the elk's path, but if they noticed she was not hot on their tails, they might turn right instead of left.

"Hó'ésta!" he commanded, and his walker obeyed with a second bellow that filled the mountain glade and sent the elk into full panic. The herd met the streambed and veered left, along the easiest course but into the walker's path. She was ready and surged forward with even greater speed. In two strides she was close enough. One doe trailed behind the rest. The walker clamped her jaws down on the elk's neck. George held on as his mount slowed and jerked her head back. The elk's neck snapped and the walker released the body, looking for another kill, but the herd was in the woods where she could not follow with any speed.

"Good, good, don't worry," George said as he patted her heaving sides. She was thin and out of shape. This kill, however, would help to get her fit for the buffalo hunting season, where she would need to make multiple kills.

She waited impatiently as George set to skinning the carcass. She chuffed and stamped. George worked as quickly as he could, sensing her hunger almost as his own, but he was unskilled in the skinning of large game. She walked closer, chuffed again, and then roared at him. He whirled on her, bloody knife in hand, and bellowed back. They stared at one another, she towering over him and he, staring upward, hands now on hips, refusing to back away.

"Hámêstoo'êstse," he ordered her and signaled with his hand. He could feel her hot breath on his head. *"Hámêstoo'êstse."*

Incredibly—or so it always seemed to him whenever he had to assert his will over a fifteen-foot-tall man-eater—she obeyed. She backed away three steps, settled down on the bright spring grass, and let him return to his chore.

When the carcass was skinned and the teeth—a valuable commodity among the People—had been removed, George stepped aside and let her free of his command. He had trapped enough for his needs and those of his neighbors, so the whole of the elk was hers. She ate loudly and with gusto—not a pretty sight—and when she was done, George climbed aboard her and they headed home at a slow, full-bellied waddle.

"A good day," he said to her as they traveled. "Could have done better if I had a rifle, though." He looked at the fox hanging from the side of his back-rest. That skin, plus the other pelts of fox, beaver, marten, and such that he'd trapped over the winter, together should be enough to trade for a rifle, but he wasn't sure.

Then he remembered the nugget of gold. *That* would be enough. Enough and more.

At home, when he presented Picking Bones Woman and Mouse Road with the elk's teeth and hide, he broached the subject.

"I thought I might make a journey to the *vé'ho'e* trading-place."

The women's faces brightened. They grinned at him. "Truly?" Mouse Road asked. "Will you truly go?"

Befuddled, George gave a little chuckle. "Yes," he said. "Truly. Why?"

Picking Bones Woman shrugged. "The men, they never want to go up to the trading-place. 'What do they have that we need?' they always ask. But if you go, I can think of one or two women who would like their husbands to make the trip with you."

"I *would* need someone's help," George said. "To show me the way, at least."

"Leave it to me," Picking Bones Woman said.

Within three days she had organized a trading party. Through the efficient use of suggestions and casual remarks to neighboring women, Picking Bones Woman had subtly undermined any objections the men had to such a frivolous trip. By the morning of the party's departure, a total of twenty-four men had "volunteered" to guide George to the nearest trading outpost.

George stood outside his lodge, loading up his drake. The mountain air was still crisp in the mornings but would heat up as the spring day progressed. George guessed it to be mid-April—he had given up on his exact count during the winter—though it might have been May. To the People, it was still the Ball Game Moon, a time of happy relaxation, the last moon in their mountain camp. The next moon would be Hatchling Moon, and the band—along with every other band of the People—would make its way down to the plains where the hatchlings could graze on the tender new grass and where the People would slowly gather and prepare for the return of the buffalo herds. George was lucky. His two hens were sitting on clutches of eggs. That left him, however, with only his drake to ride on the trading expedition, for he would not take his hungry walker on a trek with no other company than whistlers.

"One Who Flies!"

It was Mouse Road, coming up the hill with two whistlers in tow. She led them up to the drake, who displayed bars of pale gray and deep red up and down his head and neck in seasonal aggression. Mouse

Road's hens fluted and changed their colors to dark mottled green in submission, quieting the male.

"My mother has sent you these spare mounts." Mouse Road smiled and pointed to a bundle of pelts on the back of one of the whistlers. "And something extra to trade."

George was touched by the generosity of Picking Bones Woman. "Please take my thanks to your mother," he said.

"She would like for you to get," Mouse Road continued, enumerating items on her fingers, "some red Trader's cloth, at least two arm's lengths; some salt, a bag about this big; a new knife, and a good one, not one of the small ones Storm Arriving always got her; some corn, at least three large sacks; and a metal cooking-plate, like the one Little Worker has."

"All that?" George laughed. "She expects me to get all that for a few pelts?"

"Yes," Mouse Road said with a sharp look. "You will have to be very clever with the traders. But my mother says that she will have finished dressing the elk hide by the time you return."

"Yes. The elk hide," George said, chagrined at being reminded of the favor Picking Bones Woman was doing for him. "I will do my best."

"Cloth, salt, knife, corn, cooking-plate," Mouse Road said with a satisfied smile.

He repeated the list as he took his own pelts and supplies and tied them onto the pack animal Mouse Road brought. "And thank her for the loan of the whistlers, will you?"

"I will." She turned to go, but hesitated.

"What is it, Mouse Road?"

She turned back, her hand on the pouch that hung at her belt. "Will you trade something for me?"

"Of course," he said. "But what could you possibly need?"

"Something shiny," she said and touched the end of her braid. "Something silver or copper for my hair."

He signed his agreement. "And what do you have to trade?"

She reached inside the pouch and pulled out something small, held gingerly between two fingers. She held it out, and dropped it in George's open palm.

It was another nugget of gold. Smaller, to be sure, than the one Speaks While Leaving had found, this one was only the size of a pea. George took out his knife and pressed the edge against the nugget. It left a mark in the soft metal. Definitely gold.

"Where did you find this?" he asked, trying not to let his excitement show.

"Near where Speaks While Leaving found hers. I went out to the tamarack tree she told of, a few days after. Is it worth anything? Can you trade it for me?"

George swallowed. These women, he thought to himself, are picking up pure gold off the open ground. How much must be under the surface?

"Um, yes," he said. "I think I can trade it for something for your hair."

She smiled and it was a happy smile of innocent pleasure. "My thanks," she said, and bounded off down the slope. George stared after her, then shook his head, and looked again at the small nugget. His ideas of what to get at the outpost were already changing.

He rode down to the meeting place near the lower pond, absently repeating the list of items. "Red cloth, bag of salt, big knife, three sacks of corn, cooking-plate, something for Mouse Road's hair. Red cloth . . ."

Two dozen men and over seventy whistlers were converging on the field. George was glad when he saw Red Whistler riding down the hill from his lodge. It would be good to have another person at the trading post who could speak French. The young man looked worried, though; his brow was furrowed and his eyes stared at the ground in front of him. He was muttering to himself, and as he drew closer George could hear his words.

". . . one sack of sugar, three sacks of corn, three sacks of white beans . . ."

George laughed out loud and Red Whistler looked up in anger.

"Quiet, One Who Flies. If I forget something, my wife will be most angry with me."

"Wait here," George said. He slid off his whistler and went over to a cold fire-pit near the edge of the pond. With a charred twig and a parfleche, he wrote his own list on the inside flap—in French, for he had no idea how to accurately spell the Cheyenne words.

"What are you doing?" Red Whistler asked.

"I am"—the Cheyenne had no word for "to write"—"I am drawing the words, to help me remember. There." He showed him the written words. "That is my list. Now tell me yours."

"Those marks . . . they are words?"

"Yes. Tell me your list and I will draw your words, too."

Red Whistler recited his list and George wrote it down. When he was done, he read it back. "One sack of sugar, three sacks of corn, three sacks of white beans, some blue cloth, two wool blankets—"

"You can see all of that? In those marks?"

George nodded, caught himself, and signed in the affirmative. "—two handfuls of peppercorns, one large piece of hardback shell, and a long coil of brass wire."

Long Jaw rode up, having overheard their conversation. The older, quiet Indian looked at Red Whistler's baffled expression, then at the words that George had written down.

"Four sacks of corn," he began.

"No, no, no," George protested, but saw that Long Jaw was prepared to take offense if George refused. He also saw that the other men were all riding over to see what was of so much interest to Long Jaw. "I do not have enough room for everyone's list here. I should mark your list on something of yours, so it won't get confused with someone else's list."

Long Jaw handed over a beaver pelt and recited to George his list. The elder man stared at the pelt as George handed it back to him.

"Take care not to smear the markings," George said. "Next!"

The lists were generally the same: corn, beans, sugar, salt, something new for the household, something nice for the wife. The Indians handled the enscribed pelts and hides like holy relics, holding them flat and level as if the words might somehow slide off. George did not discourage their caution, and made a mental note to mix up some ink and cut some quills.

The trading party rode for five long days, down from the Sheep Mountains, and out across the vast plains. To George, however, the empty land around them was no longer the wasted resource he once considered it to be. The land *was* in use, by a people who simply did not leave their mark upon it.

The greening of the land was well under way. The grass that blanketed the earth was bright and vivid. The trees that stood in groves along streams and riverbeds were in full leaf, and when the party stopped along a stretch of running water, the ferns were thick and the berry bushes were full of flowers.

Everywhere George looked there was the activity of springtime: birds sang and gathered grasses for their nests, and bees floating lazily from flower to flower to flower. The whole prairie was sown with the colors of wildflowers and dogwoods, birds and butterflies.

The trading place, as George discovered, was near the towns of the tribes the People called the Earth Lodge Builders. At the confluence of the Big Greasy and the Antelope Pit rivers lived the Mandan, the Hidatsa, and the Arikara. When he had first seen their towns, he had been amazed. Now, a year later, they still impressed him.

George and the others rode through field after field of mixed crops. The Indians planted their crops together so that in one glance George could see the tiny

white flowers of bean bushes standing tall over the
blowsy blooms of squash and pumpkin. But still, between each crop plant, the prairie intruded.

"Where are the farmers?" he asked Red Whistler.
"I see no one out here working the land?"

Red Whistler shrugged. "What is there to do? You
sow the seeds, the plants grow."

Long Jaw spoke from a few paces back. "Long ago,
before anyone had even heard of the *vé'hó'e,* the People used to live along these rivers. We would plant in
the spring, and follow the buffalo all summer. When
we came back in the autumn, we harvested our crops.
The plants know what to do. They do not need our
help."

"But couldn't you . . ." George did not complete
his sentence. With arable land that stretched to the
horizon and beyond, discussions of bushels per acre
were meaningless. More was not better if you did not
need it.

They rode wide of the quiet town, though even from
a distance George could make out the large settlement
of cylindrical buildings with thatched, domed roofs.
After some miles they came to a place where the river
swung this way and that in a long, lazy ess. George
could see buildings on the far shore—ten or twelve
of them—built like regular houses. Their walls were
straight, their corners square, and their roofs were
peaked. Smoke rose from a few chimney pipes.
George felt his stomach flip over.

White men.

He thought of his Indian clothes, his long hair, his
scraggly beard. He hadn't bathed since they had set
off and he felt the grime of a week's travel on the
back of his neck. For the first time in nearly a year
he was going to meet some white men and he
looked like—

He stopped and considered his line of thought.

Am I ashamed? Embarrassed of my appearance?
Afraid of what these traders might think of me?

No, he decided. I'm just nervous. I haven't been among whites for moons . . . for months, that is. Everyone wants to make a good first impression.

At the near shore and also on the far side several large canoes had been pulled up out of the water. The Big Greasy was too wide to ford here, so they hobbled their whistlers, unpacked their trading goods, and three and four to a boat began to ferry themselves across. Even before they had reached the middle of the river's creamy brown flow, four men stood on the far shore.

White men. Traders.

As the boats came close the men waded in to help pull them ashore, already hawking their wares in an amalgam of French, signs, and—even to George's untrained ear—heavily accented Cheyenne.

" 'Allo, Chief. Come with me! I'll get you what you need!"

"What you need? I have everything you need!"

"Cloth! Blankets! Come! Look!"

The youngest of the four reached for Long Jaw's parcel of pelts and hides. There was a blur of motion and the trader was on his back in the riverside mud, a long, thin knife at his throat. The other traders fell silent and still. The man on the ground was wide-eyed with fear, petrified.

Then Long Jaw, usually so stern and taciturn, actually smiled. He put his knife back in its sheath.

"I thought he was going to take my list," he said, and everyone laughed. Everyone, including the traders who, though not comprehending, were glad nonetheless to see peace restored.

None of the traders, however, helped anyone with their bundles.

"Sacré mère," said one of the traders and George saw that the man was staring at him. "What have we here?"

The other traders stared, too, first with incredulity, then with derision.

"Looks like someone's gone native," said one.

"Or around the bend," said the youngest, having recovered from his encounter with Long Jaw.

"Just who in Hell do you think you are?" asked a third trader. He took a step closer and George could smell the stink of the man: sweat, dung, whiskey, tobacco, and six or seven other odors all joined in on the assault. His own fears about having not bathed suddenly felt absurd.

"Oh," the trader said, noticing George's reaction. "So you think you're better than me, *non?*"

George felt the presence of several of his friends behind him. Though none but Red Whistler understood the French trader's words, the belligerent tone was unmistakable.

"Say nothing," he heard Long Jaw say. "They are just crazy *vé'hó'e*. They do not know how to act."

The old phrase, so long applied to him, and now turned around against others of his own race, struck George as oddly humorous.

If these men were the Indians' primary contact with his own race, with their foulness and their avarice and their aggression, it was no wonder that the People had such a low opinion of the whites.

"Crazy *vé'hó'e*," George said in Cheyenne, and began to laugh.

"He's a lunatic," said the first trader, and with a sudden smile of blatant huckstership, he turned and beckoned the others to follow him. "Come with me, Chief. I've got what you need."

"Crazy *vé'hó'e*," Long Jaw said, giving George a pat on the back. Then they all picked up their bundles and headed up the riverbank toward the buildings.

To George, several of the cabins—though even that word was too kind to describe some of the outpost's dilapidated hovels—looked empty, as if uninhabited for some time. The others, those in use by the four traders, were not in much better shape. Doors hung loosely on leather-strap hinges and unglazed windows gaped from behind broken or missing shutters. Shattered glass and potsherds littered the area around each shack, as did the offal of hunting kills and—George's nose told him—ordure from the traders' own eliminations.

Red Whistler pointed to each of the traders. "That one has metal, and that one has cloth. The oldest one has tools and knives, and the youngest one has sugar and salt and pretty things for decorations."

"What about the corn and beans and such?"

"We will get those when we visit with the Ree, back on the other side of the river."

For the traders, obsequiousness and flattery were the order of the day, but the Indians appeared immune to it. The party stayed together and walked toward the first of the traders' shacks, ignoring each man's attempt to separate individuals with promises of good trades.

As they approached the shack of the trader of cloth goods, the spiels from the other three increased in urgency. When the Indians all bent to their bundles and took out a pelt or hide, the traders' entreaties grew feverish. George found their unabashed avarice disturbing. Their hands pled and their voices whined in supplication, but their lips curled in near snarls. Only the older trader maintained any fragment of dignity and decorum. He stood farthest back, a knife in one hand and an awl in the other.

"Best price to first customer," he said. "Not too many left."

But when the Indians each brought their hides to George and he read off what their cloth needs were, the traders fell silent and stared.

"*Merde,*" the metal dealer said. Then he and the other dealers stood back and let the dickering begin in earnest.

Even though the cloth dealer's supplies of blankets and fabric were dirty, dusty, and in some cases frayed and torn, the desire for them was strong. The trader bargained hard. George and Red Whistler helped with the translation when necessary, but sign language and a few words of Cheyenne proved to be adequate for all but the most complex requests.

George quickly learned that the most precious pelts were marten, fisher, fox, and mink. Though George had far fewer pelts than some of the others, he had a good number of marten and fox. He purchased a length of red wool in exchange for a beaver pelt.

From the cloth trader they went to the metal dealer. This man kept a neater cabin, with small sheets of iron, tin, and brass over to one side, and cast-iron pots, pans, and griddles on the other. Again the lists were consulted where memories were shaky. Sheets of iron were purchased for the making of arrowheads, and the other metals were bought to make decorations or bells for whistler harnesses. George looked around, but aside from a skillet, he saw none of the items he sought.

The young trader was next. The haggling over sugar and salt was perfunctory, prices having been well established over the years, but when it came to the limited selection of beads, wire, and silver, it became fierce.

"He is crazy," complained Long Jaw. "Six fox for two circles of silver. They are too small. I would not give him six *rabbit* pelts. Tell him, One Who Flies."

George complied. "He would not give six rabbit skins for those."

"I wouldn't take them," the trader said, cool and competent in this, his own realm of expertise.

George did not need to translate the trader's words, but the young trader's attitude irked him. Growing up on the Frontier, George had had ample opportunity to learn a thing or two about haggling. He turned to Long Jaw. "How much would you give?"

"Three," Long Jaw said.

"Fox?"

Yes, Long Jaw signed in confirmation.

"Two fox skins," George said to the trader.

"Two!" The young trader laughed, holding up two fingers. "Two?"

Long Jaw tapped George on the shoulder. "I said three."

"I know. I'm making a deal."

But the trader had seen Long Jaw's gestures. "He said three."

"Yes, but I told him they're not worth three."

"You what?"

"Those tiny little things? They're not worth three. Two, maybe . . . not three."

"Not worth—" The young man gaped, finally flustered by George's audacity. "Who the infernal devil do you think you are?"

George leaned close into the young trader's stink. "I," he said with an evil grin, "am the one translating your words." He turned to Long Jaw. "Look insulted," he said in the language of the People.

"What?"

"Make a face. Act like I'm telling you that he just insulted you."

Long Jaw caught on. With great theatricality he pulled out his knife and raised it over his head. "I'll kill you!" he shouted.

"Hold on, hold on," George said placatingly. "Pretend it's a smaller insult."

Long Jaw put his knife away and simply glowered at the young trader.

"And so," George said in French, "I think perhaps you get my point, *non?*"

The trader curled his lip and sulked. He picked up the two silver circles. "Two fox," he said.

"And those as well," George said, pointing to two other silver disks.

"Are you—"

George half turned back to Long Jaw. "What's that you say?"

He could hear the man grind his teeth as he picked

up two additional silver disks and handed them all over to George. "Two fox."

George smiled. *"Merci."* Then to Long Jaw he said, "One fox, and don't look surprised." George took his friend's pelt and took one of his own and handed them both to the trader. To Long Jaw he handed a pair of silver circles while he kept the other two for Mouse Road.

"I think we're done here," George said to the trader. "Many thanks."

It was at the old trader's shack that George finally saw what he was hoping to find. While Red Whistler was interpreting for the others in their purchases of knives and awls, George was looking at other, quite different items.

A barrel in a corner was filled with long hickory handles. On the floor next to it was a pile of pick- and mattock-heads. Leaning up against the barrel were several spades and shovels. There were some other tools nearby—hammers, hoes, wedges, and such—but they did not interest George. He took aside three of the pick-heads and began searching through the barrel until he found handles to fit them.

"Going to do some prospecting?"

George jumped at the sudden nearness of the trader. His question, too, set off alarm bells in George's head. If this man guessed that there really *was* gold out in Cheyenne territory . . . But he was stuck. He'd already gathered up items that testified to his intention, and he wouldn't dare use the gold itself to barter with.

George could think of only one thing to do.

"Prospecting?" he said with a wild-eyed grin. "You bet. Prospecting. That's me." He laughed in the old trader's face. "Gonna find me the mother lode. You bet. So I need these." He put the pick-heads in the trader's arms. "And these." He added the handles. "And some of these," he said, picking up a pair of shovels. He saw an ax across the room and almost ran over to get it, but caught himself.

Act crazy, he told himself, but not *too* crazy.

"I need some other things, too, but"—he grimaced as if in pain—"I can't remember what they are. Ah! My list." He dashed to the door. The other members of the trading party gave him odd looks but Long Jaw began to speak to them. By the time George returned with his list, the Indians all looked on him with a conspiratorial smirk.

"My list," George said, showing the pelt to the old trader. "Ah, an ax, an ax, I need an ax, and a big one, not a hatchet."

The trader was looking at George with an expression of mixed tolerance and skepticism. George wasn't sure if his act was working, but he decided it was still his best bet.

"An ax," the trader said. "How about that one?"

"Good, good."

George kept up his quasi-maniacal glee and eventually the trader's sidelong glances of incredulity waned. They gathered up all the tools, added a big knife for Picking Bones Woman, and topped it off with a straight razor and strop.

"Good," George said. "All this. How much?"

He dickered shrewdly with the grizzled trader, just as he had with the others. He was sure that the four white men would compare experiences after the party had left, and George did not want any discrepancies in his abilities to tip his hand. They settled on a final price that left George with enough to trade for the corn he still needed. He gathered up his purchases in a clattering armload and headed for the open doorway.

An arm came down across the opening, hindering his exit.

"I'm on to you," the trader whispered in English. "Those tramps"—he nodded toward the other traders' shacks—"maybe you fooled them, but not me. You've found something out there, I'll wager."

George felt his heart begin to race.

"I've been a prospector, on and off, for thirty-five years. I can see it when a man's had a taste of the real thing." He put a hand on George's shoulder. "But I'll tell you what, friend. I'll keep your secret. I'll keep it, on one condition. You cut me in on the deal. I'll get you the supplies you need—tools, wagons, even explosives if you want—and I'll keep your secret, but you cut me in or on my next trip up north I'll tell the whole town that *Custer's boy has found gold in Indian territory.*"

George felt his mouth go dry. "I don't know what you're talking about."

"Don't play old Vincent for a fool, boy. A crazy white man walks in with a bunch of Cheyenne warriors, but he can read and write and haggle like a horse trader and he wants to buy a razor? *Tabarnaque.* I am not an idiot. So, have we a deal?" He held out his hand.

"I haven't found anything."

"Nothing big, perhaps, but yes, you have. And you'll need more than three picks and two shovels when you make a strike. Any other trader with a brain will see through you just as I did, and he might not choose to offer you a deal. He might just follow you to your strike and kill you for it. So, those are your choices."

"I don't like those choices," George said, all pretense gone.

"*Quels dommages.*" The trader said it without sympathy, but still held out the offered handshake.

Despite his misgivings, George clasped the trader's hand. The old man smiled, revealing crooked teeth.

"Vincent D'Avignon," he said.

"George Custer, Jr."

"A pleasure, George."

The trading party left shortly thereafter, and all were impressed by George's skill at bargaining. He did not tell them of the deal he had had to strike with Vincent D'Avignon, nor did he say much of anything during the journey home. He had already, he feared, said far too much.

*   *   *

Custer put the final flourish on his signature and laid down the pen. Samuel, his attaché, leaned in and rocked a blotter over the wet ink. Custer flipped the bill's pages back to the beginning, closed the cover, and rose.

"Gentlemen, I give you the General Allotment Act of 1887."

The senators and representatives applauded politely and though a few even said "Hear, hear!" the overall response was quite tepid. Custer looked at the collection of political power that filled the White House's large oval library. Their dark frocks and dour expressions competed with the cheery white trim and yellow silk wallpaper. They were not affected by the warm sunlight of the late spring afternoon, nor by the southerly breeze that stirred the lace curtains on the curved-glass doors. Many of them, in fact, looked as if their heads ached, though Custer doubted it was from any early celebration. The bill's passage had been rocky and contentious. Not even its sponsor looked happy.

"Senator Dawes," Custer said as the staff brought in the obligatory drinks and canapés. "Surely you can summon some enthusiasm over the enactment of your bill?"

Dawes, a sharp-faced man with the intense gray-eyed gaze commonplace among New England reformers, took a cup and saucer of tea from Janie, the serving maid, and thanked her before turning to address his president.

"I regret to say, sir, that any enthusiasm I may own on the subject of this bill—which at one time was prodigious—has now been quite attenuated by the actions of my own Republican Party."

"Oh, not again," said Greaves, a senator from Illinois. "We've heard it all before."

"And yet I'll say it once more," Dawes replied, his Boston accent surfacing along with his ire. "The amendments you Westerners added have destroyed the spirit of this bill. It was supposed to *help* the Indian—"

"It allocates one hundred sixty acres of reservation land to every married adult male," Greaves said. "Eighty acres to every unmarried male, just as you intended."

Dawes sneered and looked down his nose at the Illinois senator. "But instead of holding the unallocated reservation lands in trust for future generations, it allows for the sale of that land to whites, just as *you* intended."

Robert Matherly turned and smiled good-naturedly. "But if they're not going to use it," he began, as if it were the most obvious point.

The Massachusetts senator took a step toward the big man. "It is their land, Senator Matherly."

"And if not allocated, according to *your* plan, it would lie fallow forever. Shouldn't *some*one get *some* good of it?"

"The amendments abrogate this nation's long-standing treaties with the Indians, sir. You and your fellows are advocating the misappropriation of millions of acres of Indian land. And you are using *my* bill to do it."

"Gentlemen," Custer said, stepping between the two and addressing the group as a whole. "I think we can safely say that I was wrong. There is still plenty of enthusiasm about this bill."

Matherly and most of the others laughed and returned to their private conversations. Dawes, however, remained stiff and unmoved, face flushed and nostrils flaring with frustration.

"Senator," Custer said, "the amendments were the only way to get your bill passed at all."

"Yes, Mr. President," Dawes said curtly. "I know. It is still, however, wrong. If you will excuse me, please?"

Custer nodded and Dawes turned away.

Samuel Prendergast, Custer's personal attaché and

long-time adviser, watched as Dawes handed his cup and saucer to Douglas and walked from the room. "I do feel for the man. He's such an idealist."

"Zealots always are," Custer said. "But I do not believe he truly understands the thing he hopes to help. The Indian of the plains cannot be made into a corn farmer."

"Then why not veto the bill?" Samuel asked.

Custer shrugged. "I could be wrong."

Matherly came by again, picking up on the end of the conversation. "I actually think Dawes is right," he said. "Naturally, there will be some individuals who will resist—there always are—but to use the senator's own words, if we treat them like white men, they will behave like white men."

"And what about the selling of reservation lands?" Samuel asked.

"It simply allows us to reclaim the unused acreage. Do you know how much land they *have* on those reservations?"

Samuel laughed bitterly. "Somewhat less than they had prior to our arrival on this continent, I'd guess. But what of all the land in the Unorganized Territory? Shouldn't you start giving that away now, before we have reservations out there?"

Matherly looked thunderstruck. "Why I'll be," he said. "Mr. President, I do believe that Mr. Prendergast has hit upon a great idea."

Samuel's jaw dropped.

"If you want settlers for the Frontier," Matherly said, "what better way to draw them out there than with the promise of free land?"

"Oh, dear Lord," Samuel murmured. Custer bit back on his mirth as the senator plowed onward.

"We could have a lottery. Or just open up the border on a given day." Matherly snapped two pudgy fingers. "We could coordinate it so that it coincided with the opening of the bridge across the Missouri! What an event!"

"Robert," Custer said with a crafty smile, "I do think I may have underestimated you."

"Why, thank you, Mr. President," he said with a grin and a curt bow. "I take that as a compliment. And thank *you*, Mr. Prendergast, for the idea. But excuse me, won't you? I'd like to have a little chat with some of my colleagues." He turned and walked across the room, rubbing his hands together.

"I feel ill," Samuel said.

"I should expect that you now know precisely how Senator Dawes feels," Custer said.

"Do you think Matherly will do it?"

"I believe he will try," Custer said, nodding. "Remind me to write to Herron. If Matherly moves ahead on this, I'm sure Herron and I will want to have a 'little chat' of our own."

CHAPTER 5

Summer, A.D. 1887
Near the Sudden River
Alliance Territory

Storm Arriving lay with his hands behind his head, listening to the birds of dawn while he waited for the others of his patrol group to awaken. Mornings came early during the waning of Hatchling Moon, but he did not mind much.

Less time to spend staring at the stars, he thought to himself.

He had not slept well during his weeks on patrol. He had not thought it possible to have grown so quickly accustomed to the warm smoothness of his wife beside him at night, but he had and now, feeling keenly his separation from her, he spent most of his nights watching the moon and stars perform their slow dance overhead. But morning brought the music of killdeer and lark, and painted over the stars with a slow, patient palette of violet, blue, green, red, and pink.

Storm Arriving's patrol of Kit Fox soldiers had made camp in tall, golden grass and made no fire. He heard the deep breathing of men asleep as well as the rustle of others just now beginning to swim up from the depths of slumber. The whistlers, already awake, heard the sounds of their riders' growing wakefulness. The beasts sang quietly to one another, anticipating the day's activity.

Red Hat stretched and groaned as he came awake. He looked over and saw Storm Arriving staring at the sky.

"Another sleepless night?" he asked.

"I slept some," Storm Arriving replied. "But then the moon rose and woke me."

"How impolite," Red Hat said and looked at the weather. "How long have these clouds been here?"

"A hand or two."

A puff of breeze moved the grass. Red Hat sat up and sniffed the air. "Rain coming?"

"I think so," Storm Arriving said. "Not soon, though. Late."

One by one all the Kit Fox soldiers rose and got ready for the day's ride. Storm Arriving ate a few bites of pemmican as he tied his rolled-up buffalo hide on the back of his crouching whistler.

The grass was higher than a man was tall, and the whole patrol—eight men and sixteen whistlers—were completely concealed. It meant, too, of course, that they were blind to oncoming trouble, but the breeze carried no hint of smoke and the whistlers, more attuned to scents of danger than any man, were calm.

When a gunshot cracked and echoed across the landscape, it surprised them all, man and whistler alike.

The two youngest members of the patrol leapt up onto their whistlers' backs, ready to attack.

"Lost Heart Wolf! Issues Forth!" Storm Arriving said in a harsh whisper. "Must you do everything wrong?"

The boys' eager smiles evaporated. "But I heard . . ." Issues Forth began.

"And who do you think it is?"

"I—I don't know," he said.

"Wouldn't it be better to know who and how many before you ride off on the war path?"

Storm Arriving saw Red Hat raise an eyebrow at the severity of his reprimand. He took a deep breath and let it out through pursed lips.

"I know you are new to the Kit Fox society," he said to the boys, "and that this is your first patrol. But I do not want to have to tell your mothers that you died out here because you didn't think."

The sudden wideness of the boys' eyes made Red Hat laugh.

"Yes," Red Hat said. "You can die out here. What did you think we were doing? Looking for a good place to fish?"

The other men joined in the laughter. Storm Arriving pointed to Issues Forth.

"Stand up on your whistler's back and take a look. Tell me what you see."

Issues Forth balanced on his whistler's spine and stood so that he could peer above the tall grass.

"I . . . don't see anything."

"Open your eyes," Red Hat said.

Issues Forth smiled at the teasing and began again. "I don't see anything unusual. Just the long slope down to the river and the land on the other side."

"No men? No riders?"

"No."

"Do you see any smoke?"

"No."

"Not *vé'hó'e*, then," Red Hat said. "Who else could it be?"

Storm Arriving climbed up on his own whistler, standing slowly so as not to expose their hiding place.

The land declined gently away from their vantage, down to the long, twisting cleft that held the White Water. Beyond the river, the land rolled onward in low rises to the horizon. Storm Arriving could see the hands of the morning breeze caress the tall grass in hypnotic waves that ran unhindered across the flawless vista . . . or nearly flawless.

"There," he said, pointing. "See it?"

Issues Forth squinted. "Yes," he said.

Down along the river's run, the ripples in the grass crossed over two lines where there was no grass: two scars in the growth that, as they watched, grew longer.

Two men, Issues Forth signed.

No, Storm Arriving signed in return. *Two groups of men.*

Near one of the lines three pheasants flew up out of the tall grass, wings whistling through the air. Another shot was fired and one of the pheasants fell. The lines split and extended out to search for their quarry. Storm Arriving heard the hunters talk to one another. He crouched down and spoke to the rest of the patrol.

"Wolf People. Ten of them. I wonder what they are doing here."

"Hunting pheasant," Issues Forth said.

Storm Arriving rolled his eyes. "I mean what are they doing *here*?"

Red Hat scoffed. "What does it matter?" he asked. "Soon they will all be dead."

"No," Storm Arriving said. "I think it is important to know why they are here."

"Why?" Red Hat asked, and proceeded to enumerate the possibilities. "They are not here on a whistler raid—the Wolf People ride the domesticated elk, like the *vé'hó'e*. And they aren't hunting buffalo, not on foot." He appealed to the other soldiers. "They must be here to spy for the bluecoats, and are shooting some pheasants to fill their bellies."

Men murmured their agreement. Lost Heart Wolf and Issues Forth stood slack-jawed, waiting to see what Storm Arriving would say in rebuttal.

"The Wolf People have been our bitter enemies forever," Storm Arriving said. "We drove them across the Big Greasy in the time of our great-grandfathers. But now some have come here again. It is probably just as Red Hat says—they are scouts for the bluecoats—but if they are, I want to know why. Why did the bluecoats send them? What do the bluecoats want to know?"

The group considered the arguments. Silently, and one by one, the men signed their agreement to Storm Arriving's proposal.

"Prisoners, then," Red Hat said. "And once we know all there is to know?"

"Once we know why they are here," Storm Arriving said, "it will be clear what we should do next."

They prepared their war mounts for action. Another reconnaissance showed that the trespassers had converged again into two groups moving parallel with the river. The soldiers put away arrows and took out clubs and ropes. Knives were ready, if needed, and Storm Arriving knew that some of the Wolf People would probably be killed in the attack. As long as a few were left to tell their tale, though, he would be satisfied.

Storm Arriving spoke to their two young soldiers. "This is your first taste of battle. Do not go first. Hold back and learn. Come in to assist any in need." He looked at the group. Eight men, ready for war: eyes bright, limbs taut. A sense of urgent potential filled the circle of trampled grass.

"*Nóheto.*"

From a crouch their war mounts leapt up and ran. They held their heads up to see over the tall grass and held their forelimbs out before them to push aside the waving stalks. The soldiers yipped and whooped as they tore down the slope, guiding their mounts with pressure from heel or toe. Storm Arriving saw the paths in the grass stop in their westward progression.

"They've turned back in their tracks!" he shouted.

They rode in fast. Storm Arriving held a war club in one hand and a coil of buffalo-hair rope in the other. The pale grass stung his legs as they flew through it. The whistlers sang out and changed their colors to match the gold that surrounded them. The pack of riders split to surround their quarry. Storm Arriving guided his mount toward one of the paths in the grass. He heard a gunshot. The soldiers yipped as they all closed in. He swung onto the Wolf People's trail, into the area of trampled grass. He saw them, up ahead, several of them, running, but . . .

"Hold!" he shouted. "Kit Foxes! Hold!"

The riders all swerved in to form a circle. They slowed, then stopped. Before them, in an area of flattened grass, stood an old man, an old woman, two boys, three girls, a man and two women. Not scouts, not warriors.

A family.

All of the soldiers stared at this unexpected discovery, Storm Arriving included. By their dress he could see that they were, indeed, of the Wolf People. The man wore large ball-and-cone earrings and a headpiece of deer-tail hair. His leggings were brightly banded with blue and white, and he wore a dotted red shirt of thin *vé'ho'e* fabric. The women wore *vé'ho'e*-style dresses of dark cloth and had little jewelry or decoration. The adults looked thin and the children were potbellied from improper food. They all looked very frightened. The man held his gun in his hands, ready, but not aimed. It was an old rifle—a single-shot style like the bluecoats used. Storm Arriving doubted the man had had time to reload it since his last shot.

"I am Storm Arriving, of the People," he said, nudging his whistler into the center of the circle. When it was obvious that the Wolf People did not understand him, he said it again, using the language of the Inviters. "We are Kit Fox soldiers on patrol, and you are trespassers in Alliance land. Who are you, and what are you doing here?"

The man put the butt of his rifle on the ground and leaned on the barrel like an old man upon a walking stick. "I am called Knee Prints by the Bank. This is my wife and her family. We are here looking for a new place to live."

"Go look somewhere else," Red Hat said. "Your lands are across the Big Greasy."

"Those are not our lands anymore," Knee Prints by the Bank said. "The white men have taken them."

"What do you mean?" Storm Arriving asked. "How? Did you war with them?"

"No," Knee Prints by the Bank said. "The chiefs of the white men made a new law. This law said our land was no longer our land, but that if I made my mark on a piece of paper, we could use a small piece of it for farming." He lifted his rifle and set it back down. "I am not a farmer," he said. "I do not know how. So we have come here, back across the Big Greasy, hoping to find a new home."

"Well, you won't," Red Hat said. "The Wolf People are not welcome in Alliance land."

Knee Prints by the Bank looked up at them and Storm Arriving saw the sadness in his eyes. "Don't you understand what I am telling you? There *are* no more Wolf People. There are just the few who have stayed, the many who have died, and those like us, who have scattered in search of another home. The Wolf People are no more."

Red Hat took a breath to speak but held his tongue at a motion from Storm Arriving.

"Why should we help you?" he asked. "After generations of war with you, how can the People call you friends?"

Knee Prints by the Bank's gaze hardened, and Storm Arriving saw the old warrior within the man before him. "You can call us friends," he said, "because we are your enemies no longer."

"Who is?"

He picked up his rifle and pointed to the east, to the Horse Nations.

"They are," he said, "and if you will feed my family this night, tomorrow I will show you why."

They took the family to a place some distance east, where there were trees and shelter from the coming rains. Some of the Kit Foxes went out hunting and came back with a small antelope they'd been able to kill. Storm Arriving looked on as the children were offered helpings of food. They were known as the Wolf People because of their fierceness and tenacity. Now, watching one of the boys take a chunk of roasted meat with nervous hands and run off to eat it in solitude, Storm Arriving saw that misfortune had imparted a different similarity.

Before dawn, when the new day's sun still lay dozing beneath the horizon, Storm Arriving stopped pretending to sleep. He crouched down next to Red Hat and poked him.

"What do you want?" Red Hat grumbled.

"Let's go."

"Now?"

"Yes."

"Just because you can't sleep, it doesn't mean that I can't."

"Come," Storm Arriving insisted.

Red Hat sighed. "As you wish."

Storm Arriving told the picket guard that they were leaving and in a short time, with the bleary-eyed Knee Prints by the Bank alongside them, they rode off toward the Big Greasy.

Knee Prints by the Bank was unsteady on whistler-back, so Storm Arriving set an easy pace across the night-shrouded landscape. They traveled in near-silence, the only sounds the waking birds, the wind of their passage, and the cushioned *thump-thump-thump* of their whistlers' feet.

Knee Prints by the Bank, so talkative yesterday, was sullen. It might have been the early hour, but Storm Arriving kept a sharp eye to possible ambush, just in case.

The Big Greasy was on their left hand as they traveled south. Its waters were dark and quiet. Slow, smooth ripples were the only hint that it was a river of water and not some black road of polished stone. Across the river was the land the *vé'hó'e* named after the vanquished branch of the Inviters: Yankton. This was a dangerous area of the borderlands, and they were all alert to possible danger.

"Here," Knee Prints by the Bank said, speaking at last. "I remember this stand of sweet-sap trees, and that rise of land ahead. This is where we swam across the river. It is not far from here."

"What is it that you think is so important to show us?" Storm Arriving asked again.

"You must see for yourself."

They rode on and Storm Arriving began to wish that they had brought more of the Kit Foxes with them. Then he chastised himself.

You are letting his mystery affect you, he told himself. This man would not let himself be trapped, not alone and with his family behind him.

They continued, and the dawn began to break in imperceptible waves of subtle color. The sky paled and brightened and at last the limb of the sun overtopped the rim of the world, sending its light out across the land.

Storm Arriving squinted into the glare. They all held a hand up to shield their eyes as they rode up over a low rise. Ahead, Storm Arriving saw a structure and through the brightness of the rising sun caught a glimpse of movement.

A man in front of them shouted—an alarm by its tone—and Storm Arriving tried to resolve the cluster of shadows and reflections into an image.

In the first heartbeat he saw wooden lodges and cloth tents along the near bank. In the second, he saw *vé'hó'e*, bluecoats and others, all shouting and running toward them, rifles in hand.

"Turn around!" he commanded. "Back! Back! *Nóheto!*"

He turned his whistler. Gunfire peppered the air. He looked back and saw Red Hat and Knee Prints by the Bank riding like spirits out of the dawn's light. There was more gunfire and he heard the balls zip and snap past him, tearing the air and the grass and the turf around them. They ran on, and when the third round of reports crackled behind them, the shots could not cover the distance. With a sigh of relief, Storm Arriving looked back.

Red Hat's whistler was riderless.

"When did he fall?"

"I don't know," Knee Prints by the Bank answered. "I could only think of holding on."

Storm Arriving pulled his whistler to a halt. He gathered in the loose mount and handed over the halter rope. "I'm going back. Wait here."

Knee Prints by the Bank's pallid face and shaking hands said that he would. Storm Arriving toed his mount into motion, lying low along the whistler's spine and guiding it back along the path of trampled grass and kicked-up dirt that they had made in their flight. He unslung his bow from across his shoulder as he rode and put an arrow to the string in anticipation of danger. His whistler had paled its skin and it ran like a tow-colored ghost across the rolling prairie.

"Slow," he said as they approached the top of a gentle rise. "Stop."

His feet firmly in the loops of the riding harness, he stood slowly and looked over the top of the shoulder of land. The trail of their escape stood out like three shiny stripes in the knee-high grass. Next to one of the paths was a man-sized depression. The land beyond was clear up to a farther rise. Storm Arriving dismounted and walked on ahead.

Red Hat lay in a bed of summer-slick grass. His blood colored the golden stems in crimson arcs, having sprayed out from the hole that had been torn in the side of his neck. The Kit Fox soldier's arm and chest were shiny with the gouts he had attempted to stem but now no blood flowed from the wound, no breath passed his lips, and no life lived in his dark eyes. Storm Arriving put down his bow and picked up his friend. As he carried him to his whistler, he sang the death song that Red Hat had been unable to voice.

> *. . . Nothing lives long,*
> *Only the earth and the mountains. . . .*

He laid his friend's body across his whistler's back and went back for his bow. As he leaned down to pick it up, he heard hoofbeats coming over the rise: bluecoats giving chase.

He did not run, but stood in the space where Red Hat had fallen. With arrow to bowstring, he waited, and when the two riders topped the rise, he let fly.

The arrow passed clear through the chest of the first bluecoat and the man toppled from his saddle like a child's doll. The second bluecoat reined in and aimed his rifle. The weapon fired and Storm Arriving heard the bullet slash through the grass behind him. He sang as he pulled a second arrow from his quiver.

Without moving, his own death song emerging through gritted teeth, he aimed as the bluecoat struggled to load another cartridge in his rifle. The *vé'ho'e* cried out as the arrow pierced his forearm, pinning it to his chest. A breath later, the second arrow struck him below the collarbone, twisting him around and tumbling him to the grass.

Storm Arriving ran up the gentle slope, a third arrow at the ready. The horses fled at his approach but he did not care. They were of no use to him.

The first bluecoat was dead. The second lay on his back, tugging at the arrows with a panic-weakened hand. The dying man looked up at Storm Arriving, his panic turning to terror. Storm Arriving sent his final arrow just to the right of the bluecoat's breastbone, piercing the heart, and the man was dead.

The sun was a bit higher, and the glare off the quiet river had lessened. Over the top of the rise Storm Arriving could see more of what Knee Prints by the Bank had brought them there to see.

He saw a path of wooden boards extending out over the water, suspended by upright logs. He saw boats— large, flat, wide *vé'hó'e* boats and not the slender craft the tribes used—tied up alongside the walkway and anchored out in the river's flow like giant stepping stones. On two of them were the beginnings of heavy-timbered towers. On both sides of the river were tents and buildings and piles of supplies taller than both.

They are coming, he said to himself. Again, the *vé'hó'e* are coming.

He retrieved his arrows and took the bluecoats' rifles and cartridge bags. He checked them for anything else of value, found a ring and a silver chain, and then with two quick slices of his knife he took his scalps. He felt no joy in this coup however, unlike previous victories, for despite his success, he could only think of one thing.

The *vé'hó'e* lied to us. They are coming again.

Whistlers sang and flashed their colors in excited greeting. Walkers bellowed their challenges to any and all who would hear. The Closed Windpipe band crested the last ridge and Speaks While Leaving looked down on the camp of the People.

The basin of land was surrounded by the curve of the Little Sheep River and a long ridge of land. This was one of her favorite campsites: plenty of water, hills for children to play upon, and forests filled with fruits and berries.

They were not the last to arrive—Speaks While Leaving saw several empty sections in the grand circle—but they were certainly not the first. Walkers down in camp roared back, challenging the newcomers, and across the river to the west the pale flocks of whistlers ran across the grazing grounds like a heavy liquid, flowing this way and that in their excitement. The people, too, were excited and already several groups were walking toward the new arrivals, eager to share gossip and the winter's news.

There were many people Speaks While Leaving wanted to visit, but foremost in her mind was One Who Flies. She saw in the west the camp of the Tree People, and searched for the hail and handprints of the lodge belonging to her husband's mother.

"You look for him like a lovelorn girl," her grandmother said as she rode by in her travois.

"Ke'éehe," Speaks While Leaving said in a scolding tone. "I am only worried about him."

"Tsh. Worried. Then you and your husband should have gone to visit."

"*Mother,*" Magpie Woman said. "It would not have been proper for *them* to visit anyone. Not in their first season of marriage."

"Aah," the old woman said with a wave of her hand. "Proper. I am too old to worry about what is proper. If she worries, she should visit."

"She is a chief's daughter," Magpie Woman said.

"Yes, Ke'éehe," Speaks While Leaving said with a playful smile. "And someday, perhaps, the wife of one."

Halfway down the hillside, the people from the camp and the inbound travelers came together in a cacophony of shouts, laughter, ululation, and song. Many of her father's friends had come to greet the family, and she enjoyed hearing the bits of news they brought, but she did not see the one she hoped to see.

The Closed Windpipe band walked into camp and stopped in their place just south of the sun road. The families spread out in a circle, selecting their favored sites, forming their own circles and starting the work of unpacking and erecting their homes. The air was alive with the squeals of children. Hens cooed to their hatchlings as they were led off to the grazing grounds and dogs barked and yapped at everyone's heels.

Speaks While Leaving and her mothers had just finished raising the poles for the family's main lodge when she saw a young woman standing nearby, waiting to be noticed.

"Mouse Road?" she said. "Is that you?"

The young woman smiled and ran forward to hug her sister-in-law.

"Look at you. Wait until your brother arrives. He won't believe how much you've grown."

"He is not here?"

"No, he was on patrol for all of Hatchling Moon, but they are late coming home. He will be home soon, though, but—ah, me—Mother, look at this one! She is as tall as I."

"She has become a beautiful young woman," Magpie Woman agreed.

Speaks While Leaving noticed other changes, too. While over the winter Mouse Road had grown taller and leaner, while her body was that of a woman and no longer a girl's, she had also grown in other ways. She held her head higher. She wore a woman's dress and not a child's smock. Her hair was not in the single plait made by a mother's hand, but fell in two braids as a woman wore it, each one was pinned up in a loop with a large circle of etched silver. On her wrist she wore a coiled bracelet of bent hardback shell.

"Where did you get such pretty things?" Speaks While Leaving asked admiringly.

"One Who Flies got them for me. He went up to the trader's town. I gave him the piece of chief-metal I found, but he wouldn't use it and traded his own furs for them. The others said he was a good trader."

The sound of pride in the young woman's voice was unmistakable. "And how is One Who Flies?"

"Oh, Speaks While Leaving, you will be proud of me. I did just as my brother asked. I didn't want to at first, but soon I came to enjoy teaching him. Now he speaks almost like a real person."

"It sounds as if you have found your tongue again, as well."

Mouse Road smiled and Speaks While Leaving caught a glimpse of the shy girl of the previous year.

"Yes," she said. "I am not so sad anymore. I still miss my sister, but One Who Flies has been so kind and so friendly this winter, he made my sadness just melt away."

Speaks While Leaving saw that her mother was listening to their conversation and the two women exchanged a meaningful glance. It was always dangerous when a young woman lost her heart for the first time. If Mouse Road had, and to One Who Flies no less . . . someone needed to speak to him of delicate matters.

"Where is One Who Flies?" Speaks While Leaving asked nonchalantly.

"He is digging."

"Digging?"

"Yes. For more of the yellow chief-metal. At the place where you and I found the first pieces. He says the metal will open many doors."

"Speaks While Leaving," Magpie Woman said, chiding. "We must raise our lodges before nightfall. Your grandmother has spent too many nights in the open already."

"Yes, Mother."

"Can I help?" Mouse Road asked.

"Of course," Magpie Woman replied. "Your brother speaks highly of your abilities at lodge-raising."

The first chores were to raise the lodgepoles and their covers. Then the grass was plucked from the lodge floors, the rectangular hearthpits were dug out, and the ground was swept down to the hard earth. Then the furnishings were unpacked and set up on the half of each lodge set aside for the family. Beddings were unrolled, unfolded, and laid out between the furniture. In the guest areas, blankets and hides were laid down. By then, the sacks and parfleches full of food and other goods were unpacked and ready to be stored, all neatly and orderly, each item in its accustomed place.

The women worked swiftly, sharing stories as they worked. Mouse Road told of her winter's events and Speaks While Leaving gave her news of her brother. In a little over two hands of time the family's homestead was set to rights.

Still, One Who Flies had not arrived.

"He stays out there all day," Mouse Road explained. "I bring him food sometimes. He forgets. Shall I take you to him?"

Magpie Woman spoke up. "You should see after your mother. She's been without you all afternoon."

Old enough to suspect she was being gotten rid of, but young enough to still obey without question,

Mouse Road, after another hug from her brother's wife, ran off toward her home.

"You go, too," Magpie Woman said. "Go find him. Talk to him. Make sure all is well and proper."

"I am sure he has done nothing inappropriate."

Her mother did not look so confident. "Men can be stupid," was all she would say.

Speaks While Leaving went to the flocks where their whistlers had already been taken. She whistled, two low notes and two high ones.

"Two Cuts!"

She heard his answer and saw him trotting across the plain toward her. She and he had ridden many long miles since she had captured him, only the summer before when the cloud fell, bringing One Who Flies to the People. Two Cuts had proven to be a fine addition to her flock.

She mounted him bareback. He let her settle into position and at her command he moved gently into motion. The site of the gold find was miles to the south, in the foothills of the Sheep Mountains, but it was an easy ride. The grasses here on the upper prairie were short and the creeks and streams easy to ford. She rode and felt the warm wind on her face, on her neck, like the touch of fine cloth on her skin. She could smell the summer's heat like a perfume in the air. The sun, tending now toward evening, lit the world with a light that was still bright, but had lost its noonday harshness.

They climbed up into the foothills and at last she saw the lone tamarack tree up on its ridge of rocky land.

She gasped, and Two Cuts slowed, sensing his rider's distress.

The slope beneath the tree had been covered by golden grass, broken only by the knotted roots of the towering tree and the outcroppings of pale stone. Now, near the base of the tree, three deep trenches scarred the land and the dark earth was laid bare to bake in the sun. At the end of one trench, One Who Flies toiled, swinging a pick to break the ground.

"Nóheto," she said, and Two Cuts swept into motion.

"One Who Flies," she shouted and saw his pale-haired head poke up out of the trench like a squirrel-that-barks. She saw his broad smile and his wave, but she could not feel any joy in this meeting.

The three trenches were deep. They cut down through black soil, red dust, and bright stone. Each began at the rock where she found the first large nugget, but each struck out in a different direction.

"What are you doing?" she said in the Trader's Tongue.

Still grinning, One Who Flies climbed up out of his handiwork. "I'm digging," he said, using the language of the People. "I'm digging for the yellow chief-metal."

"But you mustn't," she said. "You must not. This is . . . this is . . ." She looked at the torn land around her. "It is wrong."

His expression told her that he did not understand her anguish. She was not sure she understood it herself. But when she felt the touch of the *ma'heono* on her mind like the light from a hundred suns, she knew her instincts were right.

Her vision brightened and the world around her faded. She saw One Who Flies as through a mist, a brilliant fog that deepened and spread. She saw the concern in his furrowed brow and saw his lips move, speaking as he came to help her, his hands trying to catch her as she slipped from her seat on her whistler's back and slid down to the ground. She saw him speak, but heard nothing, for the pressure of the spirit powers was already within her. It blanked out her world and carried her to another place where time and distance did not matter. In the world of the *ma'heono,* things were real, but not real; they were true, but not in their true shape. Since childhood they had come for her and shown her visions of what had been and what was yet to be. She had long ago learned not to fight them, so now she gave herself up to the light, to the chill. She tried only to force her body to say a few calming words to One Who Flies, who did not understand such things, and then she was among the powers and spirits.

The world was white and without form. She waited and saw what seemed to be a cloud of rainbow gnats: zipping, multihued shadows. They spiraled and whorled until, one by one, they began to slow and coalesce into a shape, something white and pale against the brightness of the vision world. Then, like a ghost out of a dream, it solidified and became a white buffalo, the great spirit woman who fed and cared for the People. White Buffalo Woman stepped forward and wherever she stepped, the world reappeared, racing outward from her hooves like ripples in a tranquil pond. By the time White Buffalo Woman had reached her, the world was complete. She turned and showed Speaks While Leaving the vision.

There was a lodge so tall that its over-the-smokes were lost in the clouds. The skin of the lodge was painted with all sorts of symbols—trees, grass, rivers, buffalo, antelope, birds, and grasshoppers. In the door of the lodge stood a woman. Her skin was all brown, her hair and her eyes raven-black, and she stood like a timber-deer in the shadowed oval of the doorway, calm but wary.

Six men came up to the lodge and each wore the regalia of one of the soldier societies. Kit Foxes, Crazy Dogs, Little Bowstrings, Dog Men, Red Shields, Elk-horn Scrapers—all were there. One by one they went up to the brown woman with the long black hair and put out their hands, but she only shook her dark head and turned them away. When the last soldier came, he had in his hands a handful of summer grass and dried flowers, their heads heavy with seed. When he came to the dark woman, she gave him a stone in exchange for the grasses and flowers. Then the dark woman smiled and she turned and fled into the shadowy interior of the lodge.

The soldier turned away with his stone and the other soldiers gathered around. They all reached out and touched the stone, and as they did, it fell on the ground and broke open like an egg. Within it was a nugget of gold like the one Speaks While Leaving had found, but as she and the others watched, it began to change shape. It became first a rifle, then a large gun with wheels on it. It grew and became a boat with smoke that came up out of two stacks in the middle, and then became a chair like she had seen *vé'hó'e* use, except heavy and ornate. Finally, it became a shield and a helmet like the ones the Iron Shirt Men wore in years long ago.

Speaks While Leaving turned to White Buffalo Woman. The great spirit was now in the form of a woman with long, loose black hair and a dress of whitened deerskin.

I don't understand, Speaks While Leaving said to her guide, but White Buffalo Woman only reached out with her hand. In her open palm was a nugget of gold. It shone with a warm light and the light grew to fill her vision. It engulfed her, breached her mind, and carried her away from the spirit realm and back to the world of the People.

One Who Flies knelt at her side, worry creasing his features.

"I am back now," she said as she sat up.

"What happened? Are you all right?"

"I am fine," she said. She moved to stand but was still light-headed from her journey.

"What happened? It was like you were asleep or dreaming, but you were speaking—"

"Did you hear me?" she asked him urgently. "Did you understand what I was saying?"

"Yes," he said. "Every word."

"Good," she said, relaxing. "Then you see why you must stop your digging."

"Stop? No, I don't. Why should I stop?"

"You are not doing it properly."

He laughed, embarrassed. "I know I could be doing it better," he said, pointing to his trenches. "I can't seem to find the path of the metal. I am a poor prospector."

"No," she said, "you are not going about it with the proper respect."

He sat back on his heels, baffled. "Respect? What respect? I just have to find the right place to dig. I can't get to the gold unless I dig for it."

She touched his arm to calm his agitation. "But it must be done in the right way and with the right people. We must wait for the rest of the Council to arrive so that I can tell them of this vision. They will decide the best course for you to follow. Until then, though, you should fill in these holes."

"Fill them in?"

"Yes," she said. "To put things back the way they were before you began."

One Who Flies stared at her as if she had asked him to swallow the moon.

"Just until the full Council can assemble," she added.

"Fill them in," he said, still disbelieving.

"Yes. Of course, no one can tell another what to do, but I think that would be best."

Still he stared at her and so dumbly that she thought perhaps the *ma'heono* had come upon him, too, but then he threw his arms up and began to shake his head slowly.

"I do not understand you sometimes," he said.

She laughed. "Perhaps not, but I understand you very well. Mouse Road was right. You speak almost as well as a real person."

George watched Speaks While Leaving ride back toward the camp. He turned and looked at the results of five long days' effort: three exploratory trenches, four feet deep and about twenty feet long. He clenched his fists and felt the hot pain of open blisters crack on his palms and fingers, the grit that cloaked his shoulders and the dirt beneath his nails. He felt the pressure of the westering sun on his burnt back.

I am so close, he said to himself. I know I am. I've missed in three directions. The seam of rock can only lay in the fourth.

He looked at the sun and judged there to be at least three hands of daylight remaining. He walked over to his tools and, wincing at the pain in his hands, picked them up. He walked around to the far side of the exposed length of quartz and granite.

She'll come around when I show up with an armload of gold.

He swung the pick and broke the ground for a new trench. He pulled up the sod and then shoveled aside the dark earth beneath. When the soil turned pale and hard, he took up the pick again and cracked the earth apart, clod by clod. He dug a hole that was knee-deep. He widened it and lengthened it so that he could stand on the bottom and still have room to swing the pick.

"Where are you?" he asked, looking up at the rock that stood tall out of the ground only a few yards away. "Where do you go?"

When the hole was shoulder-deep, his walker chuffed in warning. He stood up straight to see out of the hole.

The sky had started to fill with color, nightly cobalt seeping in to wash away the bone-white pallor of day. The sun hung on the horizon like some fiery fruit, immense and Promethean. Its orange light skittered across the landscape, leaping from hilltop to hilltop, and on one height a mile or so away, he saw two dark riders. Their clothing was dark and they had painted their skin black, so they seemed to soak up the light of setting sun. They wore their hair loose, which was not the custom among the People. At that distance, George could not make out their faces, but he saw that they both carried one of the long, feathered, crook-ended lances like Laughs like a Woman owned when he was a Contrary: Thunder Bows.

George stared at them for a while, trying to see who they might be, and they stared back, not moving from their place on the hilltop. He climbed up out of the pit, his walker chuffed again, and as the sun slid down behind the purpled horizon, the men turned and rode off, disappearing down the far side of the hill.

George watched as the light slowly left the world, but he did not see the men ride up over any of the more distant ridges. As the new moon, a waxing fingernail of light, chased the departed sun, he shivered.

They must have traveled back to camp along the lowlands, he told himself. Nothing mysterious in that.

He turned back to the hole he had dug. It lay before him, open, dark, gravelike.

I am committed now, he thought. Whoever they were, they'll report back. I'd better not show up empty-handed.

He spent the night curled up against his walker, lulled to sleep by her deep, wind-river breaths and the gurgling music of her stomach. At dawn, ignoring his sharpening hunger, he began again, and in short time his hands rang with the concussion of pick on stone. He got down on hands and knees and cleared the dirt away from the rock. It was not long before his fingers found the limits of the boulder. It was not the same seam of granite, then, but simply a pebble off its shoulder.

"Hellfire," George shouted as he wiped the gritty sweat from his brow with an even grittier forearm. "Damnation."

He looked at the jagged torso-sized piece of quartz-veined stone.

"I must be getting close, though."

Using his pick, he levered the stone up out of the ground and onto its face. It hit the soil with a hollow thump. The dry earth fell away and there, in the dim light of morning, George caught a glimpse of gold. He knelt, brushed at the stone, and saw, running the length of the yard-long rock, a finger-thick vein of yellow metal.

He stared at it until the fire in his lungs reminded him to breathe. This was what he had sought: evidence of an extended deposit beyond the small vein visible up at the main outcropping.

"We have it," he said, and looked up at the granite where Speaks While Leaving found her nugget. At least fifteen yards intervened between this stone and the top of the hill. George calculated quickly and guessed that the deposit might easily yield several pounds of gold.

"We have it. Enough to buy anything we need."

With renewed energy he rolled the stone back over. A few well-placed blows cracked it open like an egg along the weakness of the vein. With the heart of the stone exposed, he found it easy to chip the gold out of its fragile bed of quartz. By the time the sun had reached the top of the sky, he had filled a small pouch with chunks and flakes and small nodules. He walked over to the tall tree and sat down against the trunk. He was exhausted in both body and mind, and his hunger had begun to knot his insides. But looking at the pouch of gold, he felt a large wash of relief. He felt as if the final obstacles to the safety of his new friends had been swept away.

He laughed at his own simplicity. It was a long way from a pouch of gold to the security of a nation, but it was not unimaginable. He laughed again and felt freed by the release.

"We have it!" he shouted, and laughed some more.

He rode down the sun road into camp, feeling like a conquering hero. The sun hammered down from a white, cloudless sky. Most of the women were out gathering wood or digging roots, but George hoped to find Speaks While Leaving at home.

He turned south and guided his walker among the lodges of the Closed Windpipe band. The men, sitting in front of their homes, resting or working on their shields or arrows, looked up at him as he passed. They did not greet him; they just stopped what they were doing and watched him as he rode by. When he had passed, they returned to their activities without comment.

He found the lodge of One Bear and ordered his walker to a halt.

"Speaks While Leaving," he called as he walked up. "Is Speaks While Leaving at home?"

There was no answer, but soon the doorflap opened and One Bear himself came out. He stood before the open doorway and stared at George, his face expressionless.

"How was your winter?" George asked, afraid he knew what he was up against. "I have some very good news to tell you."

One Bear kept his silence and only stared impassively at him.

"I think this is very important. Last summer I talked with Three Trees Together about using gold to help the People. Now I have found it, lots of it, right where Speaks While Leaving said it was. Look." He held out the pouch of gold. "There is much more, too, if we can only get to it."

More silence. Tall, dark-eyed, oppressive silence.

"I know she wanted me to wait," George said, pleading now. "But I had to know, and look, it is all fine now. The gold is there and from here on we can do it her way. Won't you please tell me where she is?"

Silence. And the sound of movement from within the lodge.

Speaks While Leaving came outside and stood next to her father. George could see by the sheen on her cheeks that she had been crying, but as she looked up at him now, there was no sadness in her eyes. George saw only anger, backed by an unbending will.

She held out her hand. George handed her the pouch. She undid the tie and poured some of the metal into her hand. The sunlight splintered against the gold, throwing up glints and gleams that danced in their eyes. She looked at George again, her eyes as hard as her father's, as hard as the metal in her hand, and she emptied her hand and the pouch onto the ground.

"No!" George shouted and dove to recover the treasure strewn at her feet. He scrabbled in the dust and frantically began to refill the pouch. "Don't you understand what this means? It's the key to the future. It's power. It's control. It's . . ."

He stopped, realizing that he had been speaking in English. He looked up at Speaks While Leaving. The anger on her face had been replaced by naked disgust. She did not say a word, but only turned and stepped back into the lodge.

From within the lodge, George heard the old grandmother ask, "What is going on out there?"

"Nothing," was the answer Speaks While Leaving gave. "Nothing."

George knelt in the dust and felt the heat of shame color his cheeks. One Bear still towered over him, unmoving and inscrutable. George did not look up. He simply scooped dirt and gold alike into the pouch and tied it closed. When he stood, he could not bring himself to look at One Bear at all, and just turned back toward his walker. No word stopped him as he mounted and left the camp.

He rode back to the rocks and the holes and the solitary tamarack tree that stood over it all, as silent and as still as One Bear in his disdain. He sat on the stony height and watched the moon follow the sun— farther away today—while words like *stubborn* and *unreasonable* and *ungrateful* bounced around inside his head until he was numb and empty of thought.

The stars came out, eager and sharp. They dressed the world with a slow, blue light that dragged at George's vision. He could see the pale stone on which he sat, the mound that was his sleeping walker, the

bright shafts of his tools' hickory handles, and the
sheen that covered the ground: the dry prairie grass.
But down at the base of his granite perch the heavens
failed, unable to light the holes where he had dug.
The pits and trenches lay on the ground like starless
voids. He stared into their blackness and listened to
the night, to the nighthawk and the coyote, the owl
and the bat. The wind ran in from the west. The prairie rippled as it whispered through the grass. Nothing,
though, nothing touched the blackness he had made.
It was impervious; alien and isolate.

By the time the morning star rose to prepare the
east for the coming dawn, George felt he understood
something of what Speaks While Leaving had said—
his digging was wrong, incorrect, not proper. But
wrong though it might have been, what he could not
see was a way to get at the gold without doing it. He
hefted the pouch in his hand. Its heaviness depressed
him, for the things it represented—work, hope, future—now seemed either futile or lost.

He stepped down from the tall boulders and walked
over to his last pit. Refusing further thought, he
dropped the pouch into its depth and, taking shovel
in hand, began to refill the hole.

The day dawned and he worked. The sun rose and
he worked. The filling went much quicker than the
emptying had gone, and one by one his trenches
were unmade.

When he stopped, the sun was setting and he was
alone. He searched the landscape for his walker and
found her, nearly a mile away, hunting field mice to
pass the time. Beyond her, on the same hilltop as the
day before—or was it two, he wondered—stood the
two dark riders with their Thunder Bows. He rubbed
at the bleariness with which fatigue had veiled his
eyes. As they had the time before, this time, too, the
men stood in the day's final light, watching. George,
however, waved at them and shouted.

"See? See what I have done? See?" He knelt and
patted the fresh earth. "See? Go tell her."

The men on the hilltop did not acknowledge his words. They only watched and as the sun's rays died out, they turned and rode away, disappearing behind the hill.

"Tell her," George shouted after them as the night advanced.

He spent the night out on the rock. Hunger had long ago left him for more fertile ground, but sleep avoided him, too, and he could do little more than watch the stars overhead play hide-and-seek among the clouds. He looked for the shapes of familiar constellations and made up some of his own—"The Aster," "The Carriage." He was working on "Washington Crossing the Delaware" when the sun began to blanch the sky with its morning fires.

"You have worked hard," said a deep voice.

George sat up, blinking, and saw Stands Tall in Timber sitting nearby on the rocks. He was an old man— his hair gray, his skin dark and lined, his black eyes set deep on either side of a strong, hooked nose. George knew him to be one of the holy men of the People, but he knew nothing more than that. Now the old man sat on the rocks next to him, his knees tucked up against his chest, the ends of his long braids dangling down near his feet, as he looked over the area of George's prospecting.

"Yes," George said. "I have."

"It still looks pretty bad," the old Indian said.

George looked at the humps of dirt, the scattered clods, and the torn edges of the earth. "Yes," he said. "I suppose it does."

Stands Tall in Timber sighed but did not look away from the scars in the prairie ground. George did not say anything; he did not want to argue anymore. Finally it was Stands Tall in Timber who broke the silence.

"Three Trees Together says that this yellow chief-metal could be very helpful to the People."

George did not reply.

"He says we could use it against the bluecoats, by

trading it for powerful weapons. I don't know if I like that idea." The old man picked up a small shard of stone, inspected it, and put it back where he had found it. "I used to be an angry man," he said, "a soldier of the Crazy Dogs, and I walked the path of war for many years. It was many years ago now, during a time of great strife between us and the Crow People. I fought many battles, took many scalps, stole many whistlers, and counted many coups. I was a very great warrior, but I was not a very good man. I thought only of myself." George watched as the old man's gaze lifted to the east and the still-new sun that hung there under the morning clouds. He squinted into the light until his eyes were slits; deeper wrinkles in a deeply wrinkled face.

"But one day, I was finished. I just left all my anger on the plain. I came home, I married a wise woman, and I learned to help others. In time, I was chosen as the keeper of the *Maahótse*, the Sacred Arrows." He chuckled to himself. "Perhaps I was chosen because of my failings. It does make it easier to understand the failings of others."

He glanced over at George and then looked back toward the horizon.

"There is a saying among the People: You cannot tell a man what to do. I think you may have heard this, now that you talk like a real person, but I don't think that you understand what we mean." He glanced over again, but George just waited for him to continue. The holy man's voice was paced and mellifluous, and his words were easy to understand. George was willing to listen to him all day.

"No one can tell me what to do," he went on. "That means that only I can tell me what to do, and *that* means that I must judge for myself whether the results of my acts are worth the acts themselves." He pointed to the dirt-filled holes. "When you began, were you thinking of what would happen if you did this thing?"

George thought back. "No," he said after a moment. "I was only thinking that I was right and she was wrong."

The old man smiled. "That is young-man-thinking. You will get over that in time. But tell me. Were you right?"

"Yes," George said.

"And was she wrong?"

"Yes," he said, and then, "No," and then, "I do not know. We weren't asking the same questions."

"Aaahh," Stands Tall in Timber said. "Now, that sounds better."

"How can it?" George asked. "If Speaks While Leaving is right, then the digging is wrong. But we can't get the gold without digging. And if we can't get the gold, then why am I . . ."

Stands Tall in Timber waited for George to finish his sentence. When George did not, he said, "And if we cannot get the gold, then why are you with the People in the first place? Is that what you were going to say?"

George clenched his jaw and frowned. With a gesture, he said that it was.

"My young friend," the old man said, "you are here because you are here; there is no *why*. There is only *how*. It is how you live that makes a difference."

Stands Tall in Timber's words flowed into George like water over a parched land. They rolled over his surface, beading up, unable to penetrate until, suddenly, the tension in his mind disappeared and they soaked straight in, down to his soul.

"The gold is important," George said. "And we must dig to get it."

"That seems so," Stands Tall in Timber agreed.

"But my digging was wrong."

Stands Tall in Timber smiled, showing worn and crooked teeth. "So we must find a way to make it right."

"You make it sound so simple," George said. "What will Speaks While Leaving say?"

"I have already talked to the daughter of One Bear. Her vision was very strong. It tells us all we need to know, and some things I do not understand. But we will bring her vision into this world and make it true."

"And the other two? What do they say?"

"Who do you mean?"

"The two Contraries that you sent to check up on me."

Stands Tall in Timber shrugged. "I sent no one."

"Then Speaks While Leaving—"

The old man signed with an upturned palm. "No, she sent no one except me. What did these men look like?"

George described the men and Stands Tall in Timber became thoughtful.

"I do not think that those were men," he said. "Not men at all. I think the Thunder Beings have taken an interest in you."

Storm Arriving led the caravan of people up the slope as the sun dipped down toward the western mountains. The evening breeze freshened and brought the sound of drums and the scent of sage-blessed smoke. He thanked *nevé-stanevóo'o*, the sacred powers, for getting them all home, and heard murmurs of thanks from those behind him as well. His patrol was more than a week overdue but they brought back with them over a hundred people, all fleeing the new laws of the *vé'hó'e*: Wolf People, Greasy Wood People, even some Fox People who everyone had thought were all long dead. Whole families had crossed the great river, hoping to find a land to live in, even if it meant begging at the doorstep of old enemies.

The refuge-seekers rode whistlers and hardbacks borrowed from the stocks the People kept at the Ree villages near the White Water. The whistlers fluted at the scents of home and chafed at the heavily laden travoises they dragged behind them. The people riding hardbacks cried out in alarm as their mounts—nearly twenty in number—answered the drums ahead by lifting their club-tipped tails and thumping the ground.

Storm Arriving had pushed them, human and beast alike, allowing little rest, wanting only to bring everything safely within the circle of the People—his soldiers, the refugees, the body of Red Hat, and especially the information he had gained about the bluecoats.

Up ahead along the top of the last low swell of land, ten soldiers appeared, all on whistlers and with bows at the ready.

"Ho!" Storm Arriving cried out, raising his own bow. "We are Kit Foxes, coming home. And we bring some new friends."

The soldiers relaxed and rode down to meet them. Storm Arriving recognized Raccoon, his father-in-law's nephew.

"Cousin," Raccoon said in greeting. "Who are all these people with you?"

"They are new friends, I think. We need to speak with the Council."

"You will have to wait until morning," Raccoon said. "There is a dance tonight."

Storm Arriving waved a hand. "What I have to say is more urgent than a summer-sweetheart dance."

"It's not a social dance," Raccoon said. "Speaks While Leaving has had a new vision, and they are dancing it into the world."

Storm Arriving felt his throat tighten and his mouth go dry.

First the people from across the Big Greasy, he wondered silently. Then the bluecoats, and now a vision dance? The world is changing too fast.

"We will wait until morning," he said, "but we must see to these families."

Raccoon conferred with his squad. "We will take them from here," he said.

They rode up over the rise, but everyone halted on the far side. The families whispered to one another, amazed at the size of the Alliance laid out before them. For Storm Arriving and the rest of his patrol, however, the wonder was in the center of the camp.

In the clearing, the dancing ground was lined with drummers and singers. Around them, people from the camp had gathered, moving with the rhythm and joining their voices in song.

Tall lodgepoles had been set upright in a large circle, and buffalo skins had been hung between them to create a great lodge with no roof, just sides reaching up to heaven. The sky lodge was empty save for a large fire and a single dancer, a deer-dancer, representing the earth. Other dancers waited outside the sky lodge—dancers representing the soldier societies, and one dancer clothed in white, representing the great spirit. Storm Arriving could feel the power of the vision and the dance that was making it true.

The dance progressed, and Storm Arriving watched as Speaks While Leaving's vision was acted out. The meaning was clear: When you take from the earth, you must give something in return.

The drumbeats built in intensity. The deer-dancer gave the soldiers the gifts of the earth. The gifts changed into rifles and wheels and smoke. The singing rose in pitch. All the soldier-dancers circled around the white spirit, dancing their thanks to the world's four corners, the earth, and the sky.

Storm Arriving felt the power build, felt his chest constrict with it. He closed his eyes and felt the drumbeat in his veins, felt the trueness of the vision. The tempo began to sprint, the sun began to set, and Storm Arriving heard new, faraway voices draw nearer—perfect voices, spirit voices—singing the vision from their world into his. The voices, spirit and flesh, ran with the drums. The sun set with a last wink of light. The voices became one. Storm Arriving opened his eyes and saw a gust of wind rush through the camp. It ran through the clearing and past people and dancers. It ran up the slope to where Storm Arriving and the others stood. It hit him in the face—cool and springlike and full of the scents of life—and then it was gone.

The drums had stopped. The singers were silent. The dancers stood still. And then Storm Arriving felt it: an elation that came from some place within his breast and from some place outside the world, a surge of emotion that welled up and came out in a whoop of joy.

The vision had been made real.

The magic that had rooted him to the earth was gone. Storm Arriving and his colleagues bade each other a good night and headed off to their camps.

He arrived home and found no one there. He tethered his whistlers and went into the lodge that his wife's parents had given them. Speaks While Leaving would be the last to come back from the dance, he knew. Everyone would want to talk to her, to ask her how she felt the dance had gone. He put a few buffalo chips on the coals and lay down on top of their bed, listening for the sound of her return.

The bed, with its willow-twig backing and its layers of hides, pelts, and blankets, was pliant beneath his weight. The fur of the buffalo hide that covered it was soft and smelled of summer breezes and the scent of his wife's hair. Never before had a one-moon patrol seemed so long. Never had he been so glad to come home.

He waited for his wife, smelling her smells, seeing her belongings—her folded clothes and her quill work, her clay pots and her cooking tools—all in the places where she liked to keep them. He saw the bundles of medicinal herbs she collected hanging from the lodgepoles. He heard the ringing of the small copper bells she had tied to the over-the-smokes. He was surrounded by her, and yet apart from her; missing her, yet comforted by her presence.

He did not know that he had fallen asleep, and awoke to the sound of singing crickets. The fire had burnt back down to coals, and in their dim light, he saw Speaks While Leaving sleeping on her back next to him, naked in the summer heat. He watched the light from the coals pulse across her form: her tiny feet, the long lines of her legs, the fullness of her hips, and the pouting curve of her belly. Her smooth skin was lit by moving light. He could see the pulse of her heartbeat in the hollow beneath her ribs, and the swell of her breasts as they rose and fell with each breath she took. Her hair was loose and it lay about her head like a dark, rippled sea, while the sculpture of her face with its broad brow, high cheeks, and strong nose was a beauty he would not compare to anything.

He sighed.

"So you *are* awake," she said in a low voice. She opened her eyes—shadow lashes unveiling onyx beads. The dim light returned her to her youth, removing the tiny lines the years had placed beside her eyes and mouth. "I have been waiting for you to greet me." She smiled and he caught the gleam of white teeth in fading firelight, and then she moved, reaching out for him. In one fluid motion she was beside him, then atop him, her arms and legs enfolding him, her breasts soft and gentle as they brushed across his chest. He could not stifle his low moan of pleasure.

"I have missed you, husband," she said into his ear.

"And I have missed you," he said. "More than I knew I could."

She reached below and pulled aside his breechclout. "I know that we have been husband and wife for only three seasons, but I think it is time for us to make a child. I do not want to wait any longer."

Her words filled him with a fire that tautened his skin. She lowered her hips upon him and swallowed him up with her own warmth. He held on to her, hugging her close to him, wanting if he could to merge their two bodies into one, to pass his flesh into hers, to become the pure being that together they made. He responded to her movements in kind, and as the light from the hearthpit died, their passion burned the brighter.

George awoke to the call of the crier, walking through the camp.

"Today is a no-hunting day. The Little Bowstring soldiers have the watch. Three Trees Together calls the Council to session when the sun is two hands high."

George rubbed at his eyes and shook his head to clear it. "Two hands high?" he grumbled. "What could be so urgent?" He heard a footstep outside his lodge door.

"One Who Flies?" the crier said.

"Yes. I am here."

"Three Trees Together asks you to join the Council this morning."

"Thank you, Fire Bear. I will be there."

The crier walked away, continuing his rounds. "Today is a no-hunting day . . ."

George looked up through the smokehole. The sky was blue and the clouds were without a touch of pink. He had slept late but was glad of it. The previous evening's dance had filled him with a sense of assuredness and peace and he had gotten his first good night's sleep in weeks.

When he dressed and stepped outside, he saw Mouse Road over at her mother's lodge, walking in small circles and frowning at the ground.

"What is wrong?" he asked her.

She frowned even more and George could see she was near to tears.

"My brother," she said, and George had a sudden fear that something terrible had happened. "He came home last night, but didn't come to visit."

George laughed with relief. "Is that all?" But he saw that he had hurt her even more. He took her hand in his. "I am sorry, Mouse Road. I'm sure that he will come and see you as soon as he can. You heard Fire Bear say that there was a special Council meeting this morning. I have to go to that meeting, and I have a feeling I will see your brother there. I will make sure that he comes here afterward."

"Will you?" she said and George heard hope in her voice. It had been a long first winter without her brother. "Do you promise?"

"On my honor," he said, and gave her hand a little squeeze.

Picking Bones Woman chose that moment to come out of the lodge. She saw first her daughter and then George, holding her hand. Her eyes narrowed and her brow creased, and George realized what she was thinking.

"Good morning, Picking Bones Woman," he said, letting go of Mouse Road's hand. "Your daughter has just given me the task of bringing her brother home for a visit after the Council meeting."

"Hunh," the elder woman said, her expression unchanged. "A son should not have to be brought."

George kept a smile on his face. "Then that will make my task all the easier." He turned and checked the position of the sun. "I must go now." And he hurried down to the river to bathe and prepare for the day.

He arrived at the Council Lodge out of breath and with his wet hair hanging down to his shoulders. The lodgeskins of the tall Council Lodge had been raised to allow the breeze to enter, and George could see that the chiefs were already seated and listening to a speaker.

Beyond the lodgepoles sat others, men and women respectfully eavesdropping on the Council's discussions. George looked around for Storm Arriving and saw that he was the one speaking to the Council. George caught the attention of one of the young chiefs who guarded the door, but the chief signed for him to wait where he was.

A man sitting on the ground tugged on George's

leg. "Storm Arriving says that the bluecoats have crossed the Big Greasy again, and that they have built a village on our side of the river."

"Damnation!" George said, incensed. "They told us—"

"Hush," said another listener nearby.

George was quiet as they all listened to the rest of Storm Arriving's report and the discussions that followed. Suggestions ranged from increased patrols to outright attack, and the sixty chiefs of the Alliance seemed split on what path to choose. When nothing new was being said, Three Trees Together raised his hand and gestured to the young chief by the door. The young chief in turn pointed to George.

"One Who Flies," he said. "You are wanted."

George walked through the ring of spectators to the doorway. All the chiefs inside watched as he entered and walked around the perimeter of the lodge to the *vá'ôhtáma* where Three Trees Together sat. The old chief pointed to an open spot next to Storm Arriving. His friend looked tired but well, and though he was quite formal and reserved as the occasion mandated, George could see a smile of greeting in his eyes. They clasped hands briefly as George sat down beside him, and then all attention was for the eldest chief of the People.

"Tell me," the ancient Indian began. "How would the bluecoats react if we made a village across the Big Greasy?"

Storm Arriving began to translate the chief's words into French, but George stopped him. *"Néá'eše, néséne. Ékánoma'e. Natsêhésenestse."* Thank you, my friend. It doesn't matter. I speak Cheyenne.

Storm Arriving smiled as George turned and spoke to Three Trees Together. "If you were to settle a village across the Big Greasy, the bluecoats would run you off or kill you, as simple as that."

Three Trees Together glanced up from his idle

study of his medicine bag. "And should we do the same?"

"No," George said without hesitation, and heard the stir his words caused among the chiefs.

"Tell me why we should not," Three Trees Together said.

"You are not ready," George said. "You need better weapons."

"Guns," the chief said. "Rifles."

"Yes," George replied. "Your bows and arrows are excellent for hunting and good in battle against small parties or against others with similar weapons. Against the bluecoats, your weapons must be able to match theirs, or surpass them, if possible."

In the silence that followed his assertion, Dark Eagle rose from his seat near the door of the lodge.

"What can be better than the rifles of the bluecoats? A rifle is a rifle." He sat down and George, after a gesture from Three Trees Together, stood to reply.

"There are different kinds of rifles. Storm Arriving has one—a gift from One Bear. It is just like the ones the bluecoats have. It can make only one shot at a time." He pantomimed the process of firing and reloading the Springfield Trapdoor that was standard Army issue. "You load, you aim, you shoot, and then you must load again." He turned and pointed to one of the chiefs of the Hair Rope band. "But Red Blanket has a different rifle. His rifle you load once with seven bullets and you can fire seven times in a row before you must reload the rifle. That is better than what the bluecoats have, and it could mean all the difference in battle." He turned back to Three Trees Together.

"There are many kinds of rifle, and you must have rifles before you attack. More importantly, bullets are not like arrows. An arrow from one man's bow can be used by another man. But bullets from Storm Arriving's rifle will not work in Red Blanket's rifle. You must all have the same kind of rifle, so bullets and parts can all be shared." He stopped and tried to encapsulate his feelings. "I am not saying that you have to fight like the bluecoats fight, but I am saying that you need to use the same tools—or better tools—in order to keep your lands." He sat down, having said all he could think of to say.

Three Trees Together let go of his medicine bag and put his hands on his knees. "Does anyone feel differently after hearing the words of One Who Flies?"

Dark Eagle stood again. "I do. I have changed my mind. I think we should increase our patrols until One Who Flies can make enough of the yellow chief-metal to trade for these guns." The young chief sat down, and George could see that many others agreed with his words.

"Is it decided then?" Three Trees Together asked. "Shall we double the patrols while we wait for the new weapons?"

There was no dissent.

"Good. Then that is what we shall do. One Who Flies, six soldiers have volunteered to work with you. Stands Tall in Timber will instruct you on the proper way to get the chief-metal from the earth. Is there anything else you need?"

George thought about it and decided that there was. Whether this was the best time to ask for the thing he needed or not . . . that he left to fate. "In truth, there is one thing I need. I know only very little about digging metal from the earth. Because of this, I might dig in the wrong place, as I already have done. I would like to ask for someone to help me."

"One Who Flies, we do not know any more about digging metal from the earth than you do."

"Yes, Grandfather," George said, using the title of respect for elder chiefs. "But I have met a man who does. He has offered to help, in return for a share of what we find. He lives up at the trading-place. He is a *vé'ho'e* of the Trader Nation."

A rumble of discord rolled around the room and George stood before it built further.

"He will also be able to provide us with the extra

tools we need, and I think he can help us get the weapons we desire, after we have enough of the chief-metal." He sat then, and let the storm break.

Dark Eagle rose again. "I do not like this. There was nothing in the vision about a *vé'ho'e* from the Trader Nation."

High Chief, one of the elder leaders, rose as his junior colleague sat down. "I do not recall anything about any *vé'ho'e* at all in the vision. Are we to say then that One Who Flies should not participate in this digging for metal? After all, he too is of the *vé'hó'e*." As he sat he added an aside to George, "Though I mean no offense by it."

George smiled and respectfully avoided High Chief's gaze to show that he was not angered by the comment.

Three Trees Together sat forward—his way of asking for the floor without having to stand. "One Who Flies," he said. "Do you trust this trader-man?"

"No, Grandfather. Not for a heartbeat."

Several chiefs stood to speak but Three Trees Together stayed them with a skeletal hand. "And how will you manage him, then?"

"I will have six soldiers with me. Between us, we can manage one old *vé'ho'e*." Again he hesitated, not liking what he had to say. "And, if he tries to run away or steal what metal we have, he will be killed for it." Such statements made him uneasy, but ruthlessness was an axiom of war.

The chiefs who had risen to voice objections were satisfied by George's words, and retook their seats. Three Trees Together looked around the lodge for a long moment, giving ample time to anyone who still wanted to speak. None did.

"Then I suggest," the old man said, "that you prepare to pay this trader-man a visit."

George and the six soldiers assigned to the mining crew left that very day. They took a northerly route to the trading post, crossing the Big Greasy many miles upstream in a place where it ran fast but remained fairly shallow.

George felt very different this time as he rode down into the trading-place. He was no longer a nervous *vé'ho'e* on a common errand. Now he rode at the head of an armed war party on walker- and whistler-back. Now he was once again a soldier with a clear purpose.

As they rounded the final bend before the trading encampment, he told his walker to sound off. Her bellow echoed off the valley walls. The traders ran out of their shacks and then shrank back toward their homes in trepidation.

"Nóxa'e," he commanded, and the mounts all came to a halt. George surveyed the scene: dirty, unshaven *vé'hó'e* standing before him, nervous and unsure amid a sorry collection of dilapidated homes. These were men living on the fringe of their own world, outcasts eking out a marginal life on the boundaries between two opposing cultures.

These were the men I feared to meet, he marveled silently. These were the men I feared I would not impress.

He looked at them. They stood staring up at George and the others, dumbfounded by the sudden appearance of a handful of capable men. Only one of them was not wavering between cravenness and cowardice.

Vincent D'Avignon leaned against the jamb of his doorway. His hands were in his trouser pockets and his right foot was casually crossed across his left. He looked at George with a constant eye and a lopsided smile, and when George with a touch made his huge walker crouch to the ground, the old trader laughed out loud with a harsh, crowlike cawing.

"I was hoping I'd see you again," he said, but even his assuredness failed when George and his six companions dismounted and walked slowly in his direction.

The Indians had dressed for war. They had painted their faces with handprints, stripes, tears of blood, and arcane symbols. Some wore headpieces made of spiky badger fur, fox tails, and grouse plumes, while others simply wore a few eagle feathers in their braids. All of them carried one of the short but powerful horn-and-sinew bows that were the mainstay of the Cheyenne arsenal. None of them looked like they were there to trade.

"Monsieur D'Avignon," George said as they stopped in front of him. "I should like to speak with you."

D'Avignon grinned. "I *knew* it," he said in a whisper. "I knew you had found something. *Mais oui,* come inside and we will talk."

There was not enough space in the small, two-room cabin for the piles of D'Avignon's trade goods and eight men as well. Gets Up Early—the Little Bowstring soldier who had slipped into the role of George's lieutenant during their journey—asked two of the others to stand guard and prevent the other traders from overhearing their conversation.

D'Avignon dragged a spavined, plank-backed chair in from the tiny back room. "Good to see you again, Young Custer. Have a seat and tell me all your news."

George put a friendly hand on the trader's shoulder. "I think perhaps it is you who should sit down."

D'Avignon's grin lost some of its toothy enthusiasm. His gaze skipped from George to each of the soldiers in turn. George turned the rickety old chair around and offered it to their host. D'Avignon wiped the back of his hand across his mouth.

"If you insist," he said, and sat down.

George decided to employ one of the methods he had seen his father use many times. George and his sisters had called this tactic "Pitching Woo" but in reality it was simply his father's technique for presenting a skittish potential collaborator with a nice, appetizing carrot before revealing what was usually a very big stick.

He took a few steps away from the trader—all that the small room would allow—and with his arms folded across his chest, he turned and smiled agreeably.

"I believe we have something you'd like to have a part of."

The trader leaned forward in his chair. "You made a strike?"

George rocked up on the balls of his feet and bounced. "We have, and we are prepared to offer you a share. Enough to make you a very rich man."

"Sacré mére!" He clapped his hands and leapt to his feet. "Good boy! Good boy. I *knew* you'd had a taste of the real thing when I saw you last. Good boy. And I've kept your secret, too. *Mais oui!* I have not told a single soul, and especially not those turds I call neighbors." His eyes widened. "A drink! That's what we need. A drink and a toast to celebrate."

He dashed into the back room and George spied him pawing through a pile of canvas. He heard the clanking of empty bottles, a muttered *"Merde,"* an exultant *"A-ha!"* and the old trader reappeared, a brown stoneware jug in his hand.

"Not the finest, and certainly not what a president's son is used to, but it will have to do." He tipped the bottle back and took a gigantic swallow.

"D'Avignon," George said.

The trader wiped his mouth and offered the jug to George. *"À santé,"* he said. "Have a drink. To seal the deal."

Time for the stick, George thought to himself.

He grabbed on to the jug and D'Avignon's hands both. "There are terms," he said.

D'Avignon froze. "Terms?"

George took the jug. "Sit down."

The trader sat down. "What terms?"

George stood over the older man and looked down upon him. "You will provide us with tools, supplies, and your expertise at mining and prospecting. You will swear to maintain the secrecy of our activities, the secrecy of our location, and the secrecy of our purpose. You will agree to stay and work with us for a period of not less than three months but no longer than a year. If you fail us in any of these regards, the consequences that will be visited upon you will be most dire." He paused to hook his thumb meaningfully toward the soldiers at his back.

"You must abide by all Cheyenne laws during your stay, one of the first of which is"—he raised the jug—"no liquor. Of any kind. They do not allow it. For me, my father was a teetotaler and I never learned to drink, so it is no hardship. For you, it might be a consideration. So here. Have another drink. It will be your last for quite a while."

D'Avignon stared up at George, stupefied, as if he didn't understand, but George knew that it was precisely D'Avignon's clear understanding that was the cause of his bewilderment.

"There are other laws, of course," George went on, "most of which are the same as those held by our own people. Punishments for breaking such laws range from banishment to beating to a peculiarly effective form of shunning. The Cheyenne do not execute their own, but I warn you that they will have no qualms against killing an outsider such as yourself."

"*Mon Dieu, mon ami!* I might as well be put in prison." He took another long swig from the jug and some of the pale brown liquor slopped down onto his chin.

"Prisoners are not paid in gold," George said.

"Ah, *oui*," D'Avignon said. He put the jug on the floor and stood. "So we have you and me and what . . . six young bucks?" He looked Sharp Nose up and down. "Though a couple of them seem a bit long in the tooth for this work."

"You are hardly one to speak on that subject," George said.

"But you're not after me for my strong back, are you?" He tapped a long finger against his temple. "It's what I have up here. Now I don't care what fraction you've agreed to give these braves. For all that you are asking from me, however, I demand a share equal to yours."

George laughed and held out his hand. "*D'accord.*"

D'Avignon grinned but did not shake to seal the deal. "You agreed to that too easily. What's the trick?"

"Nothing," George said. "Except that my share of this will be nothing. I was prepared to give you more, but—"

"What do you mean? What is this? I think that maybe I was wrong about you. I think that maybe you *are* crazy. Nothing? What do you mean, your share is nothing?"

George held up his hands to calm the old trader. D'Avignon held his tongue and his temper, but there was fear in his eyes, fear of madness and the unknown.

"My share in this is nothing. So will my friends here take nothing. We are here as representatives of the Cheyenne Alliance, the people who control the land in which you live." George paced off the few steps the room afforded him. This was the most critical part of the negotiation, he knew. Failure would necessitate a grim twist in the proceedings. "I have been empowered to offer you a position as head prospector and mining overseer for the Cheyenne Alliance, working with me and these men, so that we might be able to . . . utilize . . . some of the mineral riches of their land. In return for your help and know-how, you will be provided with a one *per centum* share—"

"A *hundredth?* You *are* mad. I would never consider such a thing for less than a tenth."

George sighed melodramatically. "Then I can only assume that you have no confidence in your own abilities to adequately exploit this deposit."

"No, no, no," D'Avignon said, his pride touched. "It is my confidence in *you* that is lacking. You're no prospector. How do I know how large the find is? A hundredth of a hundred-ounce find is little more than nothing, but of a ten-ounce deposit? Less than nothing. I have a better situation here, where at least I can have a drink on a Sunday afternoon."

D'Avignon's words were harsh, but to George's ear

they were sweet because they were not a refusal. The door had not been shut.

"A minimum, then," he said, opening the offer a bit. "A guarantee of three ounces of gold."

"And I must then wait until we see three *hundred* ounces before I see any more? No, I'll take ten ounces up front and ten percent of anything we find."

George raised an eyebrow in calm delay but within his breast his heart was pounding. "Five and five," he said. "Five ounces up front, and five percent of anything we take in. I'll go no further than that."

D'Avignon scowled. "I should not even be considering such an arrangement. This will have to be a magnificent strike if I'm to make it worth my while, and all on the word of a boy who's playing at being an Indian brave." He scratched the back of his head with dirty fingernails. "What makes you think this is such a lode? How much have you found so far? How does it lie? I can't be expected to leave my stock behind and go traipsing out into nowhere for a few flakes in a tin pan, you know."

George smiled. He grinned. He tucked two fingers into his belt pouch. "It's not a few flakes," he told the skeptical trader. "And it lies . . ." He pulled out the nugget that started it all and watched D'Avignon goggle and gape like a springtime bullfrog. "It lies on the ground, waiting to be picked up."

The trader took a stilted step forward, staring at the nugget. *"Mère sacré de Dieu,"* he whispered. He reached out for the nugget and George let it drop into his hand. D'Avignon felt its weight and brought it to his mouth. He tasted it with his tongue.

"Incredible," he said. "I've never seen its like."

George held out his hand and D'Avignon slowly, reverently gave back the huge nugget of gold.

"What . . . did you say?" the trader asked. "Five and five?"

"Five ounces now. A five hundredths' share of everything we mine. Agreed?"

"Agreed," D'Avignon said absently, still staring at the nugget in George's hand.

"And you abide by all Cheyenne law, and all instructions as to how we mine?"

D'Avignon nodded.

"And you swear to keep the secrecy of our operation, on pain of death?"

Again, a nod.

"And you supply us with tools and supplies?"

"Of course," D'Avignon said. "We will need a good weighing scale."

CHAPTER 6

Autumn, A.D. 1887
New York City
New York

"**M**r. President. Mr. President!"

Custer waved as he stepped down from his railcar and onto the platform. The newspapermen from the New York press leaned in against the linked arms of the Grand Central Depot constabulary. They shouted at him, yelling out their questions as if believing that by sheer volume they could somehow force an answer.

"Good Lord in Heaven," he said as he turned to help Libbie descend. "How I *do* hate New York."

With one lace-gloved hand his wife lifted the fabric that trailed from her bustle, and with the other she held lightly on to his hand. She stepped down with poise and grace and a friendly smile—her "out in public" smile—and as the journalists called out to her, using her Christian name, she said, "I quite agree. At least at home they *pretend* to respect us."

Custer smiled at her jest and saw her affected smile take on a hint of real humor.

"Shall we?" he said with a small inclination toward the turbulent reporters.

" 'Once more unto the breach, dear friends, once more,' " she quoted as she took his arm. They turned and the reporters redoubled their endeavors, shouting even louder.

" 'Or close the wall up with our English dead,'"
Custer completed and waved again to the press. "Gentlemen, gentlemen. Some decorum if you please."

"Mr. President!"

Custer checked the crowd of men and pointed to
one who he thought would make no trouble; a sallow
youth with a badly fitted Bowry on his head.

"Mr. President," the young man said. "Will you be
supping with Mr. Villard tonight?"

Damnation, Custer thought. Serves me right for
judging the book by its cover.

"How's that?" he said, feigning difficulty hearing
the question over the steam release of a nearby locomotive. "Our plans for the evening? Well, I'm sure
most of you have heard it all from my aide, Mr. Prendergast. Check with your society reporter, Son, and
you'll find that Mrs. Custer has once again inveigled
me into a night at the theater. We'll be dining this
afternoon at our hotel, and then we will be taking in
the performance of *Ruddigore* at the new Fifth Avenue Theater." He pointed to one of the older reporters, hoping he would be less hungry for real news.

"What's the latest from the Frontier?"

Good, Custer thought. A proper question.

"I received word just yesterday from General Herron. He is pushing out into the Unorganized Territory
and building his fortifications. He said that they had
already repulsed one attack, destroyed the enemy
force, and had suffered no harm."

"Mr. President," the reporter said. "Do you mean,
sir, that the Army has fought a battle with wild Indians and come out of it without a scratch?"

"I do, indeed, mean just that. Not a single U.S.
soldier was harmed in the encounter. I am quite
pleased with the progress General Herron has made
both in dealing effectively with the hostile Indians and
in managing the construction of the new bridge across
the Missouri River. Very pleased."

Libbie tugged lightly on his arm, but another reporter spoke up before he could turn away.

"Sir, will you be calling General Herron back to Washington to discuss future plans?"

Custer shook his head. "I see no point in disrupting General Herron's command. He has things well in hand, and we communicate frequently via the new telegraph lines that now cross the young state of Yankton. Should I pull the man away from his job, just so you boys can get a chance to needle him with your questions?" He laughed good-naturedly and the reporters allowed the barb to pass. "Now, gentlemen, if you will excuse us, we have engagements."

He turned and began to lead Libbie away.

"Excuse me, Mr. President."

Custer bristled and turned with a glower. It was the man with the poorly fitted hat. The other reporters stepped back from the young man, hoping to distance themselves from presidential disfavor.

"I just wanted to clarify," the young man went on. "You said you were dining at your hotel, but not where you will be supping. Will you visit with Mr. Villard after the play?"

"Why, yes, we shall. Mr. Villard is having a small group of friends over for refreshments."

"Is that Mr. Henry Villard?" asked another reporter. "The railroad magnate?"

"Yes," Custer replied, unable to keep the note of ice from his voice.

The reporters picked up the scent. "Henry Villard is known in New York as something of a kingmaker, Mr. President. Does this mean you have decided to run for reelection in eighty-eight?"

Custer felt Libbie's hands squeeze his arm.

"It means nothing," Custer said. "We are just visiting New York for the theater and a gathering of friends."

"Are you going to run in eighty-eight?"

"Mr. President, are you going to run?"

"It is far too early for that."

"Autie," Libbie said. "Take me out of here."

"Mr. President."

"Mr. President!"

It was not until they were safely ensconced and alone in their rooms that Libbie spun and accosted him.

"Just *when* were you going to tell me?"

"Libbie—"

"When? When were you going to tell me?" She stood, straight and imperious, the blush of her anger blotching the fairness of her cheeks. She was furious, more so than he had seen her in many months.

"Libbie, it's just a small gathering after the show."

"What are you talking about?"

"At Villard's. After the performance. Libbie, I really haven't decided if I even want another term or not. This meeting with Villard, it's just to keep the doors open."

"I don't *care* about that." Her hands shook and her features were twisted. She sat down heavily on the silk-covered couch and began to weep.

Custer saw that he'd misread her. "What is it? Libbie, dear. What's wrong?"

Through her tears, she spoke in a singsong of frustration. "I don't *care* about another term. I *know* you will run again. It's the other thing." Her hands rose briefly only to fall back into her lap as if too tired to gesticulate.

"What other thing?" he asked. "Libbie, I honestly don't know what you are talking about."

"The Frontier," she said. "Autie, when were you going to tell me? You are killing Indians again . . . out on the Frontier."

"My dear," he said, trying to calm her. "We have been working to settle the Unorganized Territory for years. This is nothing new. Now we're building forts out there. Haven't you been reading the papers?"

"I haven't read the papers for over a year! I can't bear it anymore. And you . . . you just go on as if nothing had ever happened. And now you're killing Indians again."

"We are killing Indians because they are attacking our soldiers."

"But, *Autie* . . ." Her pain was palpable. "George is still *out* there."

Custer heard his wife's words and knew he was unable to help her. "Libbie . . ." he said. "Aw, Hell, Libbie." He did the only thing he could do. He sat down next to her on the watered silk divan and held her closely. She turned toward him and wept into his chest.

"I just want to see him," she said.

"I know, I know."

"Just once more. Just once. Just so I can know he's alive."

"I know," he said. What he thought, however, was that it would have been better if their son had died, for all the pain he caused them. Just like Herron said: better off dead. But he would never say that aloud, not to Libbie anyway. "I know, my darling," he said. "I know."

Autumn tamed the summer sun and breathed cool mist across the morning land. Storm Arriving sat down on the dew-damp grass outside his lodge and unrolled the length of leather that held his fletching tools. He began to pull his arrows from their quiver but stopped and spent a moment listening to the world.

The robins and larks and wrens of early morning were quiet, having sung their songs to the rising sun and headed off on their daily business. Now came the time for daytime birds—chickadees and sparrows, waxwings and thrushes—all chattering among themselves for as long as the sun was shining, allowing no interruption save for the teasing jeers of blue jays or the raucous command of a malcontented crow.

The air smelled of autumn: the thick scent of night-born moisture on dry summer grass, the musky smoke of burning buffalo chips, the earthy smell of freshly scraped hides staked out to dry. He breathed deeply of it, relishing it, but when he exhaled, it came out in a sigh.

Speaks While Leaving came outside. She handed him the tiny clay jar with the fish-bone glue she had prepared the night before. "What bothers you?" she asked.

"Nothing, really," he said as he unsealed the jar and stirred the translucent jelly with a cherry-wood stick. "The summer has passed so quickly. With the extra patrols, there has been little time to hunt."

"But we have plenty," she said, sitting down beside him. "Enough for us, and enough to give your mother a winter's supply as well."

"And a good thing, too," he said. "One Who Flies has been digging all summer. If he didn't have to feed his walker, he would not have gone on a single hunt this season."

"You should be glad he has a walker. Otherwise he would not even have enough for himself."

Storm Arriving laughed quietly. "That is true. But that is not what bothers me."

"What then?" she asked, puzzled.

He pointed to the blank spots in the circle of the People. "The bands are already departing for winter camps. I have not had time to spend with you, with my friends, and I have not had nearly enough time with my mother and sister." He chuckled again. "I even miss One Who Flies."

Speaks While Leaving caressed his arm and took his hand in hers. "You miss him especially, you mean to say."

He did not laugh at this. He tightened his lips to hold in the truth, but she was right. The former blue-coat had spent the whole hunting season back at the Sheep Mountains, digging for his precious metal. "He has been too long absent from the People."

She leaned over and kissed his cheek. "We will visit this winter."

He smiled, embarrassed, and was about to reach out

and embrace her when they heard a shout. They both stood and looked eastward.

Out on the perimeter, they could see the picket guard waving his arms. Up and over the hill rode two men on whistler-back. They streaked down the grassy slope and sped into camp, riding down the sun road like demon spirits.

"It's Big Nose," Storm Arriving said, recognizing his Kit Fox brother. "And Kills at Night. Where is the rest of their patrol?"

"Something is wrong," his wife said. "You had better go see."

"Tell your father and then you come, too. They may be hurt."

"Yes, I will. Now go."

He ran toward the center of camp, to the Council Lodge that still stood tall in the clearing. Others were running in, too—soldiers, Kit Foxes and others, all of them concerned and wanting to see what was wrong.

Storm Arriving ran up and seized the halter rope on his friend's whistler. Big Nose had a wound on his arm and the hair on his head was matted with dried blood and stalks of pale, dry grass. His quiver was empty. Storm Arriving caught his friend as he dismounted, but Big Nose pushed his help away.

"I am fine," he barked. "See to Kills at Night."

But others were already helping the younger soldier to the ground.

"Speaks While Leaving is on her way," Storm Arriving told them and then turned back to Big Nose. "What happened?"

"Wait," the thickset man said, pointing. "I only want to tell this once."

Storm Arriving looked and saw that Two Roads and Red Eagle, chiefs of the Kit Fox society, were coming toward them along with other chiefs.

"Should we go inside the Council Lodge?" Storm Arriving asked.

"No," Big Nose said. "It is not proper." Meaning

that this would be a meeting of war, and would not involve the Great Council.

Speaks While Leaving arrived with her father and the other chiefs. Two Roads, as chief of the returning soldiers, took charge.

"Take Kills at Night to the Kit Fox lodge. Speaks While Leaving, please see that he is well cared for." Speaks While Leaving signed her assent and went along as several soldiers bore the wounded man away. "Now," he said to Big Nose. "What has happened?"

Big Nose took a deep breath to steady his nerves and then began to speak.

"I led my patrol to the new *vé'hó'e* village, on our side of the Big Greasy. We arrived in the early morning and saw that they were building something, but what I cannot tell for sure. There was dirt and wood and stone piled up everywhere and it was hard to make any sense of it. It was all very strange—we all thought so—but they had not built anything beyond that place, and so we left them alone as we had been instructed."

He knelt and made marks in the dirt. "The *vé'hó'e* village lies here, at a place where the Big Greasy turns on itself twice like a snake."

Two Roads and Red Eagle muttered their understanding.

"And here, upstream, is where the Sudden River meets the Big Greasy. We left the *vé'hó'e* place and were riding this way, toward Foolish Woman Creek off the Sudden River." He paused to ensure that everyone understood.

"Almost right away we noticed tracks in the tall grass. We saw the tracks of many *vé'hó'e* riders and many of their roll-alongs. The roll-alongs left deep ruts in the earth, so they must have been loaded down. We followed the tracks. It was not hard.

"The tracks led in a straight line to a place with long walls made of tree trunks, and tall wooden lodges perched on top of the walls like giant nests. There were many bluecoats there. When we attacked, they all ran inside the walls and closed the doors. They climbed up into the nests and stood on top of the walls and fired at us with their guns. We lost four men right away. When we rode in for another attack, we lost two more. The bluecoats have great power in that place. Even my dream shield did not protect me completely, and I was grazed in the arm and head by spent bullets."

Storm Arriving heard the emotion building in his friend's voice, and heard his shaking breath.

"We had to leave their bodies," Big Nose said, anguished. "Kills at Night wanted to go again, though he was hurt more than I, but I said we had to come back to report what we had seen." He spoke through bared teeth, his rage and grief seething in and out with every breath. "I had to drag him away from there. Better had I left him, and destroyed only my own honor."

"No," Storm Arriving said, and Two Roads put a hand on Big Nose's shoulder.

"There is no dishonor in this," the chief said. He turned to those gathered. "There is no dishonor here. A duty was done. Had Big Nose not returned to warn us, we would have sent out more to seek him, and they too might have died, unprepared for what they found."

Big Nose grabbed on to Two Roads's arm. "But I must go back," he said, the tears on his cheeks bright in the morning light. "I must. I owe it to the others to bring their bones back to their families."

"And you will go," Two Roads said. "How many bluecoats did you see?"

Big Nose thought a moment. "Perhaps four times ten. No more than five times ten."

"And the creatures they ride?"

"Yes, many, but they were all inside the walls. It was not like the bluecoat camps we saw during the war against Long Hair. I could see through the door-

way when we first attacked. They still live in square
lodges made of cloth, but all of them were inside the
walls. Everything was inside the walls. We could not
run off their mounts, we could not pull down their
lodges. We could do nothing."

Two Roads paused to confer with Red Eagle. They
came to an agreement.

"You," he said to Big Nose, "and you," he pointed
to Storm Arriving. "You two will lead a war party.
Take eight times ten men. That is a good number.
There are still many Kit Fox soldiers in camp—"

"What about us?" asked Badger, one of the Little
Bowstring soldiers. "We want to go, and so do
others."

"This is a Kit Fox matter," Two Roads said sternly.
"It was a Kit Fox patrol, and it is Kit Fox soldiers
who lie dead before the bluecoat camp. It will be a
Kit Fox war party that answers."

"We should still tell the Council," said another man.

"This is a matter of war," Two Roads said, "not
one of policy, but tell the Council if you wish. We will
go regardless. Big Nose, Storm Arriving, prepare to
select your men. You others, run through the camp
and make sure every Kit Fox brother knows: A war
party leaves before the sun reaches the top of the
sky."

Men scattered, running to all the remaining bands
to spread the news and call for volunteers. Storm Arriving turned to his friend.

"Go home," he said. "Kiss your wife and your baby
boy. Eat a good meal and wash yourself in fresh water.
Then meet me at the end of the sun road when the
shadows grow short."

The two men embraced and Big Nose led his whistler off toward his home.

Storm Arriving did not tarry. He had much to do
and little time.

When the lodge's shadow had run under its sloping
sides and a man cast no more darkness than a circle

near his feet, Storm Arriving waited with Speaks While Leaving at the end of the sun road.

"I am sorry I have to go," he said.

"I am proud that you go," his wife told him. "But you must promise that you will come home to me."

"I promise that."

Others began to arrive, some of them stern-faced, some of them smiling at the chance to prove themselves in war.

"Will you kill many of them?" Speaks While Leaving asked.

"I will try," he said.

She sighed. "Why will they not leave us alone?"

"One Who Flies tried to explain it to me . . . it seems very long ago now. He said that they think that this is their land."

"But they don't live here," she said.

"No, they do not. But to the *vé'hó'e*, that does not seem to matter."

Big Nose rode up, looking grim and unhappy. With him was his youngest brother, Wolf Robe, a youth of fourteen summers.

"He will be going with us," Big Nose said.

Storm Arriving began to object but his friend stopped him.

"He says we cannot tell him what to do. If we do not take him, he says he will follow us."

Storm Arriving looked at the young man. He was thin and still reaching for his full height. He wore a brave face—with furrowed brow and stiff-set jaw—but Storm Arriving saw that his fingers shook as they held his whistler's halter rope. He *would* follow if they tried to leave him behind. It would be better to keep him close, where he could be watched. And where they could limit the trouble he caused.

"As you wish," he said.

Over a hundred men had gathered, all prepared for a long, hard ride and a fierce battle. Storm Arriving and Big Nose weeded out the young boys who came hoping to join their first war party. With the exception of Wolf Robe, they selected only seasoned veterans. Then, with good-byes for their loved ones and their spirits high, they mounted their whistlers.

"Fight well," Speaks While Leaving said, reaching up to hold his hand a last time. "Remember to thank the spirits."

He smiled down at her. "I thank them every day."

"*Kit Foxes,*" Big Nose shouted, preparing them, "are you ready?"

In unison Storm Arriving and the others shouted the rally cry of their society. "A Kit Fox is *always* ready!"

And with yips and barks and howls, they all set their mounts in motion, riding east, off the end of the sun road, toward the camp of the bluecoats.

General Herron climbed up the ladder, felt the rough grain of the wood under his hands, and stepped up onto the gangway that ran the length of the timbered wall. The air was still redolent with the smell of freshly sawn wood. He stomped a booted foot on the walkway planks, was satisfied by their soundness, and turned to his aide Quincy and Colonel McCormack, the man he'd put in charge of building the fort.

"I want to see it from up there," he said, pointing to the lookout tower.

"Yes, sir," McCormack said, and led the way.

Herron noticed with approval that the walkway behind the parapet was a good eight feet wide: room enough to lay down a stricken comrade or to set a heavy gun. The battlements rose four feet above the walkway and were crenellated every ten feet. A man could stand and fire over the top or crouch and shoot through the embrasures. Herron had borrowed the whole design from castles he'd visited in Wales and Scotland. While they wouldn't stand against a modern force, he expected they would be able to turn the trick with the Indians.

He walked to the secondary ladder that gave access from the battlement to one of the four towers that topped each corner. The tower platforms had proven themselves during the recent attack, allowing gunners to fire along the ramparts and enfilade Indian forces attempting to scale the walls. They also gave an extended vantage of the fort and the surrounding terrain.

Herron climbed up, returned the salute of the corporal posted as lookout, and gazed outward across the land.

Trampled turf surrounded the fort, and horses grazed on pale grass beneath the protection of watchful guards. Farther away was the dark mound of earth where his men had buried the Indians killed in their doomed attack, but beyond that, the land was a flat sea of dun-colored knee-high grass. Its only features were the wandering indentation of a creekbed and the movement of the grass itself as it bowed beneath the wind that sped across the plain.

This is a different land, Herron thought. We can't fight here like we did at Gettysburg or Sharpsburg. Can't hide or move behind a screen of trees or beyond a ridgeline.

He looked all around the fort and in every direction saw the hard line of the horizon delineating land and sky.

No. You can see a man for miles in this country.

He could see the almost imperceptible bow of the earth, the curve of the planetary sphere, and with the waves in the windblown grass, he felt as if he were sailing on some alien ocean. The only flaw in the illusion was, as he looked eastward, the track of trampled grass and upturned earth that the engineering regiment had made when they had carted the tons of wood and supplies out to the site.

It had taken a week just to transport the timbers for the walls, and wagons still came, every few days, deepening the ruts that wandered their way back to the Missouri River.

But the ruts did not bother Herron. He knew that

soon the ruts would be gone, replaced by shiny rails. He knew it, could see it all, as if it had already come to pass. These forts—*his* forts—were just the first step.

He inspected the yard from the tower's vantage. The east-facing gate had been opened to allow the horses out to graze. The walls on either side of the gate stretched out to enclose the interior, nearly three hundred feet on a side. In the northern half of the yard were buildings that would serve as the commander's and officer's quarters. Across the yard on the southern side were the commissary, smithy, and carpentry shops. In between, two rows of white canvas tent shells lined the western wall. The rest of the yard—most of it, to be truthful—was unused.

"Looks pretty empty," Herron said.

"For now, sir, it is." McCormack was a thickset stump of a man with florid cheeks and watery blue eyes above muttonchop whiskers. He was well known for his tendency toward loquaciousness, but today— perhaps at Quincy's suggestion—his responses were blissfully curt. "It will be a different story, though, with a full fighting regiment in residence."

"Hmm," Herron said, nodding. "True enough." Four hundred men, he thought. Not to mention their horses and supplies. They'll be crammed together like pickles in a jar. It'll be—what was the word Greene used?—ah, yes: medieval. Still, it's all very well done.

"My compliments, McCormack. Your experience at Fort Whitley shows."

"Thank you, sir," the colonel said.

"Sirs?" the corporal said, pointing.

Herron looked back out toward the horizon. His eye caught a blur of motion far out to the west, like the shadow of a cloud as it passed in front of the sun. He looked up. The sky was clear.

"My glasses," he said and Quincy, always near, quickly produced the binoculars. McCormack called for his as well, and the two men peered out across the pale plain.

Herron turned the wheel and brought the jittery

view into focus. Stems of grass swayed, individuals in the ocean that covered the land. He swept the vista, searching for the anomaly that had caught his attention. Slowly, back and forth until *there!* it blurred past his sight. He followed it, caught it, and tried to understand what he saw.

Shapes, brown and tan in color, tumbled across the plain, altering size and hue as they went. He knew immediately what they were, even before he heard the first fluting call.

"Whistlers," he said.

Dreamlike animals in shifting colors, they ran across the plain. He could see the outlines of their curving crests, he could see the pumping legs. Their skins were colored in pale hues of dun and buck and tan, splotchy shapes that moved across their bodies, winking from one color to the next. There were dozens of them, perhaps a hundred, but it was impossible to be sure.

He watched them, fascinated, but also compelled. There was something not right about them. He'd seen thousands of whistler flocks during his years on the Frontier. What was different about this one? The flock was less than a mile away, following a curving path that would take them around the fort on the northern side.

"McCormack," he said. "Do you notice anything odd about those whistlers?"

"No, sir," the colonel said. "Not really, unless . . . I don't know that I've ever seen them use more than one color at once, if that's what you mean."

The flock was closer now, a thousand yards or so away, swinging around the northern side of the fort as they continued on to the east. Only they weren't continuing. The flock swung closer.

Herron saw it at a glance. The open gate. The grazing horses. The flock's shifting colors that didn't hide them so much as they hid something else. He looked through the glasses again, refocused, saw the whistlers, closer now, all brown and tan, saw a rope, a halter rope around the neck of one, and then, as the flock curved closer and turned toward the fort, saw Indians hanging low on their mounts' far side like trick riders in a Kansa horse show.

"Colonel," he said calmly. "I believe we are under attack."

McCormack jumped as if pinched, saw the danger for the first time, and turned to bawl at the top of his voice, *"To arms! To arms! Everyone inside!"*

A hundred men leapt into action, running for rifles, climbing ladders, corralling horses back toward the gate and the safety of the yard.

"Sweet Jesus," McCormack said. "The horses."

Herron felt the old coolness descend upon him, the clarity of mind and serenity of soul that he always experienced during battle. It was his own personal irony that he should never feel more at peace than when gripped by the teeth of war, but he accepted it when it came, and he relished it.

He took in the factors: the speed of the attackers, the skittishness of the horses, the Indians' ready bows.

"The horses are gone," he said. "Concentrate on the men."

"Yes, General." McCormack bellowed more orders. The men obeyed and ran inside the gate, having driven in less than a quarter of their herd. The gate closed as the whistlers swept in and sent the rest of the horses fleeing across the grasslands.

Got to give them credit, Herron thought. That was well done. We're as good as trapped here now, but will they be able to capitalize on it?

The attackers split up and began to circle the fort in both directions. They spread out, giving none of McCormack's men an easy target.

"Everyone to the walls," the colonel ordered, and in minutes every walkway was manned. The soldiers spread out to cover every approach.

"Fire at will!"

The command was passed and the popcorn sounds

of riflery broke out along the walls. The white smoke of black powder began to fill the air. Herron sniffed, taking in the warm scent of battle.

The Indians began to return fire. Herron watched from the tower as one of the savages coursed past, his whistler's color pale against the pale grass, as was the Indian's own clothing. The warrior rode the whistler, holding no reins, controlling it only with the pressure from his feet and knees. The beast sped, slowed, turned twice back upon its tracks in a figure eight, while bullets from the men on the walls slashed through the grass where he had been, or where he had been heading. Then he let fly an arrow. With an accuracy that Herron could barely believe, it found its mark and took a man down to his knees, pierced through the arm. Elsewhere around the wall the same dance was performed, but other soldiers were not so lucky.

"Use the wall," a sergeant shouted at his men. "Use the crenellations. That's why we built 'em, lads!"

The soldiers complied, but still, as they stood to track one target for a shot, Indians from the other direction would shoot and soldiers would go down. The exchange of fire went on, and Herron saw no Indians lying in the dust.

"Colonel," he said, "may I suggest that you concentrate your men along two of the walls and mass your fire into volleys."

"Do you think that will help?"

Herron looked at his pocket watch. "In the twenty minutes since this raid commenced, I have counted sixteen of your men wounded and two killed outright. At that rate you can last a little over two hours. The sun sets in four. You will not survive with these tactics."

"General, with all due respect, my men are engineers and carpenters, not regular army."

"Excuses won't save their skins, Colonel. Your men are dying. Take my suggestion or not, but do something before it is too late."

McCormack hesitated. Herron felt for him. The colonel couldn't relinquish direct command over his men without disgrace, but he was inexperienced in battle. His men fought with precision but without confidence, and it was confidence that made all the difference in a fight.

Two more men fell back with arrow wounds as McCormack struggled with his choice. Herron made it for him.

"Do it, Colonel," he said in a low voice so his seconds would not hear. "Do it now."

McCormack seemed almost relieved by Herron's order. He turned to his battalion commanders. "Concentrate your men on the east and north walls. You'll have the sun behind you there. Reserve Companies A and B for the west and south. Put Company C in the yard, ready to ride. For the rest, mass your fire into volleys by company. Aim for the whistlers if you must, but drive those savages off."

"Yes, sir." The two officers saluted and left to carry out their orders.

Herron peered over the tower wall. The Indians were circling closer now, and their whistlers were varying their colors from dark to light, making it nearly impossible to track them for a shot. The Indians, though, made evil use of almost every arrow, and McCormack's men continued to fall.

The soldiers hustled into their new positions and crouched behind the walls in groups of twenty. Their sergeants spotting for them, they prepared to loose their salvos upon the enemy.

Storm Arriving pulled another arrow from his first quiver and set it to the bowstring, pressing with his left foot and leaning in as his whistler rounded the corner of the fort. He saw no shot to take, and held his own fire as he swung around the eastern side. He squinted, saw a bluecoat at the wall, clenched his knees to steady his mount. He raised his bow and pulled back the string.

A score of bluecoats stood from behind the wall, bristling with guns. Sunlight glinted. Storm Arriving let his arrow fly unaimed, grabbed the first rope, and dug in with his left toe. His whistler pulled left toward the wall as a gout of smoke exploded over his head. Whistlers screamed. Men shouted. Ahead, another lone bluecoat was watching, sighting for others hidden behind the wall. Storm Arriving veered right as bluecoats stood to fire. He banked left again to face them, to give them the narrowest target. Twenty guns spewed white fire. Bullets zipped and slapped the ground behind him. Pungent smoke—metallic and sharp—stung his nostrils, a thick fog of hot haze. Down the line, another volley, more smoke, and men and beasts went down.

Big Nose was wrong about their number, he thought quickly. Wrong by half.

He held on as his whistler hurdled a fallen comrade and heeled in to turn and put some distance between himself and the wall. He halted his whistler and ordered it down into the dried grass. The drake crouched and paled his skin. Storm Arriving readied another arrow, aimed at one of the sighters along the wall, but atop the tower, he spied bluecoats who had no rifles.

Chiefs, he knew: bluecoat chiefs.

He aimed, fired, and was on his mount and riding as bullets began to rip the grass.

Herron only heard the arrow as it sliced through the air and hit with a meaty thunk. Quincy didn't say a word. He simply collapsed into a twisted heap like a broken toy. Herron stared at his aide for what seemed a long minute, saw the arrow that protruded from his chest, saw the dark brown of Quincy's irises disappear as his pupils expanded to take in eternity, saw the cabochon bead of a single droplet of bright red blood on the arrow's raven-black fletching. Then time returned and McCormack was tugging at his sleeve.

"General. You must depart the platform."

Herron jerked his arm free of the colonel's grasp. He pointed out beyond the walls. "They're changing tactics. We'll have to change ours. God damn it, man, look!"

The dust and gunsmoke dimmed the view of the field but it was clear that the Indians had shifted their methods. Only a few rode back and forth past the walls. Elsewhere, ghostly warriors appeared from nowhere, rode mounts of insubstantial air, and disappeared again. The field was littered with dead and wounded—probably two score of the enemy down—but every time a company stood to volley at a passing rider, a dozen Indians seemed to sprout from the ground itself, loosing deadly shafts and then sinking back down into the earth.

"Send out Company C," Herron said.

"Send them out?"

"Yes. Attack."

"Attack what?"

Herron pointed. "Right in front of us. A hundred yards out from the gate. The men on the ground will see them. Open the gate and attack."

"General, I—"

Herron glared. "You have your orders, Colonel."

McCormack hesitated, a moment of defiance, but an emotion Herron understood completely. He nodded once, acknowledging his subordinate's protest. McCormack saluted and turned to issue commands.

Yes, Herron thought, men will die. But it is not our job to keep them all alive. It is our job to ensure that if they must die, their deaths are useful.

Company C formed up in ranks behind the heavy-timbered gate.

"Ready!" shouted their first sergeant. The men gripped their rifles and leaned forward like foot-racers at a church picnic.

"Open the gate!"

The blocks were pulled, the bolts drawn back, and the single door swung out.

*   *   *

The rifle fire increased. Storm Arriving and a dozen others ducked back down behind their whistlers. He saw Wolf Robe a few yards closer to the wall, nearly flat on the ground. Storm Arriving readied another arrow but did not shoot. He had already emptied his first quiver—others too would be starting to run low—and he could not afford to waste any shots.

Then he heard them, the bluecoats. A throaty, urgent sound that chilled him with the memory of battles fought along the Big Salty.

"Prepare!"

The Kit Foxes were ready and the first bluecoats died at the gate. The next ones through fired their rifles and whistlers cried out in distress as they were hit. Several beasts bolted, leaving their riders exposed. More bluecoats came out of the gate, rifles in hand. Storm Arriving grabbed his mount's first rope.

"Kit Foxes, fall back. Quickly!"

Wolf Robe was still hiding, frozen by panic as the bluecoats charged the field.

"Get up! Wolf Robe! Let's go!"

Bullets sang through the thick afternoon air. Storm Arriving saw the young Kit Fox grab his first rope, saw him dragged upward as the beast leapt into motion. Storm Arriving turned his own whistler and sped away from the fort with all the others.

They rode until they were out of range of the bluecoats' rifles and then they drew up and halted. Storm Arriving and Big Nose took stock.

"This is bad," Storm Arriving said, counting the men that were with them and looking back at the field. The bodies of soldiers and their whistlers lay in the dust outside the wooden walls. Worse than that, the bluecoats, now retreating back inside the gate, had with them three Kit Fox soldiers. Storm Arriving felt his heart ache at the sight of it.

"Wolf Robe," Big Nose said. "Where is my little brother?"

Storm Arriving pointed.

"What in Hell are they doing?" Herron asked.

"General? I ordered them to take prisoners."

"Prisoners? What in Hell are you going to do with prisoners?"

McCormack was nonplussed. "Why . . . interrogate them, sir. What else?"

Herron glared at the colonel. He walked to the rail that overlooked the yard. Men, wounded and dead, Quincy among the latter, lay in the shade of an improvised awning outside the infirmary. McCormack's surgeon major moved quickly among the wounded, ascertaining criticality. In the center of the yard the survivors of Company C were assembled in a circle around the three Indians brought in from the field. Other men were joining the circle.

The Indians stood close together: an older man and a youth supporting a wounded man between them. The man in the middle stood on one leg, his other bent at an ugly angle below the knee, useless. The trio eyed the surrounding soldiers, but only the boy's face evinced any sign of fear, eyes wide and trying to look everywhere at once.

Criminal, Herron thought, to press a boy so young into action.

The soldiers began to taunt the prisoners, jeering and pushing at them from the protection of their circled strength.

"Leave them be," Herron commanded, and men— soldier and savage alike—looked up to see who had spoken. The soldiers backed off a step. Herron turned to McCormack.

"Well, Colonel? There are your prisoners. What will you do now?"

McCormack colored to his hairline. "Well, General Herron, sir. I certainly don't intend to interrogate them from here."

"Why not?" He turned and pointed to the captives. "You there," he said, his voice filling the yard. "How many in your tribe? No? Then how about: Where is your main military force?"

The Indians gave no answer, gave not even the inkling of comprehension.

Herron glanced back at the red-faced McCormack and returned to his questioning.

"Do you speak English?" he said to the Indians.

Nothing.

"Parlez-vous français?"

Again, nothing.

"Sprechen Sie Deutsche? Usted habla español?" Herron turned back to McCormack, unable to hide his loathing of the situation. "There. Your prisoners have been interrogated. Now execute them."

"Sir!"

"What did you think, Colonel? Were you going to keep them? Send them back to the territories for trial?"

"Sir, I . . ."

"No, I didn't think so. Well, now you'll have to see it through. Execute them."

"But, General—"

Herron skewered him with a fierce stare. "Colonel, take those insurrectionist bastards outside the gates and have them shot. I will not say it again."

McCormack's face was ashen, his hesitation now not defiance but an inability to execute his orders. Herron gave him a moment to master himself, which he did. The colonel took a backward step, saluted, and walked toward the ladder. Herron turned his attention back to the enemy.

The surviving Indians were gathered a thousand yards to the east—in sight of the gate and the walls, but beyond effective range of their Springfield rifles. He scanned the group through his binoculars.

They rode their beasts without attempt at concealment, though the whistlers still camouflaged them-

selves with dust-colored flanks. Herron estimated
forty, perhaps fifty riders—a little more than half their
original strength. He had hurt them, but they had hurt
him, too, and badly. He looked back inside the yard
and saw only three score of able-bodied men. Half of
the fort's current complement was down or dead.
Some would be back, of that he was confident, but he
knew, too, that probably a third of the original force
was down for good.

It will be different, he assured himself, with regulars
out here.

He looked back out at the Indians as the captives
were escorted out of the gate.

Storm Arriving and the others watched as the gate
opened. The three Kit Foxes were marched out under
guard. Little Creek and Wolf Robe held up the limping Rising Moon. Two bluecoats led them to a place
a short distance from the gate and stepped back. The
other bluecoats raised their rifles and fired. The three
Kit Foxes fell before anyone knew what was happening.

Big Nose cried out and toed his whistler into motion. Storm Arriving caught the halter rope and
stopped him.

"Let me go!"

"No!"

"I will go. I will avenge my brother's death."

"You will only kill yourself."

"Then that is what I will do."

"No. There is no purpose to it."

"I don't *care*."

"I do. I will not let you do this."

Big Nose swung with his bow but Storm Arriving
caught the other's foot with his own and toppled Big
Nose from his whistler's back. Other Kit Foxes joined
Storm Arriving to hold back the thickset warrior.

"You cannot tell me what to do," Big Nose screamed.

"No," Storm Arriving said. "But I can tell you that

you have a wife and a year-old babe at home who will curse your name when I tell them how you died. I can tell you that Wolf Robe came here as a man, of his own choice, and that he killed a bluecoat before he died. And I can tell you that if you attack them now, you will die and you will gain nothing. Your death will only mean one more body we must carry home."

Big Nose stared at Storm Arriving with tear-stung eyes, his breath shuddering through an open frown.

"Let me go," he said, his voice no more than a whisper. "You cannot tell me what to do."

Storm Arriving closed his eyes. "Release him," he told the others, and turned away.

He heard his friend walk to his whistler and mount. He heard the whistler rise, heard its feet stamp and scratch the earth, heard it turn, and heard it walk toward the bluecoat fort.

Heard it walk.

Storm Arriving turned and looked.

Big Nose was not attacking. He rode his whistler, straight-backed and proud, but only at a walk, not at a running charge. Storm Arriving squinted and saw bluecoats at the walls and on the tower. He saw rifles.

The bluecoats yelled and laughed as Big Nose rode toward them. Storm Arriving saw a puff of smoke from atop the wall, and then heard the report as the lazy bullet landed in the grass like a thrown stone. Big Nose continued to ride forward. More shots were fired, each *pop* delayed by distance. Bullets began to land closer to Big Nose, and with more force. Finally, one of the bluecoats bellowed a command and the firing ceased.

Big Nose rode without stopping, without turning, up to the place where his brother lay dead. There he halted and in the growing shadow of the bluecoat fort, with the pale faces of the enemy looking down upon him, calling to him, daring him to act, Big Nose knelt and picked up the body of his mother's youngest son. He did not glance upward. He did not acknowledge the bluecoats' insults, the men themselves, or even the existence of the wooden walls that stood unnatural and square in the flowing smoothness of the prairie. He simply turned, mounted, and as his whistler walked back to where Storm Arriving and the others watched in awe and respect, he began to sing the death song to his brother's fallen spirit.

Nothing survives.
Only the earth and the mountains.

Storm Arriving joined in the song, as did the rest of the survivors. It was the song every man hoped to sing before his death, or the song he hoped would be sung over him soon after he died.

Big Nose rejoined the group, his face full of grief and wet with tears. Storm Arriving had no words of comfort for his childhood friend, could think of nothing to say at all. Big Nose had risked his life, but not thrown it away; Storm Arriving hoped what he had said played a part in that decision, but did not know and was not going to ask. It was not important to know. It was only important that Big Nose was still alive, and that he had shown the rest of them what truly needed to be done.

Storm Arriving mounted his own whistler and headed it at a walk toward the dark walls of the bluecoat fort. Others came behind him, a solemn procession, all singing the death song for their fallen comrades, all walking into danger's shadow to bear their bodies home.

"Let them come," Herron said.

"General," McCormack said quietly. "With all due respect, sir, I don't understand you. One moment you have prisoners executed and now, when we could wipe them out in a blink, you let them live."

Herron gave a slight nod as he stood at the parapet and watched the Indians come forward to gather up their fallen. "We could wipe them out, and lose another twenty men in the doing of it," he said, "but look at them. They're beaten. I want them to take that message home, along with their dead." The Indians picked up the corpses and lay them across the backs of whistlers, one or two per beast. They sang an eerie, warbling song that started high and stepped down to a low mumble.

"They fought well," Herron said. "They deserve that much respect, at least." The Indians sang their song, loaded up their dead, and carted them away, like the French at Agincourt.

Medieval, Herron thought. Positively medieval.

George and Vincent rode through a golden forest. The slanting sun of morning heated the ground, raising a mist, but the rain-wet air held the firm promise of winter. Their whistlers walked leisurely beneath pied boughs, leaves the color of fire, of earth: deep purples and bright scarlets, pale yellows and crinkly browns. Their beasts' feet whispered through the fallen leaves. George's mount stopped unbidden and sniffed. He let the hen have her way, and she took a step toward the bole of a nearby maple, sniffing the ground. Vincent's whistler became interested and the two men let the two beasts dig down through the new carpet of leaves until they found their prize: a patch of black, bulbous, half-buried mushrooms. The whistlers argued over the tidbits in hoots and rough nudges, but soon they had consumed their treat and the men toed them back into motion.

"We've been gone more than three weeks," George said. "It's time we headed back, don't you agree?"

"Ah, *oui*, of course," Vincent said. "If you wish. But I was thinking that those hills over there look promising." He pointed to the east where, past the trees and beyond a small valley, several dark, folded ridges rose up out of the gentle land.

"No," George said. "That is the Teaching Mountain. It is a place the People hold in great reverence; a most holy place. We will not be digging there."

Vincent sighed and shrugged, and George chuckled at the trader's dismay.

"We have found six other sites already, enough to make you rich. Aren't you satisfied yet?"

"You seem immune to it," Vincent said.

"Immune?" George looked over at his companion, thinking he must have misunderstood. "What are you talking about? Immune to what?"

"The fever," Vincent explained, as if it were obvious. "You, and your Indian friends, too. Completely immune."

George continued to stare.

"*Gold* fever," Vincent said. "You seem immune, but me? No, no, no. I've got it, and a bad case, too. Six sites? A drop. Sixteen? Better. Sixty? Ah, *mais oui!* Then I might be able to think of being satisfied."

George laughed out loud. "And what would you do with such wealth?"

Vincent raised a haughty eyebrow. "Why spend it looking for more, of course."

Their laughter echoed in the still, clean air. A chipmunk scolded them from atop a fallen tree, making them laugh all the more.

They headed east, down out of the uplands and back toward the prairie that would lead them home to the mining site in the Sheep Mountains. The woods began to thin as they descended, and the two men caught glimpses of the vast plain that lay ahead. Their whistlers, too, could see the open land, and they yodeled in anticipation of being back in more familiar terrain.

"Vincent," George said. "You've been a tremendous help to us. We owe a great deal of our success to your advice and instruction. I doubt we would have achieved half of what we have without you."

"And there's more to come," Vincent said, smiling. "That seam shows no signs of weakening." He shook his head. "Though what your Indians are going to do with it, I can't guess."

"Since you mention it, I've been wanting to talk to you about that."

"Oh? Tell me."

George hesitated. He had kept their ultimate purpose a secret from Vincent. The weeks of digging had turned into months and the old trader turned prospector had been satisfied to direct the operation, weigh the day's take, and parcel out his percentage. He had never asked what George or the Cheyenne intended to use their massing fortunes for, though he had been unable to hide his curiosity.

But, once again, George felt unequal to the task before him. Once more he felt the lack of worldliness brought on by a bookish nature. He needed help—help Vincent could provide.

"We want to make some purchases."

Vincent snorted. "Purchases? You could purchase the whole of Illinois with what you've mined so far. I'll be no good to you there, but anything else, and I am your servant. What is it you desire?"

"Arms," George said plainly.

"Ah! *Mais oui!* Enfields? Henrys? Sharps? It will be a pleasure. Will you be hunting buffalo or smaller game? I know some do not care for the larger bore, but in my experience—"

"No," George said. "Not hunting rifles. Not shotguns. Arms."

Vincent looked over at George with head held back and a crease across his brow. "Arms?" he asked.

"Yes," George replied. "Arms. Military arms."

The old trader frowned. "Oh, George, do not ask me this. Please."

"Why not? Can't you help?"

"It's not that—"

"Then you *can* help."

"Well . . . yes, but—"

"But you won't."

Vincent held out pleading hands.

George was disappointed, but not beaten. He played his last card. "We would make it worth your while."

The old man winced, then shook his head. "It is not like that. Please, try to understand. I am an old *fils de pute* who has happened into a lucky circumstance. I am not a brave man, and what you ask . . . it is dangerous."

George sighed. "Well, if you won't help, I'd appreciate any advice you could give me."

"What? You? You are not thinking of . . . not you?"

"Who else?" George asked in reply. "None of the People could do it."

"Trading raw gold for military arms?" Vincent said, incredulous. "You?"

"I," George said.

"You realize it is against the law. In Canada as well as in your United States. To supply Indians with weapons—even rifles, not to speak of military weapons—it is a serious crime."

"Yes, I know, but these people need those weapons. They will be slaughtered if they can't defend themselves properly."

"Have you considered . . ." Vincent began in a solicitous tone. "I know you are fond of these people, but have you considered that perhaps this is what God intends for the world?"

George clenched his teeth, remembering the carnage of the past year; the cavalry's sneak attack on the camp of the People, the hundreds dead, including Mouse Road's older sister, Blue Shell Woman. He remembered the young woman lying in her mother's arms, her blood dripping into a puddle of rain, her eyes staring up to the heavens, her chest ripped open by American bullets.

"What I have seen," George said, "had nothing to do with God."

They rode out of the trees and into open country. In front of them the hills spilled out onto a world of long lines and subtle curves. The sun was climbing toward noon and the west held the promise of more rain. To the south, a herd of deer grazed. They lifted their heads at the sight of the men on their whistlers, and silently bounded away. George smiled as the deer displayed the distinctive tails that gave them their Tsétsêhéstâhese name: Timber-deer-waving.

"I will do this, Vincent. But I surely could use the help of a man like you."

His companion remained silent, and George did not look over to gauge the older man's reaction.

They reached the open prairie and let their whistlers run. The rainstorm that threatened held its breath as they coursed beneath its blued-steel belly, and George was grateful for it. They'd been wet enough on this trip.

The next day, when they arrived back at the mining site, they found the mining crew filling in the trenches and re-laying the carefully preserved sod over the up-turned earth.

"What are they doing?" Vincent asked.

"Closing up for the winter. Unlike us, those men have families. They've been apart from them long enough."

"Yes, all right," the older man said testily. "But why are they filling in the trenches?"

"We have to protect the land," George explained. "We have to leave as small a mark on the earth as possible."

"But we'll just have to dig it up again in the spring."

"Then that is what we will do."

Vincent made a rude sound and folded his arms across his chest. "It is a very great waste of time, I say."

"Come," George said with a chuckle. "Let's see how they did during the month we were gone. That ought to make you more tolerant of our ways."

They walked over to the lodge where they kept their supplies, the undivided gold, and Vincent's pre-

cious scales. Gets Up Early, the Little Bowstring soldier who had taken over the managing of the
operation in their absence, met them there.

"How was your trip?" he asked.

"Very good," George said. "We found other places
to get the chief-metal when this place is empty."

Gets Up Early smiled. "Remember them well, One
Who Flies. I do not think you will be needing them
for a long while."

He ushered them into the lodge. George heard Vincent swear under his breath.

On the left side of the lodge were the five beds for
the men who slept there. On the right side, along the
lodge wall, were the empty parfleches and depleted
sacks of meats and grains that had been sustaining
them during their stay. But toward the center of the
lodge, stacked up next to the dark firepit, were a number of leather bags. Some were merely fist-sized, but
one of them was the size of a five-pound sack of flour.

"Five, six, seven . . . how many?" George asked.

"Two times ten plus two," Gets Up Early replied,
using the People's accretive numbering method.

George nudged Vincent. "One of those is yours,"
he said.

"*Tabarnaque,*" Vincent breathed. "*Incroyable.*" He
looked at George, his face slack. "I am rich."

George smiled. "Indeed, you are. And there's more
than enough for me to get started as well."

Vincent looked at the sacks of gold, then back at
George. "I cannot let you," he said.

George's good humor evaporated. "I must," he said.
"I will."

"You will end up dead. They will take one look at
your boyish face and they will split your gut and divide
the profits while you lay dying."

George looked Vincent straight in the eye. It was a
thing he had learned not to do, living among the People, as they considered it very rude, but George had
not forgotten how to act among whites.

"Then help me," he said. "Watch my back, or let

me watch yours, but help me. Keep me alive, Vincent D'Avignon, because I will go. With you or without you, I will go."

George could see the battle the trader waged, the tug-of-war that went on inside his mind as his lackadaisical conscience fought with his well-developed sense of self-preservation. His breath sounded harsh and at several points he seemed about to speak, but did not. Finally, he took a deep breath and let it out, his bony hand caressing his wrinkled forehead.

"I'll want a commission," he said.

George smiled.

CHAPTER 7
Winter, A.D. 1887
Westgate
Yankton

Herron returned Shafer's salute and pointed to an empty chair.

"Shut the door, Colonel, and sit down. I'll be with you in a minute."

Lieutenant Colonel Shafer pushed the door closed and dropped his gangly frame easily into the armchair. Herron returned his attention to the reports and messages on his worktable.

The wood burning in the wide cast-iron stove shifted with a muffled *shump*. A pot of water sat atop it, simmering, humidifying the air and building fantastic geometries of frost on the rippled glass of the unshuttered windows. Outside, the world was brown and white, mud and snow, dark wood and bright ice. The only exceptions were the river—a deep, dark flow of ice-lined water slowly moving downstream—and the equally dark stone and metal of the unfinished bridge, its skeletal frame beginning to arch across the black currents.

Herron put aside the official telegraph messages that had so displeased him and Shafer's poorly typed reports that had simply angered him.

"Lieutenant Colonel," he said, and the chief engineer uncrossed his legs and sat a little straighter in his chair. "I have been reading reports on your progress and I am not pleased. Correct me if I have misinterpreted their content—and I truly hope that I have—but what I believe they are saying is that we are going to miss our target date by three months."

He paused, waiting for the desired correction from Shafer, but the colonel only shrugged shoulders and eyebrows as if to say: *c'est la vie.*

Herron silently cursed all artists before he continued. "Allow me to put it this way, Colonel. Tell me how you are going to get us back on schedule."

Shafer blinked. "Sir," he said, "I'm not."

"You're not?"

"No, sir. I can't. We're behind schedule, that's true, but there is no possible way to get us back on schedule."

Herron stood and began to pace the length of the short carpet behind his worktable. He could feel his blood pounding in his ears. "Shafer," he said, and held up a thumb and forefinger, "I'm this close to busting you to major and letting someone else build this God-damned bridge."

He picked up the telegraph messages. Strong capital letters stood in straight, bold lines. "The President informs me that he will soon introduce his 'Homesteader Act' to Congress." Herron read from the message on top of the sheaf. " 'I expect its passage to coincide with the official opening of your bridge in March.' Do you hear that, Shafer? In March. Not June, not July. *March.*" He tossed the messages onto his table. "Good Christ. Come spring we're going to have a hundred thousand desperate people out here wanting to cross that God-damned bridge in hopes of building a new life. I've got squatters out there already trying to preempt Custer's act and I don't have the men to protect them. I don't have the men because I have to ferry supplies across the river. And why am I ferrying goods across a winter-swollen river instead of sending them across by train?"

"The God-damned bridge, sir?"

"Don't be flippant, Colonel." Herron stopped and pointed a finger. "It's one of the worst choices you could make right now. Your only worse choice is to be argumentative."

"Sorry, sir."

"We were supposed to have a usable cart deck by now and be working on the rail deck. You haven't even finished the main arch yet. Now I don't want to hear *can't* and I don't want to hear *won't*. I don't want to hear *not possible* or *beyond my control*." He leaned forward, fingers on the table. "I want to hear just two things: *how* and *when*."

Shafer's brow was furrowed and he bit his upper lip. He was thinking hard, and then he sat up straight and looked Herron in the eyes. "All right, sir. It's like this: We were sent a shipment of wrought iron that was of substandard quality, courtesy of Senator Matherly's father-in-law. I can't use that iron. I won't use it. It is not possible to get a new shipment from Penn's Sylvania any faster than it is already coming. I'm sorry, sir, but it is simply beyond my control."

Herron's pulse kicked up from a canter to a full gallop. Still, and somehow, he was able to force a prim smile.

"You are a clever man," he said. "You wouldn't be here if you weren't. But as long as I am your superior, Lieutenant Colonel, be it in nothing other than rank, you will show the proper respect." He pointed to the scene outside the window. The barges and wooden scaffolding nearly obscured the otherwise graceful curves of wrought iron that tried to span the main channel of the Missouri. "Now tell me, you've got iron here, yes? And you've got two hundred men sitting on their asses, yes?"

"Yes, sir, but—"

"But nothing. You've got what you need, so cut corners, redesign, I don't care, just get those men to work."

"But, sir, the wrought iron we have is not good enough."

"It's not a work of art, here, Shafer. It's just a God-damned bridge." He stood straight and folded his arms. "Finish it, Colonel, or I'll get someone who will. Dismissed."

Gets Up Early and the rest of the mining crew escorted George and Vincent to the trading post. The Indians took all the whistlers back home and left the two white men with two weeks' worth of food, two heavy sacks of raw gold, and a dozen buffalo hides for use in acquiring a mode of transport that would be less . . . conspicuous.

Vincent traded most of the buffalo hides for two old mares and some western clothing for George—a usurious price in light of the quality of goods received—and then, keeping their gold well hidden from the traders that still lived at the post, they headed north.

George had not ridden a horse in nearly two years and he wondered how he had ever found the process the least bit comfortable. His new trousers, the old saddle, and the horse's rocking motion made him sore within a few miles. Hastening to a trot or canter did not help, either. When the wind picked up and began to howl across the wintry landscape of the Santee Territory, blowing snow up their backs, George was sure it could get no worse. In time and miles, though, he learned that he was wrong, that the discomfort with which he started the ride was only a specter, a dream portending the painful nightmare that the journey quickly became.

When they rode into little Pembina, at the border between the Santee Territory and British Canada, George felt like the definition of misery. He dismounted with ginger care and stood at the hitching rail while Vincent went into the assayer's offices to turn some of their gold into coin.

Beyond Pembina was Emerson, then Otterburn, and St. Norbert. At each town they stopped and exchanged some of their gold with a bank or assayer or goldsmith. At each town, too, Vincent insisted on buying something—a new shirt, a new suitcoat, two more and better horses—and their possessions began to accumulate.

"We don't *need* this stuff," George said as Vincent handed him a flat-topped John Bull hat and a gray frock coat.

"Yes we do, and speak English, please," Vincent said, using that language himself. "We are in Canada, not Acadia, and we need these clothes because no one is going to trust a couple of crazy backwoodsmen enough to sell them more than a slingshot."

George frowned. "Then who will they be trusting?"

Vincent smiled his crooked smile. "We are in charge of security along the Stonewell to Brandon branch of the new Canadian-Pacific Rail Road. Oh, and your last name is Carter, not Custer. Now put on the coat."

George sighed but put on the coat. "The sleeves are a little long."

Vincent shrugged. "Nothing's perfect," he said.

The city of Winnipeg lay on the switchback banks of the Red River. They reached the limit of the frozen waters at noon—according to Vincent's new pocket watch. The sky was covered by a blanket of dark clouds heavy with the threat of snow. George and Vincent rode across the stonework bridge at the south end of town. Their shadows, vague and amorphous, slid silently across the icy cobbles.

The bridge took them onto Broadway, and at the foot of the impressive, spire-cornered bulk of Manitoba College, they turned right onto Main. Main Street was broad and traversed the length of the town, running alongside the twisting river as best it could. As they traveled from the edge of town toward its heart, the smaller prairie homes became larger and more numerous. The buildings began to huddle together, as if for warmth against the frigid wind, and they grew from small, square homes with sharply sloped roofs into midsized storefronts with tall, rectangular façades that lined the boardwalks. A horse-drawn trolley appeared in the middle of the thoroughfare and the buildings strengthened: from wood to brick, brick to stone, standing taller—three stories and four—increasing in size and stature the farther George and Vincent rode.

The Cabot's Bay Company store, an immense square pylon, covered half a block and commanded an entire corner at the intersection of Main and Queen streets. The central business district lay ahead of them. Emporia and trading houses stood shoulder to shoulder. The streets were filled. People dodged carts and horses as they crossed the slushy streets, running for the trolley or delivering parcels to a patron. Boys cried out, hawking daily newspapers thick with local gossip. Men in dark frock coats and rounded hats stood outside their banks and offices, conversing as if it were springtime. Oblivious to the elements, they chatted amiably, comfortably, though their cheeks burned brightly and their words and laughter smoked in the cold winter air. Shouts, greetings, hoofs splashing in hollow rhythm down the street, the creak of wheels, and, blocks ahead, the heavy breath of locomotives. It was a busy town, full of energy and excitement.

"The place has grown up in the last few years," Vincent said. "I'd say she's doubled her size at least."

"The railroad?" George wondered aloud.

"No question," Vincent said. "From Ottawa to the Pacific in a matter of weeks. Can you imagine?" He shook his head at the wonder of it.

They rode on into the busiest section of town—the crossroads of the rail lines and Main Street—where the mercantile met the industrial and merged into a sprawling, patternless jumble of warehouses, manufactories, hotels, and saloons.

"Where are we going?" George asked as they turned north off of Main.

"To a place I've wanted to stay, but never had the coin." They turned onto Machray and the old man pointed. "The Grand Pacific Hotel. Isn't she a sight?"

To George, who, as a politician's son, had seen some of the finest homes and hotels the East had to offer, it seemed somewhat less than both its name and Vincent's estimation would deserve.

It was tall—four floors above ground level—with a cupola capping a tower at the rear. Awning-draped balconies divided the front of the upper three floors, and a man in a red coat and black topper oversaw the main entrance, ready to assist the clientele. The hotel was built with the lines of a great hotel, albeit on a smaller scale, but George's eye caught the signs of deteriorated glory.

The awnings that shaded the snow-dusted balconies were frayed and faded. The stonework was dingy with soot. The doorman was nearly as old as Vincent and only half as agile, and horse chips lay in the street near the entrance.

However, George consoled himself with the fact that he had seen no better on their trip through town, and that this place would most likely—and at the very least—be warm and dry; two things he had not been in weeks.

They hitched their horses to the rail and, taking their precious saddlebags with them, entered and checked into a suite on an upper floor.

"What now?" George asked as he took the room on the right and dropped his bags onto the small bed.

"Now?" Vincent said from his own room. "Now, a soak, a shave, a meal and a bottle, and then, *peut-être*, a soft-skinned whore with high spirits and low expectations."

George laughed as he undid his necktie. "Yes, but seriously, what do we do tonight?"

"Tonight? I just told you what I am going to do tonight."

"But . . . but what about the guns? Isn't there any-one you want to contact tonight?"

Vincent poked his head out into the common sitting room that separated the two bedrooms.

"Young Custer, this is not going to happen overnight. It will take time. It is delicate. I must make subtle inquiries and wait for people to respond. We will be here at least a week, maybe two."

"Two weeks," George blurted. "What am I supposed to do for two weeks?"

"Frankly, I think you could use some female companionship." Vincent raised an eyebrow and snickered. "I can't promise anything, but I'll see what I can do."

The old man shut his door and left George standing there, wordless.

For the next week Vincent led George through a numbing procession of saloons, taverns, pubs, eateries, and streetfront vendors. They never left their hotel before noon. Then they spent the day walking the riverfront and the rail yards, stopping here and there, chatting with stevedores and cargo masters. Great friendships were purchased for the price of a beer or a meat pie, and from burly Scots and Irishmen they learned the names of dealers and traders at warehouses and dry goods shops. These more significant men of business Vincent treated to suppers and evenings full of drink and women, and they in turn shared the names of still other men whose reputed desires and purposes lay closer to those of their hosts.

The women, with their heavily rouged cheeks, loose hair, and bawdy humor, did not appeal to George, and the general drunkenness of the soirees held even less allure. But he sat with Vincent and endured the ribaldry, nursing a beer and trying not to be tagged as a complete prig. As Vincent became less and less coherent, George kept track of the information their liquor was buying. Each evening, well past midnight, he guided Vincent back to their hotel, rang the night bell, and gave the bleary-eyed clerk a coin for his trouble. The next day, after a great deal of coffee, they began again.

They kept up the routine for ten days straight with no progress—as far as George could discern—until late one morning when they were breakfasting in the hotel's small dining room. They were the only patrons there so late in the forenoon, but the kitchen had come to anticipate their habits and had prepared Vincent's usual of eggs, toast, and syrup-drowned ham. George was enjoying biscuits and gravy, and both men had coffee: black, hot, and very strong. George ate without attempts at conversation—the wisest course, he had learned, at least until Vincent had finished three cups of coffee—and the dining room was filled with the small sounds of silverware and china.

Their waiter came to the table. "Mr. Carter?"

"Yes," George said. "What is it?"

He held out a note on a small tray. "There is a gentleman in the lobby. He asks for a few moments of your time."

George took the note and unfolded it. Finely formed letters stood tall in a single line across the small piece of hotel stationery. It read: *I can get what you want.*

George folded the note and answered Vincent's unspoken query with a quick smile. To the waiter he gave a coin. "Please, invite the gentleman to join us."

The waiter stepped back and departed. He returned a moment later followed by a tall man in a black overcoat with a fur collar. Gloves and derby in hand, he came up to their table with a confident stride. His hair was silver at the temples and forelock, combed back and pomaded. His beard, shot through with gray, was neatly trimmed. His coat, his hat and gloves, his high-collared shirt and silk necktie, all spoke of wealth and position.

George and Vincent rose. The gentleman bowed ever so slightly and held out his hand to George.

"Angus McTavish," he said in a voice that was deep and rumbled with brogue. "At yer service, Mr. Carter."

George shook the offered hand. "Pleased to meet

you, Mr. McTavish. Allow me to introduce my partner, Mr. Vincent D'Avignon."

"A pleasure," McTavish said.

"Please," George said, "join us." He gestured to the waiter and an extra chair and place setting were brought to the table. "Some tea or coffee?"

"Oh, aye. Tea would be lovely."

With another glance George instructed the waiter and the three men settled into their seats.

"About your note, Mr. McTavish . . ."

"Please," the Scot said with a gesture of denial. "Such formality. I'm sure we're all t'become fast friends so, if y'please, call me Angus. 'Tis what everyone calls me and I'd hate for y't'think I was puttin' on airs."

George nodded. "Very well, then. Angus. As for myself, George will be fine."

"Grand," Angus said. "And you, Mr. D'Avignon. Do y'mind if I call you by your Christian name?"

"By all means," Vincent said with a sour smile.

"Grand," Angus said again.

They sat for a moment, all smiling at one another. George felt like an idiot, grinning foolishly, and so he pressed on.

"Angus, about your note . . ."

"Oh, aye. Y'see, I have heard about town that you—"

He paused as the waiter brought his tea and set it on the table with a rattling of china and silver. When the server had gone, Angus leaned forward and continued in a raspy whisper.

"I have heard about town that you two are lookin' to make some purchases for your . . . ah . . . security needs."

"Well, yes," George said. "We are. It's certainly no secret. We'd like to purchase some rifles and other items."

"Ah, but such a purchase is simple enough. I've gathered though that there's a wee bit more to it than that. Am I correct in this deduction?"

"Perhaps," George said.

"*Tabarnaque,*" Vincent swore. "Quit playing games. Of course there is more to it. We've made no secret of *that* either. What I want to know is, what does he bring to the table?"

Their guest sat back in his chair, a wide-eyed expression on his face. George glared at his partner. The old man's terseness was uncharacteristic, even considering his hungover condition. He wondered if Vincent was put out because Angus had not approached him first, but then George discarded such idle speculation as useless and returned his attention to McTavish.

"As Vincent says, yes, there is more to it than that. Much more. My caution, however, is because of my concerns. Very few have the wherewithal—or the discretion—to fulfill our rather extensive needs." He touched McTavish's note that lay folded on the tablecloth. "Your introduction said you can get what we want. Do you know what we want?"

Angus shrugged. "I believe I do. I believe I do." He ticked off items on his fingers. "Y'want guns, specifically, rifles. That much you've made most clear. Repeaters, from what I've heard, and naturally, you'll need ammunition to go with 'em."

"Naturally," George agreed. Vincent said nothing, and sawed off another piece of syrupy ham and watched Angus with a gimlet eye. "How many can you provide?"

Angus puffed up with pride and a confident smile. "More than y'need, I'm sure. Now I've got several cases of Springfields—"

"No Springfields," George said. "Not sturdy enough."

"Ah, of course. Then I have some Spencers—"

"No," George interrupted again. "The magazine is in the buttstock. I've seen them explode when dropped."

"Ah," Angus said, struggling to find something George found suitable. "So it's durability yer wantin', then."

"Absolutely." George knew that on the prairie, toughness would make the difference.

"Winchesters, then. Model 1873."

Vincent sat up. "1873? We don't want any antiques here."

Angus held up his hands against the charge. "*Model* 1873. They were made but two years ago."

"How many do you have?" George asked.

"Two hundred."

"Only two hundred?"

Angus chuckled. "*Only* two hundred? How many do y'need?"

"More," George said.

"How many more?"

George looked at Vincent and the old trader gave a small nod. "Many more."

"Five hundred?"

"More."

"A thousand?"

"More. And more than just rifles. Heavy guns."

"And explosives," Vincent added. "For excavation," he said when George gave him a querying glance.

Angus looked from George to Vincent, his self-assured air suddenly weakened. He laughed and sipped at his tea. "What in th'name of Christ are y'doing?" he asked as innocently as he could. "Raisin' a bloody army?"

Vincent's knife and fork clattered to his plate. He took a long swig of his lukewarm coffee and then wiped at his mouth with his linen napkin. "Do you know how many miles are between here and the Pacific Ocean?" he asked.

Angus blinked at the sudden change in subject. "Why, no. I must say that I don't."

"Thousands," Vincent said, pointing a finger at Angus. "Thousands. And in each of those thousands of miles? Indians. Yes, Indians. Hundreds of thousands of them. And right through the middle of it all?" He slapped the tabletop and made the china dance. "The Canadian-Pacific Rail Road. All those people traveling through two thousand miles of unfriendly territory." He picked up his knife and fork and attacked the last of his ham. "Someone's going to have to protect them, eh?"

Angus started to catch on. "But I heard that y'were only responsible for security 'tween Stonewell and Brandon."

"For now," Vincent said around a syrupy mouthful. "For now."

Angus smiled and leaned back in his chair. "Well, now then. Suddenly I see just what kind o'men I'm dealin' wi': men o'vision and courage. Why, that's the kind o'bold plan that made the Cabots and the Morgans what they are today. Gentlemen"—and here he raised his teacup—"I salute you."

George refreshed his own coffee from the Spode pot at their table. "But can you do it, Angus? Can you get us what we want?"

The Scot pursed his lips and shook his head. "Thousands of rifles? Artillery? Explosives? Nae. None could." He saw George's look of disappointment and quickly continued. "Not right away, that is. But given time, aye, I can. It's a grand big risk for me, though. Financially. And legally."

George glanced at Vincent for help and the old trader stepped back into the conversation. "We have more than enough to cover the costs of what you can provide us now. Whatever is left, you can also have, as an advance on our account. The rest, well, you'll just have to trust us, as we will be trusting you."

Angus sipped his tea as he considered the offer. Then he set down the cup and laced his fingers over his belly. He looked at George and then at Vincent.

"It'll take 'til summer," he said, "and I'll most likely call m'self a fool in the mornin', but I'll do it."

Now it was George's turn to smile and offer his hand to seal the deal.

*   *   *

Storm Arriving stopped his work when he heard the returning patrol. Their whoops and shouts echoed up along the rocky hills that surrounded the valley of the Closed Windpipe band's winter campsite. His whistler quit her pawing of the calf-deep snow and lifted her head to listen for her returning kindred. Then she let out a long-necked, low-pitched rumble that tickled the hairs on Storm Arriving's arms and made his head hurt. When she stopped, she pawed at the snow again, but this time in anxiousness, not hunger. Storm Arriving let out the breath that he didn't know he'd been holding. He grabbed his whistler's halter rope, mounted, and headed off down the long, crooked path that would take him toward home.

The sky was a patched quilt of blue and white. The snows had come late this year, and were lighter than normal. The firs and pines that covered the hillside were still unburdened by white winter coats. Their needled boughs remained dark and glossy green, and their evergreen scent was sharp in the sunlit air. Storm Arriving rode down the slopes, wondering what news the patrol had brought back with them.

He heard their agitated voices long before he could make out the words, but even by the tone he could not tell if the news was good or bad. Some of the voices sounded angry, the words gruff and clipped, while others sounded excited with high-pitched words tumbling together. When he came around the bend in the narrow path that led into the wide canyon where the Closed Windpipe band gathered every winter, he saw a large group of men and whistlers. The returning patrol of Red Shield soldiers was surrounded by those eager for news. Everyone was talking at once. Two Tailfeathers, one of the men of the patrol and a cousin to Storm Arriving through his marriage, saw him and beckoned the others to be quiet.

"Quiet, all of you! Storm Arriving is here, and he will surely want to know this news."

The group ceased their jabbering and Storm Arriv-

ing rode up close to them. "What is it?" he asked.
"What is this news that I should want to know?"

They all began to talk at once, the angry ones and
the excited ones both. He cut them off with a gesture.

"You," he said, pointing to Rising Bird, one of the
angry voices. "What is your news?"

Rising Bird was a mature man who was near the
end of his years on the path of war. He pointed to
the south and east where, for many days, his patrol
had ridden through the prairie lands. "On our side of
the river," he said, his voice steady and his words
strong. "Many *vé'hó'e*. Bluecoats, in two of the
wooden forts. And others, too. In wooden lodges."

"Settlers?" Storm Arriving asked, his brow creased
and his eyes intent on the men before him.

"Yes," Rising Bird said, and others signed their
agreement. "We did not count the bluecoats in the
wooden forts, but there are two times ten plus four
of the lodges, each with at least two *vé'hó'e* in them.
Some with as many as eight."

"The *vé'hó'e* have brought their animals with them,
too," said one of the other men. "They mean to stay."

"They will not," Storm Arriving said. "Not if I have
anything to say about it." Rising Bird and the other
worried men seemed to take heart at his words.

"Then our other news," Two Tailfeathers said with
a smile, "you will be glad to hear. One Who Flies
comes, with Long Teeth, the trader. We found him
on our way home. They have been to the north, to
Grandmother Land, and they have traded the yellow
chief-metal for rifles."

Storm Arriving could feel the smile grow upon his
face. "One Who Flies? Rifles? Truly?"

His young cousin and the others all smiled. "He
comes," Two Tailfeathers said. "With many boxes and
crates. We will be able to attack the bluecoats now!"

"He did it," Storm Arriving said, still smiling. "I
did not think he could do it, but he did it." The former
bluecoat continued to surprise him. "Where is he?"

"He is a hand of time behind us. We left them at Three Owl Creek."

"Please, Cousin," he said. "Tell my wife. And tell Two Roads and the chiefs, too. They will want to plan for a war party."

"Where will you be?" Two Tailfeathers asked.

"I go to meet him." He turned his whistler back onto the trail and nudged her into a run.

Even though the sun warmed his back, as he rode down out of the valley and onto the lowlands the air bit his cheeks and the backs of his hands. Down here, the snow was even less, lingering only on the northern slopes, the rest having melted away into the ground under the attentions of the slanting winter sunlight. He rode around the foothills, toward Three Owl Creek, looking forward to seeing his friend after being separated by duty and distance for so many months.

Three Owl Creek was a hand's ride away, but before he got halfway there, he saw them: five riders and a long train of whistlers ambling toward home. Three of them were soldiers from the patrol who had stayed as an escort. The trader, whom they all called Long Teeth, was easy to spot as the one bundled up in furs against the cold like an old woman. But it was One Who Flies that Storm Arriving sought, and he found him, riding up and down along the long train of whistlers, inspecting every travois and checking on every tied bundle.

"Haooo!" Storm Arriving cried out and waved. The soldiers started but then saw him and waved back. One Who Flies looked forward, concerned, but then saw him, too. He recognized his friend and waved with both arms. Storm Arriving heard his distant cry of greeting, and both men toed their whistlers into a run.

They rode toward one another like boys on a summer field, calling out and laughing. He could see his friend's broad grin as they grew nearer. Storm Arriving held a hand out to one side and so did One Who Flies. Their whistlers tried to stop as they closed but only slid on the wet grass and patchy snow. The two men laughed again as they passed each other by, their reaching hands missing entirely. One Who Flies slipped as his whistler tried to pivot and Storm Arriving saw him disappear off the animal's far side. The whistler fell, too, and in scrambling to rise showered the former bluecoat with mud and dirty slush. Storm Arriving leapt down off his own mount and stood over One Who Flies as he wiped dirt from his face.

"You are a sorry rider," he said with a grin.

One Who Flies looked up, his teeth and pale eyes stark in his mud-smeared face. "You must be kind to me," he said. "I've been riding a horse for the past moon. I'm having to learn how to ride one of those creatures all over again."

Storm Arriving extended a hand to help him up. "That's not all you've forgotten. What are those clothes you're wearing?"

One Who Flies pulled at the edges of his *vé'ho'e* clothing. "Nothing I'm not anxious to get rid of." He stood back and looked Storm Arriving up and down. "I am glad to see you, my friend," he said. "I have not seen you since early summer. It has been too long a time."

Storm Arriving beamed. "It has," he said. "Too long. But what is all this?" He pointed to the long train of whistlers that were now just catching up with them. "You have succeeded?"

One Who Flies signed his agreement as they both retrieved their whistlers. "Yes, we succeeded. We have over two hundred rifles with us, with ammunition, plus some explosives for this year's mining."

"Two hundred?" Storm Arriving asked, suddenly concerned. "Two hundred? Is that all?"

One Who Flies stopped, his smile weakening. "It's all we could get right away. More will be coming. Many more."

"When? How many more?"

"Next summer. When we have more of the chief-metal. What's the matter? You knew we weren't going to get them all right away."

"But two hundred? What are we to do now?" Storm Arriving could not believe that this was happening, not after so much work and hoping. "The bluecoats are building forts on our side of the river. There are *vé'hó'e* in our lands, building lodges, grazing their animals. They are here *now*. How many *vé'hó'e* can we kill with only two hundred rifles?"

One Who Flies looked at him, his expression unreadable, and Storm Arriving felt all of their boyish elation blow away in the icy wind. They stared at one another as the convoy of whistlers and the escort caught up to them.

"What is it?" he heard Long Teeth ask in the Trader's Tongue as he drew near. "What is wrong?"

One Who Flies continued to look at him, his gaze cold, his eyes hard. "It seems," One Who Flies replied, "that our efforts may be insufficient. Certainly they are unappreciated, at least by some."

"One Who Flies," Storm Arriving said. "I did not mean—"

"What?" Long Teeth exclaimed. "He doesn't like the deal we made?"

"No," One Who Flies said. "Not very much."

"Well, then, he doesn't have to partake of it. I'm sure there are plenty who'll stand in line for a free rifle."

"Yes," One Who Flies said. "I'm sure there are others who will gladly take what we have brought, and who will have the manners to show some appreciation for our work and effort." He told his whistler to crouch and climbed up onto her back. The hen stood at his command and fell into step with the others. Storm Arriving stood there, holding his own whistler's halter rope, boiling with a stew of emotions as he watched them continue onward toward the camp.

"Why do you argue with him?" one of the Red Shield soldiers asked. "They came to find us." When

Storm Arriving looked at him blankly, he explained
further. "One Who Flies did not go home to his own
band. He wanted to share the new guns with us first.
He wanted to share them with you." The soldier
frowned. "And all you can do is argue with him." He
headed off to catch up with the others.

Storm Arriving grit his teeth as he mounted his own
whistler to follow.

During the meeting of the war chiefs, One Who
Flies ignored him. Not even when Storm Arriving volunteered for the war party and took for his own one
of the new rifles did One Who Flies do anything but
stare at his hands.

One Who Flies showed them all how the magazine
under the barrel could hold ten cartridges at a time.
He showed them how the rear sight flipped up and
how the small slide on it was used for aiming at distant
targets. He showed them how to fire the gun, how the
lever pushed the spent cartridge out and pulled the
new one into place from the magazine. He told them
a man could fire from a hiding place or a ditch and
have greater protection than a bow and arrow would
allow, and he showed them how a man could fire ten
shots in the time it took to draw two breaths. He
showed them all the things that this new weapon could
do, but through it all, he refused to speak directly to
Storm Arriving.

The war party assembled on the last day of Big
Hard Face Moon, one hundred fifty men from all the
soldier societies standing in the clearing at the south
end of the camp with their wives and families. The
first real snowfall of winter drifted silently down upon
them. Storm Arriving stood with Speaks While Leaving, saying their good-byes. One Who Flies stood off
to one side, watching the preparations and the leave-
takings, his face clouded by stormy thoughts.

"Go talk to him," Speaks While Leaving said. "Do
not leave with an uneasy heart."

"I do not think he wants to talk to me."

"Go," she urged him. "If he does not talk to you, he will talk to me. Tell him that."

Storm Arriving chuckled in spite of his sorrow. "We will be home soon." He kissed her hands and walked off toward One Who Flies.

The former bluecoat was wrapped in a buffalo robe. He had once more put off his *vé'hó'e* clothing and taken up the attire of the People. Many people had given him gifts in thanks for the rifles he had brought to them, and his garments were quite fine. His hair was still long, and someone had given him the tail feather from a red-tailed hawk and a leather lace. He had tied back his hair and stuck the feather in at the nape of his neck. His features were troubled and sad, but when he saw Storm Arriving walking toward him, his countenance took on an even harder edge.

Storm Arriving did not confront his friend face-to-face, but walked up and stood beside him, watching the farewells.

"The rifles are a good thing," Storm Arriving said. "They will make us strong against the bluecoats."

One Who Flies did not speak at once, but after a few moments said, "Yes. They will."

"I am sorry," Storm Arriving said, "that I did not show the proper respect for what you did. The People are grateful. I . . . am grateful."

He heard One Who Flies sigh and saw that he had covered his mouth with one hand. His brow was furrowed and his eyes were bright with tears. "It's not that," he said and he pulled his buffalo robe closer about his shoulders.

"What then?" Storm Arriving asked. "Tell me, my friend. What is it, then?"

One Who Flies breathed in through clenched teeth, his eyes still watching the scenes of quiet tenderness that passed between soldiers and their loved ones.

"I have brought you weapons," he said, his voice shaky with emotion. "I know it is the correct thing to do. But you put it so plainly when we met . . . I had never thought of it that way."

Storm Arriving thought back. "What was it that I said? I do not remember."

"You said . . . you said, 'How many *vé'hó'e* can we kill with only two hundred rifles.' " His breath caught in his chest, and then frosted in the cold air. "*I* am a *vé'ho'e*," he said. "I am one of them, and I am making it possible for you to kill my people. I don't know how to feel about that."

Storm Arriving heard his friend's words and took them into his heart. He tried to feel the emotions his friend must feel, but knew that it was wrong, that his friend was wrong.

"No," he said to One Who Flies. "This"—he touched the hawk's feather that his friend wore in his hair—"and these." He touched the thick skin of the buffalo robe that he wore and the supple deerskin of his leggings. "They are things of the People, not of the *vé'hó'e*. And so are you." He held up the new rifle that One Who Flies had brought back for him. "And this, this too is now of the People, thanks to you." He looked toward the men and women who bid one another farewell. "And they, they are *your* people. You are no longer one of the *vé'hó'e*. You are no longer of the Horse Nations. I do not know when it happened, but it did. You have seen the heart of the land, and you have felt the spirit of the world. You are not of that other place anymore. You are a real person, now. You are one of us."

One Who Flies looked at the snow that was gathering on the ground at his feet. "But people will die," he said.

Storm Arriving put a hand on his friend's shoulder. "That is true," he said. "We are at war, and one way or the other, people will die. If not them, then us." He took a step forward and turned to look One Who Flies straight in the eye. "Who shall it be?"

One Who Flies met the challenge of his gaze, and Storm Arriving saw the tragedy and the struggle that lay within him. The snow had started falling more heavily and thick, feather-like flakes clung to his hair and settled on his robe-covered shoulders. He reached out and touched the barrel of the rifle that Storm Arriving carried.

"Be careful," he said. "I will bring greetings to your mother and sister."

Then he turned and walked away.

Storm Arriving watched him go. He felt a touch at his shoulder and turned to see that Speaks While Leaving was beside him. "What did you tell him?" she asked.

Storm Arriving shrugged. "Nothing he did not already know," he said. "But perhaps something he was not ready to accept."

Within a few days the war party had ridden across the Sudden River and was approaching the place where the bluecoats had built their wooden forts. Storm Arriving, Red Bear, and Sees Far were in charge. Red Bear was younger than Storm Arriving and still impetuous. Sees Far was older, and knew the value of caution. Together, the three of them made a good balance.

The weather had followed them, laying down snow in their path. The whistlers disliked this cold, wet weather, and despite their riders' attempts to cover and cloak them as they rode, the beasts piped their complaints often and to any who would listen.

From sky to earth the world was white. Clouds hid the sun. The snow concealed the land. They were only a short distance from the Sudden River, but already the warriors were cloaked in bleached deerskins and their whistlers had paled their bodies to hide themselves in the wintry landscape. The wet flakes that clung to the riders' buffalo robes only helped to camouflage them.

"Over there!" shouted one of the soldiers and Storm Arriving turned to see where the man pointed. Off to the east he saw black shapes standing tall: dark giants in the wintry distance.

"Thunder Beings," said a man nearby, and "The Spirits walk the earth with us," said another.

Storm Arriving ignored them. "I do not think so."

"What then?" asked the soldier beside him.

"I do not know," he said. "Let's find out." He started that way but none others followed. As he rode closer, the veils of falling snow pulled back to reveal the truth.

The dark shapes became the trunks of tall, straight trees all stripped of limbs and bark. They had been upended and set in the ground, a group here, another there. The snow had only just begun to drift up at their bases, clinging to the barkless sides in bright patches. There were four groups in all, framing the four corners of the new bluecoat fort. In between the unfinished corners, more logs lay on the ground in snow-covered mounds the height of a man. Storm Arriving saw a deep track in the ground, a path used by the *vé'hó'e*, slowly being obscured by the falling snow. The track led off toward the southeast in a straight line. It was not hard to guess where that path might lead.

"Come," he shouted to the others, and waved them on. "Do not sit like potbellied babies. Let's go. By tonight we will see how our new gifts perform."

They rode on through the thickening snow, following the straight path that was becoming ever fainter in the white land. The storm intensified and they called back their scouts rather than risk losing men. The struggling winter light could only color the snow an icy blue and all the world's shadows merged together. They rode onward through the gloom, their line now single-file. The day passed, the men were silent, but the whistlers called to one another with cautious songs to keep the flock intact.

Storm Arriving heard the crack of a rifle shot from his left. Another shot, and whistlers and men alike shouted in alarm. The snow was thick and the light was dim but through it Storm Arriving could see the dark bulk of the *vé'hó'e* fort. They had ridden right up to it and nearly passed it by.

Soldiers scattered as more gunshots broke the quiet air. The bluecoats were firing at them from the walls. Storm Arriving fired back. The kick of the new weapon surprised him with its force and he nearly lost his seat. His whistler, unused to such noise, shied and turned unbidden. He worked the lever and the used shell sang. He aimed, cursed, tried to settle his mount with pressure from his feet, and aimed again. He could barely see the heads of the bluecoats as they peeked out through the slots high in the wall. White faces through white snow, dark blue cloth against dark wooden walls. He fired, but the shot carried high and did not even hit the wall. Others were missing their targets as well, as most were still aiming as if they were firing a bow. While they could fire faster than the bluecoats, they were not doing any damage and blossoms of fire were coming back at them from atop the wall.

"To the rear," Storm Arriving shouted. "Pull back! Keep together!" The soldiers retreated and the wooden wall was lost behind a curtain of snowfall. The war party gathered together and the leaders assessed the situation.

"What are you doing?" Red Bear said. "Why did you call off the attack?"

"We were not ready," Storm Arriving answered him. "We were not in a good position."

"I agree," said Sees Far. "But what is the best thing to do now? I do not think we should attack them now."

"I agree," Storm Arriving said.

"What?" Red Bear was furious. "Of course we should attack them. Why else are we here?"

"To do what damage we can," Storm Arriving said. "But they know we are here, and they will be waiting for us to come back. You were not here the last time we attacked one of these forts. You do not know how bad it was."

Red Bear would not be put off. "We are here to kill the bluecoats. I will not leave here without doing that. I will not face my people and be called a coward."

Storm Arriving moved his mount a step forward and spoke right into Red Bear's face. "Is that what you think I mean? Do you think that I am afraid to fight the bluecoats?"

Red Bear sneered as he spoke. "I do not see you wanting to fight them."

"No. Not now. A good chief picks his battles wisely. I do not want to kill our soldiers."

"Or yourself, it seems."

Storm Arriving put his hand on his knife. "I will not permit you to speak of me so."

"But you would attack me before you will attack the bluecoats?"

Sees Far rode in and pushed the two men apart. "Stop this!" he ordered. "We must be of one mind or we will surely fail." He glared at each of them. Storm Arriving and Red Bear snarled at one another, teeth bared like wild dogs. "Stop. And act like grown men."

The moment subsided and Storm Arriving retreated a step. Red Bear's smile was haughty and cruel.

"As I suspected," he said.

Storm Arriving kicked his whistler forward. He grabbed Red Bear by the shirt and pulled him off his mount. Red Bear fell to the snowy ground and Storm Arriving leapt down after him. He had his knife out of its sheath and pointed up under Red Bear's ribs. With his free hand Storm Arriving pulled open his own shirt, exposing his chest and the rectangular scars he bore there.

"Do you see these, Red Bear? Do you see these scars?"

Sees Far spoke quietly, as if he were dealing with a rogue walker. "Storm Arriving. Do not be a fool."

But Storm Arriving was not listening. He ignored Sees Far and he ignored the other men who were gathering around the scene as well. He saw only

Red Bear, heard only Red Bear. He smelled the scent of Red Bear even through the winter's cold, a scent hot and pungent with sudden panic. Red Bear's eyes, full of stark fear, were fixed on Storm Arriving's face.

"Look, Red Bear. Look at my scars."

Red Bear tipped his head downward but kept his gaze on Storm Arriving's face. Then, at last, he looked down and saw the two shiny patches of skin, each the size of a child's hand.

"Do you know what those are?"

Red Bear swallowed hard but did not speak.

"They are the marks of the skin sacrifice," Storm Arriving said. "From when I hung by my own skin under a full day's sun and then had it sliced off as a sacrifice to the spirits. From when I rode with One Who Flies to the City of White Stone and counted coup on the bluecoats and their war chiefs. Let me see if you carry such scars."

He pulled open Red Bear's shirt. The skin across Red Bear's chest was smooth and unmarked.

"No," Storm Arriving said. "I see no such scars on you." He put his knife back in its sheath and stood up. "Nor will I, I suspect."

Red Bear got up but Sees Far put him back on the ground. "That is enough," the older warrior said. "The bluecoats are too strong in this place. They will be prepared for us, and we will accomplish nothing except the death of good soldiers. Storm Arriving is right; a good chief picks his battles. I choose against this one."

Red Bear got his feet underneath him and shook the snow off his clothes. "Then what are we to do here?" he asked, frustration cracking his voice. "Are we to go home? Without even striking a blow against the *vé'hó'e*?"

Storm Arriving looked out through the failing light. Out beyond the snowfall was the bluecoat fort, but beyond that? What of the land beyond that? "Why are the bluecoats here?"

"What?" Red Bear asked. "I don't know why they are here. They are here because they want our land."

"For whom?" Storm Arriving asked. "For themselves?"

"No," Sees Far said. "For other *vé'hó'e*. Like the ones already out there. Two Tailfeathers and the others from the last patrol, they spoke of the bluecoat forts, but they also spoke of wooden lodges out on the prairie."

Storm Arriving signed his agreement. "One Who Flies once told me that his people are not like us. We are what he calls *nomads*, an always-traveling people, but the *vé'hó'e*—once they stop in a place, they stay there."

Red Bear collected what dignity he had remaining, standing tall and resettling his deerskin shirt across his broad shoulders. "Then we must make sure that they don't stop here. And if they aren't here, then there's no reason for the bluecoats to be here."

"No," Sees Far said. "No reason at all."

Storm Arriving frowned into the snowy darkness. He thought of the *vé'hó'e* that lived out in the distance beyond the gloomy circle of his sight. There were families out there, he knew; fathers and sons, but mothers and daughters, too. Perhaps, just as with his and his wife's family, the *vé'hó'e* lived with their old ones as well, grandfathers and grandmothers, other-mothers and uncles. Out there, living together in their small wooden lodges, raising their animals and growing their crops.

On our land, he reminded himself.

"We should leave this place and bed down until the weather passes. Tomorrow . . . tomorrow we will be very busy."

The sputter of gunfire echoed up the valley and Speaks While Leaving felt her heart skip a beat.

"Bluecoats," she breathed. She left the rabbit she was skinning and ran inside the lodge. "Bluecoats," she said to her family.

Her grandmother frowned. She and Magpie Woman began to douse the fire. Speaks While Leaving's father reached for his quiver and bow.

The sounds of shots were closer now, but along with them Speaks While Leaving heard voices; whoops and howls. Her father heard it, too, and stopped to listen.

"Not bluecoats," One Bear said and smiled at his daughter. "The war party is home."

Speaks While Leaving tried to smile, but her fear was still with her. Though the possibility of danger to all was gone, there still remained the possibility of danger to one—a very important one. She did not like the return of patrols and war parties, for always, riding in ahead of them was Anxiety, and often, riding in behind came Sorrow. So far, Sorrow had never come riding in for her, but someday . . . someday.

"Come," her grandmother said, sensing her worry. She wiped the dust from her hands. "Let us go and meet your husband."

Speaks While Leaving took a deep breath and signed her agreement. The gunshots were close now, and she could hear whistlers around the camp singing to returning friends and mates.

"Whistlers never worry when family comes home," she said.

Healing Rock Woman took her granddaughter by the hand. "Whistlers are always glad to see old friends," she said. "Whistlers are lucky that way."

They left the lodge, stepping out into the powdery snow. The towering tops of dark conifers swayed in the wind and wisps of smoke danced through the branches. Other people were leaving their lodges and heading down toward the clearing at the bottom of the camp. Speaks While Leaving looked back and saw her mother and father step out of the lodge. Her mother was still forbidden by custom to speak to her new son-in-law, and her father, as a Council chief, needed to keep himself apart from the activities of war. They would wait at home and be satisfied with hearing stories around the family fire. They waved and Speaks While Leaving waved back.

The two women—one young, one old—walked down the snow-covered path. They got caught up in the flow of people, and Healing Rock Woman did her best to keep pace. The whoops and shouts of men were joined by the ululation of women. Gunsmoke filled the air. The clearing was thronged when they arrived, and Speaks While Leaving held back, using the vantage of higher ground to find her husband amid the crowd. Healing Rock Woman looked, too, and the two women held on to one another as they stood on tiptoe and craned their necks.

More riders were arriving. Speaks While Leaving saw bound wounds and limping whistlers, but she also saw bloody scalps tied to belts, blankets and Trader's cloth bundled on whistler-back, and many tired smiles. Then, there he was, riding slowly up the forest path.

He rode with the older soldiers, and Speaks While Leaving saw right away the difference between them and the younger men who had ridden in first. The young men were smiling and already trading stories, and showing off their trophies and weapons to family and friends. They laughed. They teased. They corrected one another, making large or small of the particulars of their tales.

The older men were stern-faced, solemn. They held their heads high, but did not smile. Speaks While Leaving looked and noticed that their belts did not carry trophies of scalps or ears, and their whistlers carried no booty, no prizes from vanquished foes. Their eyes did not hold the fire like their younger comrades, and what they did hold was something Speaks While Leaving could not divine, but remained masked and hidden from view.

Storm Arriving searched the crowd. Speaks While Leaving and her grandmother waved and he saw them. The fleeting smile that he showed them touched only his lips. His furrowed brow and the darkness that encompassed his eyes remained.

He rode around the crowd and dismounted before them.

"What is it?" Speaks While Leaving asked immediately.

"What kind of greeting is this?" He chuckled and smiled again, but still the shadow dimmed his features.

"Something is wrong," she said. "I can tell. You can't hide these things from—"

Her grandmother had put a hand on her arm. Healing Rock Woman shuffled forward and touched, too, the arm of Storm Arriving. "My heart is glad to see you," the old woman said to him, and then with a sidelong look at Speaks While Leaving, said, "we are all glad to see you."

"Yes," Speaks While Leaving said, and forced herself to smile. "Of course we are. Are you hungry?"

For a moment the shadow left his face. "Very hungry," he said.

"Good," Healing Rock Woman said. "That is good."

Speaks While Leaving did not think her grandmother was speaking of Storm Arriving's hunger.

At the family camp, Storm Arriving begged off joining the others in her father's lodge.

"I am too tired," he said.

"As you wish," she said, and went to make her apologies to One Bear.

Later, after he had eaten, he went to lie down on the bed.

"I am tired," he said when she asked what was wrong. "Just tired. That is all."

"No," she said calmly, carefully. "You are lying to me."

Her harsh accusation stung and he sat up. She sat by the hearth, legs folded to one side. She looked at him through the heat of the fire. He shimmered and wavered and seemed like a spirit being: handsome, broad of shoulder, his chest and arms scarred by battle and sacrifice, his black hair frosted with the gray of maturity. His dark eyes danced with firelight, but his mouth was a firm line, taut with concealed emotion, and his fingers clenched the fur of the buffalo pelt that covered the bed.

"If you want to sleep," she said, "then sleep. If you do not want to tell me what is wrong, then do not. I cannot tell you what to do." She looked down, escaping the intensity of his gaze. She looked into the fire-pit, at the coals that glowed with auroral light. "But if you lie to me, I will call you a liar."

She heard him take a deep breath and let it out slowly.

"I do not want to tell you what is wrong," he said. He lay down and pulled the covers over him. "I want to sleep."

She left the fire and went to the bed. He lay on his side facing away from the fire. She tucked the blankets in around his feet and pulled them up to cover his shoulder. She brushed a few loose hairs away from his face and leaned over to kiss his cheek.

"I love you," she said.

"Thank you," he said.

She put a few more sticks on the fire and then left to spend the evening with her family.

It was late when she left her parents' lodge. She stepped out into the cold and the moonlight, her moccasins crunching in the new snow. The sky was clear and star-shot. The trees were shadowy giants and the lodges around the valley were children hiding behind skirts that glowed with the yellow light of fading hearthfires. A coyote up on the ridge cried out, singing to the moon. Another joined in from farther away and their songs mingled, echoed, and died. She breathed the night air into her lungs, felt it cold in her nostrils. Somewhere down toward the valley floor, men were singing, probably one of the soldier societies in a late-night feast. She sighed and her breath came out in a cloud.

The fire was low when she stepped inside, the coals glowing dimly through their blankets of ash. Storm Arriving still lay in bed, on his side, facing away from the fire. She fed the fire a few pieces of wood and then took off her moccasins and her leggings. She sat down on the empty side of the bed and listened to her husband's breathing. It was slow and even, but not deep enough for sleep. She reached out to touch his shoulder but halted herself. Instead, she untied her belt and slipped her dress over her head. Then she was under the blankets and up against him. He was cold, and she pressed her body against his back. Her arm stole across his side and over his belly. Word-lessly, he sighed and held her hand close to his chest.

The flames bit into the new wood. She watched the single shadow they made as the firelight made it move and jump on the inner lodgeskins. She felt his breath-ing shorten and hold, as if he wanted to speak but wouldn't. She did not say anything, did not move. She waited. The fire spat once and hissed, then subsided.

"The stories you will hear about this trip," Storm Arriving said quietly, "they will not please you. You will hear of things done that have no honor."

She did not reply, not knowing what to say, afraid that the wrong word would stop him.

"Things were done that should not have been done," he said. She could hear the emotion in his voice, feel it in his breathing. "Families were killed. Wives and children. No prisoners were taken. Nothing was left behind." He paused a moment for control. "We . . . we wiped the prairie clean of them. All of them. All except the bluecoats. The bluecoats—" His voice broke and she could feel the tension grip his body. "They never even left their forts," he said through clenched teeth. "Even when we dragged the bodies up to their gates, they would only fire at us from atop their walls." He took a shuddering breath. "There was no honor on this trip. None."

Words, she now knew, could not help him, and so

she simply held him. Offering neither condemnation nor approval, she held him as his silent weeping tore at her heart.

"No, not there!" Vincent shouted in French, then swore. "I mean, *Nóxa'e. Anoo . . . Tabarnaque!* How do you say that again?"

George chuckled and hefted his own box of explosives. Vincent's struggles with the Cheyenne language had done nothing to improve his demeanor during the nearly two weeks it took them to travel from the Closed Windpipe camp to the winter camp of the Tree People. George stepped up the hillside toward the lonely lodge at the limits of camp, looked inside, and saw the problem. He motioned to the other side of the hearthpit and spoke softly to Gets Up Early.

"Tsêhéóhe, néséne. Énánôtse tsêhéóhe." Over here, my friend. Put it down over here. "And gently, too," he added.

Gets Up Early stepped away from the square crates and put the keg of black powder down on the other side of the lodge floor. Vincent wiped the sheen of sweat that covered his bald forehead in spite of the deep cold. Gets Up Early simply shrugged, but George understood. Never having seen the materials he carried in action, the Indian had little appreciation for what these parcels contained.

The other men brought in their loads and set them down. Then they all trudged back downhill to the creek where George and Vincent had left the wagon. The wagon had barely made it to the winter camp, and would never have made it up the steep sides of the ravine to the storage lodge. One by one they carried the heavy crates and kegs more than a mile uphill from the creekside. After several more trips, the last of the cargo was safely up the hill, far away from the rest of the community.

The small kegs of black powder on one side of the lodge were lashed together. Then the men covered them with an oilcloth tarpaulin and tied that closed as well. The crates of ammunition and the small boxes marked EXPLOSIVES were assembled into a low, stable pile. The coils of corded fuse were stored on top in parfleches, and they covered those with tarpaulins, too. When they were done, there was little room left in the lodge. George closed the doorflap as they exited and tied it closed with a strip of leather.

Vincent shook his head. "I'd feel better if it were all in storage up in a Winnipeg warehouse."

George thanked the men who had helped them and then started walking back toward his own lodge. "We had to get it out here sometime," he said to Vincent. "Better to make one trip than two."

"All right," Vincent said. "Then I'd feel better if *I* was in storage up in a Winnipeg warehouse. At least until spring."

George laughed. "Anytime you want to go," he said. "But that ends our deal. And with the dynamite plus the extra men that Three Trees Together has agreed to let help, well, that's just a whole lot to miss out on."

Vincent scowled. "You are a heartless man," he said.

They walked on down the hillside path and George watched chickadees chase one another from tree to tree, knocking snow to the ground as they flew. Young boys hollered as they slid down the snowy slope on old buffalo hides. Down at the frozen pond, the women and older girls played a sort of football with a deerskin ball and sticks.

"Actually, I'm not," George said. "I'm just happier here is all." He smiled at Vincent's doubtful look. "You may yearn for the city and all the hubbub—"

"The business, you mean!"

"And the stench—"

"The perfume!"

"The crowds—"

"The society!"

"And the loose morals—"

"The loose morals!"

George laughed. "Yes, yes, you relish all those things. But me?" He motioned to the world around him. "Here it is simple. Uncomplicated. Basic. That is what I crave."

Vincent snorted. "This you crave? This?" He shook his head, unable to comprehend. "And surrounded by the most virtuous women in the world? It's just as well that it is cold enough to freeze a man's balls. No, you are a heartless man," he said. "Heartless."

"And you are nothing but a base scalawag!"

"Mais oui!"

George put an arm around the trader's shoulder. "Come. Perhaps if we beg, we can get my virtuous young neighbor to make us some skillet bread."

"Ahh," Vincent said with real appreciation. "Now, my friend, perhaps there is some hope for you after all."

CHAPTER 8

Spring, A.D. 1888
Washington
District of Columbia

The wind howled around the White House and whistled through the gaps beneath the library's French
doors. Custer stopped pacing and turned to toast his
backside by the fire. Matherly sat in a deep leather
chair and sipped his tea. A gust of wind pushed a puff
of smoke back down the chimney and into the room.
The president took a step away but stayed near
enough to enjoy the warmth.

"Read that back," he said.

Samuel put down his pen and picked up the piece
of paper that was now covered not only with even,
typewritten lines, but also clumps of tiny scribbles con-
nected by looping lines and arrows. The aide held the
paper up to catch more of the light from the window.

" 'And provided, further,' " he read, " 'that in case
of the death of both father and mother, leaving an
infant child, or children, under twenty-one years of
age, the right and fee shall inure to the benefit of said
infant child or children; and the executor, administra-
tor, or guardian may, at any time within two years
after the death of the surviving parent, and in accor-
dance with the laws of the State or Territory in which
such children for the time being have their domicile,
sell said land for the benefit of said infants, but for
no other purpose.' "

Custer let the words roll around but shook his head. "I don't see the difference one way or the other."

Matherly put down his teacup and leaned forward. "The way it reads now, Mr. President, is much more specific as to the way in which the land can be passed on. I believe it is crucial, especially after the many deaths of this past winter, that we provide for the perpetuation of those homestead grants in the control of widows and heirs."

Custer blinked at the senator. "Sakes alive but you talk like a lawyer. I don't understand you any better than I do the bill." He left the fire and walked toward the window.

"Mr. President," Matherly began again. "The difference between the two versions—"

Custer held up a hand. "Samuel?" he said as he looked outside. "What do you think?"

There was a pause as his aide considered his response. "The new version is less ambiguous, sir."

"Good. Keep it, then."

The daylight from outside was muted but full like pale velvet. The blizzard that had struck the whole northeastern seaboard had abated overnight. Like an invading horde it had swept in, paralyzed the populace, and moved onward. From the library's mullioned windows Custer looked out across the south lawn and the Ellipse. The winds still blew, wailing like some monstrous child and piling last night's snow up into twenty-foot drifts. The first floor of the White House was entirely snowbound and out beyond the Ellipse, the immense white spire of Washington's monument was nearly lost in the blowing snow.

Custer sighed silently as he regarded the tall monument. To be honored like that, he thought to himself. To be so loved. To be nearly deified, like a Caesar.

The huge obelisk pointed up to heaven. Custer's next breath was less wistful, held more remorse.

How in Hell can a man compete with that?

"Sir?"

"Hmm?" Custer turned. By the expectant looks on

the faces of the two other men, he realized that he
had missed some of the conversation. "My apologies,
gentlemen. My mind was . . . elsewhere. What was it
you were saying?"

Samuel cleared his throat. "The senator suggested
some modifications to limit the homestead grants to
lands in the territories only."

"It's just that recent history has shown us how seriously some states take their sovereignty," Matherly
said. "Since it is our intention to encourage settlement
and cultivation in the Frontier, I suggest we include
such a limit explicitly in the bill. That will defuse any
argument along those lines."

Custer smirked. "And keep your own state from
being overrun by squatters."

Matherly stammered but had the good grace not to
look affronted.

"Go ahead," Custer said. "Add it. Regardless your
motives, I think you're right. We'll need all the allies
we can get on this one."

"Yes," Matherly said, picking up his tea again. "The
debate has already started."

"Up on the Hill?"

"No. But in the lobbies and dining establishments
around town, which is perhaps where the more important conversations take place."

"What is your feeling on it?" Custer asked.

Matherly gave a slight grimace. "Not good," he said.
"Fortunately, though, the opposition has devolved
into two camps. One side opposes you completely just
on basic principal."

"Speaker Carlisle," Samuel muttered.

"Just so," the senator agreed.

"And the other camp?" Custer asked.

"The other, and smaller camp believes that we are
creating this bill simply to fulfill a political promise;
that it will ultimately fail, politically and practically;
and that the best strategy is to simply go along and
let it do so, taking you down with it."

"Duchesnes," Custer said, naming the new Senate majority leader.

"Correct, as well."

"Why does the distinguished gentleman from New York think the bill will fail?"

Matherly became uneasy. "There were . . . quite a few settlers who died this winter."

"It's a frontier," Custer said, walking back toward the fire. "It's dangerous out there."

"But your General Herron was unable to protect them."

"They were squatters. He didn't even know they were there."

"Well, if you can't protect even a few squatters, how can you possibly protect half a million homesteaders"—Matherly stopped, having forgotten to whom he spoke—"or so goes their argument, Mr. President."

A breathlessness tightened beneath Custer's ribs, expanding like some yawning pit until he felt as though it would consume him. "Do you mean to tell me," he managed to say, "that there are members of Congress who believe that I would put half a *million* citizens in harm's way just to achieve a political goal?"

"Mr. President," Samuel said quietly. "You know there are those who do not hold you in high regard."

"High regard?" Custer spat a laugh. "This isn't a simple lack of regard. To believe this . . . you'd have to think me a monster." He turned his back on the two men to hide the rage he knew he could not keep from his face. The anger that built within him was a solid thing, a tumor of terrible emotion. He walked to the French doors that led out onto the balcony, and pushed the door open against the wind and snow.

The wind whipped his collar-length hair and he squinted as it lashed around his eyes. He made his way to the rail, pushing through the foot of snow that had accumulated on the balcony overnight. The railing was cold beneath his hands. He gripped it, feeling the iciness seep into his fingers, feeling the pain invade his palms.

How could they? he asked the world silently. How could they possibly?

The pain in his hands faded as numbness took hold. The cold crept in past his clothes, chilling his skin, his muscles, his bones. With the silence of the snow-shrouded city before him, the only sound he heard was the chattering of his own teeth, and the words of damnation that filled his head.

He turned and stormed back into the library.

"Samuel," he said. "Take a message."

Herron undid the button in the middle of his frock coat, put his hand into the inner pocket, and retrieved Custer's telegraphed message. He shook it to unfold it and handed it to the engineer. Shafer stepped closer to the lamp and read it while Herron ground his teeth.

The rain beat down on the roof of the small office. Two tin buckets, one near the door and one by the window behind Herron's desk, caught the water that leaked in, each tiny splash magnified into a harsh, metallic *plang*.

Shafer handed back the piece of paper.

"Well?" Herron asked.

"He seems rather insistent," the colonel offered.

"That's hardly the way I would characterize it."

"How would you put it, sir?"

"He's good and God-damned mad is how I'd put it. He's furious. I'm surprised he didn't order my ass onto the next eastbound train so he could bust my balls in person, is how I'd put it, Colonel." He folded the message, put it back in his coat pocket, and continued in a calmer tone. "But he did not say those things, and so here I am. And here, also, are you. You've read the president's request. As far as the bridge is concerned, will you be able to accommodate him?"

Shafer shrugged. "Sir, the late winter has slowed our schedule and the blizzard that hit back east, well, sir, it's delayed some critical shipments."

"Is that a 'no'?"

"I'm sorry, sir. We just need more time."

Herron pressed his lips into a thin line and sighed. "Very well," he said. "That's what I needed to know. Thank you, Colonel. You are relieved."

Shafer saluted and turned to go. "Excuse me, sir," he said, hand on the doorknob. "Did you say dismissed?"

Herron sat down at his desk and pulled out a sheet of paper and a pen. "Hmm? Dismissed? No. I said you are relieved."

"Relieved. Sir . . . but . . . the bridge . . ."

"The bridge," Herron said as he wrote, "will continue on without you. It will be completed without you." He dipped his pen again and wrote some more. The nib met the paper with the sound of rat scratchings. "You, Colonel Shafer, are hereby reassigned. McCormack will take over your duties."

"McCormack? Sir, McCormack is a dullard and a ditch-digger. You can't turn a project of this magnitude over to him."

"I can, and I will. In fact"—he put his signature at the bottom of the page—"I just have. And if you, Colonel, don't rein in the attitude, you're going to find yourself reassigned to duties far beneath your abilities. As it is, I know they'll be far beneath your opinion of yourself."

Herron could see his point finally strike home. Shafer slowly pulled himself up to attention, facing Herron like a condemned man before a firing squad. Herron put aside the first paper addressed to McCormack, took out another sheet, and began a new set of orders. The colonel stood silently before him, awaiting the words that would spell out his future. Herron glanced up and saw Shafer leaning in, trying to make out the upside-down letters in the dim lamplight. Herron finished the orders, redipped his pen, and moved to sign them.

"What'll it be, Shafer? Levees in Mississippi? Or working here to fulfill the request of your commander-in-chief?" The tip of the pen hovered over the blankness at the bottom of the page. The colonel's face was rigid: jaw tight, nostrils flared, brows beetled low, his eyes hidden by the reflection of lamplight in his spectacles.

"Last chance," Herron said. No response. He shrugged and looked down to sign.

"No. Wait . . ."

The general looked up again.

"I'll stay."

"I don't need you to do me any favors—"

"I mean," Shafer interrupted. "I mean, I'd like to stay. Sir."

"You'll finish the bridge?" Herron asked.

"Yes, sir."

"In six weeks' time?"

"Sir, six weeks? McCormack couldn't do it that fast."

"Shafer, if I let you stay, it's because you can do something that McCormack cannot."

"Yes, sir."

"Can you do it in six weeks?"

Shafer struggled with it, then gave in. "Yes, sir. In six weeks. Trains will be rolling across that bridge by the time the president arrives."

Herron studied his colonel. Shafer had not lost the passion of his youth nor the idealism. Yet, despite his experiences, neither had the younger man acquired a sense of proportion. For an engineer, Herron found him impossibly impractical.

"Shafer, you are a zealot, and a zealot is the most dangerous kind of man there is." He leaned his elbows on the desktop and looked up at the colonel's lamplit eyes. "You've placed your faith in something beyond this world. You believe in ideals but not in reality. You believe in perfection but not in fallibility. Something tells me that if I send you down into Mississippi, you won't learn anything. You'll just bitch and moan and make yourself into a martyr for your own cause."

He picked up the two sets of orders. "No," he said, ripping them in half. "I think you'll learn more here in this next month than you would if I sent you to the bayous for a year."

A smile curved Shafer's lips but he remained at attention. Herron stood and pointed at him, the torn orders crumpled in his fist.

"But if you fail, Colonel, I swear by God Almighty that you will spend an eternity engineering nothing more than latrines. Do I make myself clear?"

"Absolutely, sir."

"Dismissed."

He returned Shafer's salute and waited until the colonel left. Then he sat, leaned back, and put his feet up on the desk. The crumpled orders were still in his hand.

Were you bluffing? he asked himself. Would you really have put that mediocre dunderhead in charge of this thing?

He reached into his pocket and unfolded the message he'd received only an hour before. The operator's bold letters only added emphasis to Custer's words—an emphasis that the words did not require.

YOUR FAILURE . . . NO EXCUSES . . . YOUR DUTY . . .

Strong words—made more terse by the medium—pounced upon him from the page. He folded it up and took it as if to tear it up as well, but stopped himself. Instead, he put it back in his coat pocket and, patting it to feel it there, buttoned his coat again.

A zealot, he reminded himself, learns most through humility.

In the days that followed, Herron watched as Shafer shook the crews from their hibernation. The work that had slowed and eventually stopped with the onset of winter now began anew, revitalized by the colonel's passion. Shafer did not renew his objections to the use of substandard iron. Nor, to his credit, did he complain of anything: not the weather, the hours, the conditions, or even the food.

When the rain slowed the progress of the welding teams, he simply made them work double shifts. When the mud became too deep for the drays to work at dockside, he conscripted a dozen of the crop-haired Indians who lived upstream. They came in with their turtlelike hardbacks and Herron watched in amazement as the near-naked savages stood knee-deep in muck—the rain and thunder pounding down upon their heads—and with no more than a touch or a short whistle they maneuvered the ox-sized beasts into precise formations.

The construction began to pick up pace. The trestled sections had been completed for some time, as had much of the arch. The trestles stretched from concrete footings on each riverbank out to huge pylons that stood a quarter of the way out from either side of the Missouri. Crisscrossed iron beams made the X's and V's that formed the long sides and top, and their decks—completed before the rains of autumn—had been laid with railroad tracks and were now used to cart out supplies and men for the main effort now under way.

And it was that main effort that had frustrated Herron—and fascinated him—during the long, dark months of the winter.

Between the two tall stone-and-concrete pylons and across a full half of the river's breadth was an intricate and disorderly collection of barges, pilings, piers, cranes, and scaffolding; a tortuous skeleton of metal, wood, stone, ropes, and cable.

The barges at the base of each pylon set pilings into the soft river mud, and on those pilings piers were built. The piers supported scaffolds built of timbers and logs, clumsy constructions that rose up higher than the pylons and slowly reached out toward the opposite side. Atop each pylon was a crane of wood, metal, and thick, twisted cable. The buttressing support of the barges and piers worked in tandem with the lifting power of the cranes to extend the scaffolding outward.

The scaffold became thinner and narrower as it neared the center, and it was on this fragile array that the first pieces of iron were laid.

Through the past months of cold and ice, Herron had looked out his window to see the awkward, ungainly structure stand idle and unworked as sleet fell and the occasional snow blanketed the spars and boat decks. Now, with the warming rains and Shafer's new-found resolve, the uncompleted arch was like a thing come alive.

Every morning, his fire-blackened enamelware cup filled with steaming coffee, Herron stepped outside what the men mordantly called The Devil's Den: the small, leaky-roofed building that held the administrative and command offices, including Herron's own. With his coffee cooling in the harsh air of the prairie morning, he looked out at the tremendous structure that leaned out over the water, silhouetted by the awakening sky.

Lamps glowed in the nascent dawn, hanging like a hundred yellow eyes along the back of a myth. The blowtorch stars heated rivets to a volcanic glow, and the rivets shed bright meteors as they were pounded into place, joining metal to metal, beam to beam, section to section. The cranes atop the pylons wove webs of cable and rope like colossal spiders hunting for the men who worked at their feet.

Along the river's edge, men drove teams of horses, mules, and hardbacks. They oared boats through the midnight waters and manned the great barges and rafts out beyond the pylons. They operated the huffing steam-powered winches that pulled loaded trams up the trestles' inclines. They tended the fires that burned in the bellies of pistoning machines that belched black smoke and white vapor with each gasping breath.

Men climbed on the bones of the beast itself, walking the beams and spars that hung over the water. They clambered along the span in a hundred places, hung from ropes, leapt from girder to girder. They hammered, sawed, worked bellows and pumps. They cut wood and metal. They pounded and hefted and grunted and shouted and cursed and laughed and sang as they all, a thousand and more, worked and sweated together: two full regiments, a hundred teamsters and drivers, a score of cooks, ten smiths, four surgeons, and one very overwrought colonel.

And the bridge grew.

Ironwork sprouted upward along the scaffolds like rime. Trestles formed and interwove their straight lines into twin curves of dark filigree, two arcs canted in toward one another until, at the apex, they became one elegant structure that crossed the wide Missouri in a single, graceful step.

The arch was complete, and the scaffolding was dismantled. The river foamed as timbers and boards plunged down from a hundred feet above, then only eighty, then just forty. The Missouri carried it all away, a scrap at a time, until the only thing left was the arch, as beautiful and dark as a lady's eyebrow.

Herron sipped his coffee, tasted its bitterness, its bite, and watched men swarm the arch. First, the welders with their tiny suns, dripping fire onto the water below. Then the riggers, dragging miles of cable behind them, lacing it into the pulleys like ants threading a series of gigantic needles.

The riveters returned, and more welders, and hundreds of men surrounding small, steam-driven cranes. With a cacophony that made the air shudder, they assembled the planks of the bridge deck, attached it to the cables, and moved forward, using it as a platform from which to assemble the next plank.

They met in the middle and then retraced their steps to solidify and strengthen the deck. In their wake came the carpenters, and the railmen, and more. And more.

Herron drained the last cold swallow from his cup as the locomotive hissed and sighed its way up the incline for the first weight tests. Shafer was headed his way, slowly, the grime of days and the debility of sleepless weeks on his face. He stopped in front of his general and hooked a thumb over his shoulder toward the bridge.

"Done, with time to spare, sir."

"Three days," Herron said.

"Yes, sir. Three days." There was no tone of pride in the colonel's voice. Only weariness; weariness, and something else.

"How important was it?" Herron asked. "The iron, I mean. The quality of the iron."

Shafer sniffed the fragrant air of a full spring morning and turned to view his creation.

"If she makes it through the first subzero winter, she'll last for a while. Beyond that, I'd say she's good for ten years. Maybe twenty, eh?"

"Not a thousand?"

Shafer expelled a breath of bitter humor. "No, sir. Not a thousand. Not this gal."

Herron shifted his feet, feeling uncomfortable for no reason he could specify. "Well, even so," he said as he regarded the reflection of the rising sun off the arc of metal. "Even so, well done, Colonel."

The colonel did not turn and Herron could tell by the tightness in the other man's shoulders that there were some strong emotions flowing through his subordinate. "Thank you, sir," the younger man said. "I hope the president makes good use of it."

The plume of smoke drove upward from beyond the rise of land. It was a long black trail that shoved its way up into the air above the green prairie. Storm Arriving could hear the machine, even from this distance. He and his small patrol rode up to the top of the rise.

The huge iron hardback wheezed like an old bull as it rolled down the twin rails that scarred the land. It left a smudge in the sky and a stink on the wind. It pulled several gaudily painted cars behind it. Some of the cars had openings in their sides, and out of two of those Storm Arriving saw the puffs of gunsmoke bloom. The muffled reports came a breath later, but the train was too far away for the *vé'hó'e* inside to do them any harm.

The patrol watched in silence as the train continued onward. Far away, miles away down the dark line of the train's metal road, lay a larger darkness like the shadow of a single, unseen cloud on the land. To one side of the metal road they could see the dark walls of the bluecoat fort, and on the other side of the road were the dwellings of other *vé'hó'e* who had come out into the People's land.

As Storm Arriving scanned the landscape, he saw more of the square *vé'hó'e* lodges scattered through the prairie. Around each lodge the earth was no longer green with spring growth. Blackness surrounded the *vé'hó'e*, for the first thing they all did was to plow up the ancient grass and tear up the earth. Nearly everywhere Storm Arriving looked he saw their buildings, their marks.

"We cannot bring the People here any longer," he said. Others around him agreed.

"Nowhere south of the Sudden River," Black Willow said. "It is no longer safe here."

"Not anymore," Storm Arriving said. "This is now a place of war."

"What shall we do?" asked Issues Forth, the youngest Kit Fox in the patrol.

There is nothing we can do, Storm Arriving wanted to say, but he refused to utter words of such frustration. He looked back at the others in his small patrol. "We are not a war party," he said. "We cannot beat the bluecoats with sixteen men, and no one expects us to do this." He turned once more to face the prairie, the metal road, and the dark, sprawling stains that the *vé'hó'e* put on the earth. "We shall do what Three Trees Together sent us here to do. Look, listen, and return with news."

His soldiers grumbled at this. They wanted action,

and blood. They wanted to protect their lands and drive off the invaders. Storm Arriving understood them well.

"And once we have seen all there is to see and heard all that we can hear, we will draw lots. Six will fulfill our mission. They will return with our news. Ten will stay."

There was general acceptance of this plan, but Storm Arriving wanted to be sure. "Does every man agree?" he asked them.

"Yes," they all said. All except Issues Forth.

"What will the ten who stay do?" he asked.

"You are new to the path of war," Storm Arriving said to the young soldier. "And you do not yet think like a soldier. The ten stay behind to do what other patrols are surely doing to the south and the east." He pointed to the *vé'hó'e*. "Burning homes, killing animals, drawing the bluecoats out of their fort and slaying them on open ground."

He looked directly at the young Kit Fox, a look of challenge. "It is a shame that we have been reduced to raiders in our own country, but we will stay. We will stay and we will make it as dangerous here for their families as they have made it for ours."

Issues Forth met his gaze, and when Storm Arriving raised an eyebrow, the young man smiled.

"Come," Storm Arriving said to them all. "We will rest at Killdeer Creek and wait for nightfall. Then we shall see what there is to see."

"No," Vincent said. "The cap has to be tighter." He reached over and with thumb and forefinger rocked the blasting cap off its seat at the end of the stick of wood carved to the shape and size of a dynamite stick. "If it's not on tight, the primer will blow the cap off the dynamite. The cap goes bang, but not the stick. Try again."

George and the old trader sat outside on a lonely hillside, far from the work site and even farther from the lodge where they stored the explosives and fuse. On the ground between them were several knives, pliers, and other tools, scattered wood shavings, and a length of Bickford miner's fuse.

The afternoon was warm and pleasant with a gentle wind from the west—the birthplace of all weather according to the Cheyenne—and George would have liked nothing better than to lie back on the spongy grass and bask in the gentle sunlight while watching the clouds tumble across the sky.

But he could not. Time was limited, and George wanted to make sure they got the gold they needed by the end of the Moon When the Whistlers Get Fat. If they could do that, he and Vincent could travel back to Winnipeg with the gold, pay off McTavish, and return with their weapons and supplies by the end of summer. With that end in mind, he tried again with the blasting cap.

The copper-clad cap slipped easily over the end of the carved stick of wood. George handled it gingerly, for the cap itself could deliver a hurtful explosion. While half of the cap was just an empty sleeve that slid over the main charge, inside that sleeve was the primer—fulminate of mercury—that would detonate the explosion. And while Vincent had said that they could play catch with a stick of dynamite, he had repeatedly pointed out that these blasting caps were not nearly as forgiving.

George picked up the wide pliers and, keeping the entire assembly as far away from himself as possible, gripped the lower portion of the cap's sleeve.

"Easy, now," Vincent coached him. "Remember that the wood is harder than the dynamite stick, so it will give you more resistance. It won't take half the pressure to crimp a cap onto the real thing. There you go. *Bon.* Now the fuse."

George put the capped stick down on the soft grass while Vincent picked up the coil of cord.

"This," Vincent said, "is your common, everyday

miner's fuse." He took the end of the coil and with a
knife cut off a yard-long piece. He handed it to
George.

It was like a stiff but still flexible rope, nearly a
quarter of an inch thick. He inspected the end and
saw a dark internal core wrapped by a twisted fabric
sheath. He picked at the core with his thumbnail and
chipped off a piece.

"It's made from a paste of black powder," Vincent
said. "This type will burn one foot each minute. There
are other types—faster, slower—but they're all basi-
cally the same." He slapped George on the arm with
the coil of fuse. "Important," he said. "Always test a
length of fuse so you can see how fast it burns. You
must test your fuse, so you know for sure what it is.
Not knowing can kill you . . . or someone else."

George looked at the length of fuse in his hand with
a bit more respect. "I thought fuse was just . . . fuse."

Vincent smiled. "Generally, yes. Usually, yes. But
don't bet your life on it."

"Have you tested this?" George asked.

Vincent made a face of indignation. *"Mais oui,"* he
said and smirked. "Now, put the fuse in the cap."

George took up the stick again. In the end of the
blasting cap's copper jacket was a hole. He put the
cut end of the fuse into the hole. It was a tight fit but
the fuse cord was stiff enough for him to push it—
gently—inward.

"Bon," Vincent said. "Now you just light it and back
away." He rattled a box of matchsticks. "Ready?"

George grinned. He took the matches and the stick
and walked to a spot several yards away. He set the
stick down and knelt, his back to the wind. Normally,
matches would have been a precious commodity out
here on the prairie, but Vincent had brought several
large boxes' worth back from Winnipeg. George took
out one match, slid the box closed, and scraped the
stick across the surface of a nearby stone. The match
lit and he brought it to the fuse. Nothing happened

as the small flame encircled the end of the fuse. Flame and black powder shared the same space for a moment, and George watched the jute fibers begin to darken and curl. Then the powder came alive with smoke and hissing sparks. He leapt back in surprise, his heart pounding in his chest.

"Back away," Vincent said. George complied.

Steadily, the spitting fire crept along the length of fuse. George, now back at Vincent's side, watched it with fascination. He heard everything around him— the friendly chatter as the crew worked the slope of the mining site, the thud and check of pick and shovel, the songs of birds, the whispering wind—but his eyes were unable to look away as the sputtering flame slowly consumed the fuse. He was entranced by the power it represented. His life, his career, all had been put to the exercise of control over nature. But *this* . . . this was the essence of that nature.

This was raw power.

The fuse shortened. The fire approached the cap. George prepared himself. The flame touched the cap, disappeared.

Silence.

Bang!

The stick jumped in the air. Men looked up from their work. The stick tumbled end over end. The remnants of the copper cap fell to the ground with a timid clink, followed by the thud of the stick.

"That's it?" George asked. "That's all it does?"

The old man looked up at him, quizzical. "What did you expect?"

"I expected—I don't know—an explosion. Something bigger, anyway. Not just a Fourth of July noisemaker."

Vincent got up and retrieved the stick they had used. The end of the green wood was frayed like a hank of old rope. "Noisemaker?" he asked calmly. Then he walked over to the small wooden box that held the other blasting caps. He took one of the caps.

"Noisemaker?" With a smooth underhand motion he lofted the cap up and away. It landed ten yards away, exploding with a sharp report that spat dirt back to where George stood. He held up a hand to ward off the debris.

"Noisemaker?" Vincent asked again, and then chuckled. "Show some respect." He closed up the box and picked up the coil of fuse. "Anyway, you'll feel differently tomorrow after we clamp one onto the end of a real stick of dynamite. Believe me."

The next morning the crew stood at the mining site, waiting expectantly. During the past few weeks they had followed a promising vein of gold down deep into the ground as it plunged under the shelf of rock that formed the backbone of the ridge. To follow it farther, they needed to break up that rock—a solid mass of a hundred tons at least—and move it all aside.

The medicine men had not been pleased at the prospect. The war chiefs, however, had been convinced by the obvious, albeit limited success achieved by patrols using the small number of rifles George and Vincent had brought back from Canada. They wanted more, and to get more they all agreed that more gold was needed.

Thus, as the sun rose and light flowed out across the plain and up onto the ridge like a tide, George and Vincent waited with the others and watched as Stands Tall in Timber presided over the rituals that would allow the excavation to continue.

Four men from the mining crew had volunteered for the honor of participating. They sat facing the rising sun, in a semicircle around a whistler-hide drum. Behind them, Stands Tall in Timber stood near a small fire. The holy man, keeper of the Sacred Arrows, sang in wailing tones of the spirits, of honor, and of sacrifice. He tossed dried sprigs into the fire and George smelled the sharp bite of juniper, the earthy caress of sage. The song was sung once to each corner of the world, once to the earth, and one final time to the sky. The men beat the drum slowly, a deep and constant pulse, and the sacred herbs played sensuous counterpoint.

The drumbeat stopped and Stands Tall in Timber drew from within his shirt a bundle of red cloth. He unrolled the bundle, producing four pieces of roughly woven cotton and a small, thin-bladed knife.

George, his emotions an admixture of revulsion and awe, watched as the Cheyenne holy man went to the first of the four volunteers. With sure, practiced movements, he took the man's left forearm, touched the knife to the skin, and slid the blade underneath. The man grimaced but did not cry out, his every muscle, every tendon, tautened as he fought his own body's desire to protect itself. The knife cut through the skin, leaving a rectangular flap the length of a finger. Stands Tall in Timber reversed the blade, severed the flap of skin, and handed the man a piece of cloth with which to bind the wound.

"Tabarnaque," Vincent swore as Stands Tall in Timber took the piece of skin, laid it by the fire, and moved on to repeat the rite on the second man.

George looked over. The old trader's skin was ashen, his eyes wide, his mouth slightly agape, his upper lip curled in disgust. George had known of this sort of ritual; Storm Arriving had undergone a similar sacrifice and bore the scars on his chest with pride. Having lived with the People for two years, George now felt he almost understood this rite that Vincent only saw as the acme of primitive behavior.

But it was not savagery. George had learned that much. It was simply the point at which the traditions of the People were furthest removed from the world of the *vé'hó'e*, the point of greatest disparity.

"It's inhuman," Vincent whispered.

"No," George said as the last man's offering was placed by the fire. "It's nearly godlike."

Vincent turned with a start. "Are you mad?" he asked.

"No," George said. "And neither are they. This re-stores the balance."

"What balance?"

"The balance we will upset when we blow the earth apart."

"Pff. Nonsense. Heathen nonsense. How can you condone this? It's brutal."

George smiled a little. "It is their way."

Stands Tall in Timber began to sing again, a slow, low-toned prayer of thanks. George felt the hair on his neck prickle. There is a power here, he said to himself. Though perhaps only in my mind.

The song ended and the four volunteers, their fore-arms wrapped in red cloth, stood. Stands Tall in Tim-ber spoke quietly to each of them, and then walked down the slope toward George.

"It is done," the holy man said. "The sacred persons who guard the world have been properly honored. You may proceed."

"Thank you, Stands Tall in Timber. I know you were against this. I am grateful for your help."

The holy man blinked his eyes slowly, accepting George's thanks. "The world, I think, is changing. We all must try to change with it." He walked over to his whistler, mounted, and bid it rise. "One Who Flies," he said. "Use well the gifts given here today."

"I will do my best," George said.

Stands Tall in Timber set his whistler in motion and headed north. George watched him ride away, part of him wishing he could ride along, back to join up with the People who were gathering up along the Milk River.

Vincent slapped George on the back, jolting him out of his reverie. "Ready, then? Done with all the mumbo-jumbo?"

George bit back a sharp response. "Yes," he said. "Done."

"Good. Let's get busy, then."

The trench had already been prepared and the holes

for the charges dug. George directed everyone back to the campsite, a quarter mile away. Only Vincent, Gets Up Early, Standing Motionless, and George himself remained within the blast zone.

The four worked slowly, deliberately. Four charges were capped and given fuses. George and Vincent set charges in the holes, each one twenty feet from its neighbor. The fuses were trimmed so that the explosions would start at one end of the line and proceed down to the end. Lit simultaneously, the four men would have six minutes to clear the area.

Vincent handed out the matches, three to a man, and they all went to their designated hole. Vincent went to the near end while George took the farthest hole. He looked back toward the camp and saw the entire crew standing patiently, expectantly at the boundary Vincent had marked, waiting for the release of what George had only been able to describe as "the spirit of thunder."

"Let's go," Vincent yelled from the end of the line. George returned his attention to his tasks.

"Ready?" he called out in Cheyenne.

"Ready," Gets Up Early said.

"I am ready," said Standing Motionless.

"Vincent? Are you ready?" George shouted in French.

"Yes, yes, ready," Vincent replied.

"Fire the fuses!"

He struck his matches, three at once, and held the flame to the fuse. A second passed, a heartbeat, a breath, and the fuse sparked into fiery life. The hole filled with the acrid smell of gunsmoke and burning jute. George scrambled up out of the trench. The others were doing likewise.

"Go!"

They all ran. Vincent was slowest and George and Stands Motionless caught up to him quickly. They took the old trader by the arms and sped him along toward the camp. George was breathless when they reached the rest of the crew, but not from exertion. They all stopped and turned to watch.

The ridge was a finger of land that jutted southward out from the foothills. At its end, the lone tamarack tree stood above the exposed stone that they now knew was the tip of a long seam of granite and quartz. The eastern side of the ridge was scarred by their digging. Long trenches wandered the slopes of it, delineating the limits of the ridge's stony skeleton. It was quiet, peaceful, and completely at odds with the hammering of George's heart and the violence about to be unleashed.

Time ticked past.

"What's wrong?" George asked.

"Nothing," Vincent said.

"Did they fail? Did we do something wrong?"

"With all of them? Don't be ridiculous. They'll go." He took out the pocket watch he had brought back from Winnipeg. "Any moment now."

George felt it before he heard it, felt it in his feet. The earth rumbled. The front of the line up on the ridge seemed to sink down and then it leapt up into the air with a roar that sent every man to his knees in reflex. The second explosion punched up out of the earth, a titan awakened. Then the third. Men were shouting, crying out in surprise. The sound engulfed them. The fourth charge exploded. The air was filled with dust. Bits of gravel pattered down upon them with the sound of a fresh spring rain. The earth trembled, then quieted. The dust began to settle and drift on the wind.

As the air cleared they saw what they had done.

The upper flank of the ridge had been ripped open, lifted up, and dumped down onto the lower slope. Slowly, George and the others began to walk toward the site. As they came close, George could see exposed stone, tons of shattered rock, and everywhere, it seemed, the glint of gold.

"Good God," he said, reverting to English. He

looked back at Vincent. The old trader was beaming with pride.

"Not bad, eh?"

George grinned. "Not bad at all," he said. "This will keep us busy till summer."

Vincent laughed. "Let's get to work, then, eh?"

CHAPTER 9

Summer, A.D. 1888
Washington
District of Columbia

"**G**rover Cleveland?"

"*Autie.* Keep your voice down." Jacob closed the door to the smoking room where the men had gathered after dinner for brandy and cigars. Custer, as was his habit, eschewed both, but right now he felt a strong desire for a drink.

"Hellfire," he said as he sat down in an overstuffed chair. "There goes our hold on New York." Jacob eased himself down at one end of the leather davenport while Custer's other guest, his brother Nevin, took the other end.

"It's not as bad as all that," Jacob said. "There's also Fisk from the Prohibition Party and Streeter from Union and Labor. They're sure to take some votes away from Cleveland."

"And from me as well," Custer said.

"Yes, but they'll take more away from a Democratic governor than from a Republican president. Especially Streeter."

"Damnation," Custer muttered. "When did he announce his candidacy?"

Nevin reached forward and chose a cigar from the humidor. He was Custer's junior by only a few years, and had the same good looks as his presidential brother: wavy blond hair, a piercing blue gaze, and a strong aquiline nose. When he lit the cigar, the matchlight reflected in his deep-set eyes.

"The governor announced within hours of your vice president breaking his own bit of news," Nevin said. "I heard it at the station."

"Hell and damnation," Custer swore. "They figure that without Hayes's strength on the ticket I'll be an easy mark in November. Damn Hayes, anyway."

"Autie," Jacob said in a tone meant to placate. "He always said he only wanted to serve for one term."

"You say that like people believed him. I certainly didn't. Did you?"

"Well, not really."

"Nevin?"

"No one believed the old coot," Nevin said.

Custer slapped the arm of the chair. "Aw, Hell. Let the old man go. Let him go back to lawyering in Nowhere, Indiana—"

"That's Nowhere, Ohio," Nevin corrected.

"Fine. Ohio. It doesn't matter. He's off the ticket. But what are my other choices?"

Jacob spoke around his snifter of brandy. "The leadership is fairly well set on Harrison. I have another preference, though."

"Why not Harrison?" Custer asked. "He may be ineffectual, but who could be better than the grandson of a former president?"

"Morton," Jacob said with a sly smile.

"L. P. Morton?" Nevin said. "The banker?"

"The *New York* banker," Jacob said. "He'll help deliver against Grover C."

"But he's ancient," Nevin said with a laugh. "He's older than Harrison."

"But he has money. And power," Jacob insisted.

Custer sighed and looked up at the ceiling. "These are my choices?" he asked the universe. "Thank God I didn't announce my own candidacy yet."

"Why?" Jacob asked, his eyes wide with shock. "You're not thinking . . . Autie, you *are* going to run for a second term, aren't you?"

Custer sneered.

Nevin put down his cigar and went to his brother's side. He squatted down and put his hand on Custer's shoulder.

"Don't tell me that you're not going to run," he said. "Not just because you're not sure of a win."

Custer shrugged off his brother's well-intentioned hand. "Do you know what this job costs? Do you have any idea?" He stood and paced the length of the square room. "It's not all parades and ribbon-cutting, you know."

Jacob tried to appease him. "We know, Autie."

"Do you, Jacob? Do you? Everything I want to do is a battle. Even when my own party was in control of the House *and* the Senate, it was a battle. And the press!" He threw his hands into the air. "Every item of our lives is grist for their mill. Libbie . . . Libbie." His breath caught with an anguish too long held within.

"Autie," his brother said.

"Libbie. The bastards won't even let her grieve." The pain broke through in a single, harsh-edged sob. "Our son," he managed to say. "We can't even grieve."

Nevin walked up to him, embraced him. Custer got his emotions under control and pushed Nevin gently away. He nodded, saying, "I'm fine. I'm fine."

Silence ruled the room as the three men—two brothers in blood, two brothers in service—let the moment of Custer's outburst fade.

Nevin sat and relit his cigar. Jacob freshened his brandy.

Custer returned to his chair; he sat, hooking a leg over one of the arms. He frowned, contemplating his future.

Beyond the presidency, what was there for him? He

was not a lawyer like Lincoln or Hayes. He wasn't a political boss like Arthur. He was a soldier; like Grant and Sherman, he was a soldier.

And where were *they,* now? Dead. Sherman, assassinated, killed by the political machine he hated and vowed to change; and Grant, who loved that same machine, had been forgotten by it and left to die, alone and afraid.

And me? Custer wondered. What choices lie before me?

At only forty-nine, he couldn't count on Grant's cancerous deliverance. He chuckled.

Maybe, he thought, if I stay on, I'll be given Sherman's release.

"So," he said. "Whom shall we ask to replace Hayes?"

The noonday sun hammered the color from the sky, making a pale mirror to reflect its light. The ground, still damp from days of rain, simmered in the heat, making the air thick and wet. Spring, having long overstayed its usual time, had been evicted during the night and Summer had immediately set about making itself at home.

George felt as though he were asphyxiating in the open air. It was like breathing in a steam bath: heat, vapor, and the heavy, windless air. He lifted a patch of prairie sod and carried it back toward the mining site. A hundred men were doing likewise, bringing seeds and sod to the slope that they had blown open two months ago, covering it over and returning it as best they could to its original state. A dozen other men were taking down lodges and packing travois, striking camp and preparing for the trip home.

There was a joy in the otherwise oppressive air; excitement, and a definite sense of anticipation. There was singing and laughter, teasing and friendly banter. Certain words that had been set aside during the long weeks of their labors were now picked up again like treasured objects: Home, Family, Hunt, Dance.

George carried his patch of deer grass and little bluestem up the slope and, digging out a depression in the soft, fragrant earth with his hands, set it into its new home.

"Grow," he asked of it simply. "Thrive."

He wiped the dirt from his hands and stood. He saw Vincent down at the campsite, a lone figure, immobile amid the motion of the others. Behind him, eight whistlers, laden with supplies and the heavy product of the camp's labors, munched on the grass. Vincent waved. George waved back. Vincent waved again and beckoned. With hands to his mouth he bellowed, *"Let's go!"* Others looked over to see who was being so ill-mannered, but saw that it was only the old trader. George knew what they were saying; they used to say it about him: crazy *vé'ho'e.*

"Perhaps they still do," he said. Refusing to shout back and forth, he walked down to Vincent. "Impatient today, aren't you?"

"We should have left at daybreak," Vincent said.

"You weren't ready at daybreak," George reminded him.

Vincent scowled. "Well, I'm ready now."

"So I see. Where is Gets Up Early?"

"There."

George looked where Vincent pointed and saw the Little Bowstring soldier helping others secure lodgepoles to a recalcitrant whistler.

"Gets Up Early, are you ready?"

The Indian who had been so important to their success had also agreed to accompany them north to the borderlands. "Yes, One Who Flies," he said. "I am ready." He came over and with him came the five other men. The original mining crew stood before George: Howling Hawk of the Elkhorn Scraper society, Sharp Nose of the Red Shield soldiers, Grasshopper of the Dog Men, Pine of the Kit Foxes, Standing Motionless of the Crazy Dogs, and Gets Up Early from the Little Bowstring society. Their pride showed in their smiling eyes and broad grins.

The other men who had been added to the crew this year stopped in their work and walked toward the group. Soon a crowd of a hundred men and more all stood in respectful silence around George, Vincent, and Gets Up Early. They seemed to be waiting.

Vincent nudged George with an elbow. "Say something, Young Custer."

George felt the blood rush to his cheeks and some of the men laughed at his embarrassment. He did not like making speeches and had not expected to make one now. Still, he felt as though he should say *something*. After all, they had all worked so hard to fulfill this dream.

No, he thought. Not a dream. A vision.

He fumbled at his belt pouch and took out the nugget that Speaks While Leaving had given him, the nugget that he carried with him always.

"This," he said, holding the lustrous lump high for all to see. "This is what started it all. This and a vision. You have all worked very hard. You have all done your part. The result of your efforts is here behind me." He waved a hand toward the sacks filled with hundreds of pounds of gold nugget and flake. "And for now, your work is done. Go home. Hunt. Eat good food. Dance. Kiss your wives."

Grins flashed through the crowd of men and George and his companions mounted their whistlers. As the three whistlers stood and they readied to leave, George regarded the crew. Strong feeling swelled in his throat, but the People had no words for leave-taking—no "good-bye" or "farewell"—so George simply raised his hand, a sign that transcended language and culture. The men responded in kind.

"*Nóheto,*" he said, and he, Vincent, and Gets Up Early all rode out of camp, followed by the five whistlers that carried the sacks that held the future.

During the next days they followed much the same course George and Vincent had taken the previous winter. At Pembina, Gets Up Early stayed hidden in a nearby woods with the whistlers while George and

Vincent walked on into the small frontier town that hung like a cocklebur stuck to the threads of the iron railroad tracks. In town they exchanged raw gold for coin and purchased horses, a wagon, some clothing, and four small heavy-sided chests. They drove the wagon and goods back out to where Gets Up Early waited. The sacks of gold were put into the chests, the chests were locked, and then one by one each two-hundred-pound chest was slid up onto the buckboard behind the driver's bench.

The horses disliked being so close to the lizardlike whistlers, and the whistlers' natural curiosity did not help matters. With small, almost mincing steps, George's hen sidled closer to the hitched team. She crept up on the rearmost horse until she was close enough to properly inspect the mare by sticking her nose under the mare's switching tail. The mare whinnied and bucked, the other horses stamped. The wagon shifted, the men cried out in alarm, and George's hen retreated, her green eyes wide, her muzzle and neck alive with shifting bars of red and white. George grabbed the reins of the wagon team while Gets Up Early calmed the whistler, scratching her withers until her colors calmed and her song fell from a shrill piccolo down to a throaty French horn.

With the gold all on the wagon and with George and Vincent both in new clothes more befitting their pretended station, they were ready to part from Gets Up Early.

"We will meet at the trading-place, where Vincent used to live," George said. "At the full of the Moon When the Cherries Are Ripe." He checked with Vincent. "That will be a month from now. Enough time?"

Vincent chewed on his mustache. *"Oui,"* he said. "Enough time."

George felt giddy. It's going to happen, he said to himself. It's really going to happen.

Winnipeg was in full leaf when they arrived in town.

The tree-lined avenues of the town's west end formed
green tunnels that invited all to stroll beneath their
canopies. Toward the town center, churchyards and
tiny parks with spreading maples made shaded oases
among the bright, sun-filled streets. Children played
in alleyways, women walked the boardwalks on their
errands, and men, as in winter, stood in street-corner
conversations, but everyone was a bit slower, a bit less
boisterous. The sun of summer and the humid air,
even this far north, sapped the town of its vivacity and
life, slowing it to a leisurely pace.

George, however, now fairly well accustomed to
the stronger summer of the lower latitudes, found the
weather most pleasant, even in his heavier *vé'ho'e*
clothing. He smiled as they passed through town, tip-
ping his hat to pretty women and touching the brim
as they passed businessmen and bankers on the
street.

They turned onto Machray and sighted the Grand
Pacific Hotel. The aged doorman recognized them immediately. He poked his head inside to tell of their
arrival and by the time they had pulled the wagon up
to the steps, the doorman, the bellboys, the clerk, the
manager, and even the cook were there, waiting to
greet two of their very best customers.

The manager grinned as he greeted them. "Mr. Carter. Mr. D'Avignon. How nice to see you again. Will
you be staying with us?"

"Indeed we will," Vincent said.

"Your same rooms?"

"If you please."

George and Vincent kept careful watch as the bellboys labored to carry the small but surprisingly heavy
chests upstairs. They went away with sweaty brows,
broad smiles, and a two-dollar tip that would double
both their wages for the week.

"My, my, my," Vincent said as he undid his tie and
unbuttoned his collar. "I have to say it, my friend: I
did not think you would do it." He laughed lightly

and slowly eased himself into an upholstered armchair. "No, I didn't. A year ago when you came to me I thought: I'll go along. I'll even make some money, *peut-être*, enough to start a ranch or set up a decent shop in a nice town like this." He leaned forward, elbows on knees, and waggled a finger back and forth.

"But let me tell you, I did *not* expect it to be like this, sharing a room with a quarter million dollars in gold, nor did I expect to have over twelve thousand dollars to my name." His finger stopped and jabbed at the air. "You, young Custer, are without a doubt, the most pigheaded, single-minded, mule-stubborn, no-quarter bulldog I have ever met."

George smiled. "You haven't met my father."

"No," Vincent said with a sigh of relief. "And I don't care to. But enough chitchat. We must prepare. I sent one of the boys to find McTavish."

"Now wait a minute," George said. "I'm not leaving this gold here to trail after you and Angus while you bounce from tavern to tavern."

"Relax. I wouldn't dream of leaving this fortune unattended. We'll entertain Angus with the best our hotel chef can offer. You have the keys, yes?"

George patted his coat pocket. The keys to the chests jingled.

"There, then," Vincent said. "The chests are secure. The dining room is just off the lobby. I don't think anyone will be able to pound off the locks or sneak one of these chests past us to the street without our notice, do you?"

"No," George said with a chuckle. "I suppose not."

"Good. Now, why don't you go down and tell the cook to kill the fatted calf and put the champagne on ice while I make use of the facilities."

After George had spoken with the cook about supper, he repaired to his own room to clean himself up. A quick scrub-down at the dry sink, a long-needed shave, a clean shirt, and a freshly starched collar made him feel ten years younger. A supple brush took the dust of the road off his coat and trousers, and a shout and a nickel got his shoes shined until they gleamed.

He stopped, though, as he was combing back his hair, and looked at himself in the silvered glass that hung over the dry sink. He leaned in and for the first time in many months really *looked* at himself.

His eyes were still the pale Custer blue, though he noticed the first seams of weathering at the outer corners. His skin had been darkened by the sun and toughened by the wind. His nose was strong and aquiline, and with his blond hair long down to his shoulders, he resembled more than ever his father, President Custer, the Boy General, the Savior of the Battle of Kansa Bay. To the People, though, while his father was simply known as Long Hair, there were other words used to describe him.

Murderer. Liar. Evil.

It troubled him, this similarity to a man he understood so little, a man so reviled by the people to whom George himself owed so much.

Who knows, he thought grimly to himself. After this, I may have a similar reputation among my own people.

He met Vincent in the common room that separated their bedrooms. The old trader, too, had scrubbed and shaved. With his fine waistcoat, golden watch chain and fob, high collar, and a tie of watered silk, he was transformed.

"You look almost respectable," George said.

Vincent shrugged on his dark frock coat. "Thank you," he said quietly, not rising to George's bait.

"Something wrong?" George asked.

"Eh? Wrong?"

"You seem distracted."

Vincent smiled weakly. "Just nervous, I suppose. Nothing more. Just nervous."

Someone knocked at the door. George went to answer it. It was William, one of the bellboys.

"Mr. McTavish is here, sir. He's waiting for you downstairs."

"Thank you, William." George gave the youth a coin. "Please ask him to wait. We will be down presently."

"Yes, sir, Mr. Carter. I will, sir." He headed off toward the stairs and George closed the door.

"Angus is here."

"Yes," Vincent said, checking his watch. "A little early. He must be anxious to start reaping the rewards of his investment."

"Can you blame him? He must have had quite an outlay of cash."

"Don't forget that we gave him some on account."

George shrugged. "Compared to what we brought? It was a pittance."

Vincent regarded him frankly. "You are a kind man, do you know that?"

Embarrassed by such an unusual display from the other man, George busied himself with straightening his cuffs.

Vincent changed the subject and they talked for a time of little things. Then Vincent stood and stretched. "It's nearly seven," he said. "Angus has waited long enough. Let us go down to supper."

Angus was as convivial and forthright as ever. Over sherries in the sitting room he displayed the manifests for the goods he had purchased.

"Eight thousand rifles," he said. "With enough ammunition for a year."

"What about the heavier guns?" George asked.

Angus produced another piece of paper. "Here y'go, Mr. Carter."

The manifest listed four crates carrying the parts and assemblies for two Gatling guns, ammunition, and mounting tripods.

"Good Lord," George breathed. He looked up at Angus. "You are a marvel."

Angus beamed.

Dinner was the best the town and the cook could offer. After a puree of tomato soup came a stuffed trout in a dark ham-flavored Spanish sauce. This was followed by a selection of roast beef, roast loin of pork, and shoulder of mutton in a piquant Sauce Soubise made from sweet onions and heavy cream. Vincent insisted on the best *vin d'hôte*, a French champagne that he selected himself, and he further insisted that George partake.

"No excuses," Vincent said. "This is a celebration."

George was feeling light-headed by the time a light salad was served to finish off the supper. When the choice of either rice pudding or apple pie with melted Edam cheese was offered him, he could only nod.

The trio retired to the upstairs suite for cigars and brandy. George found himself sitting out on the balcony, a snifter in one hand and a lit cigar in the other. Before him, the long evening of the Canadian summer colored the sky a greenish-blue. Streetlights flared as they were lit one by one. Horses clopped by, their hoofbeats echoing in the emptying streets. Occasionally a merchant would rush by, shop apron fluttering, hurrying home after a late evening at the store.

George sniffed the brandy, unmindful of the quiet conversation that engaged Vincent and Angus, happy to simply be here on the far side of the mammoth task that had consumed him for the past year. He tasted the liquor and coughed at its harshness. His head swam and Vincent was there, patting him on the back.

"Perhaps you should turn in for the evening, my friend. I will entertain our guest."

"Ya," was all George could manage. The world tilted as he was taken inside. Vincent and Angus helped him to his room.

"Poor lad," he thought he heard Vincent say.

"Cannae hold 'is drink," Angus said.

"No, nor that."

The room began to spin and the dark figures above him split apart and joined together.

"I think I'll sleep now," George said.

"Aye," Angus said. "That y'will."

Aeons later, George began to become aware of certain things. The first of these was an incredible pain in his head. His skull felt like it had been split like a soft-boiled egg. Of course, the thumping didn't help.

The thumping was the second thing. The double-pulsed, metallic rhythm was like some giant mechanical hammer pounding on a steam-driven boiler. It shook the room with each *ba-bang ba-bang*, and the split in George's head widened as it thudded against the floor. The piercing train whistle only made it worse.

Train whistle?

George sat up quickly, regretted it, and turned to vomit. His flesh went cold and clammy as he realized where he was.

Strong sunlight slipped through the cracks between the boards of the boxcar, spearing the darkness. The car was empty but for some hay strewn across the floor. It smelled of cattle and manure, now mixed with the acrid stench of bile from his own upheaval. George inspected himself.

He was fully clothed in shoes, shirt, tie, trousers, and frock coat. He saw his hat lying on the floor near the sliding door. A small leather valise lay beside it. George winced as he crawled over to it and opened the flap.

Inside were a small bag of coins and a folded piece of paper. He checked his coat pockets. They were empty. Gone were the keys to the chests, and also the nugget that had been the gift from Speaks While Leaving. Tears sprang to his eyes. He took the paper from the valise and unfolded it, knowing what it said before he even read it.

Sincere apologies for the tap on the head, young Custer. And much gratitude for all your hard work.

It was in Vincent's handwriting.

"You son of a *bitch*!" He crumpled the paper and threw it into the darkness of the far corner. "*Damn* you, Vincent D'Avignon! God *damn* you!" He collapsed into the straw. His hand found the pouch of coins. He lifted it, ready to throw away anything that had to do with his betrayer, but felt something larger inside. George undid the ties and poured out the contents.

A fistful of copper and silver coins tumbled into the straw, catching bits of light and scattering it about the dark interior. He shook the pouch again and the larger object fell to the floor with a solid thunk. With reverent hands, George picked up the gold nugget. The gift from Speaks While Leaving. He squeezed it, pressing it into the flesh of his palms, and held his clenched hand to his forehead as he crouched down, curled up on the thumping, straw-covered floor, and wept.

The sun was a bright circle in the hazy sky. The heavens lowered down upon the land like a stove-pot lid, holding in the heat. Crickets sang despite the noon hour, their reedy hymn a lonely susurrus beneath the somber proceedings in the cemetery. The air was a thin soup: humid, hot, and sloppy with the scent of wild onions. Custer stepped up to the lectern. He looked toward the crowd that was gathered on the cemetery hilltop, but he did not look at their faces. He looked past them, down the gentle slope toward the white-trimmed red-brick houses in the quiet cross-roads town of Gettysburg. The place had infected him. From the moment he stepped down from his train, it had seeped into his brain and swathed his every thought in black crepe.

On the far side of town was a rise of land. Custer spied the splash of pale green that was the cupola atop the seminary tower. His gaze swept along the spine of Seminary Ridge, southward along the dark line of oaks that cloaked its undulating length, and then back east across the awful ground that lay between the far ridge and the one on which Custer himself now stood.

In front of him, at the top of Cemetery Hill, lay a broad semicircular sward. Set in the earth were curving rows with thousands of low marble markers—most carved with a name, some with only a number—each indicating the grave of a fallen soldier from those three terrible days that to Custer did not seem so long ago. At the apex of the semicircle was the grand, Gothic monument—a column of fine Connecticut marble flanked by four seated figures of white bronze, topped by a fifth figure, standing, who looked out across the graves in silent wisdom.

Around the monument, men in black coats and high silk hats stood still and upright in the late summer heat. The few women in the crowd, their gowns dark and sparkling with beads, lazily fanned themselves with their programmes.

Custer cleared his throat.

"I am not here today," he began, "in my capacity as the President of our United States. I am not here as a former commander or officer. I am not even here as a decorated hero." The audience's attention was focused upon him, but he did not feel the pressure of their regard. Instead, the day seemed to open up before him, a panorama of memory. "This terrible and hallowed place has the power to strip me of every title, every accomplishment. Here, I am reduced, but not diminished. Here, I am rebuked, yet elevated. Here, mindful of the ghosts and prayers that live in this place, I am simply: Soldier.

"Twenty-five years ago, the greatest battle known to Man was fought in these hills. We have gathered on this consecrated ground with the greatest respect and resolve to rededicate this ground, and ourselves, to the same spirit of Unity with which it was first sanctified."

He continued reading the words that he had written several days before, but his mind continued to wander, drawn down old paths. The faces of old friends passed before his mind's eye, faces long gone, some buried beneath the very grass at his feet. But his battle had not been here, at Cemetery Ridge. His venue had been a few miles to the east. The clash of saber, the pounding of hooves, and the shouts of men filled his memory.

God, he thought. I was so young. So brash. I never knew that any of us could die.

He concluded his brief remarks and left the podium to the polite applause of the assembled guests. As the final speaker, his departure was the signal that the rededication ceremony was about to end. The gathering began to fragment, re-forming in smaller groups divided along party lines.

So much for Union, Custer thought as he was greeted by fellow Republicans.

He nodded and shook hands with senators and congressmen, handing out pleasantries and platitudes like they were candy.

"Wonderful speech, Mr. President."

"Thank you, Senator."

"Very much like what Lincoln might have said."

"Well, Senator, if we learn nothing else from him, it should be brevity."

His security detachment helped him make his way through the crowd.

"Congratulations, Mr. President," said a reporter on the sidelines.

"Congratulations? For what, sir?"

"On the Homestead Act. It passed, sir, by a margin of twenty-four votes."

Custer stopped in his tracks.

"Please, Mr. President," said Higgins, the security guard on his left. "We must keep moving."

"When did you hear this?" Custer asked the reporter.

"It just came in over the wire."

Custer felt the weight of the day slip away, and had to consciously keep from breaking into a silly grin. Such a display would not be proper in this place.

"Do you have any comment, Mr. President?"

"I'm very pleased," he said. "Very pleased."

"Thank you, Mr. President."

"Mr. President, please, keep moving." Higgins urged him along with a meaty hand.

He yanked his arm away and turned on his bodyguard with a scowl. "Do you think someone is going to assassinate me here? In this place?"

"No, Mr. President," Higgins said coolly. "Not while I'm here."

He and Higgins stared at one another for a long moment. "I will not be ushered about like a schoolgirl. Clear?"

"Yes, Mr. President. Now if you'll please come with us, sir, your train leaves in twenty minutes."

No apology, Custer noted. Well, that's all right, I suppose.

He turned and walked briskly down the cemetery path, gravel crunching under his feet. Though he tried, he found that not only could he not keep up his anger, but that the spell that Gettysburg had cast upon him had been dispersed as well. With the Homestead Act in place, with Morton effectively fracturing the Democratic voting bloc, with the bridge at Westgate complete, and with the railroads advancing out into the territory, everything—*everything*—was going according to plan.

Herron's new aide was an officious prig named Graham Noyles. He was lanky and weak with thin blond hair and rabbit-pink skin, and his heavy-lidded eyes gave the impression that he doubted everything he heard. He never laughed at Herron's humor, and always scowled at his profanity.

But, Herron thought as Noyles laid out the map,

prepared the coffee, and ushered McCormack into the office, he's efficient, ambitious, and thorough; three things more important to the post than a winning personality.

McCormack saluted. Herron responded and they walked over to the table.

"Coffee?" Herron offered.

"Yes, sir," the colonel said. "Thank you, sir."

Before Herron could ask, Noyles had readied a cup. "Cream or sugar?" the aide offered. Herron left the niceties to his aide and turned his attention to the map.

The narrow oblong of paper ran the table's length and covered half its width. On the right side was the serpentine course of the Missouri. Hash-marks denoted Herron's headquarters, the growing town of Westgate, and the Robert Matherly Bridge. On the left of the map was the Niobrara, but as its course was still a matter of some guesswork, the lines that represented its banks were less crisp than those of the grand Missouri.

Creeks that drained into the two rivers were noted as well, but the main focus of the map was the extension of the Chicago & Rock Island Rail Road, a solid double line that extended in a west-northwesterly fashion from the bridge at Westgate. In straight segments and shallow arcs, it pushed outward from Westgate into the middle of the map, at which point the line sputtered and thinned into penciled dashes that wandered onward into the wilderness.

Herron put his finger on the end of the solid line. "Here," he said to the colonel. "That's all the track we've laid this year." He pointed to a place only two-thirds of the way to that spot. "Your forts are complete only to here."

"General Herron," McCormack said with polite deference. "Your delays were mine, as well."

Herron nodded. "Perhaps, but only so long as the bridge was incomplete and the railroad was behind you. That is no longer the case."

"Yes, sir. And our rate of progress has increased."

"Good. Then let me tell you what I want to happen now." He moved his finger beyond the solid line and out onto the dashed line of the proposed track. "The track will continue, keeping well ahead of you and eventually reaching the Niobrara where Colonel Shafer is laying the groundwork for a wooden trestle. You will continue *your* work building our stockade forts. I want three more by the time winter hits us."

"Three?" McCormack said abruptly, then glanced at his general. He sipped his coffee. "Begging your pardon, sir, but that's a tall order."

"McCormack, the President's Homestead Act has passed and goes into effect in the spring of the new year. That means plenty of folk headed our way. I need completed forts that I can garrison. It cannot be like it was last winter."

"Yes, sir. But three, sir?"

Herron straightened. He motioned to Noyles for a cup of coffee and invited McCormack to take a seat by the desk. The two senior officers sat. Herron took a long whiff of the strong black coffee before he sipped it.

"Colonel, I know you to be a sensible man. You don't make promises you can't fulfill."

"Thank you, sir."

"That also means, however, that you don't stick out your neck."

McCormack shifted in his seat, suddenly uneasy. Herron held up a hand to put his colonel at ease. "Let me lay it out simply. Come November, Custer is going to take this election in a cakewalk. He's fulfilled or begun work on every promise he's made, and the fiasco with his son back in '86 has somehow made him even more sympathetic to the public. The man is scandal-proof, and all of Cleveland's mudslinging is working to Custer's advantage. He's still playing the golden-haired boy, and it's working for him. So—and I shouldn't be telling you anything you haven't already figured for yourself—Custer is the man who will be calling our shots for the next four years."

He leaned forward a bit, affecting a conspiratorial tone. "Please him," Herron said, "and your future brightens."

McCormack swallowed with difficulty. Herron leaned back in his chair. "But, to please him, you must be willing to take a risk or two."

"Yes, sir."

"And you understand what that means."

"Yes, sir. Three forts by winter."

Herron stood. "Thank you, Colonel. I'm glad we are in agreement. Dismissed."

The colonel stood, saluted, and turned to go.

"McCormack."

"Sir?"

"Leave the china."

McCormack looked blankly down at the china cup and saucer in his left hand. He handed them to Noyles, mumbled an apology, and left the room.

"He seems fairly well rattled, sir," his aide said.

Herron grunted. "It'll be good for him."

Outside, a train whistle broke the quiet of the peaceful afternoon. Herron reached inside his coat pocket and checked the time on his watch. "Quarter hour late," he said as he turned to look out the window.

"Yes, sir," Noyles said. "I'll make sure it's properly noted in the day's reports."

The china on the table began to rattle as the train neared the bridge. Herron waited, gazing out toward the footings. He heard the subtle shift in the engine's tone as it stepped up onto the incline of the bridge's approach. Then it came into view: all black and appointed with shiny brass. The glass of its lanterns gleamed in the sunlight. Gouts of black smoke erupted from its stack and the whistle blew again, releasing a lonely pair of notes and a billow of steam.

Herron smiled grimly as the locomotive rumbled up

onto the bridge deck, pulling its line of cars filled with iron, timber, and supplies for the men farther on down the line.

A hundred miles to the end of the line, Herron said silently. And a hundred more before winter if I have anything to say about it.

A hundred more . . .

Cli-*clack*. Cli-*clack*.
Click-*clack*. Click-*clack*.
The rhythm of the wheels slowed like a runner with a stitch in his side. George woke slowly, awakened by the change. After a week sleeping on trains and in railyards, he'd become attuned to the sound and shifts of the great machines. He cracked open an eyelid.

Afternoon light spilled through the slats and into the boxcar. Crates and boxes were stacked eight feet high. George nestled in his cubbyhole and watched dust swirl in the slanting shafts of light, pushed by drafts that moved and cooled the air, but never cleared it. He reached into the crate beside him and took out another orange, biting through its bitter rind and into the meat. Sweet juice ran down his fingers and down his throat. He squeezed and mashed the orange and he sucked out the juice and the pulp.

Still listening for changes in the train's motion, he cast the empty rind into a far corner. He heard no change, which meant that they were not slowing for a stop. But what, then? The car answered his question as it tilted up an incline.

A hill? he wondered. In Yankton?

Then the shafts of sunlight began to break and flash in regular rhythm. George scrambled to his feet and lurched toward the door. He pulled, slid it ajar, and looked out.

Metal beams and braces rushed past. The sound of the wheels on the iron tracks had changed from a dull clatter to a hollow, open sound, like a lone man applauding in an empty theater. Below the rails, there was no ground. George was high up in the air—three or four stories high—and far down beneath him was the turbulent expanse of a great, muddy river.

He looked up as the boxcar passed by a tower of stone and leveled off. An arc of metal shot up from the tower, rising overhead like the iron trail of an artillery rocket. Cables hung from the arc like strings on a colossal harp; strings that kept the bridge deck above the water. The whole of it—strings, arc, and deck—rang with the train's percussion as it crossed the rails.

It was a marvel and George realized instantly that this was the new bridge that crossed the waters of the Big Greasy. He must have been asleep for much longer than he'd intended, but he didn't care. After a week of hiding in trains and in railyards, after a week of nursing a cracked skull and waking up headed in the wrong direction, after a week of drinking from puddles and eating what scraps he could buy with the few coins Vincent had left him, he finally felt a twinge of joy and the lifting of the pressure that had sat upon his chest and shoulders. He looked out of the boxcar door. Now across the bridge and back on solid ground, the train settled back into its old rhythm. George took a lungful of relief. He was back on the right side of the Big Greasy, heading home.

But that thought turned around and slapped him as he remembered the whole of the events that still hung, fogged and vague, in his bruised brain.

Homeward-bound, but as a failure. Vincent's chicanery had stolen a year's worth of work and all of George's hope. He slid down in the open doorway, one leg dangling over the blurring ties, and took an honest inventory of himself.

His shoes were split and wrecked from mud and miles. The knees of his trousers were out from a fall he'd had running for a train. He was hatless. His coat was filthy and rumpled, his shirt was stained and torn. He'd used his tie to replace his broken belt, and he had no idea where he had lost his collar. His chin bore a ten-day beard. He stank. He was hungry. His every joint, bone, and sinew ached or throbbed or just plain hurt. Aside from the questionable clothes on his back, he had—he checked in the pouch he still carried—precisely seventeen cents and a chunk of gold the size of a child's fist.

And where to from here? He didn't know how far the railroad would take him, but even at the farthest he could imagine, he would still be hundreds of miles from the People. His only chance was to wait until the train stopped, buy what food his penurious means allowed, and head out onto the prairie. With luck, a patrol would find him. With good luck, it wouldn't be an Army patrol.

George slid the door closed and set himself up against a crate. He ate another orange and wished that his coat had pockets.

It was dark when the train began to slow. George grabbed two oranges and slid open the boxcar door.

The air was cool and fresh and the sky was deep and full of faraway stars that shimmered like lights through water. George looked ahead and saw the wan, yellow lamps of a small town. He stepped onto the rung of an iron-bar ladder set into the side of the car and pulled the door closed. When the train had slowed sufficiently, he jumped off and hit the ground running, heading off into the shadows of the town's outskirts.

The place was hardly worthy of the title *town*. He saw a station house near the tracks with a hand-lettered sign that read FORT ASSURANCE. A stone's throw away he spied a lonely street with three stores, two taverns, and a small chapel at the end. He scanned the horizon and saw a few lights, miles out on the prairie to the north. To the south, though, less than a half mile off, he saw the black bulk and towers of an Army fort, an unmistakable silhouette beneath the quarter moon.

He heard voices from up ahead at the station house

and saw a gang of men walking back along the length
of the train. Heavy doors slid open with a rumble and
a clang, and George decided that he didn't care
whether or not they were looking for stowaways; he
didn't want to be in the vicinity. He crept away, keeping low behind the brush.

He came up behind the two taverns. The sounds of
a raspy concertina and sour voices issued forth from
the tavern nearest the tracks, and the air surrounding
it was laden with the smells of food and bread. George
stowed his two oranges around the side. He dipped
his hands into a rain barrel to wash the worst away
from his hands and face and he raked his hair back
with his fingers. He straightened his lapels, brushed
his shoulders as clean as he could, and after a deep
breath, he stepped up and into the smoke and noise
of the tavern.

And panicked.

The clientele was almost entirely military—forage
caps, blue wool, brass buttons, gray cotton shirts, and
suspenders filled the room—privates and corporals
and sergeants. Without thinking, George, the traitor-
ous son of the most famous officer alive, had walked
into the midst of the U.S. Army.

His instinct was to turn and leave, but faces had
turned his way already, and he knew that to walk out
now would raise more eyebrows than would his staying. Besides, he reasoned, if this was where the regulars gathered, the other tavern was probably the *de
facto* officers' club. So he continued inside, approaching the proprietor with a courteous air.

The man behind the bar looked like he might have
been a sergeant himself, years ago. His ruddy cheeks
were grizzled with gray stubble. His hair was thin on
top and gray as well. His vest puckered, the buttons
straining to keep the fabric stretched across his girth,
but his arms were meaty, not flabby, and he glared at
George with a merciless eye.

"What do *you* want?" he asked.

"No trouble, sir," George said. "Just a meal and something to drink, if I might . . . I have money," he added quickly.

The taverner was not impressed. "Let's see it."

George put his coins gently on the scarred bar-top. A dime. A nickel. Two pennies. In any civilized town it would have been enough for a three-course meal of hefty proportion. In frontier towns, however, George knew prices were often overblown. "Should be enough for something," he said.

The taverner looked at the coin and then at George. He glanced at his other patrons nearby, but they had lost interest in the quiet bum who had wandered into their favorite haunt. The taverner reached out to take the coins, hesitated, and then took just the dime. "Sit down over there," he said, pointing to a dark corner of the room. "I'll bring you something."

"Many thanks, sir." George smiled and made his way to the corner. There were no empty tables, but there was one with only a single occupant: a lone sergeant, mute and motionless, one hand on an empty bottle and the other on an empty glass.

"May I?" George asked, indicating one of the empty chairs. The sergeant looked up and blinked. He gestured with a lethargic hand. "Psh," he said.

George took that as permission granted and sat down.

"Soldier, you are out of uniform," the sergeant said. Despite his inebriety, the man spoke with precision, his German accent audible beneath the liquor's effect.

"I'm a civilian, Sergeant. Just a civilian."

"Ah. That would explain it." He looked back down into his empty glass.

The taverner came over to the table. He set down a large bowl of brown stew and a half loaf of hard-crusted bread. Next to that he put a quart tankard, brimming with foam-topped beer. George saw potatoes, carrots, and hunks of meat in the thick gravy, and his stomach leapt at the aroma. The bread was brown and heavy—a meal in itself. He looked up and the taverner winked at him.

"Y'looked like you could use a break in your run of luck," he said.

"I surely can," George said. "Many thanks."

The taverner left and George turned to his food. "Thank you," he whispered, unsure if he was thanking the taverner, God, or the spirits that guarded the world. Nor did he care. He just felt grateful for the kindness. Then, slowly, he began to eat.

His companion moved little and said less. He sat as a statue might sit—immobile and frozen in a moment of time—though George noted to himself that no sculptor would have chosen to immortalize such a banal and homely subject. The soldier's thick, peasant features were neither lovely nor noble, and he wore an expression of insensibility on his face. When he did speak again, it was as if to no one, and to everyone.

"My father was a soldier," he said. "As was his father. My great-grandfather was a soldier as well; he fought against you colonists in Penn's Sylvania. He liked it here, in America, and always wanted to come back and live here. He wanted to be an American soldier."

George ate as the sergeant spoke, nodding politely though the man paid him no mind at all.

"A long line of soldiers, and I am the first one—" He looked at George and poked himself in the chest with a meaty finger. "The *first* one to become an *American* soldier. *Me.*" He stared into his glass once more. "Me. Ülrich Schmidt. An American soldier. And a good one, no matter what they say."

George paused in his meal. "No matter what who says?"

The soldier rounded on George with the same pointed finger. "I am American soldier, now," he said, his speech starting to slur. "And I should not have to work with them. Side by side with them. I should not have to."

"With whom?"

The sergeant tried to focus on George, failed, and turned back to his glass. "The *Schwarzen,*" he said. "They make me work with *Schwarzen.* Me. An American soldier, down in the ditch with *Schwarzen.*" He shrugged. "So I get into a fight. And now they throw me out. *Me.*"

"You've been discharged? For fighting?" George knew the type of man this was—bigoted and fearful, hanging on to prejudices that placed him at a comfortable height above the black man. He did not care for such men, but fighting was hardly a court-martial offense.

The sergeant shrugged again. "The *Schwarze* died," he said. "But to throw me out, after twenty years of service, and now, just when things are getting better."

Now that's a first, George thought. A soldier saying the Army is improving. "How is it getting better?" he asked.

The sergeant waved a vague hand. "Everything," he said. "New forts. New quarters. New quartermasters. Even new rifles, and repeating rifles, to boot."

George's heart thudded. If the Army soldiers were given repeaters, that would wipe out any advantage the People's soldiers could achieve. "When did you get repeating rifles?" he asked.

"Not yet. Not yet. Soon, though. But by then I'll be out."

"You mean they haven't distributed them yet?"

"No." The sergeant was becoming annoyed. "They have not even arrived yet. There's a shim . . . a shipment due in a month or so. An armory shipment."

Now George's heart began to pound. "When? When is the shipment?"

"A month or two," the sergeant said.

"When, exactly?" George pressed.

The sergeant glared at him. "Do you think they would tell me? I do not know. Ask the stationmaster."

George's mind was racing. Repeaters. For the

Army. To keep them out of the Army's hands would be a boon, but if he could get them to the People instead . . .

He ate the last two bites of his meal, took a long draught of the beer, and left.

The station office—little more than a shack by the tracks—was dark. The train that had brought George into town had headed out after its brief stop, and the stationmaster had obviously closed up for the night. George crept around the outside.

It was a one-room office with two windows and a door. The door was locked when George tried it, and the windows were as well. Peering through the dusty panes, he could see a desk, a table, two chairs, and some cabinets. Papers, both loose and bound with twine, covered the tops of the desk and table. He could not see a safe of any kind, so the schedules were somewhere in the piles of paper. He inspected the window. If he broke out the small pane in the middle, he could reach the latch and—

"Can I help you?"

George spun and found himself face-to-face with a man who had come around the building. He was small and bespectacled. He carried a sheaf of papers in one hand and a key ring in the other. His shirt was coming untucked and a tuft of his hair stuck up like a rooster's comb.

"Are you the stationmaster?"

"Yes, I am," the man said, his words slow and suspicious. "What can I do for you?"

"I need some information. About a train schedule."

The stationmaster visibly relaxed. "Oh, is that all," he said. "It's rather late, but let's see what we can do." He stepped forward and jingled the keys until he found the right one. He undid the lock and the hasp, and the door creaked open with a push. "Just a moment while I light a lamp."

George stood by the door, frantically wondering what to do. He didn't want to hurt the man, and if the stationmaster became too suspicious, he might report George's visit to the Army officers and the schedule might be changed.

A match flared in the darkness and the stationmaster touched it to the wick of a chimney lamp. The wick took and its soft light filled the room. George saw that papers not only covered the table and desktop, but lay in stacks on the floor and protruded from behind cupboard doors. Pages peeked out of drawers and a small pile of them lay underneath the uneven leg of one of the chairs.

"There, now," the short man said as he sat down behind the desk. "What was it you wanted to know?"

George cleared his throat. "Quite a lot of papers here," he said, stalling for time while he tried to come up with the best approach.

The stationmaster blew air and shook his head. "You don't know the half of it. It's the Army. Eventually, the railroad will be privately owned, but until it is, it belongs to the U.S. Army, and the Army loves paper."

"So I've learned," George said, remembering his days as an engineer for the Army.

"Ah," the small man said. "So you've experienced it yourself."

"Yes, sir. Firsthand. I know what it is to be swamped in forms and reports."

The stationmaster sighed. "They don't pay me enough to do this job. But I digress. You wanted some information. A schedule, wasn't it?" He began lifting the corners of pages and looking through the papers on his desk.

"Actually, I was hoping you'd be able to tell me about a particular shipment."

"Shipment?" He paused in his search. "What do you mean?"

George could tell that he was approaching a delicate subject. He hooked his thumbs in the vest pockets. A lump in his coat's inside pocket reminded him of the nugget that he carried there, and his mind latched on to the seed of an idea. "Yes," he said. "There is an important shipment due in the next month or so. A very important shipment. The men at the fort are quite excited about it. New equipment. New supplies. New weapons . . ." He let his voice trail off.

The stationmaster's brow contracted. "But that information is secret. They shouldn't be telling you about it. Nor shall I. Why do you want to know, anyway? I should report this to the colonel."

George held up a hand to calm him. "Just a minute. Don't go off half-cocked. Hear me out, please."

The stationmaster scowled but waited. George dragged over the other chair and the stack of papers for its uneven leg.

"Now here's what I'm planning," he said as he sat. "I want to open a shop here in town."

The stationmaster laughed. "You? You're joking."

"I know I don't look the part of the entrepreneur. I had some unfortunate luck on my way here and ran afoul of some rather unsavory fellows. They stole my money and left me senseless in a ditch."

"Oh, my," the man said, never thinking for a moment of any reason why George might lie.

"I still had my ticket, though, so I decided to continue onward. My partner, you see, back in Chicago, is expecting me to begin preparations."

"But what can you do?" the stationmaster asked. "They stole your money."

"My money, indeed," George said, reaching into his coat pocket. He took out the gold nugget and laid it on the paper-covered desk. "But not my wealth."

The man's eyes widened, his brown irises encircled by white. "Oh . . . oh, my. I see." He reached for it, drawn like a drunk to liquor, but stopped and looked up at George. "May I?"

"Be my guest," George said, and smiled as the stationmaster picked up the nugget and gasped at its weight.

"Now as to this store," George continued. "We intend to supply the soldier as well as the settler with whatever they might require for their protection. Everything a man might need for the proper care and maintenance of his armaments. You know what I mean: holsters, rifle bags, ammunition, even weapons for the civilians. Surely you can see why knowing how the soldiers will be equipped is so very important to my inventory plans."

The stationmaster looked up from his inspection of the nugget. "Yes. I can see that. Surely. Say, is this solid?"

"Indeed it is. And surely you can see how knowing when these new rifles are to arrive is crucial to the timing of my proposed operation."

"Oh, absolutely. This is an enormous piece of gold."

"And I have more like it," George said. The stationmaster looked up in surprise. "It is how I will be financing my operation," he explained.

"Oh, my," the stationmaster breathed.

"And, of course, I will be extremely appreciative to those who assist me in starting this endeavor."

"Oh, of course," the man said, and then he blinked, his eyes large behind his lenses. "Oh," he said again, and put the nugget down at arm's length on the cluttered desktop. "I see."

"So," George said slowly. He pushed the nugget back toward the stationmaster. "If you could see a way to supply me with the information I requested, I assure you it would make all the difference to my plans."

"Well, I . . . ." The small man sank back into his chair, his eyes still staring at the nugget. It glowed in the lamplight, throbbing with each flicker of the wick's flame. "I suppose . . . ." He licked his lips and his brow was beaded with sudden sweat.

"What harm?" George whispered. "I get a jump on the competition. You get a well-deserved raise in salary."

A secret smile crept onto the stationmaster's face. "When you put it that way," he said hesitantly.

"Go on," George urged. "What harm?"

"What harm, indeed?" the man said. He snatched up the nugget and giggled as he held it close to his chest. Then he began riffling through the papers on his desk. "Arms shipment, you said. I know the copy of that requisition is around here somewhere." He began to open drawers one at a time, and on the third one exclaimed aloud. "Here it is." He sat up, a handful of folded papers in his hand. He opened the papers flat on the desktop and pressed out the crease with a knuckle. George noticed that the fingers that gripped the nugget were white.

"Yes, this is it," the stationmaster said, reading down the lines. "Cases of Winchesters, rounds of ammunition. Dry goods, flour, beans, salt pork, et cetera, et cetera."

"Good," George said. "When is it due?"

The man flipped forward to the last page. "October," he said. "Supplies for the winter garrisons."

"What day in October?"

"Hmm? Oh. The, um, the ninth. The shipment is due here on the morning train on the ninth of October." He looked up at George. "Does that give you enough time?"

"Let me see," George said, pretending to calculate. He had no idea what day it was and hoped the stationmaster would fill him in. "Today is the . . ."

"The seventh of September. That gives you about four weeks. Not a lot of time."

George grimaced. "Well, I may be selling my wares from under a tent, but I think we can make do. I can't thank you enough for your help."

The stationmaster grinned and held up the fist that was clenched around the nugget. "Oh, but you *have*!"

George held out his hand and the stationmaster shook it with true fervor. "Will you be staying in town?"

"Oh, no," George said. "I plan to visit some of the folks out on the land, the civilians. To see what needs they might have."

"Well, be careful," the stationmaster said. "The plains are crawling with wild Indians."

George frowned. "You don't say." He wished it could only be that easy.

CHAPTER 10

Fall, A.D. 1888
Beyond the Sudden River
Alliance Territory

Teeth bared, Storm Arriving rode into the rain, his head low along his whistler's back. His three companions kept pace. Up in the clouds, the Thunder Beings struck steel to flint. The day went white as lightning flashed and drums rolled out thunder across the land. Storm Arriving's gritted teeth became a ferocious grin.

Back, behind his riders, twenty bluecoats pursued them. Storm Arriving could hear their shouts above the storm's din. He looked forward again, searching for the mark.

"There," he shouted, pointing to a coral-berry bush with a long forked branch. "This way."

He swung his whistler around the shrub as he turned to the right. His men whooped as they passed it. Storm Arriving heard the small yips of squirrels-that-bark-like-dogs as they rode around the rodents' village of burrows and holes, and looked back. The bluecoats had veered to the right as well, but their course would take them to the inside of the coral-berry bush.

Across the squirrel-dog village.

"Prepare!" The men reached back and slipped rifles out from under their seat pads. The bluecoats neared the squirrel-dogs.

"Now!"

The group of four stopped and wheeled. Rifles ready, they aimed. The bluecoats saw the challenge and rode to meet it.

The first rider was halfway into the squirrel-dog village when his horse found a burrow. His mount's leg sank and snapped off below the knee, pitching horse and rider to the rain-slick grass. Another horse fell, man and animal screaming. A third stumbled. Others reined in and the riders behind them piled up on their rear.

"Fire," Storm Arriving shouted.

The four Kit Foxes fired. Bullets tore into the group of bluecoats, ripping through flesh and bone, knocking men from their saddles. The Kit Foxes fired twenty shots before the enemy thought to return fire. By then it was too late; only six bluecoats remained. They turned to flee.

"Split up!" Storm Arriving ordered and the men took off in pairs, flanking the retreating bluecoats. The vé'hó'e soldiers rode in a panic. Their horses' eyes rolled white as they looked back at the larger whistlers gaining on them. The Kit Foxes raised their weapons, steadied their mounts, and fired. It took very little time to finish the fight.

When it was over, they returned to kill the wounded and search for anything of use or value. The four Kit Foxes were silent as they collected weapons, ammunition, trinkets, blankets. Storm Arriving glanced at his fellows as they went about their tasks in the lightening rain.

There was no celebration, no joy. Their jaws were set and tense, their eyes deep and narrow. Their motions were efficient, but filled with fatigue. It had taken them half a moon to draw out these bluecoats from their fort. They had only been able to do so by burning families from their homes and letting some survive to run for help. Only then had the bluecoats come out.

Half a moon to kill twenty *vé'hó'e*. Storm Arriving frowned as he took the cartridge belt from a dead man. With new forts being built and the iron hardback bringing more *vé'hó'e* every day, they could never hope to keep them all out.

Not for the first time, he thought: This is no way to fight a war.

A distant shout sent the four Kit Foxes down onto the wet grass, rifles in hand. Storm Arriving did not want them all to get caught in a group, so with signs he asked two men to creep to the right while he and the fourth soldier headed left, trying to use the grass and the subtleties of the land to hide their movement.

Storm Arriving heard a second shout. He turned to his companion.

"Did you hear that?"

"Yes," the other said. "It sounded like 'I see you.'"

Storm Arriving cupped a hand to his mouth and shouted at the sky. "Who are you?"

The answer was weaker than the first shouts. ". . . friend of the People."

"Stay down," he told the other Kit Foxes. Then he levered a cartridge into his rifle and stood, aiming.

The man, a *vé'ho'e*, stood a quarter mile off, waving a coat over his head.

"Great spirits of the world," Storm Arriving said and waved back. "One Who Flies!"

He saw his friend's smile, even through the drizzle. Then One Who Flies dropped his coat, put a hand to his head, and collapsed.

The Kit Foxes ran to him. Storm Arriving reached him first. The former bluecoat was thin, his cheeks sunken beneath the auburn stubble of his beard. His clothes—*vé'ho'e* clothes—were torn and ragged. His feet were bare. His skin was cut and scraped and bruised, but when his eyes fluttered open and he saw his friend, he smiled.

"Merci à Dieu," he said, thanking the spirits in the Trader's Tongue. But then his face turned serious. "I

must talk with Two Roads," he said. "And the other war chiefs. We have seventeen days. We can make everything right. Seventeen days." Then his eyes rolled up into his head again and he fell as limp as a deerhide doll.

"Get the whistlers," Storm Arriving said. "We have seventeen days."

"Until what?" one of the men asked.

"I don't know. But I don't think we should wait until he wakes to start moving, do you?"

One Who Flies slipped in and out of consciousness as they traveled. When he was awake, Storm Arriving made sure he ate some food and drank some water, and his lapses quickly grew to be more like sleep. In his waking moments, he told of their betrayal, and of his failure to get the new weapons from the *vé'hó'e* up in the Grandmother Land.

"But Speaks While Leaving," he said. "She has given us another chance. The nugget that began it all. We have another chance."

He told them of the iron hardback and the shipment of weapons bound for the bluecoats. Storm Arriving understood the importance of the opportunity, and they sped across the prairie. When they reached Two Roads, the war chief's decision was clear and immediate.

"The People have already separated for the autumn," he said. "Send riders to every band, to every society. Gather the soldiers. Gather everyone you can."

They had eight days left.

The next day they were riding out again. One Who Flies was still light-headed and weak, but insisted on coming with Storm Arriving and the fifty other riders that accompanied Two Roads. To aid in retrieving the hoped-for weapons, each man rode with two spare whistlers instead of one.

The bluecoats had placed their forts fairly close to one another, so no matter where they attacked the iron hardback, the bluecoats would always be within a few hours' ride. More important was the fact that, according to the information One Who Flies supplied, the only place for them to attack the transport was between the river and the first of the bluecoat forts. That stretch of the iron road was the oldest and the fort was the best supplied. It was also the longest distance between forts, and for that Storm Arriving was thankful. Apart from surprise, speed would be their best weapon. He knew they would have the former, but could only pray for the latter.

They rode for three days, stopping little—only for a bite of food or to let the animals catch their breath. They reached the northern shore of the Sudden River at midday and stopped in a forest of beech and walnut trees. Two Roads prepared to make camp, and the men followed his example. One Who Flies became concerned, his eyebrows attempting to meet one another over the bridge of his nose.

"Why are we stopping?" he asked. "It's only noon and we still have nearly a hundred miles to travel."

Storm Arriving untied the bundle from his whistler's back. "Two Roads will not admit it," he said, "but he does not want to do this alone. Word was sent to the other bands, and we wait for others to join up with us."

He sat down and pointed across the muddy river. "I have spent most of the year out there. Riding patrols. Fighting bluecoats. Trying to send the *vé'hó'e* home." He sighed. "That is not our land anymore. Two Roads knows this. He has heard our reports, and so he will wait and hope more soldiers will be able to join us."

One Who Flies stared out through the trees and across the river. The land rose slightly on the far side—as it did behind them—hiding the expanse of the prairie.

"You say it is not your land anymore. Whose is it then? Theirs?"

"No. It is not theirs."

"But you don't think it is yours, either."

"No," Storm Arriving said. "It does not feel that way."

"Have you given up, then?"

Storm Arriving snorted. "I would not be here if I had." He noticed that in this talk One Who Flies spoke of "theirs" and "yours," but did not include himself in either group. "What about you?" he asked. "Where is your land, One Who Flies?"

He saw the former bluecoat's shoulders stiffen at the question. He just stood there at the edge of the trees, arms folded across his chest as he looked across the mumbling waters.

"I have no land," he finally said.

Storm Arriving reached into his belongings and pulled out a small parfleche. He stood and walked up beside One Who Flies. Unrolling the packet, he took a strip of dried buffalo meat and offered it to One Who Flies. His friend accepted it with a sign of thanks and they stood quietly for a time, chewing in silence. The meat tasted of sunshine and sweet summer grass, and it reminded Storm Arriving of home and family.

"If you have no land," he said to One Who Flies, "why do you fight so hard for ours?" He glanced over and saw a great sadness in the other's face.

"It is the right thing to do," he said.

"You have no other reason?"

"No."

"The bluecoats . . . don't they fight because they think it is the right thing to do?"

One Who Flies looked over at Storm Arriving—not as a challenge, but a look of serious attention. "Men only fight for things they believe in or for things they truly want."

Storm Arriving avoided the gaze of One Who Flies. He took another bite of meat and stared across the river as his friend had been doing. "And what is it that you believe in? What makes you fight for us?" he asked.

One Who Flies got angry. "What is it?" he asked, turning. He stood defiant, fists on hips, and now Storm Arriving saw a challenge in that gaze. "What is it you are trying to get me to say?"

Storm Arriving kept his gaze fixed on the southern shore. "I want you to choose. One side, or the other. Ours . . ." He nodded toward the far shore. "Or theirs."

"Why you—" One Who Flies took a step and shoved Storm Arriving with both hands. Storm Arriving staggered back and crouched to face his friend's rage.

"How can you doubt my loyalties?" the former bluecoat asked. His voice was taut like a rope stretched to its limit. "What do I have to do to convince you?"

Storm Arriving straightened. "It is not me you have to convince," he said. "You must convince yourself."

"What?" One Who Flies ran a hand through his hair, pulling at it in frustration. "Convince myself? Don't you think I already have?"

Storm Arriving tapped his temple with a fingertip. "Up here, you have." He tapped his chest. "But not here. In your heart, you still doubt yourself. In your heart, you are afraid to give up the thing that you were for the thing that you have become."

"You think I still want to be one of them?" One Who Flies said, pointing across the river.

"No," Storm Arriving said. "I don't think you want to be a *vé'ho'e*. But I think you are afraid to be one of us. In this war, you cannot be both. You cannot be a soldier of the People and a *vé'ho'e*, as well. You cannot be a *vé'ho'e* and do what you know must be done."

One Who Flies opened his mouth as if to speak but made no sound but for a small choking gasp. The anger in his eyes drained away and the tightness left his shoulders and arms. His gaze drifted. He stood as a man stunned by a heavy blow and he turned, not toward the river, but toward the forest.

The walnut trees were nearly bare and their leaves covered the ground like a dirty yellow quilt. Whistlers crouched in the leaf litter, their skins mottled yellow and gray to match the scene, their eyes half-closed in wary rest. Men sat near them or leaned up against them, tending small fires or cleaning their weapons. They chatted, shared stories, and now and again someone would grouse or laugh as a green-coated walnut fell on the unsuspecting head or back.

One Who Flies then looked down at himself, at his leggings of antelope skin, his moccasins of buffalo hide, his breechclout of red Trader's cloth, and his shirt of fringed deerskin. He lifted the scabbard that hung across his shoulder and pulled out the long knife that had been the gift of Laughs like a Woman, now more than a year dead.

"Are we so alien," Storm Arriving asked, "that you cannot accept us in your heart? Are we so different that you cannot bear to be one of us?"

One Who Flies stared at the blade of the knife. His fingers pulsed on the horn handle. "How can you accept me?" he asked. "I *am* a *vé'ho'e.*"

"Not anymore—"

"Yes, I am!" He pulled back the collar of his shirt, revealing his pale white skin. "Underneath all this, I am one of them. I will *always* be one of them." He turned and walked off toward the river.

Storm Arriving jogged to catch up, but One Who Flies kept walking along the river, scattering a mob of fishing lizards that had gathered on the muddy bank.

"One Who Flies. That is just the color of your skin. It is not who you are."

"Is that so?" One Who Flies asked. "You would feel differently if I said I wanted to marry your sister."

Storm Arriving stopped, confused. "Mouse Road? You want to marry Mouse Road?"

One Who Flies squinted. "What if I did?"

"I wouldn't let you."

"There," One Who Flies said with perverse satisfaction. "You see? You say you accept me as one of your own, but you don't want me to marry your sister."

"Of course I don't want you to marry my sister. You've not courted her properly."

"But what if I had?"

"But you haven't. I can speak to her . . . I didn't know that you had any intentions—"

"You miss my point entirely," One Who Flies howled and sat down on the ground. He put his head in his hands and tangled his fingers in his hair. His breath was harsh and heavy.

"My friend," Storm Arriving said as he squatted beside him. "I do not understand you. I say you are one of us. You say you are not because your skin is pale where the sun does not touch it. I say that this makes no difference. You say it does." He put a hand on his friend's shoulder. "This is just what I have been telling you. It only matters because it makes a difference to *you*. You are not one of *us* because you are still afraid of no longer being one of *them*."

The muscles along his friend's jaw bunched and tensed. A tear fell from his eye and skittered down the side of his leggings. "Why would you ever accept me as one of your own, after all that my people have done?"

"Because of all that you have done to try and make up for it."

One Who Flies looked at him in surprise. "Is that what . . . I suppose that is what I have been trying to do."

"And you can never succeed," Storm Arriving said.

One Who Flies took a deep breath and let it out slowly. "No," he said. "I don't suppose I can. I don't suppose anyone could."

Storm Arriving patted him on the shoulder and stood. He held out his hand to help One Who Flies to his feet. The former bluecoat looked up through pale hair that had come loose in his anger.

"Should I stop trying?" he asked. "Stop trying to atone?"

"Yes," Storm Arriving said. "Do things because they are right, and because you believe in them; not to rid yourself of the stain of someone else's crimes."

One Who Flies took his hand and stood.

"Now," Storm Arriving said. "What is this I hear about you wanting to marry my sister?"

Storm Arriving laughed at his friend's sudden apprehension, and they walked back along the riverbank.

More soldiers arrived the next day. They came in groups of ten and twenty—Little Bowstrings from the Northern Eaters, Crazy Dogs from the Flexed Leg People, Red Shield soldiers from the Hair Rope band—and by evening the forest was filled with the quiet voices of nearly two hundred men and the tuneless songs of their whistlers. Small cookfires scented the air, but most men, of the opinion that starting fires, along with drawing the day's water, was a woman's job, ate their provisions in the cold and dark.

George walked through the camp, weaving between lichen-clad boles of the tall walnut grove, greeting familiar faces, learning the names of new ones. He felt the steel bands that had constricted his chest throughout the day begin to relent. With fifty men the attack was risky, but with two hundred, they would have the game in their hands. The train would be protected, to be sure, but even for a shipment of weapons they would not be prepared for a force of this size.

He checked on his whistler, scratching her neck until she crooned, and then moved to check and recheck the two small crates he had set down on opposite sides of a large tree trunk. He lifted the oiled leathers on the first case and opened it. Inside, swaddled in cotton and pale, dry summer grass, was the smaller box that held the blasting caps. Around the other side of the tree was the second crate with their last sticks of dynamite and some coiled fuse. George saw that each bundle was secured in its cushioned nest and then, satisfied, tucked the oiled leathers in around them, putting them to bed like treasured children.

On his way back toward the others, he looked up through the lacework of dark branches. The sky was clear and edged with turquoise after the sun had set. It promised to be a cold, clear night, and many soldiers were preparing for it with blankets and buffalo pelts. George envied them their calm: These were seasoned veterans, while he had only seen combat on two occasions—and both times he had been fighting against his own countrymen.

He looked down at his left hand and the stub of his little finger. He wiggled what remained of the high joint, contracting it, curling it, and could feel the missing two phalanges. He closed his eyes and could feel the finger whole, could feel the missing joints curl and he half expected to feel the long-gone fingertip touch the heel of his palm. His breath caught in his throat.

Like my heart, came the thought. Trying to reach out with a limb that has been cut away. Trying to reach out. Trying to touch. Trying to . . . hold on.

"One Who Flies."

George jumped, startled from his thoughts. It was Storm Arriving. In the gloaming, he was a figure of blue and gray, made of night and shadow except for the white feather at the nape of his neck. "Am I disturbing you?"

"No," George said. "I was just . . . thinking."

"The fathers," Storm Arriving said, glancing back at one of the few fires that flickered under the bones of the autumn branches. "They would like to discuss plans for tomorrow."

"Yes. Good." They went together to join the meeting.

George did not sleep after he left the war council. He leaned against his whistler's warmth, smelled her spice, and listened to the darkness. Storm Arriving slept nearby, a shoulder and arm bared to the night's chill. George watched his friend's breathing for a time, and then looked for shooting stars. Hours later, the morning star appeared, shining on the horizon like a fisherman's lure in the deep waters of the nighttime sky. Around him, men began to stir, awakened by some inner sense or by some silent signal George could not hear. Whistlers croaked and complained as they were made to rise. George saw the leaders move among their men, laying out the morning's plan by starlight.

Before the morning star was half a hand high, they were across the river and riding.

The sky retained the cold clarity that only autumn could provide. They followed a wandering route that George did not understand until he saw the dark mound of a settler's shack in the distance: The war party was winding its way among the homesteads scattered across the plain. The sun, when it rose, did not warm, but only blinded them as they rode into its light.

Finally, a dark, raised line appeared, a welt across the land ahead of them: the railroad. The sun was less than a hand high, its low rays ricocheting off the shiny tracks. The men stopped a quarter mile from the railroad, and Two Roads looked at George.

"We wait on you, One Who Flies."

George set his jaw and dismounted. He gathered the items he required—charge, fuse, initiator, and the all-important matches—and walked ahead to the tracks. His heart was clog-dancing in his chest as he knelt along the rail ties. The scent of creosote was strong, even in the cold. George scraped away the dirt alongside one of the black-stained timbers. He cut the fuse, giving himself a few minutes to run back to the others. He placed the cap on the end of the charge, crimping it in place, hoping that a single stick would be enough to dislodge the rail. He inserted the fuse in the cap and laid the explosive under the rail, next to the tie. The concavity would focus the blast upward, forcing the rail up against its spikes. At the very least, he hoped it would loosen the spikes so they could unseat the rail. He

took out a match and struck it to life, touched it to
the fuse and waited one . . . two . . . three seconds
before the fuse spat, burning his finger with a jet of
hot gases. He swore and put the finger to his lips as he
backed away. The fuse continued to burn and George
turned and ran.

He waved to the others. "Down," he shouted. "Get
down." But none of these men had ever seen the explosions at the mining site, and even when they
dropped to the ground, curious heads still popped up
above the short grass.

"Stay down!" he yelled as he reached the line and
fell prone. A long minute passed and George could
hear the hissing of the fuse.

"What is wrong?" someone asked.

"Stay down," George cautioned. "It won't be long
unti—"

The explosion shook the ground with a cracking
rumble like a lightning strike. Men flattened and
George looked up to see the iron rail flying up into
the air, a bent hairpin flung by a giant's hand.

One stick seems to have been plenty, he noted
silently.

Rocks and gravel pattered down like hailstones and
then the men were up, standing, staring at the damage
and exclaiming to one another.

"It *is* like thunder."

"Look at what it did!"

What George had prayed would at least dislodge
the rail had in fact blown a wide, shallow hole in the
roadbed. The rail directly above the charge had landed
a hundred feet away and the ties and the other rail
had been blown almost as far in the opposite direction.
There was no way the train would make it past the
damage.

George looked at the hole again and saw a problem.

"They'll see it," he said. "They'll see it. We've got
to fill the hole. Two Roads, we've got to fill in the
hole."

Two Roads and the others, still grinning at the display of power, turned to him with puzzled looks.

"If the men on the iron hardback see the hole too soon, they will stop. If they stop in time, they might even go back. We have to cover the hole so that they do not have time to stop."

Two Roads heard his words and took a silent poll of his fellows. They all agreed. The war chiefs whistled at their men and issued instructions. In moments, five score men were working, scooping earth back into the hole, smoothing out the damage, camouflaging the area with uprooted scrub.

A huffing on the horizon told them that time had run out. "Back," the chiefs ordered. "Back to the line." The men retreated and hid behind crouching whistlers and clumps of tall grass.

George could barely catch his breath. The train pounded its way toward them, blazing the sky with smoke. The men kept low, made ready. Rifle levers clacked all around him. Those without rifles tightened bowstrings and loosened quivers. The locomotive approached, its lantern glaring into the early morning, a cyclopean eye in the circle of its black face. Steam spewed forth from either side like the breath from the nostrils of a monstrous bull. It loomed large, bringing along its own brand of thunder: harsh, mechanical, driven. It came onward, within a half mile of their position. George saw the cars behind the locomotive, more cars than normal, more even than he had expected. Sunlight glinted off the sides of the cars, flashing off glass, off windows. Railcars with windows.

George thought: Oh, dear God. Passengers. It's not just freight. It's a troop transport.

Brakes locked as the engineers spied the broken track. The train shuddered, compacting with deceleration. Iron screamed as metal pulled on metal. Sparks danced at the train's feet. The locomotive, massive with the crush of tons of steel and cargo behind her, slid inexorably onward with a sad grace, sliding for-

ward into the gap in the rails. Her prow dug into the
ground, tearing up the earth, tossing ten-foot ties like
pencils, bending the rails in her path. Her coaler
slipped the track behind her and pushed the locomotive to the left. She dug her trench into the prairie
grass, wheels half-buried in black earth. Fire gouted
from her stack, and the sound of tearing metal bellowed above the roar. Behind the coaler, more cars
jumped the rails, crashing right and left in terrifying
succession. Baggage cars broke ranks and then the
windowed cars—the passenger cars—leapt up and
onto the open plains. George saw men behind the
shattering glass, heard their shouts. One car slipped
and rolled, flinging men into the air as it spun. A shot
like an artillery shell blasted the air as the locomotive's great boiler cracked in a scalding fount of steam
and fire. More passenger cars skipped and slid, tumbling men to death in their play. Behind them, other
cars had slowed enough to keep upright or nearly so
as they jumped track. Farther back, boxcars pushed
forward, crushing the lighter cars. The din of mechanical death diminished and George heard instead the
voices of men. Screams and shouts were everywhere,
pain and fear given up to the prairie sky. Bluecoats
poured out of the broken cars, hollering to the heavens. Only along the line was there silence, only among
George and the soldiers of the People. They waited
beside their whistlers, stunned, two hundred men suddenly faced with an army.

Good Voice, chief of the Red Shield soldiers,
grabbed George by the shirtsleeve. "You said there
would be few."

George waved at the wreckage and the hundreds of
bluecoats. "I was wrong."

"We are outnumbered four to one, at least. We cannot kill this many, not without heavy loss." He began
to signal his men but Two Roads stopped him.

"If you leave, we will never get the weapons we
need."

"Look," Good Voice said. "There are hundreds of bluecoats out there."

George gritted his teeth and grabbed the chief's arm. "Yes," he said, struggling with his emotions. "Look."

Out at the wreck, men in blue staggered and stood. Some helped others from the cars. Some tended the wounded. Here and there an officer asserted his command. Ten cars or more, all filled with men. Eight hundred men. Maybe a thousand.

"Look," George said again. "They are the winter garrisons. Leave them here, and you will only fight them later."

"I will gladly fight them later," Good Voice said. "When the odds are more in my favor."

"Look again," George said. "How many rifles do you see?"

Good Voice looked. George knew what he saw. "These are green recruits," he continued. "Only the officers are armed. The soldiers have not been issued their rifles. The weapons are all in the rear cars."

Good Voice looked again and smiled slowly, but the contemptuous expression George saw on Two Roads's face echoed his own feelings.

"How are the odds now?" George asked, unable to keep a sneer from coloring his words. "Your rifles against unarmed men? Do you think you can handle it now?"

Good Voice heard the insult. He jerked his arm from George's grasp. "I see no weapon in your hands," he said.

"No," George said. "I gave all I had to you."

Good Voice snarled and struck George a back-handed blow across the face, knocking him on his back. Two Roads held back the second attack. George looked at Two Roads.

"Go," George said. "You will never have this chance again."

Two Roads released Good Voice and the Red

Shield chief turned to command his men. Two Roads did not move, and George saw the pain that creased his brow like a heavy crown.

"This is no way to fight a war," he said. "This is shameful."

"Yes," George whispered as gunfire began to chatter and war whoops curled the air. "It is shameful, but we must choose. We must choose."

Two Roads stared at George, his eyes brimming with tears. "Kit Fox," he shouted. *"Attack."* Then he stood, lifted his rifle, and walked to join the slaughter.

George wanted to die. He wanted to stand up and cry out to the nearest officer with a sidearm. His countrymen were dying—*his* countrymen—men dedicated to protecting the citizens of the United States . . .

. . . and who would do so by killing the Cheyenne. By killing the Arapaho. And the Yankton. And the Hunkpapa, the Lakota, the Mandan, Ree, Shoshone . . .

. . . By driving these People off the land they had inhabited for a thousand years . . .

His countrymen . . .

George looked at the battle, a frenzy of gunsmoke and running men. He scanned the land with a tactical eye: the captain shouting for the attention of his men, the cluster of officers' wives, the Indians on whistler-back firing into fleeing bluecoats, the group of infantry running toward the rear cars. He leapt onto his whistler and drew his knife. He rode out and into the battle.

"I choose," he shouted. *"I choose."*

It was not a battle. It was a massacre. George ran down men in blue wool, slaying them—at first hand-to-hand with his knife, and later gunning them down with a dead officer's revolver. He slew them in the shadow of the wrecked cars. He chased them out onto the prairie and slew them on the golden grass. Against all code of military honor, he targeted officers and threw the enlisted men into further panic. When the sun was only two hands high, he stopped. It was over.

He was sticky with the smell of death and spattered head to toe with blood. All around him, the ground was strewn with bodies. His breath quavered as he saw them, men and women, tumbled and lifeless across the landscape. He could not speak, for the two warring halves of his soul still vied within him. One half wished to cry out in horror, while the other wanted merely to shout his thanks at having survived.

He rode toward what had been the rear of the train. Storm Arriving was already there, and he stared at George as he rode up to the scene.

"I did not recognize you," he said.

George could not keep back the small, bitter laugh that escaped him. "There is little left that is not changed."

Storm Arriving squinted; a long, appraising look. "I believe you," he said.

In the boxcars they found all they had hoped for, and more. Crate after crate of Winchester's repeating rifles represented a definitive policy shift for the U.S. Army—one that concerned George, not for what it meant in itself, but more for what it portended for their future. They found revolvers, too, and nearly a whole car of ammunition, powder, and casings. Men were coming up to George, asking him what this item was or what the purpose of that object could be. Everything from clothing to compasses, haversacks to hardtack. They found supplies of beans, coffee, peas, and rice. They found salt pork and flour by the barrel, bolts of cloth, dried apples, canned sardines and oysters, and, of course, cases of liquor. Long ago a holy man of the People had warned them about the vé'ho'e and his liquor. The Council of chiefs had taken the warning with great seriousness, and the tradition of abstinence was still strong. George watched as the soldiers pounced on the liquor, taking out the bottles and throwing them up as targets to be shot in a game that filled the air with the sharp scent of whiskey. But then a Kit Fox soldier brought an unusual cylinder over to George.

"One Who Flies, what kind of bullet is this?"

George took the offered object. It was like an oversized bullet and casing, more than an inch in diameter and six inches in length. It weighed more than a pound. He looked up at the cars of cargo. "Where did you get this?"

The Kit Fox soldier pointed.

"Take me there."

The last boxcar—the last car before the ten or twelve cars of horses and other livestock—was nearly empty compared to the others. The first thing that George saw when he looked in the door was the stenciled word: EXPLOSIVES.

"Everyone out," he said.

Some of the soldiers began to take offense but George simply cut them off with a gesture. "Do not speak. Do not touch anything. This car holds thunder-sticks."

The soldiers froze. They had only just seen what dynamite could do. Quietly, they stepped down from the boxcar.

"Keep them away from here," he told the soldier who had brought him the artillery shell. The soldier signed his concurrence and George pulled himself up into the boxcar.

In the crates marked EXPLOSIVES he found more dynamite; shorter sticks than he had been using with Vincent, but thicker, too. They looked new, and were probably more stable than the few charges George had left. Five crates, each with forty sticks. Twenty times what he and Vincent had brought back from Winnipeg.

Across the car were the blasting caps, also of new manufacture and designed specifically for the Army's thicker charges. Another crate held coils of fuse, stiff loops wrapped and tied for stability.

In the next corner he found the crates of ammunition. Artillery shells like the one the Kit Fox had brought him, they were set in groups of ten, a hundred shells to the crate. He stopped counting crates at twenty-five. But what were they for?

In the last corner was a jumble of wagon wheels and long, rough-sided boxes. George lifted the wheels and axle bars off the boxes. Other pieces of wood and wrought iron—fashioned to some purpose and tagged with paper labels marked with one of the Army's obscure part numbers—were stacked in the corner in disarray. George shoved them all aside and looked at the boxes. They were unmarked. With a stout metal bar he cracked one open and pulled off the wood slats. Within, nestled in a bed of excelsior, was a huge, six-barreled rifle. To one side was a book. George picked it up, opened it, and began reading about the Hotchkiss Flank-Defense Revolving Cannon.

Except for chairs that stood empty along the walls, all the furniture had been removed from the State Dining Room. It was a week before the election and the place was full. Colored servants with white cotton gloves moved soundlessly on gum-soled shoes, serving drinks from silver trays. Ladies whispered in groups, the silk of their dresses doing likewise, and men in white ties and black tails clumped together like penguins on icebergs. Everywhere Custer looked he saw smiling faces, and the boisterous chatter nearly drowned out the Brahms coming from the double quartet at the north end of the room.

The string players finished their piece and started another. The cellos and violas laid down the base on which the violins floated their melody. Custer recognized the opening strains of a waltz by Strauss the Younger. He smiled and looked across the room.

"Excuse me, gentlemen," he said. He walked across the dark, hardwood flooring to a group of women, one of whom was his wife. He extended a gloved hand to Libbie. "A wheel about the room?" he asked.

Libbie glanced at the women with her and actually

blushed, her thin lips turning upward in a shy smile. "Autie? A dance?"

"Why not?" he said. "We have this grand room. Shame to waste it, if you ask me. Besides, I like the old standards, not like those new ones that Wagner or those French fellows are coming up with. Can't dance to those, don't you agree, ladies?"

Libbie's companions—governors' wives, congress-men's wives—all smiled in concurrence, never daring to contradict a man in public.

"Come along, Libbie. Let's dance. Just like Satur-day nights back in Monroe."

Libbie's smile went all girlish and she put her gloved hand on his arm.

"If you ladies will excuse us," he said with a nod. He led his wife resolutely to the center of the room. Guests cleared away, giving them space, smiling indul-gently at their host's sudden whim.

The tempo was quick and the players gave the waltz the elongated first beat preferred by the Viennese style. Custer found his feet moving effortlessly. Libbie beamed at him, at home in her fine clothes, at ease in the center of attention.

"You are lovely," he told her.

She smiled. "And you, my Beau Saber. It's been a long while since I've seen you in a swallowtail coat. I do believe that you are by far the most dashing gentle-man in the room."

Custer laughed. "That's not a hard task," he said, "considering all the bulldogs we invited tonight." He pressed his hand into the curve of her corseted waist, led her into a grand sweeping curve, and then spun her in a half turn so that they were side by side, prom-enading up the length of the room like skaters on a frozen lake.

Some of the other guests decided to emulate their hosts. Couples began to twirl their tentative way into the rapidly clearing center of the room. Custer swung Libbie back around to face him as they danced.

"I'm sorry that this year has been so difficult," he said. "Next year I'll—"

She shushed him with a gloved finger against his lips. "No promises," she said. "Not tonight. You've been campaigning for six months, making promises everywhere. You'll have a hard enough time keeping those without making dubious ones to me."

Custer nodded. "As you wish," he said.

The waltz came to an end and the guests applauded, their gloved hands muffling their praise.

"A two-step," a young governor suggested.

"No," said an older statesman. "A galop." The crowd approved the latter choice and turned to their host for a decision. Custer nodded toward the musicians.

"Whatever they want," he announced.

"Now, there's the mark of a *true* politician," someone commented loudly, and friendly laughter spun through the room.

The music began, lively and cheerful—the "John Peel Galop," an old favorite. Custer turned to his wife, but before they stepped back onto the impromptu dance floor, he caught sight of Jacob at the tall double doors. Jacob motioned, asking for Custer's attention.

"Aw, Hell," he murmured.

Libbie looked over her shoulder. "Don't worry, Autie. The election is only a week away. There are bound to be interruptions tonight."

"Yes, but this is the first one to interrupt me after I've started to enjoy myself."

"Well . . ." She straightened his tie. "It won't be the last, I hope. Thank you for the dance, my dear."

Custer leaned over and kissed his wife's hand. Then, with a casual smile he did not feel, he walked over and met Jacob outside in the hallway. Samuel was with him.

"What is it?" he asked as he strode to the cross hall and started up the stairs two at a time. "Problems with our numbers?"

"Oh, no, sir," Samuel said, trying to keep pace with his president and retain his air of dignity at the same time. "The numbers still look good. We will lose New York—"

"That is expected, even with Morton's help."

"Yes, sir. And some of the South is going to be too close to call—"

"But not the North?"

"The Union & Labor Party is drawing ten percentage points in the cities. That is helping to break Cleveland's bloc with the Democrats."

They reached the upper floor. "But that's not what you wanted to see me about, is it?" He turned toward his office.

Jacob and Samuel stopped at the landing. Custer turned.

"What?"

"In the library, sir," Samuel said.

Custer felt the ruffled edge of anger touch him. "What's going on here? Jacob?"

"There's been an attack," the secretary said. "On a trainload of recruits heading into the Territory."

Custer noted that even though there were still several territories that had yet to achieve statehood, whenever someone said simply "the Territory," they meant the only territory that mattered now: the Unorganized Territory.

"How bad?"

"As bad as it's ever been."

"When?"

"Early this month. On the ninth."

"Three weeks ago?"

"Word just came in this week. We've been keeping it quiet since then," Jacob said.

Custer's mind whirled. An attack. On a train. In the Territory. He looked toward the library door. "What's going on here?"

Jacob looked embarrassed. "It's a reporter. From *Harper's*—just a stringer, really. He heard the story from a relative. He says he'll hold it until after the election if . . ."

Samuel finished the sentence. "If we pay him one thousand dollars."

Custer felt his blood rise to his face. "Get Higgins and Campbell."

"They're already in there."

Custer walked to the library doors and pushed them open. The gas lamps wavered, and in their unsteady light he saw his two bodyguards standing on either side of the doorway. Near the desk, coming quickly to his feet, was a thin, dark-haired man of about thirty years. He wore an old gabardine raincoat and held his round-topped hat in his hands.

"Mr. President," the man said. "I believe I have some information that—"

"Shut your lousy little mouth," Custer said. The man blanched. Custer walked up to him and stared him right in the eye. The reporter tried to look brave, but Custer noted a narrowing of his eyes, like a dog expecting a blow. He turned and began pacing back and forth before him. "Secretary Greene and Mr. Prendergast, here, have informed me that you have learned of the tragic and terrible attack on our forces in the Unorganized Territory. Is that true?"

"Yes, Mr. President. I got a letter from—"

"They also tell me that you freelance for a newspaper."

The man nodded.

"And that you are willing to hold off on reporting this story."

"Until after the election, sir, if—"

"If we pay you a thousand dollars." Custer stopped and turned on the man. "Correct?"

The man looked right and left. His face broke into a grin and he laughed nervously. "A thousand dollars? Is that what they said?"

Custer looked at Jacob. The Secretary of War gave a slight nod.

"Not a thousand, Mr. President," the man was going on. "Not a thousand . . . but if you could see your way clear to staking me to something . . . enough to get me and my family out there to the Frontier . . . for one of those homestead claims, sir." His gaze touched on everyone, searching every face for a hint of sympathy. "A few hundred, sir . . . I'd gladly hold off on this story . . . forget all about the letter my cousin wrote me . . . until after the election's over."

"Gentlemen," Custer said, turning to the men present, "you heard him clearly?" Four heads nodded.

"Higgins. Campbell. Arrest this man."

"What?" the reporter cried out. "Mr. President! I didn't do nothin'."

Custer slapped the man across the face and stared at him, allowing all the hatred and viciousness he felt seep into his expression. "You have just tried to blackmail the President of the United States and affect the democratic process. You're lucky I don't plan to have you charged with treason."

"But, Mr. President—"

"Get this trash out of here."

The guardsmen each grabbed an arm and led the man to the door.

"Take him down the back stairs," Custer said.

"Autie," Jacob said when they were gone and the door was closed again. "Is this wise? Locking up a stringer from *Harper's*?"

"You think I should have paid him off?" Custer shook his head. "No, we'll lock him up until after the election. That will keep him quiet and save us the problem of dealing with an extortionist. The story might break anyway, but at least we've plugged this one hole in the dike." He looked at Samuel and Jacob, still angry. "Why did you tell me?"

Jacob looked at the floor. Samuel simply frowned.

"We didn't want to distract you from the campaign," Jacob said. "There was nothing you could do, anyway. We told you as soon as it even threatened to get into the papers."

Custer calmed himself. They're not the enemy, he reminded himself. He smoothed back his hair and took a deep breath.

"Never keep me in the dark again," he said calmly. "Never." He glared at each of them in turn. "Now, let's get back to the party before we're missed."

"Yes, Mr. President," the two men said.

Herron and his entourage rode westward through the early snow, on their way toward the fort. The wind pushed and shoved at them like a schoolyard bully, slapping at hat brims, tugging at cloaks, shoving them back the way they'd come. Herron snarled at the unseasonably early storm.

Even the weather wants us out of this place, he thought.

A gust shot a fusillade of ice at them. Herron's horse spooked and spun and he pulled at the reins to keep his mount under control. Looking around in the blowing snow, he found the long, snow-covered mound of the railroad that they had been following like a lifeline.

"General, are you all right?" Noyles asked.

The wind fired at them again with cold, cutting shards of ice and snow, and Herron was heartened to see even the overly capable Noyles raise a hand to ward off the sting. They held there, hiding behind cloak and arm until the wind released them.

Herron reached inside his coat and grabbed the small, leather-clad flask he kept there. He offered it first to Noyles, who refused with a silent gesture. Herron took a swallow of the old single malt.

The first swallow was always the worst: a mouthful of charcoal and peat. But it was necessary in order to achieve the second swallow, which was full of warmth and heather. He finished with yet a third, and tasted oak wood and felt the heat turn to a burn that crept down his gullet and filled him with pungent fire. He sucked air through his teeth as he corked the flask and returned it to his coat pocket.

"There," he said. "Now I'm all right."

The wind weakened, keeping its edge but losing some of its enthusiasm for the attack. He and Noyles started off again, riding side by side, their horses' hooves shuffling through the snowy grass. The world around them was made smaller by the enclosing weather, but seemed also endless, as if they traveled in a bubble surrounded by a pale void. The sounds of harness and tack, of horse and man were all that existed in their tiny world. Herron studied the railroad tracks that lay on their right hand, watching as they appeared out of the void before them and disappeared behind, as if consumed by the thing that created them. He shivered at the image, and was glad when Noyles spoke and broke the spell.

"Sir, may I speak frankly?"

Herron nodded.

"Well, sir, I don't intend to criticize. I simply wish to understand . . ."

"Noyles, you gutless rabbit. I've given you my permission to speak. Just say what you mean."

The pink-cheeked man coughed to hide his unease. "Yes . . . well . . . I was only wondering, sir, considering the tragic results of the attack, why you still insist on moving out to Fort Hannibal?"

Herron smiled grimly. "You mean why move out there, without a proper garrison?"

"Well, yes, sir. Not to put too fine a point on it, but, yes."

He looked over at his aide. "Afraid, Noyles? Afraid of life out on the wild frontier, unprotected, surrounded by belligerent savages?" Noyles frowned and Herron laughed. "You are," he said. "You figured a post as a general's aide would keep you safe and warm and well at the rear, didn't you?"

"I was only thinking of the general's safety, and the security of the command."

"Like Hell you were." Herron laughed again. "You're thinking of your own pale hide."

"General, I assure you—"

"At ease, Noyles," he said with a wave of his hand. "I know your background. I know of your family. Hell, your father wrote to me personally after the attack on the train."

"My father? Why, sir, I—"

Herron cut him off again. "Don't worry. He said nothing inappropriate. Didn't have to, did he? The senatorial letterhead was message enough."

He glanced over at his aide. The young man was thoroughly furious and holding it in bravely, staring into the snowy nothingness, his cheeks nipped red by more than just the cold, the leather of his gloves creaking on the reins.

Herron took out his flask again, uncorked it, and handed it to the young lieutenant. This time Noyles accepted the offer. He put it to his lips, took a deep swallow, and grimaced.

"Take another," Herron said. "The second one is worth the first." The lieutenant did so and handed back the flask.

"Thought you were doing it all on your own, didn't you?"

Noyles nodded.

"Well, don't worry about it. I don't give a damn whose feathers get ruffled by my actions, senatorial or otherwise. I'm going to do as I see fit, when I see fit." He took a mouthful of whiskey, let its astringency pull at the tissues of his tongue and cheeks, and then let it burn its way down as he swallowed. "That's why we're out here, riding through this, instead of waiting for the train to make its way out here again."

His aide looked at him, not understanding, but as far as Herron could remember, it was the first time

that the senator's young son had ever really listened
to his commanding officer. Herron decided to speak
plainly.

"Noyles, if the Indians attacked one train, they can
attack the next. Safer for us on horseback and moving
without a schedule than on the first train in a month
and a half, wouldn't you say?"

His aide nodded, comprehension seeping in past his
frown. "But the garrison, sir . . ."

Herron chuckled. "Don't fret, son. The Indians
haven't had the guts to attack one of our forts in over
a year. The men out at these forts are only at half
strength, but they'll be enough, at least for the next
few weeks until we get more recruits out here. Those
savages killed plenty of our boys in that train attack,
but soldiers, as you'll learn, can be replaced." He
sighed, his breath frosting in a cloud around him. "I'm
more worried about the loss of the arms and muni-
tions. *Damn.*" He struck his thigh at the thought.
"How did they know? The one train among dozens.
Who would have told the Indians a thing like that?"

"Sir?"

Noyles looked puzzled again, but Herron was suddenly out of patience. "What don't you understand
now?" he said in irritation.

"No, sir, it's not that. I just . . . well, isn't it
obvious?"

"Obvious? Isn't what obvious?"

"How they got their information about the
shipment."

Herron bit back an overly harsh reply and succeeded in saying only, "If it was obvious, then I would
know, wouldn't I?" He took a slow breath. "So tell
me, Noyles. How did they know?"

"I'm sorry, sir. It just seemed clear to me. They've
obviously got a spy."

"Well of course they've got a spy. That's what I've
been saying. But who? Who would help the Indians
do such a thing?"

Noyles's face was a wide-eyed mask of innocence. "Why, Captain Custer. The president's son, sir."

Now it was Herron's turn to gape. "Custer's boy?" he said, distracted by his whirling thoughts. "Alive?" He recalled his talk with the president before the bridge had begun; a conversation of loss, death, and finality. He'd thought no more on it; he had taken his own advice, considered the young captain dead, and driven any further thought of him from his mind. But now, yes, it was all too clear.

"You're right, Noyles," he said. "It's perfectly obvious. You've got to speak up more often, Son."

"Yes, sir," Noyles said.

"Sergeant Tack!" Herron bellowed.

"Sir," the sergeant said, reining in.

"Send two men back to Fort Sherman. I want all regiments alerted. Any white man seen riding in the company of the enemy is to be shot on sight."

"Sir!" The sergeant saluted and wheeled to carry out his orders.

Rainstorms rose from the shallow waters of the Big Salty like vast trees sprouting to the heavens. With violent winds they battered back the early snows of the Big Hard Face Moon and drenched the southern lands with oceans of rain. Storm Arriving, returning from an unsuccessful dawn hunting foray, forded the Sudden River and crossed back into the contested lands. His whistler slipped and slid on a riverbank turned to mud by the passage of the hundreds who had crossed before him. The hen warbled in distress, her face pulsing in bars of anxious red and white. He calmed her with a word, driving her onward with steady pressure from his feet. His war mount, a drake and stronger-limbed, dug his three-toed feet into the muck to push himself up the slope. The hen took heart and pushed harder to keep up with her companion.

They reached the top of the bank and Storm Arriving slowed to take in the view. His throat tightened with pride and he could not keep a smile from his lips as he looked out on a thing that, just a few weeks before, the world had never seen.

It was not just a war party. It was an army. Soldiers from every band, from every society. Soldiers even from the allied tribes and from the people from across the Big Greasy. Tied by blood or honor, clan or friendship, they were a thousand strong, the greatest assemblage of might in the People's long history. They stood or sat in groups that formed and dissolved as he watched, men moving from one group to another, visiting with old friends, telling stories, gossiping like old women.

But unlike old women, each man was armed, and heavily so. The soldiers carried not only one of the traditional weapons of bow and lance, ax and club, but each also had one of the rifles taken from the attack on the iron hardback. One of the new weapons rested across every man's legs or leaned up against his belongings, and hanging from bedrolls and slung across backs were packets filled with the small cartridges that the rifles fired. Ten shots the rifles would fire, one after another before it needed more. Storm Arriving gripped the smooth wooden stock of his own rifle and thanked the spirits for the strength of these new weapons. But even a thousand men with *vé'hó'e* weapons was not enough to do what needed to be done.

He toed his whistler into a trot and rode up to Two Roads and the other chiefs who had been selected to lead the army. "Any word from One Who Flies?" he asked the Kit Fox war chief.

"No," the older man said. "He was supposed to meet us here after testing the bluecoat thundersticks."

"We should not depend on your *vé'ho'e* to save us," said Good Voice, chief of the Red Shield soldiers. "Look what happened at the attack on the iron hardback."

"We won that battle," Two Roads said.

"By luck," said the chief of the Red Shields. His blunt features wrinkled at the memory. "Besides, he is probably in pieces on the wind by now. I do not trust his thunder-sticks."

The chief of the Little Bowstrings strode up. "Do we wait?" he asked, his tone indicating that he thought they should not.

"I say we go," Good Voice said.

"We can't go without One Who Flies," Storm Arriving said.

"Look at the sky," Good Voice said. "How long do you think we can count on this easy weather? We must attack."

Two Roads looked at Storm Arriving, his face creased with concern. "We cannot wait any longer," he said. "He should be here already. The Hoop and Stick Game Moon is past full. We must go."

One of the Red Shield soldiers whooped and pointed eastward. "One Who Flies," he shouted. Men stood and shaded their eyes as they peered into the rising sun. Word spread. Whoops filled the air.

Seven men on whistler-back rode in at a run. Storm Arriving saw One Who Flies in the lead, his pale hair tied up behind in a short braid, his eyes as bright as his smile. With him were Gets Up Early, Pine, Standing Motionless, and the rest of the soldiers who had first worked with him digging for the yellow chief-metal. They whooped and shouted their greetings as they sped in.

Storm Arriving goaded his whistler into a lope and reached the new arrivals just as they met up with the main body. One Who Flies spied his friend and grinned even more broadly than before. He said something to Gets Up Early. The Little Bowstring soldier signed his understanding and rode on toward the chiefs while One Who Flies waited for Storm Arriving to join him.

"My friend," One Who Flies said, his mood beyond joyful.

"The bluecoat thunder-sticks worked?" Storm Arriving asked.

One Who Flies laughed out loud. "Even better than we had hoped. The bluecoat supplies are far superior to what we had before. Stable, reliable, easier to use. We have a few surprises for our enemy."

"So we are ready?"

"We are ready."

Storm Arriving shouted his joy and startled the whistlers. The men laughed together as they got their dancing mounts back under control. Then they rode to the chiefs. Good Voice had heard the news and looked as if he could not decide between disapproval and suspicion. Storm Arriving laughed at the chief's consternation.

"Do not worry," he told Good Voice. "We still might fail. Then you will have been right all along."

The other chiefs chuckled at the teasing, but grew quickly quiet. They all looked at one another in silent conversation. Finally Setting Sun, war chief of the Crazy Dog soldiers, said, "Let us make ready."

Whistlers sang. Men laughed and joked. Spirits were high as the army split into two groups and got under way. They rode quickly, letting the whistlers fly across the flat lands. The beasts shifted colors to match the landscape—tawny brown for the fallen grass of summer; a pale, attenuated green to mimic the mosses that thrived only in winter. The sky was clear and the sun strong, but the air was cold with the speed of their passage. They raced southward and after a few hands of travel, with whoops and good wishes, the two groups parted.

Storm Arriving rode with the other Kit Foxes. The Wolf Men and the Crazy Dogs and some from the other tribes were with them, as well. One Who Flies and three of his mining men were with the group, too, though they rode to one side, apart from the main body. The soldiers rode, and as the miles passed, their target grew near and their jubilance waned. Storm Arriving knew why, for he shared their thoughts.

For some of us, today is the final day.

The short winter day was half done before someone shouted and the chiefs called the force to a halt.

"There," someone said.

The bluecoat fort seemed so small, so harmless against the expanse of the land around it. It was still miles away, and from this distance, it was little more than a dark patch on the ground, its smoke barely a smudge in the pale blue of the afternoon sky. It was alone, isolated, surrounded by miles and miles of flat, unwelcoming land. It was not swarming with bluecoats. It was not the nexus of an invasionary force.

"We can hardly have feared this," he said to no one in particular.

"Fear it," said One Who Flies, suddenly at his side. He reached into bags on his whistler's rump and withdrew a variety of tools and items. He jutted his jaw toward the bluecoat fort. "It is the canker from which will grow the plague that will kill us."

Storm Arriving turned to his friend. "Us?" he said with a kindly smile.

One Who Flies looked up from his ropes and pieces of metal and Storm Arriving saw no humor in his eyes. There was no room in that gaze for anything that was not hard or edged.

"Yes," One Who Flies said. "Us."

Grasshopper, Pine, and Standing Motionless rode up. Their rifles had been stowed and they all carried their bows. They each handed One Who Flies an arrow with an extra-long shaft, and he worked on them with leather laces and his rope.

Two Roads came up to them. He said nothing, only watching the work in silence, patiently waiting for its completion. When all was ready, he turned and signaled the other chiefs. A great whoop went up from the soldiers and they wheeled their mounts and rode toward the fort.

Storm Arriving looked at his friend, at the three soldiers with their bows beside him.

"I will see you after," he said.

"Yes," One Who Flies said. "And I will see you."

"Let's go," he said to his whistler, and headed toward the bluecoat fort.

He rode in at full speed, keeping low over his whistler's spine. He had his rifle in one hand and held on to the first rope with the other, barking and whooping as he rode. The dark, uneven line of the fort grew in his sight, walls sprouting up from the ground, towers lifting their sinister heads. He saw the bobbing faces of bluecoats looking over the walls, smelled the savor of their cookfires. He levered a cartridge into his rifle. Muffled gunfire popped, like corn kernels thrown into a fire.

The attacking force split in two, flowing around the fort like water. He heard shouts above his head as he swung left past the main gate and under the bulk of one of the square towers. He could even hear the pounding of feet on the wooden ramparts as bluecoats ran to man the walls.

They rode around the fort, circling it as they had always done before. Storm Arriving fired up at the bluecoats, but not often and without aiming. On his second circuit around the fort he saw the three miners ride in. Smoke trailed after them. They halted fifty yards from the gate and pulled back their bows. They fired, and Storm Arriving saw the sparks and smoke arc through the clear blue sky.

"Thunder comes!"

The arrows sailed toward the fort, one toward the timbered wood of the tall gate, and the others up to the towers that commanded the corners on either side. The riders barely had time to retreat before the thunder-sticks tied to the arrows struck.

Fire exploded across the fort. Bluecoats screamed in terror and agony. Storm Arriving turned and saw the hole where the gate had been, the fire that burned there, the smoke and flames that rose from the ruins of the towers. Splinters of wood rained down from the sky, and through the smoky gap in the wall, Storm

Arriving saw bluecoats—some sitting in the dirt, some still standing—staring at the damage the thunder had wrought. Horses began to pound out of the yard and onto the safety of the prairie.

A rider sped past. Storm Arriving saw pale hair and the glint of the afternoon sun off a rifle barrel.

"Let's go!" he shouted.

They poured through the gap and into the fort. Bluecoats on the undamaged walls fired at them and men and whistlers went down. But as the bluecoats reloaded, Storm Arriving and the others fired again. And again.

And again.

And then it was over.

Later, Storm Arriving found One Who Flies sitting on his war mount outside the broken walls.

"How many did we lose?"

"Three dead," Storm Arriving said. "A dozen men wounded. One may die."

"Is Good Voice happy?"

Storm Arriving heard the bitterness in his friend's voice. "Good Voice will never be happy," he said, and won a smile. "Do you think it went as well with the others?"

"Yes," One Who Flies said. "I'm sure of it."

"That's two forts, then."

"And four to go."

Two Roads and the other chiefs rode out of the ruined fort. Behind them, soldiers led whistlers laden with goods taken from the commissary and armory. Two Roads motioned to the spoils of their victory. "We have regained all that we expended and more," he said.

"We will grow stronger as they grow weaker," One Who Flies said. "But we should not take anything that will slow our progress."

"Such supplies can help families at home. We will cache what we do not need for battle," the chief said. He glanced behind him and they all saw Kit Foxes setting fire to the rest of the fort. "We are done here. We ride now to the meeting place."

Herron ground his teeth together. Private Andrews stood before him, bruised and bloodied. Smoke smeared his face and soiled his uniform. Colonel Lewis Grey, the commander of Fort Hannibal, stood behind Herron at the shuttered window. A single hurricane lamp lit the room, its flame turned low to conserve oil. Noyles stood near the door, hidden in the shadowed corner where the dim lamplight could not reach.

"How many?" Herron asked the soldier.

"Hundreds, sir. More'n I've ever seen afore."

"And they used explosives?"

"Blew a hole big enough to drive a train through, sir. And then they just . . . just poured in. Like the sea. And then it was nothing but injuns and lizards and gunfire. The horses stampeded an' I . . . I . . ."

"You what?"

"Sir? I know it looks bad, sir. I know it does." The private's eyes were wide with remembered terror, his lank hair plastered to his sweaty brow. He leaned forward onto the lip of Herron's desk, his hand wrapped in a bloodied kerchief. Herron could smell the smoke on his clothes, the scent of gunsmoke clinging to him. "Honest, I didn't run, sir. I didn't. I mean, we were done for. Our sixty-five against their hundreds. Someone had to come. Someone had to come and warn you. I didn't run, General. I swear I didn't."

Herron nodded, accepting the man's explanation. "Don't worry, Private. No one's accusing you of anything. Now go and talk to the quartermaster. He'll see to your needs."

"But General Herron," the private said, his eyes wide, his tone urgent. "We've got to pack up. We've got to get out of here. They'll be comin' this way."

"Private Andrews," said Colonel Grey from his sta-

THE SPIRIT OF THUNDER

tion near the window. "Thank you for your report. You are dismissed."

The soldier suddenly remembered that there were others in the room. His gaze shifted from colonel to general, and Herron could see sanity return to the young man's face. He stood straight, attempted a snap to attention, and saluted.

"Thank you, Private," Herron said, and watched the young man leave. Noyles closed the door, and Colonel Grey came around and sat down in the chair before the desk. Grey was a precise man, fiftyish but still with jet-black hair and mustache. His dark brown eyes glittered like obsidian in the lamp's light.

"When is the next train east?" Grey asked the lieutenant.

"Day after tomorrow," Noyles said. "Noon."

Herron scowled. "What are you thinking, Colonel?"

"Of decamping, sir. If Andrews is accurate, we'll be overrun by this time tomorrow. I recommend a full withdrawal, and as soon as possible."

"I do not intend to surrender all our gains—"

"General . . ." Noyles stepped forward from the shadows. "If Andrews is telling the truth, both of our westernmost positions have been annihilated. That means that you, sir, are now at the front line, with only one hundred men to protect you against a force many times greater."

"But evacuate?"

Grey leaned forward in his seat. "Not evacuate, sir. Withdraw. Pull back our lines to a defensible position. You've been fighting a defensive campaign all along, sir. Now would be the worst time to change that strategy."

Herron tapped his fingers on the desktop. They were right, he knew, and the best way for a commander to commit suicide was to ignore good counsel. He went to the window and pushed open the shutter. Outside, the yard was quiet. Lanterns swung and guttered in the wind. Horses whickered among themselves and friendly voices could be heard from inside the smithy where a supposedly clandestine poker game was being played.

We were safe, he told himself. As long as the Indian remained thwarted by our forts, we were safe. But now he has weapons, and explosives . . .

And confidence.

"Send riders out to the homesteads. Send a rider to Fort Beckwith as well. Have them wire Westgate. I want a train out there to meet us. We're pulling back."

"How far?" Colonel Grey asked.

"We'll combine all our strength at Fort Assurance and send as many of the civilians as we can back across the river to Westgate. If there's a war coming, it'll be on ground of my own choosing."

George crawled up to the limit of the low rise, the others close behind him. He reached into his bag and took out the binoculars he'd taken from the first fort they'd attacked. With them he scanned the landscape.

"This is the place," he said. "Fort Assurance. This is where they're going to make their stand." He handed the binoculars to Two Roads. He and the other chiefs—all part of an advance scouting party—reviewed the scene and eventually passed the glasses back to George.

The town that hung on the tracks was empty despite the midmorning hour. No smoke rose from chimneys, no horses stood at hitching posts. It was just as desolate as the other forts and homesteads they'd encountered on their way here. The Army had taken every article of possible use with them in their retreat—food, tools, supplies of every kind. Nothing had been left behind except the buildings themselves, and those the People's forces had burned to the ground. As George looked out on the town, he saw the same signs of orderly evacuation.

But the fort before them was a different story. It

sat beyond the town, a squat structure south of the railroad. He could see men on the towers and walking along the battlements. Two pale trails of woodsmoke rose from within the fortress walls, slanting to the east in the west-born wind. The gate was open, and riders moved in and out as patrols came and went. Around the perimeter, outside the walls, barriers with sharpened poles had been erected and breastworks had been dug. In the trenches, George could see more soldiers. He put the binoculars away.

"We are most definitely expected," he said.

Good Voice grunted. "We still outnumber them."

"Those breastworks will make a difference," George said.

"Perhaps," Two Roads said. "But I saw nothing there that would make us change our plans. Did you?"

The other chiefs, Good Voice included, indicated that they had not.

"Are the men prepared?" Two Roads asked.

"They are," the chiefs answered.

"And yours?" he asked George.

"They are waiting for your command."

"All is well," Two Roads said. "Let us begin."

The wind smelled of the sea. Herron stood at the tower rail and looked westward. The clouds were piled up above the world's rim like a Roman shade, ready with tomorrow's weather, waiting for the wind to pull the cord and unroll them across the land.

More rain, Herron fretted, is not what we need.

He studied the young lookout who shared the platform with him. The private stood at the rail, his eyes scanning the horizon, his hands clasped behind his back. From a lanyard around his wrist hung the bright metal whistle that he would blow at the first sign of an attack force.

"Make sure you watch more than just the horizon," Herron told the young soldier. "Keep an eye on the middle distances, beyond the edge of town, as well."

"Yes, sir, I will."

A lieutenant pounded up the ladders to the tower. "General Herron, sir," he said. "Colonel Grey wished to inform you that the western patrol is overdue."

Herron nodded. "My compliments to the colonel. Please return and tell him to prepare the men. We should see action within the hour."

"Very good, sir."

Herron turned his attention to the landscape. He felt his blood cool and his heart calm at the certain prospect of battle. He turned to ask Quincy for his glasses and found that it was not Quincy, but Noyles at his side.

Of course, he reminded himself. Poor Quincy's gone.

He held out his hand and Noyles gave him the binoculars.

"I can't see anything out there, sir," Noyles said. "What are you looking for?"

"Ghosts," Herron said. Through the dark-walled tunnel of the binoculars' enhanced vision, he scanned the horizon, searching for anything that seemed out of place. He found nothing, and continued his scan around to the north and east.

"How can you hide in this land?" he asked his unseen enemy.

A whistle blew at the southwest tower, sharp and shrill. Herron looked and saw men pointing. "To your posts!" he bellowed. Inside the walls, men ran across the muddy yard and scaled ladders to the walls. Outside, men ducked down in their trenches. Another whistle sounded from the opposite corner of the fort. Two forces, then, Herron thought; out of the west and east, flanking our gates. He looked beyond the walls, expecting to see the enemy charging in from miles distant.

The enemy was not miles away. He was nearly at their doorstep. Less than a mile away, to the east as well as the west, a line of whistler-borne Indians had appeared. Herron cursed again the savage's skill at stealth and surprise, but could not understand why they were not attacking. The two lines, several hundred on a side, simply stood their ground, beyond effective rifle range.

"What are you planning?" he asked them and raised his binoculars again.

The Indians, faces painted with white and black, red and ocher, sat atop whistlers mottled to match the winter terrain. Each man, to Herron's chagrin, carried a new Winchester repeater across his knees, spoils of the attack on the supply train. But they did not attack.

You've got our rifles, Herron said to himself. And our explosives. What are you planning, if not an attack? A siege? Has Custer's boy taught you siege warfare?

His mind worked, the clarity of battle taking over his senses. Siege warfare. What would Custer teach them? To draw us out? To goad us beyond our defenses? What about the heavy guns from the train?

Herron checked the enemy lines again. Just Indians and rifles. He checked the fort's perimeter. Men manned the walls and towers, rifles ready. Men down in the trenches were prepared as well. Horses at the back of the yard were saddled, and carbine-armed troops stood by, waiting to sally forth when the Indians began their standard circling attacks. They were ready for an attack, but not a siege.

And then the enemy began to move.

It wasn't an attack. It was an advance. They started forward in a slow, measured progress. Herron looked through his glasses and saw the whistlers take a step and then pause; another step, and a pause.

A murmur swept through the men along the walls. Herron heard it and hated it. The Indians were playing with his men, toying with them, eroding their confidence. Custer's boy *had* taught them something. Warfare of the mind.

More steps, and the Indians began to chant in

rhythm with their hesitant advance. The chant built, and Herron saw his soldiers glance from one side to the other, realizing that the enemy was closing in.

"Don't fret, boys," he heard Grey shout from his position on the far tower. "Let them walk right on up. Makes it easier to blast them on to Hell." Laughter followed the colonel's remarks and Herron silently approved. Still, he could not understand what the Indians intended.

A whistle pierced his ears. The lookout on his own tower was pointing north, toward the town. Herron saw Indians in among the buildings and along the tracks, less than a half mile away. Some carried bows, and they fired. Arrows leapt upward, sputtering flame and drawing lines of smoke across the sky. One was heading for his own position.

"Down!" he cried. "Off the towers. To the south."

He shoved the lookout toward the ladders. Another man leapt down from the tower to the ramparts. Noyles pulled at Herron's arm, urging him to safety. Herron grabbed his aide and pushed him ahead. He had his hand on the ladder when the arrows hit.

The explosion ripped away the footing of the tower and Herron grabbed the railing as the flooring slewed and bucked. Another explosion blasted the gatework and he felt his face and arm struck by splintered wood. He pulled himself up to the lip of the tower platform, toward the ladder that still, somehow, hung to the side. He got a leg up over the edge and looked over to find Noyles, blood smearing his cheek, holding the ladder in place for his general. He gave silent blessing for the senator's only son and grabbed on to the ladder. A third explosion detonated and Herron saw the platform of the northeast tower lift up in the air like a feather in a gentle breeze. It tipped in midair, spilling men, and slowly came crashing down upon them.

Gunfire chattered from the flanking forces and Herron heard bullets spatter the wooden walls. That was

just for show, he thought, knowing the main attack
was still to come. He clambered down the ladder to
the parapet, almost lost his footing again as the tower
shuddered, but was seized by soldiers and saved a fall
to the yard below.

"General," Noyles said. "Are you all right?"

His aide's voice sounded muffled. Herron shook his
head and realized his ear was full of blood. He pulled
a kerchief from his pocket and put it to his brow. It
came away bloody. "Just a cut. I'm fine. We've got to
barricade the yard."

The gate was a ruin. The northeastern tower was
damaged but still structurally sound; only the platform had been wrecked. The front of the northwest-
ern tower—Herron's position—was a pile of broken
lumber. The whole front of the fort was open to
attack. By the time Herron reached the yard, Grey
had already set men stacking timbers to form barricades.

"Colonel, are we still defensible?"

"I believe so, sir. We never planned on having to
withstand explosives, though."

"I know. Make do with what you can." He stopped
as gunfire began again outside the walls. "Sounds like
they're coming in. Let's use this to our advantage.
Place our Gatling guns in the gap."

"Yes, sir."

The heavy Gatling guns were slogged and pulled
into position behind low barricades. Herron climbed
up onto the southwest tower to get a view of what
was happening.

The Indians had begun their attack in earnest.
While some sped around the fort in a wide circle,
firing the occasional shot toward the ramparts, others
rode their whistlers to a harsh stop and ducked behind
their beasts' camouflage and fired with lethal accuracy
into the defenders.

The trench-bound shooters were doing deadly work
in turn. From their low vantage they could see the

whistlers against the flat horizon and the still-blue sky. Firing was erratic but not panicked, and Herron watched as Indians fell from their mounts and dropped from behind the screen of their whistlers' stippled flanks.

The Gatling guns were in place. Grey shouted the order and the multibarreled weapons opened fire. They spewed short bursts of heavy-caliber shot into the circling attackers. Men died, torn to pieces by bullets nearly half an inch wide.

He saw movement at the town. "My binoculars."

"Lost, sir."

He squinted, but was looking across the smoke-filled yard as well as an intervening half mile. "Look," he told Noyles. "In the shadows between the buildings. What is that?"

"I can't quite make it out, sir. Looks like some sort of animal."

Bullets from the Gatling gun chewed into the tavern wall. George touched the hardback's front foot with his stick, trying to stop him before he left the building's protective shadow. Pine did likewise, and the thousand-pound beast bleated like a monstrous lamb and slowed. On its back, the frame of willow-twig wicker and hewn lodgepoles creaked. The huge, five-barreled Hotchkiss rifle it supported swayed. Finally, the beast lumbered to a halt, half in the sunlight. George moved to the gunning position and Pine went to one of the wicker baskets that held the ten-shot magazines. He handed one to George.

"Are you ready?" George shouted over the rooftop to Gets Up Early.

"I am ready, One Who Flies," came the response from the other side of the tavern.

"Send the signal!"

An arrow rose into the air, a half-stick tied to its shaft. It exploded midair with a boom that echoed off what was left of the gate and northern towers of Fort

Assurance. The soldiers circling the fort parted, pulling back away from the northern side. Pine put his hand to the crank and George dropped the magazine into place.

"Begin," he said.

The barrels began to turn, picking up one of the six-inch-long, one-pound cartridges and carrying it around to the firing mechanism; not too fast—the manual warned that a fast fire rate could overheat the barrels. George clenched his teeth and squinted, anticipating the percussive shot. The first cartridge neared the top. George turned the wheels and capstans to line up the iron sights with the barricades where he had seen the sputtering fire of the Gatlings.

The Hotchkiss fired, the sound magnified by the buildings to either side. The rifle rocked backward. The hardback squalled, but held his place. Inside the gate, a bloom of fire erupted. George grinned and trimmed his aim. The second cartridge came up toward the firing pin.

"Oh, Christ," Herron said aloud as his fears became reality. The artillery round ripped into the barricade protecting the Gatling gun. A second round plowed into the soldiers behind it, tearing one man in half, his torso cartwheeling off to the side. The soldiers manning the second gun dropped their post and ran. Another round exploded behind them. The yard filled with smoke.

Herron abandoned the platform, Noyles quick on his heels. He grabbed a rifle from a dead soldier's hands. "Come with me," he ordered a squad of soldiers.

They ran along the parapet, heading to the north side. Gunsmoke filled the air with the taste of metal.

One-pound rounds from the Hotchkiss cannons flew into the yard, punching into the corralled horses, exploding against the far wall. Colonel Grey hollered orders down in the yard. Soldiers mounted up and headed out for an attack that was safer than sitting inside the yard like fish in a barrel.

More rounds came in, pounding the walls, finding the limits of their inner defense.

God help us if they hit the armory, Herron thought.

He reached what was left of the northern wall, slipped a cartridge into the rifle's block, and clamped it shut. He pointed, showing his squad the men and animals partially hidden by the shadows between the buildings beyond the tracks.

"You four, take the right. The rest of you, with me on the left. Take out those guns."

They aimed and fired. The Hotchkiss cannon continued fire. Herron put another cartridge in the rifle block and slammed it shut. He lifted the rifle to his shoulder. At the Hotchkiss, the gunner leaned forward into the sunlight, and Herron saw the blond hair of a white man. He grinned.

"All of you, with me. Take down that pale-haired bastard on the left."

He aimed.

Empty casings sang a song of hot brass as the cannon kicked them loose. The empty magazine clanged in the holder. Pine tossed it behind him and replaced it with a full one. The hardback slammed the ground with its clubbed tail, unhappy with the noise of the cannon. George aimed to compensate for the hardback's movement as Pine put his hand back to the crank.

A bullet spanged off the barrel housing. Another zipped past. Pine cried out, hand to his face, and fell back. George turned but felt a huge hand grab him by the arm and spin him the other way. An unseen fist slammed into his ribs, and another cracked him across the brow like the kick of a mule. Dazed, he stepped down off the hardback, blinking at the white spots that suffused his vision. He stumbled and fell to one knee. He blinked again. His vision cleared a little, and he saw Pine was by him, lying motionless in the dirt, a wound below his eye. George felt the searing rod of pain in his side. He looked down and realized that he'd been hit.

There was a hole in his deerskin tunic. He reached for it but his left arm refused to move. Another hole told him of a wound to his upper arm, but there was no pain for it. All agony was reserved for his torso. With his right hand he explored the wound in his chest, feeling the space where the bullet had punched through his rib. A thick droplet of blood landed on his leg. He touched his brow and found blood there as well.

Aw, Hell, he thought as the white spots across his vision were exchanged for dark splotches. Now I'm going to die. Aw, Hell.

Storm Arriving led his squad around the side of the fort. He ran his whistler past the barricades, up the breastwork, and directly into the trench. Bluecoats shouted and screamed as he drove his whistler through them. The animal's bulk filled the trench, its spade-clawed toes breaking men, cutting men, as it ran. Ahead of him, bluecoats scrambled up out of the trench as fast as they could. Behind him, the rest of his squad trampled anyone he missed, leaving death in their wake.

He whistled, three notes, and hung on as his beast climbed up out of the shallow trench. He swung back away from the gate and the explosions from the great rifles One Who Flies commanded. He glanced over and saw that one of them stood unmanned.

Horses ran out of the yard, some with riders, but most with empty saddles. Another thunder-stick exploded overhead; the last signal. War cries filled the air as the soldiers of the People turned and took their assault inside the fort.

"Inside," Storm Arriving shouted, and they swung

back in the direction of the breach. Again he looked toward the mammoth rifles and One Who Flies. He saw men lying on the ground.

He kicked his whistler into motion, streaking out toward the hardbacks. One Who Flies and Pine both lay in the dirt, faces upturned to the sky. He leapt off his mount and checked them both. Pine was dead. One Who Flies still lived.

He tried to remember all the things Speaks While Leaving had told him about her healing arts, and he cursed himself for not having listened more attentively. One Who Flies was wounded in the arm, in the head, and in the chest. The blood was not terrible, but there was a lot. He had to stop the bleeding. What was it his wife had said about bleeding?

He took his knife and began cutting at clothing, exposing the wounds, making strips of cloth and leather to bind them.

"Do not die," he pleaded. "I do not think this is part of the vision."

The sound of battle intensified. Riders on horse and whistler chased one another out of the yard and into the open. The firing of guns was constant, like hard hail against a lodgeskin. Soldiers retreated, driven back by the bluecoats on horseback. Storm Arriving tied off the last binding, grabbed his rifle, and mounted his whistler.

"Do not die," he said, and rode back into the fight.

Custer slammed the door so hard it failed to latch and swung back open. He turned, grabbed it, and rammed it closed. Then he turned and regarded his "guest."

General Charles Brandeis Herron stood near the desk in Custer's private office, at stiff attention despite the cane and the arm in a sling. He seemed a stark, angular figure against the ethereal light from the world of snow and marble outside. His uniform seemed nearly black, the brass buttons almost white. The dark wood of the furnishings and the pale, shell-jacquard silk that covered the walls combined to create a scene of contrasts; everything dark was limned in light, and everything bright was tinged with shadow like an artist's chiaroscuro. Custer took a breath, and stepped into the painting.

"I've called you here to talk about your performance, General," he said as he walked around his worktable and sat down in the straight-backed chair. "Would you please tell me how you account for it?"

Herron's gaze remained fixed on some indefinable point on the far wall. "I cannot comply with your request, Mr. President."

Custer blinked. That, certainly, was not what he had expected. Excuses, perhaps. Reasons, certainly. Even a certain amount of mea culpa would have been comprehensible, anything but a flat refusal.

"General, explain yourself."

"I cannot, sir."

Custer felt his fingernails digging into the flesh of his palm. "General Herron," he said slowly. "Please explain yourself, or lose any hope of ever again holding a command."

"Mr. President, sir," he replied, and Custer heard the rough edge of emotion in his voice. "We both know I'll never again command men in the field."

Custer sniffed. "True enough. Your career is over. You know it. I know it. But if that's true, you have nothing further to lose and can answer my question. How do you account for your complete failure to achieve any of the objectives laid out for you?"

In the light from the window, Custer saw the hard edge of the general's jaw pulse and clench. Still at attention, still staring at that infinite point, General Herron took a long breath and said, "I cannot comply with your request, Mr. President."

"Damnation, General, you *will* comply, or I'll have

you up on charges and ruin more than your career! You *will* comply, and you will tell me how you managed to lose four installations, fifteen hundred men, and every inch of ground gained in the past year and a half. *Now*, General."

Herron's nostrils flared and his mouth wrinkled in barely suppressed anger. "Sir," he said, and Custer saw him working to collect himself. "I failed, sir, because the enemy has advanced, in the course of less than a year, from a tradition of small-force strike-and-retreat tactics to a campaign of fully cohesive, well-coordinated, large-force combat strategy, including the demonstrated knowledge of demoralization tactics, supply-line dependencies, demolition techniques, siege warfare, and use of artillery. They have in effect, sir, progressed through fourteen hundred years of military history in ten months."

"And to what do you attribute—"

"If you will permit me, sir, I will tell you how they achieved this. Simply put, sir, they were taught. Someone taught them, someone coached them." He broke from his stance and looked Custer straight in the eye. "Someone educated in such things, sir." Then he resumed his pose at attention.

A feeling of dread began to worry at Custer's soul. An educated man. Educated in military history and tactics. An Army officer.

"Sir," Herron continued, "it is my opinion—"

"I have heard enough, General."

"No, sir, you have not. You will hear the whole of it."

"General, I am warning you—"

"Sir, I do not care. My career is over. Retirement or insubordination, it makes little difference to me. But by *God*, you'll hear that it was your son, sir, your son who taught them."

Custer's vision paled, the white silk on the walls bleeding out across the world, covering it. "My son?" he whispered. "How do you know?"

"I know because I saw him," Herron said. "Laying into my men with a cannon looted from the train he derailed. I know because I killed him. He's dead."

The air went out of Custer's lungs, stolen as if by some passing demon, sucked straight out of him at the utterance of that one phrase, that one word. Dead.

"Thank you, General," he said softly. "That will be all. Samuel will see you out."

CHAPTER 11

Winter, A.D. 1888
Near the Red Paint River
Alliance Territory

Speaks While Leaving patted the corn cake into shape and flopped it on the iron griddle. The griddle cake sizzled and hissed and filled the lodge with its warm scent of toasting corn. On the other side of the fire, soaked beans were cooking in a pouch made from an antelope's stomach. She rolled the pouch to let the other side cook for a time, spooning some water over it to keep it moist. It sputtered as the water steamed, and she went back to the cakes.

Her mother, Magpie Woman, and her grandmother, Healing Rock Woman, sat opposite the fire from her, working on their quilling and mending. With so many men making war against the bluecoats, One Bear had been pressed into picket duty, so the women had come together for the evening. Speaks While Leaving welcomed the company and the opportunity to provide the meal. Storm Arriving had spent most of the past year walking the path of war, and Speaks While Leaving had been relying on her relations for provisions and food from the hunts. Meager and insufficient as it was, this evening gave her the chance to repay in part her family's long kindness and generosity.

Healing Rock Woman used her iron awl to punch another hole in the strip of elk hide. Squinting, she threaded the strand of sinew through a piece of red-dyed porcupine quill, then passed the sinew through the hole she had made. She pulled the sinew tight, punched another hole, picked up a piece of black-dyed quill, and repeated the process. She sniffed the air as the cakes began to cook through.

"More grease," she said without looking up.

"Yes, Grandmother."

"And make extra," Magpie Woman said. "Your father will be hungry when he comes in."

"Yes, Mother." She smiled as she dipped two fingers into a jar and worked another touch of rendered fat into the corn dough.

Small sounds filled the lodge: the seething of the pouch of beans and the sizzle of the griddle cakes, the sibilant shifting of feet and the gentle rustle of hides as the women worked their sewing. The lodge had been so quiet for so long . . . it was nice to have some noise to liven things. Of course, that would change. She smiled again.

"Which do you hope for, Mother? A granddaughter? Or a grandson?"

She glanced up from under thick lashes. The two older women stared at her.

"Is it true?" her mother asked. "So soon?"

Her smile broke into a grin. "Yes," Speaks While Leaving said. "I know it is soon, but I felt it was time. Storm Arriving and I have wasted years enough."

Healing Rock Woman had not moved. She sat there, mouth slack, hands frozen in midpunch.

"Grandmother?" Speaks While Leaving said, worried that the ancient mother would disapprove of a child so soon.

The old woman reached over to slap Magpie Woman's leg. "Ha!" She put her quillwork back in her sewing bag, got to her feet, and walked around the fire. She stopped in front of Speaks While Leaving and gave her a kiss on the forehead. "My thanks," she said. "I did not know how much longer I could wait." Then she walked back around the fire and sat back down to continue with her quillwork. "Ha."

Speaks While Leaving was pleased. Most women waited four or five years after marriage to have their first child, and she had been afraid of what the family might have said about having a child after only two years.

A distant wail interrupted them—a woman, anguished. She heard the crunch of footsteps in the snow outside the lodge, and the doorflap opened. It was her father, One Bear, his face a thundercloud.

"They are coming in," he said. "The army. There are many wounded. Many dead."

She stared at her father, searching his face for some hint of disaster. "Storm Arriving?"

"I do not know," he said, and left, leaving the doorflap open.

Speaks While Leaving looked to her mother and grandmother. "My apologies," she said.

"We will tend to things here," her mother said. "Go where you are needed."

"Thank you."

"Send us word," Healing Rock Woman said. "As soon as you know."

"Yes," she said. "I will."

From behind one of the wicker backrests she took the parfleche that held her healer's tools and supplies. Then she left as well, following her father out into the wail-filled night, out through the blue, moonlit snow.

The men were coming in to the lower end of the hillside encampment. Wives were coming down the slopes to meet their returning husbands or receive their returning dead. The snow-draped forest muted the sounds of grief, dark trees collecting dark moans, an empty sky passing shouted prayers to the stars. Laughter, too, Speaks While Leaving heard, highpitched and hemmed with tears of relief. She looked from face to face, searching for her husband, and she saw in the eyes of the returning men a darkness for which the night did not account.

"Storm Arriving?" she asked one of them. He lifted a doleful arm, pointing back along the way he himself had arrived.

"He comes," the soldier said.

I seem always to be waiting for him, she lamented as she headed toward the back of the line. When will we have time to live?

"Daughter," her father said, calling her away from her search. "Over here."

A long line of wounded were being pulled in on travoises. She went to them and began her work, inspecting each man, speaking to the lucid, trying to determine whose needs were most urgent. But one after another, she found, they could all wait. The soldiers had done their best on the field, and those who needed a healer's immediate care had simply failed to survive the trip home. She recognized faces, but she did not see her husband. How far back was he? If not with the wounded, with the dead?

She felt a hand on her shoulder and turned to find him standing beside her.

Can it be as simple as that? she wondered. She looked up into his eyes, and saw the same darkness in him as was in the others. She saw the bloodstained bindings on his arm and hands. But it was him. Her husband.

Is that all I have to do? Simply turn around, and he is there? And all my fears can fly?

She reached for him, slowly, through a veil of blurring tears. She felt his hands on her shoulders, around her back. She took a breath and smelled his scent, his warmth, his closeness, and did not want to let the air from her lungs, fearing that in her next breath, he would be gone. But he squeezed her in his embrace, and her breath came out in an exhalation of joy and liberation.

But he said nothing. The muscles of his arms and

back were still tense. She looked up into his face. There was something in him, something she had never seen before. He took her by the hand and led her toward the end of the line of wounded men.

Moonlight reflected off the blond hair sticking out from under the deerskin that swathed the head of One Who Flies. She ran the last few steps to his side. His eyes were closed. His skin was pallid and cold despite the buffalo pelts piled high atop him. She put her ear to his mouth to listen. His breath was short and shallow, with little energy. She touched the great vein in his neck and felt the quick, weak pulse. She turned to her husband.

"He has been like this since it happened. He bled for two days on the way home. I am sorry. I could not remember all the things you told me."

She understood it, then, the thing in her husband's eyes. He was afraid. That was what it was, the thing in him she had never before seen. Fear. She reached out and touched his cheek.

"We will do what can be done."

They moved One Who Flies into their lodge where she could watch over him whenever she was not tending to others around the camp. The wounds the soldiers suffered in this new kind of war were strange; they were not the clean wound of an arrow or lance, nor were they the blunt crush of a club. Many had died on the way home, and of the ones who had survived the trip, more would die still.

Her husband's wounds were minor—cuts and stabs—nothing worse than what he had experienced in a whistler raid or during the ritual of skin sacrifice, and for it, she thanked the powers of the world. For One Who Flies, however, a different speaker wove the tale.

On his brow, a bullet had made a long gash, cut his scalp, and creased the skull, but it was not serious. The wound that pierced his upper arm, aside from the threat of fever, was likewise not a worry to her. These she drained, cleaned, treated, and dressed without a second thought.

But the wound to his chest was of great concern. The bullet had passed through him, breaking a rib on the lower left side on its way in, and coming out beneath his ribs in the rear. She found pieces of cloth and leather pulled into the wound, and was silently thankful for his unconsciousness as she cleaned it. He had bled a great deal, though, and there was nothing she could do for that except keep him quiet and warm, ward against any fever, and pray the spirits chose to save his life.

One Who Flies fluttered on the edge of death for three days, a moth around an open flame, seeking life in the deadly light. Speaks While Leaving took care of him as best she could, tending to his body, but feared it was not enough.

"Do you think Ashes would agree to come and sing over him?" she asked her husband.

Storm Arriving squinted one eye in mistrust. "That old trickster? He will do anything if it means a free meal."

She resisted the urge to speak sharply. "Can it do any harm?" she asked.

He considered this. "I suppose not," he said.

Storm Arriving rode out to hunt for something to supplement their meager supplies while she prepared the lodge for the holy man's arrival. By the time Ashes arrived, her home was neat, tidy, and smelling of fresh-cut juniper and roasting grouse.

Ashes was a man of many years and few teeth. His hair was metal-gray and wiry, constantly struggling to escape the bonds of its braids. When he entered the lodge, his gaze went immediately to the place where One Who Flies lay. Speaks While Leaving ushered him in to an honored place next to Storm Arriving at the back of the lodge.

"The food smells good," he said, his eyes still on the invalid.

"Thank you," Speaks While Leaving said. "Will you eat?"

A few heartbeats of silence passed, as if he were thinking about it. "Yes," he said at last. "I think I would like to eat."

Storm Arriving rolled his eyes and she glared at him; it was one thing to disbelieve in the man's abilities, but quite another to be discourteous to a guest. He subsided and she relented. Then, with a knife, she cut a piece of meat from one of the cooked birds, showed it to the four corners of the world, the sky, and the earth, and laid it near the hearth as an offering to the spirits.

Ashes ate with a zeal that belied his years. Storm Arriving watched the old man devour an entire bird by himself, cracking the bones between two of his remaining teeth and sucking them clean of marrow. He ate in wordless appreciation, and when he was done he sat back, greasy hands on grease-stained knees, and smiled a black, toothless smile.

"That was good," he said. "My thanks. And now, I think I would like to spend some time with our friend over there." He pointed to One Who Flies. "Alone," he added.

Storm Arriving began to say something but Speaks While Leaving stopped him with a hand on his arm and a poking finger in his ribs. "Of course," she said, and grabbing a buffalo robe, led her husband from the lodge.

They stood outside for a few moments, unsure of what to do. A light snow had begun to fall, tiny flakes twinkling with reflected firelight like dust from the stars. They saw the old man's shadow on the lodgeskin as he took out his rattle and leaned over One Who Flies. He began to sing in a soft, high-pitched voice, the rattle sizzling and snapping like fat in a flame. Speaks While Leaving took her husband's arm.

"Shall we take a walk in the moonlight?" she asked.

He took the buffalo skin and put it about both their

shoulders. The buffalo's fur was soft, softer than hair, softer than feathered down against her neck. They walked off under the snowy sky, arm in arm, wrapped in warmth, and left their guest to weave his songs of healing.

When they returned, Ashes was gone. So were the leftovers from dinner.

On the fourth day, One Who Flies began to rock his head slightly from side to side. His eyes rolled beneath his lids. Speaks While Leaving tried to give him water, pouring a small amount in his mouth, but he only sputtered and coughed, and his wounds began to weep once more. She tried trickling drops of water on his cracked lips, and was pleased to see his tongue come forth at the taste of it. A few droplets at a time, she squeezed the water from a piece of soaked deer-hide onto his lips. He took it in and swallowed, and thus was she able to address his thirst.

On the evening of the fifth day, she came home from tending others to find her mother waiting for her outside the lodge. Fearing that something had happened, she ran inside. Healing Rock Woman sat next to the bed where One Who Flies lay, her thin hands with their dark, leatherlike skin holding his with its long pale fingers. Storm Arriving sat nearby, an odd expression on his face.

Relief. He was relieved.

She looked at One Who Flies. His breath was slower, longer. His head turned, and he opened his eyes.

"Speaks While Leaving," he said in a rasped whisper. "The sight of you makes my heart glad."

She kept her composure and did not let him know how worried she had been. "My heart, too, One Who Flies. I am very glad to see you."

"Now," said her grandmother. "Will you please rest? Your husband says you have not slept in three days."

Speaks While Leaving looked at her grandmother.

The old woman slowly closed her eyes and opened them again. The danger was gone. One Who Flies would live.

"Yes," she said. "Yes. Sleep would be good."

One Who Flies stayed on with them in the days that followed. She gave him no choice, and he could not argue as his injuries had left him not only too weak to travel, but even too weak to rise. Mostly, he slept, soundly and peacefully, which she knew to be a good sign. His thirst was overpowering, and at times he gulped the snowmelt so fast that it made his head ache. His invalidity, however, also left him no option but to endure the indignity of relieving himself into a vessel for her to empty. Against her husband's wishes, she sent a buffalo robe to Ashes, but the old man sent it back, saying that One Who Flies needed it more than he.

And then one night as he ate he wanted to talk.

"Storm Arriving," he said. "Tell me what happened."

Her husband hesitated, glancing her way, then tried to laugh it off. "You were there. You know what happened."

"No," One Who Flies insisted. "I don't remember."

Speaks While Leaving felt a frown pull at her face. As Storm Arriving began to relate the tale of their strategy and attack on the final bluecoat fort, she felt her frown deepen and sink into her flesh like a hot iron into leather, searing her emotions onto her face. She busied herself with the duties of the meal—anything to keep her mind occupied. Still, she could not help but listen, could not stop the anger that built within her breast.

"When you fell," Storm Arriving was saying, "we were carrying the battle inside the walls. They defended themselves well from behind lodges and rollalongs. Many of the bluecoats ran away or rode out on horses, escaping into the coming night. Our soldiers wanted to follow, but the chiefs argued against it. The bluecoat fort was the target. That was what mattered."

"So," One Who Flies said. "We won."

"Yes," Storm Arriving said. "We won. We took all of the supplies they had and burned the fort to the ground. Many died; more than in any other war since the war with . . ."

"With my father," One Who Flies finished.

"Yes," Storm Arriving said. "But yes, we won."

Speaks While Leaving gripped the ladle she had used to serve the stewed meat and white-root for dinner. She felt her knuckles creak.

"We won," she said under her breath.

The two men stopped talking. "What was that?" Storm Arriving asked. "I didn't hear you."

She looked up at him, her frown having turned to a fierce glower. "We won," she said, and heard the bitterness in her own voice. "We won. We won. That's all that matters, isn't it?"

Storm Arriving looked at her, worried. "It is what we went there to do. To win the war."

"The war. To win the war." The words started to pile up in her head. "Always the war. Win the war. Fight the bluecoats. Drive them out. The war." The words spilled from her like snow sliding down a hillside, building up in speed and ferocity. "How long has it gone on? How long will it go on? Years? Tens of years? Tens of tens? Is it to be our whole life?"

"Please," Storm Arriving said. "You and I can talk of this later. By ourselves."

"Why? Because we might upset One Who Flies? He wants this war most of all."

"No one wants this war."

"No one? Then why do we have it? Why have I been alone for most of this last cycle of seasons? Even in winter you make war. No civilized person makes war in the winter."

"We did not have the new weapons—"

She threw the ladle at him, spattering him with gravy. "Weapons! I am not talking about weapons. I am talking about men, families. Dead men. Hundreds dead. And for what?"

Storm Arriving and One Who Flies just stared at her.

"You have accomplished nothing!" she shouted. "Nothing! You have killed bluecoats, you have counted terrible coup, you have destroyed their forts, but it is all nothing. They will just come back when the warmth returns. They will just come back across that bridge of theirs, and we will have to do it all over again. Forever."

She was empty. The words had tumbled down, and now she was empty. And like the forest after an avalanche, what followed was the terrible, ominous silence. She looked from Storm Arriving to One Who Flies and back, and saw the bafflement on their faces. She ran from the lodge, into the cold night.

She walked for hours along the hillsides below the sacred mountains, questioning the spirits and herself as well, asking the world what it meant to do and why it couldn't find a better way to do it.

When she returned home, cold and very tired, she saw the shadows of men on her lodge's buffalo skin walls. Several men. She heard the low music of serious discussion, and recognized the voices of the leaders of the band's soldier societies. She swallowed against a lump that had risen in her throat, and went to the lodge her family set aside for women during their moon-time. She sighed at the irony. She had not yet told her husband about the child growing within her.

In the morning, she awoke, cold and lonely. The fire she had built had long since guttered out and smoldered to ruin. She looked up through the smoke-hole and saw a sky overcast with clouds and the promise of more snow. From outside came the sound of shuffling footsteps.

"Speaks While Leaving?" It was Storm Arriving.

"Yes," she replied from within.

"May we speak?"

"We are," she said.

She heard his growl of exasperation. "I must tell you something."

She wrapped the blankets closer around her shoulders. "Tell me."

Feet crunched in the snow. "As you wish, then. I must tell you that I have to go. One more trip against the bluecoats."

Tears welled up in her eyes, and a defiant rage closed her throat. The only thought: What about me? What about me?

"Speaks While Leaving?"

Emotions rose, built, and burst forth. She cried out, howled, a wordless keening that cut. She did not hear the footsteps depart through the muffling snow.

Storm Arriving, Gets Up Early, and Standing Motionless rode with their backs to the weather. Their whistlers—their fastest—were tired after a three days' run back across the Sudden River, back toward the Big Greasy.

The wind was from the southwest, however, and that meant warmth, or something like it compared to the snows of home. Still, the whistlers were unhappy, for this was winter, and winter was a time for gathering the flocks and conserving strength for nesting in the spring. Storm Arriving was sure that his drakes would rather be huddled together with their hens, warding off the snows and frigid winds, instead of loping through the rainstorms of the southern lands. Storm Arriving empathized: better snow that one could shake off than rain that only soaked and chilled.

But what the whistlers wanted—and the men as well—was immaterial. What was needed was, simply, what was needed, and complaining only soured a man's stomach. Storm Arriving tried to think of happy times, of happier things ahead. His mind's eye only saw gloom, and his heart feared that this one last trip was one too many, and that it might mean the end of seven years of courtship and two years of marriage, the end of his story with Speaks While Leaving.

"Almost there," Gets Up Early said. "Do you want to continue on downstream?"

"No," Storm Arriving said. "I don't want to get close until tonight. One Who Flies says that this is the night when the *vé'hó'e* celebrate the ending of their year. All of the *vé'hó'e* will be drunk with their water-that-burns-the-throat, but not until tonight." He looked ahead and saw a gully at the foot of a low knoll. "There," he said. "That looks like a good place."

Gets Up Early looked at the sky behind them and the clouds that covered it. "I don't think any place is a good place tonight."

Standing Motionless laughed. "You old woman," he chided the other rider. "You would be cold in a sweat lodge."

They all chuckled, but to Storm Arriving, the humor seemed thin. As they descended into the narrow cleft in the hillside, ducking under the scratching arms of bare-boned trees, Storm Arriving felt his grasp on his own life slipping away. He could remember nothing but fighting, battle, and pain. He felt as though he had been at war his whole life: with his father, with Speaks While Leaving, with One Who Flies, with the blue-coats. He sat down with the others in the detritus of twigs and dead leaves, his back against a rough stone, a Trader-wool blanket around his shoulders. The sky began to mist, like a cloud brushing the earth, and jewels began to form in his hair. He looked down the length of their narrow hiding place.

The whistlers huddled together along one of the shadowed walls. Their breath poured out in long, slow rhythms, creating gouts of vaporous fog that slowly filled the gully. Overhead, wintry branches reached for one another like the hands of ancient lovers. He saw stubborn leaves hanging here and there on the branches, fluttering in the wind, until one of the leaves fluttered up to another branch, and he saw that they were birds, each the color and size of an old, dead leaf. There were dozens of them in the boughs over his head, quietly flitting from twig to branch, tugging on lichen, searching for food. Dead leaves, living birds; it made him smile, and the smile made him remember her. He was tired of the path of war. He longed for peace. He longed for a time when duty meant living instead of killing, and honor came without a weapon.

He chided himself for whining complaints. I am a soldier of the People, he reminded himself. I will do my duty. Even if it means my life.

A drop of water plopped down his back. He pulled his blanket tighter around his neck.

Still, he prayed to the spirits, I would like a chance for a life beyond the end of this struggle. I would like to see my grandchildren play in the summer's sun. I would like that very much.

The evening encroached, and the sun prepared to set behind the western clouds. In the gloaming, Storm Arriving and his two companions rose and made ready for their night's work. From bundles on their whistlers' backs they unpacked the thunder-sticks, the noise-makers, and the fire-cord. Storm Arriving held a blanket to keep the rain off while Gets Up Early and Standing Motionless put the pieces together.

"It is dangerous, putting these together here," Gets Up Early said.

"It will be more dangerous to do it later," Storm Arriving said. "We will just have to be careful."

Gets Up Early frowned up at him. "Very careful," he said.

When they were done, Gets Up Early handed Storm Arriving two large bundles of thunder-sticks. He wrapped them in oiled deerskin and put them in back in the bundle on his whistler. It was now full dark.

"Here," Gets Up Early said. He put a small packet in his hand.

"What is it?" Storm Arriving asked.

"The little-fire-sticks One Who Flies uses to light the fire-cord. Scratch the end against something rough and it makes a tiny fire. You have to work quickly, though. They do not last long, especially in the wind."

Storm Arriving put the little packet in his shirt, under his belt. "Let's go," he said.

They rode off into the night. The clouds covered the sky, and they trusted their whistlers to see with their eyesight what the men could not. As they traveled, the mist returned. By the time they heard the sound of the winter-swollen river ahead of them, the mist had become a drizzle. Storm Arriving felt his hands tighten up in the cold, and he chafed them and gripped them to keep the blood flowing to his fingers.

Up ahead along the riverbank, they soon saw lanterns, their light glittering off the waters like broken stars. The men rode a bit farther, and then dismounted, leaving the whistlers with Standing Motionless. Gets Up Early and Storm Arriving took their rifles and slung them across their backs like bows. Then they took the bundles and headed off on foot.

The river mud was cold and soaked through their moccasins. Storm Arriving slipped on a rock and heard Gets Up Early suck in a breath as he landed on one knee.

"Sorry," Storm Arriving said as he took off his ruined mocs and threw them into the bushes. The drizzle had become rain, and bare feet would be surer than mud-slick leather.

When they got to within a bowshot of the lights, they could hear the singing: raucous, jovial, but also sluggish and uncoordinated. There was a great deal of laughter and shouting and general noisemaking that filled the air as well. The two men snuck along the riverbank, and when they came to the waterfront buildings, they kept to the shadows beneath the warmly lit windows. Their target lay ahead.

The bridge stretched across the river like a dark rainbow. Gets Up Early gripped Storm Arriving's shoulder.

"Wait for my signal," he said. "I will give you about two fingers' worth of time."

"Yes," Storm Arriving said, and then his companion

was gone. Storm Arriving looked up at the bridge. He thought back to his last night at the camp of the Closed Windpipe band. One Who Flies had struggled up on one elbow as he and the leaders of soldier societies had discussed their idea, an idea born of the words of Speaks While Leaving.

They will just come back across that bridge of theirs, and we will have to do it all over again. Forever.

He envisioned in his memory the drawings One Who Flies had made on pieces of leather, and the tiny model of the bridge he had built of sticks. He went over his instructions in his mind and looked up through the rain at the immense structure.

The bridge did not reflect any light from the lantern-yellow windows around it. It ate the light. It stood, huge and enormous, the black bones of some great preternatural monster that died in the murky waters of the Big Greasy. Storm Arriving let his gaze wander its height and its length. He studied it, and remembered the points where One Who Flies said the charges should be placed: high atop the arch, out over the middle of the river.

He crept forward to the base of the bridge. Stone and metal pilings rose up from the river's swell, but the winter-fed current was too swift for him to get to them. He would have to go out along the short span first.

A small building guarded the entrance to the smaller span, its windows bright with flickering lamplight. Storm Arriving came up to the railbed and listened at the wall of the guardhouse. Nothing. Knife in hand, he sidled up along the window and peeked inside. Nothing. He stood and looked in. A *vé'ho'e* stared back at him, a bottle in his hand, a question on his face.

"'Ey," the man said, pointing.

Storm Arriving came around the building and yanked open the door. The *vé'ho'e* stood up from behind a table, small brightly colored cards scattering on the floor. He dropped his bottle. It broke with a crash as Storm Arriving lunged for him. The *vé'ho'e* gasped through an opened throat, breath bubbling through blood. His eyes lolled, and he fell. Storm Arriving stepped back and hissed at the pain in his foot. He snarled as he pulled the shard of broken bottle from the flesh in his arch. Blood dripped, dark in the lamplight. He looked around, found a rag of cloth, and tied it around his foot. Then he went back outside and ran along the tracks, out onto the metal gridwork, trying to ignore the pain that shot up from his foot into his leg.

The railroad ties were slick in the rain and he had to move slower than he wanted to or risk slipping through the gaps. He'd lost track of the time. How long until Gets Up Early gives the signal? he wondered. The towers that guarded the main span loomed before him.

The rain began to come down in earnest. His feet started to numb in the cold, and he thanked the spirits for small gifts. He reached the towers and looked up. Smooth stones and huge iron girders met over his head. He looked back toward the small town. He saw another *vé'ho'e* in the light cast by the open door to the guardhouse. The man shouted.

Storm Arriving began to climb, his fingers holding on to the girder, his toes jammed into the mortared joints. At the top, he slipped. His toes tore on the sharp stone, and his hands grabbed the rough edge of the girders. He felt warm blood trickle back down along his wrists as he pulled himself up. He looked back. More men had gathered around the tiny guardhouse. He shouldered his bundle and his rifle, and turned to face the span.

The arch of metal rose even higher into the night sky, leaning out over the water. Below, the iron rails on the bridge deck were already nothing more than two silver lines against the dark waters. Storm Arriving grasped on to the cold metal of the arch and continued his climb.

Rainwater sluiced down along the arch and the wind gathered its daring with every step he took toward the apex. His fingers began to cramp in the cold, and he stopped to shake life back into them before continuing onward. He heard shouts behind him, voices raised in heated argument. He looked back. The men were looking at the ground outside the guardhouse.

The cut on my foot? he wondered. Surely the rain has washed the blood away.

But the men had turned toward the bridge and were peering out into the darkness beyond their lanterns' glow.

He kept climbing, the cables below him humming in the wind. He did not know how high he was above the water. The wind pushed and buffeted him, toying with him like a fox with a mouse. The top of the arch was just ahead, where the girders came close and leveled out. He clambered along the final length, and sat.

Men from the guardhouse began walking out along the bridge deck. Storm Arriving saw them peering this way and that, shining their lanterns into every nook, behind every pillar, inspecting the bridge step by step. Storm Arriving wasted no more time on them. If they saw him, they saw him. They would still have to reach him.

He took off the bundle and opened it. He took out a coil of braided buffalo-hair rope and shook it loose. Then he took out the first bunch of thunder-sticks, six sticks all bound around a seventh. He tied the rope around the sticks, and then lay down along the cold girder. He could hear the men as they reached the tower that supported the main span.

He tied the bundle of thunder-sticks to the underside of the arch, according to the instructions One Who Flies had given him. Leaving the fire-cord to dangle, he trimmed the extra rope, grabbed the second bunch of thunder-sticks, and looked across to the opposite side of the arch.

The twin arches were joined by thinner girders,

nearly twenty feet across and a little wider than Storm Arriving's bandaged foot.

Don't think, he told himself, and stepped out onto the girder.

He held his breath, but the wind did not. It pushed and he swung his arms for balance. He grabbed for the far side. A man shouted out from below, but further words were lost in the explosion that lit up the night.

Fire ballooned upward from the center of the little town. The men below looked back toward the explosion, then up at the arch. A second blast of fire rose toward the darkness. The men turned and headed back toward town.

"Thank you, Gets Up Early."

He tied the second bunch as he had the first. Then he took out the small box of little-fire-sticks. Holding the end of the fire-cord, he scraped one against the rain-wet girder. It sputtered and died. He tried again and got nothing. He took out another, wiped the rain off the girder, and tried again. It flared into flame. He touched it to the fire-cord, held it there, and nearly whooped with joy when it hissed to life.

He headed back across the girder. The light from the fire in town made it easier to walk the thin length of metal, but halfway across he heard a gunshot from the bridge deck. A bullet hit metal and sang past him. He stumbled and slipped, lunged for the metal of the arch, and landed hard on the girder, his feet hanging in air, his breath coming hard, and his ribs screaming in pain from the impact. Another shot hit the metal with a heavy clang. Storm Arriving got his legs back up on the arch, unslung his rifle, turned, and fired three quick shots at the man down on the bridge deck. The *vé'ho'e* ran for cover behind the tower and Storm Arriving reached for the little-fire-sticks.

They were gone.

He swore. He turned and fired two more shots out of anger. They hit the stone tower and went zipping out into the night. From behind the tower, the *vé'ho'e* took another shot. It hit the cross-girder in a flash of sparks.

Sparks!

Storm Arriving shouldered his rifle and reached for his belt pouch. Numb, bloodstained fingers fumbled with the tie and he poured the contents into his hand. He grabbed the flint and let everything else fall away to the waters far below. He put the flint near the end of the fire-cord, took out his knife, and scraped the blade along the flint. Sparks spilled from the stone, hissing on the rain-wet girder. He smelled the sharp scent of burning metal. More shots came from below. Men shouted to one another. He tried to hide himself with as much of the girder as possible. He dragged the blade along the flint again. More sparks, lots of them. He did it again, again. Faster, he struck and struck. Sparks settled on the cord, sputtering as they died. More sparks. The cord spat, died. More sparks. A hiss. A spout of flame. It was lit.

He looked behind him. Four men at the towers. He had five shots left in his rifle. He looked at the fire-cords. He had taken too much time with the second one. The one on the far side had only a foot or so to go. No time.

Squeezing the girder with his legs, he leaned out. He fired two shots, saw one man fall, and saw all the others run for cover behind the towers. He fired two more shots, sending shards of stone about their heads. He fired his last shot, and tossed the rifle out over the river. Holding the empty bundle that had held the thunder-sticks, he leaned down alongside the girder. He wrapped the bundle's heavy leather around one of the cables that hung down to the bridge deck, gripped it with all his might, and slackened the hold of his legs on the girder above. He began to slide down the cable, the leather growling against the cable's braids. His speed increased and he held on tighter to the cable itself. The leather began to heat beneath his hands.

He could smell it burning, the heat rose, the growling became a moan, a wail. His hands held on. The bridge deck came up fast to meet him. Too fast. He gripped with his legs, felt the leather of his leggings give way, felt the cable burn his flesh. He let go, hit the rail, heard a snap, and hit hard on the deck. He scrambled to his feet and went back down with a lancing pain behind his shin. Back at the tower, the *vé'hó'e* came out from behind the stonework. They aimed and fired. Their shots went wide in the rain and darkness, but they could see he was down and unarmed. They ran forward.

Storm Arriving looked up and saw the twin stars of his work hissing overhead, so close to their goal. The men came for him, reloading as they ran. He rolled to the side, squeezed through the gap between the deck and the rail, and fell.

He hit the water with a shock that rivaled his landing on the bridge deck. The pain in his leg was intense, and the cold water on his seared flesh was like fire all over again. He pulled for the surface and spluttered for air when he reached it. The current carried him downstream, and he caught sight of the bridge just as the first charge detonated.

The explosion lit the bellies of the clouds and blew girders up into the sky. The second blast tore the peak out of the arch, and Storm Arriving heard a groan that seemed to come from the river itself. He watched as the bridge's perfect arch folded in upon itself, as the flat deck bowed and twisted. The footings pulled loose and the stone towers cracked. Huge chunks of stone tumbled into the water, cables snapped, girders buckled, and slowly, grudgingly, the massive structure surrendered. It fell into the river, sending up a spume of water higher than it had ever stood itself.

Storm Arriving swam for the riverbank. When he reached it, the fires in the town still glowed. As he lay in the river's death-cold ooze, he looked upstream at the two ruined towers, at the tortured metal that hung from them, and at the span of empty space that stood between them. He looked at the scene, and he smiled.

The White House was quiet on New Year's Day with both family and staff all sleeping in after staying up for punch and toasts at the midnight hour. Custer, however, was restless as usual. He rose with the wan light of dawn, wrapped himself in his robe, and slippered his way downstairs to the library.

The library, with its leather-bound volumes, its curving windows, and its balcony that provided a vista of the Ellipse, Washington's monument, and the river to the south, was Custer's favorite room in the drafty, hundred-year-old mansion. It seemed a place for a president, surrounded by the knowledge and wisdom of Western civilization; a place where at any point a leader could turn and find the silent, private counsel of the ages. He walked slowly alongside the shelves, touching a binding, the embossed letters of a title. He stopped at a set of five old volumes. Their ribbed, leather-bound spines were covered with hand-stamped gold filigree, but they had no titles other than "I" through "V." He couldn't remember having ever noticed them before. He pulled the fifth volume off the shelf. The leather-clad cover was shiny with age, the pages stippled with red on the cut edges. He touched the thickness and opened it up. Hand-set letters stood in uneven lines on thick, textured paper; the text, in Latin and French, kept rank in two columns. Custer turned to the front of the book.

LE DEUTERONOME
TRADUITS EN FRANCOISE
M. D C C. I.

Who, he wondered, among this house's previous tenants, had brought home this book, an Old Testament that had been an antique when his country was just being born? He leafed through the first few pages and found the simple inscription: To John, from Poor Richard, 1789.

He shook his head in wonder and looked up at the hundreds of books stacked on shelf after shelf all around the room. What other secrets were up there, hidden among the biographies and atlases, what history left behind by legends? He looked down at the book in his hand, now close to two hundred years old.

What legacy will I leave? he wondered. What will I leave behind me for future occupants to find and ponder? Anything? Anything more than failure upon failure?

A quiet knock at the door brought him back to the present. "Yes?" he said.

The door opened and Douglas stepped inside. "Mr. President, sir? Mr. Greene is wanting to see you, sir."

Custer frowned. It was far too early for Jacob to be here without a very good reason. "Send him up."

"Yes, sir. Some coffee, sir?"

"Yes. Thank you, Douglas."

The butler closed the door with a quiet snick. Custer put the ancient book back in its place and waited for Jacob's heavy footsteps to ascend the staircase. He was still touching the gilded spines when the door opened again and Douglas ushered Jacob into the library.

"Autie," Jacob said.

"Bad news?" Custer asked without turning around. He saw only the cracked leather of the spines, the decorations with their fleurs-de-lis, their lions rampant.

"Yes," Jacob said. "It's the bridge."

A smile of sadness wrinkled Custer's face, and he felt his eyes sting. "Of course," he said. "It was the only thing left."

"It's destroyed. They blew it up."

Custer swallowed. He could not turn around. He could not bring himself to face another human being. He thought: Now the failure is complete.

"Shafer's at a loss," Jacob said, his voice tight and

pitched high with frustration. "He's blaming everything from the quality of the iron to God-knows-what. He can't understand it. He says they knew just where to place the charges. How in Hell's name did they know how to do that?"

Custer's smile widened, and he felt a mixture of sadness and joy swell within him. "I suppose," he said, "they had some help." He turned and looked at Jacob, chuckled at his friend's consternation. "From an engineer, I'll wager."

Storm Arriving woke up slowly. He heard the quiet breathing of his wife beside him, heard the small *tick-tick* of coals slumbering in the hearthpit. He looked up through the smokehole. Chickadees pipped and squabbled in the evergreen boughs far above the lodge, and somewhere up the snowy hillside a vixen called for her mate.

Speaks While Leaving turned in her sleep, rolling up against him, her breasts warm against his aching ribs, her arm a comforting pressure across his chest. The sun poked its head out from between the clouds and the world brightened, grew sharp and focused. Storm Arriving looked down on his wife's face and sighed. She mumbled in her sleep and he felt her arm hold him a bit tighter.

A child, he thought. A child. He wished he could see his mother's face when she heard the news, but the idea of another trip away from Speaks While Leaving was unthinkable. Not now. Not for a long, long time.

He was glad, though, that it would be One Who Flies who told his mother and sister the news. Such news should come from family, and One Who Flies was nearly that. His friend's insistence on traveling back to the camp of the Tree People for his recuperation made it easier for Storm Arriving to stay.

The sun ran back behind a cloud and the day turned back to dawn. Speaks While Leaving sighed, and he felt the curve of her waist as her legs entwined in his.

One Who Flies should be there by now, he thought

briefly, and then Speaks While Leaving began to stir, and his mind was filled with other things.

"Are you all right, One Who Flies?"

George blinked and shook his head—a mistake—and felt his gorge rise. He held up a hand to assure Gets Up Early that he was fine, but only half believed it himself. He had felt so much better when they had left the camp of the Closed Windpipe band. Now, though, the four days' journey to the Elk River had sapped him of every bit of strength he had regained during his three-week convalescence.

"I will be fine," he said, "once we reach the Tree People. How far are we from the camp?"

"Not far," Gets Up Early said. "A hand, maybe more."

George took a deep breath and let it out through pursed lips, trying to dispel the wave of nausea that gripped him. He looked over his shoulder to where the sun's glow hung low in the winter sky. The wind freshened, sharp and bitter out of the north, but it carried a scent that revived his spirit and quickened his heart. Woodsmoke.

Home.

"Let's go."

Within a hand of time, they heard the first shout from the hilltops. Gets Up Early grinned and whooped in response, his voice echoing across the rising land. Their whistlers stamped in the snow and cried out with long yodels. The valleys ahead awoke with distant replies, and the air was filled with whistlers' music. As anxious as their mounts, they headed into the valley mouth at a brisk pace.

People lined the trail that wound through the camp.

"What is the news?"

"Did we succeed against the bluecoats?"

"What about the bridge?"

Gets Up Early grinned at George. "We will eat all winter on the stories we will tell."

George smiled, too, but wanted only one thing. He looked up at the tree-covered slopes, searching. Then he glimpsed it: through the evergreens, a lodge decorated with black handprints over white spots and jagged lines.

"Where are you going?" Gets Up Early asked as George turned away from the crowds of people wanting news and nudged his whistler into a run.

"Home," he shouted over his shoulder. "I'm going home."

His mount wound its way past trees and around snow-covered boulders, spade-toed feet digging into the steep slope. George hung on, pressure from his heels keeping the beast headed in the right direction. He held on to his wounded side. The whistler pushed uphill, passed close beneath snow-clad boughs, and George was dusted with snow. When he had wiped his face and eyes clear, he could see his destination.

Mouse Road stood outside her mother's lodge, still several yards away. She waved, and George saw her teeth bright in a wide grin. The grin faded as he rode up, and her hand went to her mouth, eyes wide with worry as she saw the bandages that bound his head, his arm, his torso.

He reined in before her, swaying atop his whistler's back, suddenly light-headed. Mouse Road took a step toward him but stopped, her eyes filled with concern. He bade his whistler crouch, and slowly, painfully, he dismounted. He stood there, one hand on his whistler's spine, gathering his strength and balance. Steam rose from the beast's flanks and its cinnamon scent was sharp in the cold, wet air. But his wounds were not the only thing that stayed him.

How long have I been gone, he wondered, that this woman should have blossomed from the child I knew?

He walked toward her with measured care.

"Mouse Road," he said when he came up to her. "I have missed seeing you."

She reached out and took his hand in hers. Though

her concern for him had not left, her smile returned, and her gaze was filled with only him.

"Mother," she said over her shoulder. "One Who Flies has come home."

Then she led him inside.

Cheyenne Pronunciation Guide

There are only fourteen letters in the Cheyenne alphabet. They are used to create small words which can be combined to create some very long words. The language is very descriptive, and often combines several smaller words to construct a longer, more complex concept. The following are simplified examples of this subtle and intricate language, but it will give you some idea of how to pronounce the words in the text.

LETTER	PRONUNCIATION OF THE CHEYENNE LETTER
a	"a" as in "water"
e	"i" as in "omit" (short "i" sound, not a long "e")
h	"h" as in "home"
k	"k" as in "skit"
m	"m" as in "mouse"
n	"n" as in "not"
o	"o" as in "hope"
p	"p" as in "poor"
s	"s" as in "said"
š	"sh" as in "shy"
t	"t" as in "stop"
v	"v" as in "value"

LETTER	PRONUNCIATION OF THE CHEYENNE LETTER
x	"ch" as in "Bach" (a soft, aspirated "h")
'	glottal stop as in "Uh-oh!"

The three vowels (a, e, o) can be marked for high pitch (á, é, ó) or be voiceless (whispered), as in â, ô, ê.

Glossary

Ame'haooestse	Tsétsêhéstâhese for the name One Who Flies
Bands	Cheyenne clans or family groups. Bands always travel together, while the tribe as a whole only gathers in the summer months. Bands are familial and matrilineal; men who marry go to live with the woman and her band. The ten Cheyenne bands are:

- The Closed Windpipe People (also Closed Gullet or Closed Aorta)
- The Scabby Band
- The Hair Rope Men
- The Ridge People
- The Tree People (also Log Men or Southern Eaters)
- The Poor People
- The Broken Jaw People (also Lower Jaw Protruding People or Drifted Away Band)
- The Suhtai

• The Flexed Leg People
(also Lying on the Side
With Knees Drawn up Peo-
ple, later absorbed into
Dog Soldier society)
• The Northern Eaters

The Cloud People Tsétsêhéstâhese phrase for
the Southern Arapaho

Contrary One of up to four men who
had an overwhelming fear of
thunder; by accepting owner-
ship of a thunder bow (*hoh-
nóhkavo'e*) they gained some
of the thunder's power, but
also had to live a "contrary"
life, living apart, remaining
unmarried, and speaking and
acting backward. A Contrary
was an exceedingly brave
soldier.

The Cradle People Tsétsêhéstâhese phrase for
the Assiniboine

The Crow People Tsétsêhéstâhese phrase for
the Crow

The Cut-Hair People Tsétsêhéstâhese phrase for
the Osage

The Earth Lodge Builders Tsétsêhéstâhese phrase for
the Mandau Hidatsa Arikara
(Ree) and other non-
nomadic peoples

Eestseohtse'e Tsétsêhéstâhese for the name
Speaks While Leaving

Ée'tótahe He is afraid.

Eho'eéto It is snowing.

Ékánoma'e It doesn't matter.

Énánôtse Put it down.

Éoseetonéto It is very cold.

The Greasy Wood People Tsétsêhéstâhese phrase for
the Kiowa

Hámêstoo'êstse (singular), Sit!

Hámêstoo'e (plural)

Héehe'e	Yes.
He'kotoo'êstse (singular), *He'kotoo'e* (plural)	Be quiet!
Hó'ésta	Shout!
Hohkeekemeona'e	Tsétsêhéstâhese for the name Mouse Road
Hohnóhka	Tsétsêhéstâhese word for Contrary
Hová'âháne	No.
The Inviters	Tsétsêhéstâhese phrase for the Lakota
Ke'éehe	Child's word for grandmother
The Little Star People	Tsétsêhéstâhese phrase for the Oglala Lakota
Maahótse	The four Sacred Arrows of the People
Ma'heo'o (singular), **Ma'heono** (plural)	A word that can be loosely translated as "that which is sacred," referring to the basis of Cheyenne spirituality and mystery
Mâsêhavé'ho'e	Crazy white man.
Mo'e'haeva'e	Tsétsêhéstâhese for the name Magpie Woman
Náháéána	I am hungry.
Natsêhésenestse	I speak Cheyenne.
Néá'eše	Thank you.
Né'éstséhnêstse	Come in.
Néháéána	Are you hungry?
Némâsêhanee'e	You are crazy.
Nenáasêstse	Come here.
Nénâhahe	You are wild, uncivilized.
Néséne	My friend (said by one man to another).
Nevé-stanevóo'o	The Four Sacred Persons, created by Ma'heo'o, who guard the four corners of the world
Nóheto	Let's go!

Nóxa'e	Wait!
Ota'tavehexovona'e	Tsétsêhéstâhese for the name Blue Shell Woman
Pévevóona'o	Good morning.
The Sage People	Tsétsêhéstâhese phrase for the Northern Arapaho
Séáno	The happy place for the deceased
The Snake People	Tsétsêhéstâhese phrase for the Comanche
Soldier Societies	The military organizations within the tribe. Membership in a society was voluntary and had no relation to the band in which one lived. The six Cheyenne soldier societies are:

- Kit Foxes (also Fox Soldiers)
- Elkhorn Scrapers (also Crooked Lances)
- Dog Men (or Dog Soldiers)
- Red Shields (or Buffalo Bull Soldiers)
- Crazy Dogs
- Little Bowstrings

Tsêhe'êsta'ehe	Long Hair (General G. A. Custer)
Tsêhe'êstoo'onahe	Tsétsêhéstâhese for the name Long Jaw
Tsêhéóhe	Over here.
Tsétsêhéstâhese	The Cheyenne people's word for themselves.
Vá'ôhtáma	The place of honor at the back of the lodge
Vé'ho'e	The Tsétsêhéstâhese name for the Spider-Trickster of legend

Vé'ho'e (singular), **Vé'hó'e** (plural)	Lit. spider, from the word for "cocooned," and now the word for whites
Vétšêškévâhonoo'o	Fry-bread
The Wolf People	Tsétsêhéstâhese phrase for the Pawnee
The Year the Star Fell	In the year 1833, the Leonid meteor shower was especially fierce. The incredible display made such an impression on the Cheyenne of the time that it became a memorable event from which many other events were dated